Endorsements

"Think of the novel *Madness* as a national birthday present—Happy Bicentennial, War of 1812—telling us of an unsung time in our early history that was as dramatic, and as dangerous, as any.

"But *Madness* does more than take us back to a time we should know better. It is a choice yarn of war and intrigue. It is the kind of yarn Tom Clancy, say, might tell us about 1812—if Clancy were as sweet a writer as Dennis Byrne. Or put it another way: Don't buy the book for your bedside table. It is the kind of book that makes you want to read on. You likely will stay up too late reading it."

—Zay N. Smith, Contributing book
reviewer, Chicago Sun-Times

"It is one thing to brush history's dust from the past but quite another to bring the past back in vibrant detail. Dennis Byrne has done that and more in *Madness: The War of 1812*, offering a compelling cast of characters in an action-packed tale. Grounded solidly in deep historical research and understanding, this is a remarkable accomplishment that makes terrific reading."

—Rick Kogan, WGN Radio Talk Show Host
and Chicago Tribune writer

Madness

The War of 1812

a novel

Madness

The War of 1812
a novel

Dennis Byrne

TATE PUBLISHING
AND ENTERPRISES, LLC

Published by Tate Publishing & Enterprises, LLC
127 E. Trade Center Terrace | Mustang, Oklahoma 73064 USA
1.888.361.9473 | www.tatepublishing.com

Tate Publishing is committed to excellence in the publishing industry. The company reflects the philosophy established by the founders, based on Psalm 68:11,
"The Lord gave the word and great was the company of those who published it."

Book design copyright © 2012 by Tate Publishing, LLC. All rights reserved.
Cover design by Errol Villamante
Interior design by Caypeeline Casas

Published in the United States of America

ISBN: 978-1-62147-212-4
1. Fiction / Romance / Historical
2. Fiction / War & Military
12.08.29

Dedication

To Barbara, Kati, and Don.

Acknowledgments

My immediate family—wife, Barbara; daughter, Kati; and son, Don—inspired this book. Not because of their interest in history or in the War of 1812, but because they believed I had a book in me. Despite my doubts, with their encouragement, *Madness: The War of 1812* emerged after five years of gestation.

Then Sheila Whalen, editor and book reviewer extraordinaire, got her hands on it. Gentle massaging and some major bone cracking focused the story and brought characters to life. Her patience and wisdom were as valuable as her deft editing.

Many others contributed to this work. Zay Smith, one of Chicago's finest writers, praised an early manuscript, stoking my determination. Joe Rizzo, Wally Johnson, Bob Meyer, and other friends seemed to genuinely enjoy the manuscript, providing more encouragement. John Glavin, my high school English teacher, showed up decades later to provide valuable counsel, sharing his experience about writing and publishing his own novel, *Trapped on The Wheel: Chicago's Columbian Exposition of 1893*.

The Off Campus Writers' Workshop, an aspiring writer's dream, yielded constructive advice, especially from one of its guest speakers, E.E. Knight, who critiqued the opening pages of my manuscript. I'm grateful to Joel Weisman, my agent, who valiantly swam upstream, trying to pitch a first-time author's manuscript to major publishing houses that have all but closed their doors to new talent.

There are too many people who taught me, either directly or by example, how to write professionally. The old *Chicago Daily News*, considered to be the "writer's newspaper," was loaded with more writing talent than I have ever seen in one place. There I was proud to be considered a colleague with such greats as Mike Royko, Ray Coffey, M. W. Newman, and Lois Wille. Tom Vickerman, the crusty night city editor and one of the many who labored out of the spotlight to make the paper great, was my drill sergeant, now fondly remembered.

Others contributed in ways they didn't know, such as agent Sterling Lord, who, in rejecting the manuscript, was kind enough to take the time to explain why, which led to a better book. The American Society of Journalists and Authors provided a torrent of resources for a would-be author confused by a complex and changing publishing industry.

Finally, my sincerest thanks to Tate Publishing for being one of the few, if only, publishing houses to accept unsolicited manuscripts and for selecting mine from the thousands it receives every month. Among them are Ashley Luckett, Lauren Downen, Terry Cordingley, Rachael Sweeden, and Sunnie Atkins. Kristen Polson collaborated to ably illustrate the major battles.

Introduction

The War of 1812, in which the United States invaded Canada, may be the most crucial and most bungled, the least understood and least remembered war the young nation ever fought.

It was the first time that America invaded another nation, with near-disastrous results. It was just twenty-two years after the ratification of the Constitution that created the United States we know. It was the first critical test of democratic leadership on an international scale that would decide whether the grand experiment of self-government would survive or collapse.

The latter was a distinct possibility. Never in the history of American warfare has this nation witnessed such an exhibition of cowardice, indecisiveness, incompetence, and laziness in the army's senior officer ranks. Battle after battle was lost, untrained troops were sacrificed in fights they could never win, territories won were quickly squandered, and the chain of command was ignored to near-treasonous levels.

More important, an American defeat likely would have resulted in Canada's annexation of New England or in the return of those former colonies to the British crown. The Southern and Middle Atlantic states might have gone their separate ways. New wars could have broken out on the North American continent—involving Britain, France, Spain, or Mexico—over control of the newly purchased Louisiana Territory. Five New England states met in secret convention to debate secession from the Union.

Considering the critical role that the United States has played in global affairs in the nineteenth, twentieth, and twenty-first centuries, a defeat could have changed the face of today's world.

The idea of separate states united under a central government was fragile and untested. The Civil War lay some fifty years ahead, but the economic, political, and social fissures that caused it had already appeared. Former Vice President Aaron Burr had conspired with army officers and planters to slice off southern and western lands to forge a new nation. From every corner, America was challenged: by Barbary pirates looting America's shipping; by battling European nations intolerant of America's neutrality, who wanted to draw the young country into the Napoleonic wars; and by Native Americans armed by the British to stymie westward expansion.

The young country was provoked, even bullied, into the War of 1812. Great Britain routinely violated maritime law and interfered with American shipping. American sailors suspected—often for the flimsiest of reasons—of being British deserters or even British-born were forced to serve on British warships. Garrisons like Fort Mackinac in upper Lake Huron, ceded to the United States by treaty after the War of Independence, were slowly and grudgingly surrendered.

So the United States had ample reason to take up arms, but it harbored intentions beyond simple self-defense: to extend America's hegemony beyond its borders into

British Canada and Spanish Florida. Such nationalist stirrings eventually would become embodied in the idea of a Manifest Destiny—an America that was fated to extend from ocean to ocean.

Whatever America's motives, the men who took on the army and navy of Great Britain were woefully unprepared for the task. It was a comedy of errors from the outset. Communication was badly mishandled or utterly ignored. Never before or since was a field general court-martialed for incompetence and sentenced to be shot. Soldiers, often ill trained and poorly supplied, lurched from defeat to defeat at the hands of the British, the Canadian militia, and their Indian allies. One miscalculation triggered another and another. Public enthusiasm for the war cooled and criticism was first whispered and eventually led to outright condemnations and recriminations. Funding for the war dried up. Commerce and trade ground almost to a halt. Political crises dogged President James Madison. Troops that hadn't deserted were starving, freezing, or dying in bogs and swamps.

The war's promoters never imagined that it would be fought on American soil, but the abortive invasion of Canada brought the fighting home. On Chesapeake Bay, British ships attacked Maryland and Virginia settlements, encouraged slave uprisings, and laid siege to Washington, D.C. British warships blockaded ports and strangled commerce. The economy turned sour, and the federal government scrounged for loans.

America had virtually no navy—its warships numbered in the single digits—while Great Britain had nine hundred. The oceans of the world were virtually a British lake. America's regular army comprised about five thousand officers and men; Britain's numbered in the hundreds of thousands. America thought it could rely on its motley militias of the separate states, some of which refused to fight outside their states and all of which were comprised of undisciplined, inexperienced citizen soldiers who often had to supply their own arms and provisions.

In the face of such odds, America—astonishingly—declared war on Great Britain.

The War of 1812 was, in a word, madness.

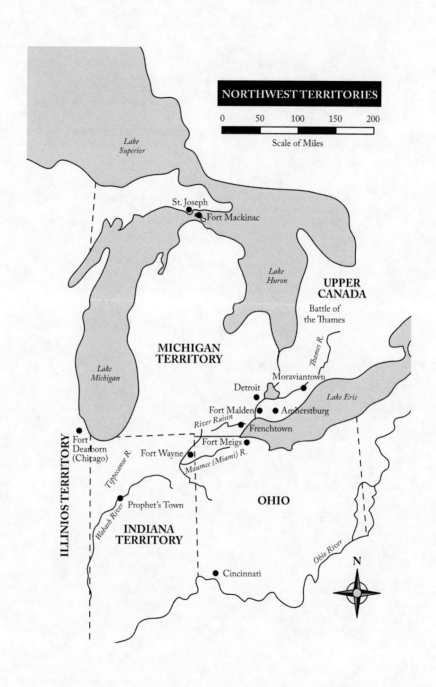

NORTHWEST TERRITORIES

| 0 | 50 | 100 | 150 | 200 |

Scale of Miles

Lake Superior

St. Joseph
Fort Mackinac

Lake Huron

UPPER CANADA

Battle of the Thames

MICHIGAN TERRITORY

Lake Michigan

Moraviantown

Detroit

Lake Erie

Fort Malden

Amherstburg

River Raisin

Frenchtown

ILLINIOS TERRITORY

Fort Dearborn (Chicago)

Fort Meigs

Tippecanoe R.

Fort Wayne

Maumee (Miami) R.

Thames R.

OHIO

Wabash River

Prophet's Town

INDIANA TERRITORY

Ohio River

Cincinnati

N

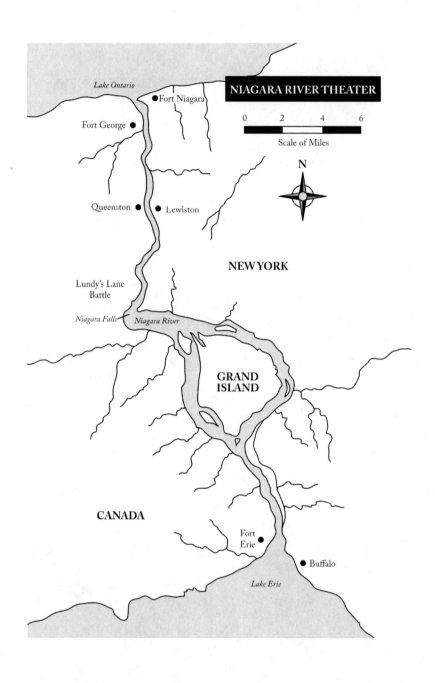

NIAGARA RIVER THEATER

Lake Ontario

Fort Niagara

Fort George

0   2   4   6

Scale of Miles

N

Queenston   Lewiston

NEW YORK

Lundy's Lane
Battle

Niagara Falls   Niagara River

GRAND
ISLAND

CANADA

Fort
Erie

Buffalo

Lake Erie

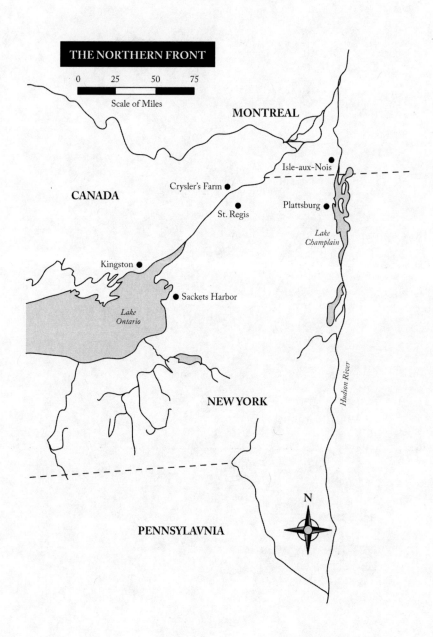

THE NORTHERN FRONT

0   25   50   75

Scale of Miles

MONTREAL

CANADA

Isle-aux-Nois

Crysler's Farm ●

Plattsburg ●

St. Regis ●

Lake
Champlain

Kingston ●

● Sackets Harbor

Lake
Ontario

NEW YORK

Hudson River

N

PENNSYLAVNIA

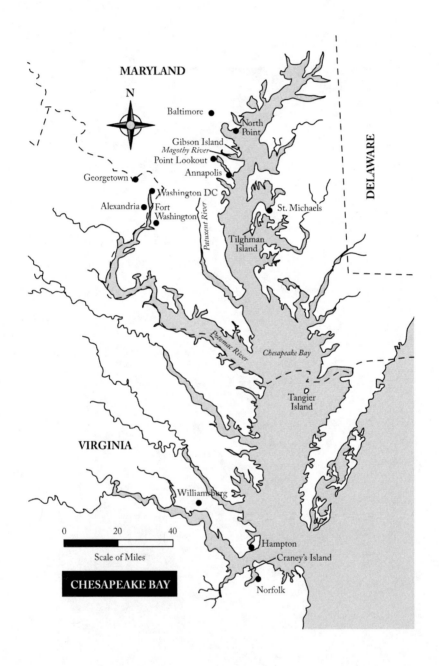

MARYLAND

N

Baltimore

North
Point

Gibson Island
Magothy River
Point Lookout
Annapolis

Georgetown

Washington DC

Alexandria   Fort
Washington

St. Michaels

Tilghman
Island

Patuxent River

DELAWARE

Potomac River

Chesapeake Bay

Tangier
Island

VIRGINIA

Williamsburg

0   20   40

Scale of Miles

Hampton
Craney's Island

Norfolk

CHESAPEAKE BAY

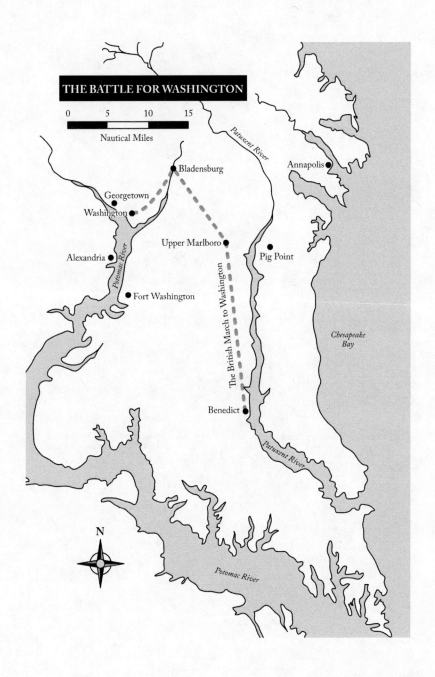

THE BATTLE FOR WASHINGTON

0   5   10   15
Nautical Miles

Patuxent River

Bladensburg

Annapolis

Georgetown

Washington

Upper Marlboro

Pig Point

Alexandria

Potomac River

Fort Washington

The British March to Washington

Chesapeake Bay

Benedict

Patuxent River

N

Potomac River

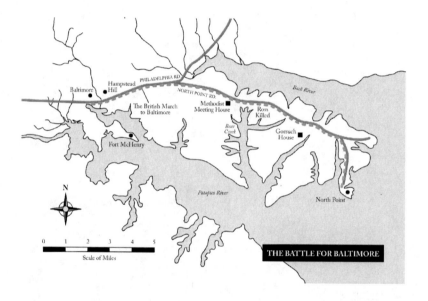

Baltimore ● Hampstead
Hill

PHILADELPHIA RD.

NORTH POINT RD.

Back River

The British March
to Baltimore

Methodist ■
Meeting House

Ross
Killed

Bear
Creek

Gorsuch ■
House

Fort McHenry ●

Patapsco River

North Point ●

N

0   1   2   3   4   5

Scale of Miles

THE BATTLE FOR BALTIMORE

Cast of Characters

Fictional

Will Quinn. Young regular army officer and Irish immigrant.

Sally Martin. A seventeen-year-old frontier woman whose family was massacred.

Judah Frake. A seasoned Kentucky sharpshooter and volunteer soldier.

Henry. A fugitive slave.

Caleb Kilfoyle. A merchant, Henry's owner.

The Quinn family: Agnes, Malachy, Aengus, and Cavan.

Actual

Adams, John Quincy. U.S. delegate to Ghent peace talks.

Anderson, Elizabeth Knagg. Michigan settler.

Armstrong, John. Secretary of War.

Aisquith, Capt. Edward. Officer in the Baltimore militia.

Barney, Joshua. Commodore of American gunboat flotilla in Chesapeake Bay.

Brock, Isaac. British general.

Chase, Maj. Elijah. General Hull's staff officer.

Chawcawbeme. Pottawatomie wise elder

Clay, Henry. Speaker of the House and leading War Hawk.

Cochrane, Adm. Alexander. Commander of British North American forces.

Cockburn, George. Admiral of the British Fleet in Chesapeake Bay.

Curtis, Ens. Daniel. Officer at Fort Wayne.

Dearborn, General Henry. Commander of U.S. forces in the Northeast.

Dausman, Sgt. Michael. Fort Mackinac garrison.

Eustis, William. Secretary of War.

Flint. Trapper at Fort Mackinac, known only by his last name.

Frye, Col. Joshua. General William Hull's chief of staff.

Gallatin, Albert. Secretary of the Treasury and delegate to the Ghent peace talks.

Hamilton, Paul. Secretary of the Navy.

Hampton, General Wade. Commander of U.S. forces in the Northeast.

Hancks, Lt. Porter. Commander of Fort Mackinac

Harrison, General William Henry. Commander of U.S. forces in the Northwest.

Heald, William. Commander of Fort Dearborn

Helm, Lt. Linai. Fort Dearborn garrison.

Hull, Brig. General William. Commander of U.S. forces in Northwest Territory.

Kesegowaase. Aging Pottawatomie chief.

Kinzie, John and Eleanor. Early Chicago settlers.

Lee, William. Master of the sloop *Friends Good Will.*

Madison, Dolley. Wife of James Madison and First Lady of the United States.

Madison, James. Fourth President of the United States.

Maw-kawbe-penay. Pottawatomie chief also known as Black Partridge

Monroe, James. Secretary of State, Secretary of War.

Ostrander, Lt. Philip. Fort Wayne officer.

Pike, General Zebulon Montgomery. American officer at Battle of York.

Prevost, George. Governor of Upper Canada,

Procter, Col. Henry. British officer.

Rhea, Capt. James. Commander at Fort Wayne.

Ronon, Ens. George. Ford Dearborn officer.

Ross, General Robert. Commander of British invasion of Washington, D.C.

Roundhead. Wyandot chief.

Scott, Col. Winfield. Officer in the Northeast.

Sheaffe, Sir Roger Hale. British general at York.

Smith, Samuel. Maryland militia general and U.S. Senator.

Smyth General Alexander. Second in command on Niagara River.

Stricker, General John. Maryland militia officer.

Tecumseh. Native American leader for Indian confederation.

Van Rensselaer, Col. Solomon. Leader of amphibious assault across Niagara River.

Van Rensselaer, Maj. General Stephen. Commander U.S. forces on Niagara River

Waterford, Capt. James. British army surgeon.

Winamac. Potawatomi chief.

Winchester, General James. Second in command to General Harrison in Northwest Territories.

Winder, General William. Army officer charged with defense of Washington.

Wool, Capt. John. U.S. officer in Niagara campaign.

1812

29 March 1812

Fort Mackinac, Michigan Territory

" *W*hose shoes did ya piss on, boy? Can't think of no other reason they'd send you here."

The newly minted Ensign William Quinn, U.S. Army, turned toward the voice rising up to him from the dock and sneered. "Piss off yourself, ya fleabag," Quinn said, tossing his grip and satchel from the deck of the sloop *Friends Good Will*, nearly hitting the fetid trapper.

Quinn, having caught the sloop four days earlier at Fort Detroit, shielded his eyes against the sun while taking the measure of this, his first posting. Not much to see. Fort Mackinac stood high on an isolated three-mile-wide island in the desolate reaches of northern Lake Huron.

Worse than I expected, Quinn thought as he jumped onto the dock, where nearly everyone living in the tiny town nestled below Fort Mackinac had gathered.

They always did when any contact arrived from the outside world. But now their thirst for news was heightened as word of a possible war with Britain had reached even this distant outpost. All eyes were on Quinn.

"Hands off that clutch, shitloaf," Quinn growled as the trapper moved to pick up Quinn's bags.

Although a rookie officer, Quinn didn't mean to be intimidated by this scrounger. Quinn had witnessed and survived the worst kind of intimidation—the violence the English portioned out on his countrymen back in Ireland.

"Oh, pardon me, your lordship. I guess we ain't had proper introductions," the trapper said, touching his hand to his greasy forehead in a feigned salute. "The name's Flint, and if'n I ain't out of line, what's yours? I mean, *sir*."

Quinn stepped close to Flint's face. The old man's breath was as insulting as his insolence. Quinn wore the uniform of a regular army officer—the tall shako hat, dark blue short coat with piping and tassels, and the single epaulette signifying his rank as a junior officer. That alone should have commanded some respect.

"I'll handle it," Quinn said, bending to snatch the bags.

But Flint, surprisingly agile for a wizened sot, beat him to the satchel. "No, I got it, governor," Flint said, brushing past Quinn. "Ya can always count on Flint for whatever's your needs here at Fort Macky."

The old man's attitude was galling rather than ingratiating, and Quinn was trying to figure out a way of ridding himself of the coot when another voice boomed out.

"Get outta here, ya piece a garbage."

It was the sloop's master, William Lee. Flint dropped the satchel and backed off.

"And if ya know what's good for ya, weasel, you'll get off my dock. I got supplies for the garrison, and you're in the way, you heap a stinking vomit."

Flint turned and made his escape though the small crowd that was enjoying the unexpected entertainment.

Lowering his voice, Lee explained to Quinn, "Don't let the looks fool ya. He's as crafty as they get. Been up here trapping and trading for as long as anyone can remember.

Surviving that long among the savages and wild cats is a triumph in itself, worthy of admiration."

"I could have handled him," Quinn muttered.

Him and anything else his new circumstances could throw at him. Irish immigrant or not, his character aligned with his young nation's—too cocky to fear consequences. Perhaps too inexperienced to imagine them. He shared with his adopted nation a deep abhorrence of Europe, especially of its dynasties and sovereigns. Like his country, Quinn was ambitious and could only imagine the future in broad stokes. Their mutual hunger for freedom and opportunity were as vast as the unexplored wilderness of the Great Lakes, Mississippi River, and the incomprehensibly huge Louisiana Purchase.

Like his adventuresome nation, he yearned to explore and discover. He could see himself with Colonel Zebulon Pike, ranging over the Rocky Mountains in search of the Missouri River headwaters. Not stuck in this godforsaken outpost.

Quinn liked to portray a certain amount of grittiness, but self-doubts crept through the façade. He hoped that his face didn't betray any insecurity. "Don't waste your time with Flint. Just don't underestimate him," Lee said, turning to the sloop's chief mate with a familiar motion that said, "Let's get unloaded." "One thing about Flint, he knows the value of information, and seeing you come ashore in that dandy uniform, he probably figured you might know something of worth."

Quinn figured he knew what Flint and everyone else— their eyes comfortably rested on him—wanted to know. When Quinn had left his family in Baltimore, long weeks ago, war talk was only worthless speculation. Asked everywhere about the rumors, Quinn could only describe the fierce debates underway out East between anti-war Northern Federalists and pro-war Southern Republicans.

Even if he had had any solid information, it would have been obsolete by the end of his trip.

"Shame that your first taste of this place had to be Flint. They're not all like that," Lee said, nodding toward the knot of civilian locals. "Got no news for ya!" Lee shouted matter-of-factly at them, ignoring their disappointment. "That, by the way, is Lieutenant Porter Hancks, the fort commander," Lee said, directing his gaze toward the half-dozen blue uniforms making their way through the crowd on the dock. "Decent fellow. You'll like him."

Quinn instantly did. Hancks's face, although carved by the frontier sun and wind, spoke of a decent and caring man. As Hancks stopped, Quinn snapped to attention and saluted.

"No need for ceremony," Hancks said, extending his hand. "Welcome to Fort Mackinac. What are your orders?"

Of course, Quinn thought as he reached inside his coat. *He doesn't know I've been assigned here. Word could not have gotten here before I did.*

Hancks did a quick read of the orders and looked up, puzzled. "You're reporting for duty? Here? Really? We haven't had any relief for months. I just assumed they forgot we're here."

Quinn couldn't tell if Hancks was joking. "Yes, sir. I mean, no, sir. If they had, I guess I wouldn't be here." Quinn cringed, sure the lieutenant would think him a dunce.

If Hancks did, he gave no sign.

"A good point, ensign. Let's go up to the fort and get you settled. I'll fill you in, and perhaps that'll explain my surprise. Gentlemen and ladies," Hancks said, addressing the crowd, "I'll let you know if Ensign Quinn here has anything important to relate."

Quinn was puffing by the time they had climbed up the two hundred-foot incline to the fort itself. Looking back, he was treated to a dramatic view—water glistening in the bright sun, extending for miles into the narrowing strait's throat.

"The British built this place decades ago to control shipping to the Orient," Hancks explained. "That's before they concluded there was no easy northwest passage to the Pacific, at least not through here. Please sit, ensign. Water?"

"Sure. I mean, yes, sir. A bit parched after that climb."

"Understandable. Still, it's a good way to stay fit. Not much else to do up here." Hancks gave Quinn's orders a second look, shaking his head. "I'll assign your duties after I've had time to think over this pleasant surprise."

"Yes, sir."

"Relax, ensign. We're quite informal up here. I see your first name is William. What do you prefer—Will, Bill, Willie, or just straight William."

"My friends and family call me Will. I think I've outgrown Willie."

"So, Will, tell me something about yourself."

"Well, sir, my family immigrated from Ireland when I was nine. Lost a little sister in the transit over. Rotten, stinking conditions aboard that transport, if I can say so."

"Must have been an abomination."

"Yes, sir, it was."

Quinn began relating how his father and his family had found the religious, economic, and political freedom they sought in Maryland, a colony founded by Catholics. The Quinns had been in the linen business in Dublin, and now, without the punitive tariffs imposed by the English and aided by an exploding American market for their products, the family business prospered.

"Then why'd you leave Baltimore?" Hancks asked.

Quinn had never really settled that question in his own mind. With three other brothers in the business, it felt a little crowded. And there was more. Quinn wanted a taste of America's freedom and opportunity. He thought a stretch in the army would let him assay his choices, and it was easy to sign up. With only five thousand officers and men in the unpopular regular army, a fit young man was always welcome. Most of those interested in a military career opted to serve in the more highly valued state militias. Americans still mistrusted a standing army, thanks to their subjugation as British subjects.

Quinn quickly discovered, though, that influence mattered, even in the lowly regular army. Young officers with political connections secured choice posts in the nation's new capital city or in one of the nation's emerging metropolitan areas like Philadelphia, New York, or Baltimore. But Quinn had little clout. Thus, his posting to the fifty-seven-man garrison so far out of sight that it well might have been above the Arctic Circle.

He tried, somewhat haltingly, to explain all this, but he couldn't easily hide his disappointment with his posting. Hanks let it pass. "My good fortune," he said. "I don't need anyone here who got where he is because of his father's connections." Apparently, Hancks too lacked such connections.

"Thank you, sir. I kind of prefer it that way too."

Just a little lie. In truth, if war was coming, Quinn wanted in. He grandly imagined killing some English to avenge his family and all the Irish under the British heel. But why would the British want this isolated outpost? The whole war could pass, Quinn feared, without his ever seeing a Brit.

"Now, this's the situation here," Hancks began, interrupting Quinn's thoughts. "The British didn't give up this fort for years after the end of the war. When they left, the brass figured we had to occupy it, even though we were short on troops.

"As you could see on the way up, the island is crawling with natives. We keep an uneasy truce. Except for a few incidents, things are fairly peaceful. If the British would just stop stirring them up, we all could go home."

Again, the damn British, Quinn thought.

"Can't say for sure how many Indians call this home, but on any day I'd say there are five hundred or more stomping around in the woods beyond. Whites, we've got a couple a hundred, blacksmiths and the like. I don't count the trappers who are in and out all the time."

Quinn understood. Fort Mackinac was alone—in time and place.

"Now, let's hear what you know about impending war. Being from out East, what you know has to be fresher than what we've got."

1 June 1812

The White House, Washington, D.C.

On June 1, Madison sent a war message to Congress, where a clerk in secret session droned on for forty-five minutes, reading it out aloud. It never directly asked for a declaration of war, but its intent was clear.

In the House, where the War Hawks led by the Republican House Speaker Henry Clay held sway, the vote was seventy-nine to forty-nine for war. The Senate deadlocked until June 17, when it voted nineteen to thirteen for war.

The war wasn't Madison's idea, but political and economic circumstances had finally, in his mind, required it. And now it was to be "Mr. Madison's war."

In the first of many blunders bedeviling the war effort, messages alerting the troops and settlers on the far frontiers went out by regular mail to arrive late or not at all—while Canadian spies sent the news north in letters franked by Treasury Secretary Albert Gallatin.

16 July 1812

Fort Mackinac

" War canoes, lieutenant."

"How many?" Hancks asked as he slid alongside Quinn on the western, windward parapet.

"Looks like four this time," Quinn said, squinting into his telescope. "Heading north. As before."

Quinn's first sighting of a war canoe months ago had been awe-inspiring. Big enough to hold five Native American warriors on each side paddling in perfect unison, the canoe sliced through the water at speeds that could challenge over a short course some Great Lakes sloops. The shirtless warriors, skin glistening with sweat and spray, could cover miles at a time. They were a frightening sight in groups and more frightening when they came straight for you.

"Where?" Hancks asked.

The persistent wind blowing at them through the straits nearly carried away the question. The midafternoon sky was painfully bright, making the distant canoes difficult to spot in the silvery waters.

Quinn pointed, then handed Hancks the glass, trying to read the lanky commander's face.

"What do you think?" Quinn asked, knowing what Hancks thought. For days they had watched a procession of war canoes pass. That was good and bad. Good in that the soldiers felt that enough Indians were hovering about the island—bad in that they assumed the Indians were up to something. Their appearance on nearby waters usually meant they'd stop to trade pelts for tools, weapons, and whiskey. Now the stream of bypassing Indians signaled they had something other than commerce in mind.

Hancks and Quinn didn't have to guess their destination: the newly built British Fort St. Joseph on the Canadian side of Lake Huron.

"Cheeky," Quinn muttered. Hancks collapsed the telescope and handed it back to Quinn. "They don't even bother to sneak by," Quinn continued. "Insulting. Do they think we're blind? Or stupid?"

Hancks remained silent. Quinn knew Hancks's dilemma: shoot at them and start another Indian uprising? Quinn favored shooting.

For almost nine full months now, Hancks had heard nothing from his superior officers, ensconced in the new capital in Washington. It was as if Mackinac no longer existed. In front of his junior officer, Hancks long ago had stopped trying to hide his disgust at the incompetence of his commanders.

"Just incredible. We could have been slaughtered up here for all they know," he had said once. "The Brits and the savages at this very moment could be marching on Fort Detroit or Fort Dearborn."

Or us, Quinn thought.

Hancks slid down the ladder to the parade grounds. Quinn followed, more questions unsettling his mind. Do the Indians eat a fallen enemy's still-beating heart? Better to fight to the death than to be taken back to the village to be tortured, burned, or buried alive.

Quinn, understood that help was not nearby. Fort Detroit was three hundred miles away and Fort Dearborn more than four hundred. Between those two outposts and the populous East Coast were more empty miles of the Northwest Territory in the hands of Chippewa, cougars, and snakes. In all of Michigan territory, only five thousand white people—a generous estimate—resided. At best, civilization was well over a week away by canoe on the treacherous lakes, a little less by sloop, and much more by land—all through hostile territories.

Months ago, Hancks had sent the reliable Private Michael Skinner, accompanied by an escort of supposedly friendly Ottawas, to Fort Detroit for updated orders and intelligence. That was the last sight of Skinner. Captured? Betrayed? Lost? Deserted? Dead? Hancks had no clue. Quinn had suggested that someone else be sent, even him, if not just to escape the dreary fort. Hancks had refused. He told Quinn he couldn't afford to deplete his already tiny garrison with more missions into the unknown.

Quinn, even as a novice, saw that operating in the dark in Indian country was a recipe for disaster. The last word from the occasional trapper passing through was the rumor that a couple thousand American militiamen were heading to Fort Detroit from Cincinnati, reportedly under the command of William Hull, Michigan's governor and a Revolutionary War hero who had grown old in mind and body. He had wangled from President Madison the additional title of brigadier general, supposedly to lead an invasion into Canada from Detroit. But it was only rumor.

Hancks and Quinn hustled to the officers' stone quarters for a meeting with the town's leading gentlemen. Quinn had grown to know them, like them, and appreciate their rough-hewn wisdom. They engaged in trading, trapping, fishing, exploring, and supporting occupations, such as carpenter, cobbler, blacksmith, and tanner. They totaled 538 souls.

They were Americans, English, and a few descendents of the French who had come here 140 years ago after Father Marquette planted a cross on the island during his explorations. They were what passed for village elders, and Hancks now needed their experience, wisdom, strength, and most of all, cooperation.

Quinn had learned to enjoy their company, but that didn't mean that he could trust them all.

"Lieutenant, these people...I'd bet a fortnight's pay they know a lot they're not telling us," Quinn had warned Hancks.

"We don't have a choice, Will. We need their cooperation—badly. We can't lock them out. Expose them to the danger. We need them willing to join us in the fort if necessary."

Hancks and Quinn, entering the stone building, didn't have time to adjust to the darkness or to the collective smell and August warmth of twenty-three men before they were hit with the first shouted demands.

"Fer Chris' sake, Hancks, what the hell's going on?"

"Why the hell don't you tell us what's happening?"

"As you know, the Indians have been moving north," Hancks began. "What for, we can only guess. Four war canoes were passing just before I came down from the west blockhouse. That's thirty-two altogether so far. And they're only the ones we've seen. Tibbins here says he saw more when he was checking his trap lines up on Les Cheneaux. Wallace said he saw some leaving here from the other side of the island. That's at least three hundred warriors going somewhere."

"C'mon, Hancks, we know all that."

Hancks let it pass. "Now, we all know what's north of here—the British garrison at Fort St. Joseph. If the Indians are going there, it's to join with the British and make trouble for us."

Flint, the boozy old trapper, interrupted. "Doesn't matter to me," he said of the Indian movements. "I'm minding my own business. That's how ya git along with them savages. The less we make of it, the better off we are."

Karl, the usually reserved blacksmith, jumped in. "Porter, the British garrison there is one hundred eighty strong. Isn't that the last you heard?"

"Maybe more now," Hancks replied.

"Maybe more now," Karl repeated with unaccustomed urgency. "We're only guessing. With all those Indians, that's over five hundred men under arms. This place is theirs for the taking. You're right. We need to know what's going on up there. Knowin's the smart thing."

Murmurs of agreement filled the room.

"They ain't going there to trade," said Flint, stating the obvious as he spit. "Unless they're trading in scalps. Them war canoes ain't packed with no pelts nor anything else the Brits want. The Brits want their tomahawks."

"Well, don't expect them to come and let us know what they's up to," advised another voice, drawing murmurs of agreement. "We've got to send someone up there to take a look."

Hancks was ahead of them. He already had sent Sgt. Michael Dausman out that morning.

Scouting, they call it, Quinn thought. *Also known as spying, a hanging offense.* Quinn figured that *this* was information Hancks thought best not to mention. No telling who'd run off to inform the British.

"Good idea. I'll work on it," Hancks replied. But getting suggestions about military intelligence wasn't why he called the meeting. He had to know whose side they would take.

Flint didn't hold back. "What the hell do you expect us to do, just wait around for the British to show up? You don't have enough men to give them pause! We ain't going to fight your battles."

Clearly, their loyalties were weak. Quinn had learned that national allegiances here weren't as important in the wilderness as simple survival. Some had settled here under the British flag, and if the Union Jack flew above the fort again, so be it.

Quinn could see where Hancks was going, and he wondered if these savvy, self-reliant men saw it too. To keep the fort in American hands, Hancks had to persuade the civilians to seek shelter in the fort—not just for their safety, but also to keep them from cooperating with the British. Hancks played on their fears.

"What about the Ojibwas? You've been seeing them leave the island and heading to St. Joe's. I'd guess if we're going to have British visitors, the Ojibwas would be coming along. And not just to watch. They'll be in war paint."

Quinn could tell by the way they looked at each other that Hancks had made his point. Indians weren't the British— they were primitives who would just as soon kill you as look at you. The Ottawa, Ojibwas, and Pottawatomie were separate branches of the same Algonquin nation, but they had spent much of their history cutting each other's throats. What brought them together now was carving up white folks—not without some cause for how they had treated the Indians. The men knew that whites who weren't butchered were enslaved or taken to the village to run the gauntlet or to be beaten to death by old women. The thought of the British turning the natives loose was something never far out of mind, and now it surfaced again, real and urgent. Some shuddered.

Hancks didn't waste the moment. "The smart thing would be for everyone to come into the stockade. At least until we make out the lay of the land. Even a force of hundreds would have a hard time standing up to our big guns. After a few canisters of grapeshot mows 'em down, I doubt that we'll see much of them again."

Again, murmurs. Quinn couldn't tell if they signaled agreement or skepticism.

Hancks pressed on, recounting his meeting that morning with the fort's interpreter. "This morning, gentlemen, I was approached by Mr. Franks with troubling news. He had sought out Chief Etchemin yesterday to ask what was going on. It wasn't just his braves crossing the waters that concerned Franks. The Ojibwas who remained behind are acting distant. Not talking. Restive. As if they know something. I'm sure you've noticed it."

A few *yeahs* were heard.

"The chief assured Franks that everything was normal. He told Franks not to be troubled, that they have warm feelings for us."

That brought groans, and Hancks spoke over them. "He told Franks the canoers were just forming a hunting party for beyond the Sault. The omens, he said, are for a hard winter, and they need to lay in extra food. '*Nde'bwe*,' he told Franks, 'I speak truth.'"

That brought more groans.

"But Mr. Franks had gathered very different information on his own. The British *are* coming, and they're bringing the Indians with them. They're assembling now at Fort St. Joseph."

Hancks waited a moment to let it sink in.

"The war has started?" someone asked.

"Hancks, wouldn't Detroit or somebody tell ya if a war started?"

"I would hope so. But it's probably a good idea to prepare ourselves. The best we can do for now is defend ourselves. That means that everyone has to get behind the walls. Right now."

Flint didn't miss a beat. "Forts don't mean much. Picking the right side means more. Maybe we should just bide our time. If we come behind the walls, we've taken a side, maybe the losing one."

Flint might be a smelly old drunk, but he had survived in the wilderness for decades. Among settlers who knew what that took, it counted for a lot. Besides, for the group, comfort lay in indecision for now.

"Maybe some of you just want to weigh it," Flint said.

Quinn began to wonder what Flint was up to. Obviously, he had no property or business here to worry about. Just get in his canoe and go somewhere else if the British came. Then why was he so anxious to keep the families outside the safety of the walls? Treachery?

Quinn, standing on Hancks's left, felt opinion shifting. A cacophony of side conversations followed.

"What would it hurt to think about it?"

"Anyone thinks he'd be safe behind walls could go ahead and spend the night."

"What, spend months groveling in there until we get starved out?"

"Ya can't count on Detroit or anyone else sending help. Look how they's already forgot us."

Or maybe they hadn't. A messenger, sent by the parapet watch, excitedly broke into the room with news.

"*Friends Good Will* is tying up in the harbor!"

16 July 1812

Fort Mackinac

"*I*'m telling ya', there ain't nothing new from Detroit!" Lee yelled at the crowd. "Nothing but confounded speculation. Now will you remove your arses from the dock so's I can get on with my business?"

As usual, Lee had departed Detroit with supplies for forts Mackinac and Dearborn. Also aboard were the axes and knives, costume jewelry, whiskey, and other wares that were traded to the Indians for furs and feathers the men and women of Paris, New York, and London coveted. The Indians thought they got the better of the deal, receiving manufactured essentials they couldn't make in exchange for plentiful and, to their minds, cheap pelts.

Lee and his crew started hoisting cargo onto the dock while Hancks and Quinn waited in the background for the crowd to disperse.

"Good trip?" Hancks asked.

"Good weather," Lee said. "And if you're aiming to ask for news, I'll tell you what I told that multitude of the curious. There ain't none to be had."

Hancks asked anyway. "Nothing? No letters, no orders from the brass at Detroit?"

"Nothing."

"Are those idiots still there at Detroit?" Quinn couldn't help himself. He now understood the frustration of being officially ignored for months. "Or did they all run back to the safety of Pittsburgh or someplace?"

Hancks jumped in before Quinn could launch a tirade. "I didn't expect to hear anything," he said. "But since I only have rumors to sustain me, can you describe what you've heard? Any niblet might prove useful."

"Well, formal announcements being scarce, I can share with you what the last scavenger who stumbled out of the woods said before I left. He said old man Hull is still tramping his way to Detroit. Hull allows as how he is a Revolutionary War hero, so I suppose that allows him to keep everyone in the dark about his intentions. As if he was still young enough to swing his fat, sloppy old arse onto his horse without help."

"Any idea where he's at now?" Hancks asked.

"None. Hey, you there, handle that hooch carefully. Break it and I don't get paid. Meaning you don't neither."

As Lee and his crew manhandled more barrels and crates onto the docks, Hancks turned to Quinn. "Hull is marching a couple thousand men to Detroit. Probably figures it'll be a cakewalk from Detroit all the way to Montreal. Hell, Will, the war may already have started, but I doubt Hull knows what's up. If his lines of communication back to Washington are anything like the ones he has with us, he's probably marching blind. Has no more an idea than us if the war's started."

"Truth be told," Quinn said.

"Could be marching straight into a surprise attack," Hancks continued. "If British preparations are going on at Fort Malden across from Detroit like they're going on here, all they have to do is sit and wait. Hull'll march right into the arms of British regulars and hundreds of Wyandottes."

Quinn knew what Hancks meant. Just as the British had built a fort on St. Joseph Island on Lake Huron to oppose Fort Mackinac, they had also constructed one at the mouth of the Detroit River on Lake Erie to oppose the U.S. stockade at Detroit. From Malden, British guns and sloops could control all Lake Erie traffic to and from Detroit, cutting an important American supply route to and from Buffalo and farther east. The British, garrisoned along the Niagara River above Niagara Falls, could turn Erie into a Canadian lake. And that would scotch whatever plans Hull had to cross into Canada and march overland to York, the capital of Upper Canada.

Hancks interrupted Quinn's thoughts. "Well, if Hull won't tell me what's going on, maybe I should tell him. Will"—he turned, fixing his eyes on his subordinate—"I'm sending you to Fort Dearborn with Lee."

"Aw, for the love of..." Quinn muttered below his breath, dreading the thought of going from the isolation of Mackinac to the earth's edge at Dearborn.

"Ensign, did you hear me?" Hancks asked as they began heading back up the hill to the fort.

"Yes, sir, I did. I'm anxious to hear more of what you have in mind."

"You and I both know that we're about to be attacked by the British and their savages. We don't know who started the war, but we know that we're gonna get hit. We can't delay getting this information to Hull and the rest. We could easily be the tripwire. So your job is to warn Fort Dearborn. Then head to Fort Wayne to pass the word there—assuming it's still in American hands. Fort Wayne's maybe a hundred and fifty miles from Dearborn. The folks there can give you directions."

Quinn knew it too. He had put his time in the wilderness to good use, learning not just survival skills, but about the importance of the Northwest to America. He had learned, for example, that General "Mad Anthony" Wayne, a famous Indian fighter, had built a fort in Indiana Territory almost twenty years ago and named it after himself. The fort was intended to protect the critical portage between the Maumee and Wabash rivers, which connected the Great Lakes and Mississippi River watersheds. From Fort Wayne, Quinn could make his way to any number of more secure fortifications to the east, or even to Detroit. But after that, what?

"Begging the lieutenant's pardon, but why not go directly to Detroit? It's nearer and more settled."

"My first instinct too," Hancks replied. "But suppose the war has started. Suppose Detroit is already in British hands? Lee, I'm sure, wouldn't think too highly of sailing back to Detroit and finding it a Limey port. They'd seize *Friends* and press him into service."

"I guess you've thought a lot about this," Quinn said resignedly.

" Maybe the whole thing's a fool's errand, but there's not much else left for us to do."

Hancks had stopped on the path and turned back to face the lake. Quinn noticed Hancks's gray eyes urgently scanning the horizon, as if he could find on it some answer, some certitude, some solid fact on which to rely. The young ensign started to appreciate the rigors of command. Facts arrive in different shades and shapes, while decisions are, of their nature, black and white—act or don't act. Act this way or that.

"Begging your pardon," Quinn said, "but why me? Aren't I more valuable to you here? How can you spare me when you need every man you've got?"

"I send you on a noble mission, Will. Hull needs to know. The rest of the nation needs to know. And I've grown to trust you."

Quinn shrugged. Noble? He didn't like being sent far from the battle or leaving behind men he had lived and trained with for the past four months. Endless hours of eating dust with wheel rights, column lefts, and about faces. Countless thrusts and parries in bayonet practice. He feared some might think badly of him, ducking out at the most dangerous moment—a quitter. Besides, he didn't want to miss his first taste of combat against the Brits. Might even kill a couple or take a bunch prisoner.

Like all novice soldiers, Quinn had a romantic view of combat. Yes, he knew intellectually about the dangers and the horrors of war, but there was the glory, the tests of courage successfully faced. Afraid of death? No, the threat was always there, whether you were on a dangerous mission through hostile territories or simply groping in the darkness toward the privy out back. In this unsettled land, dangers constantly lurked. Being stranded and lost. Falling prey to one of the great bears or cats of the wilderness. Being set upon by the savages.

Actually, Quinn's safer course would be to journey to Dearborn rather than risk capture by the British. Capture meant death. The British rationale for impressing American sailors hung on the assertion that once you were born in Great Britain, you always were a subject of the Crown. You never could renounce your British citizenship; you were stuck with it for your entire life. Hence, American sailors, even if they were U.S. citizens, were impressed onto British ships even on the suspicion of being born in Ireland, Canada, or wherever else the Union Jack flew.

For Quinn, an Irish immigrant who had become a naturalized American citizen, the idea of capture by the British haunted him. By British law, reasoning, and prejudice, Quinn could be taken back to England and hanged as a traitor. That would be the outcome because impressing Americans into the British army would be much more difficult than making them serve on a British vessel on the high seas. He would be have been accused of taking up arms against his monarch, the worst kind of sedition. His life would serve no purpose except as a wretched example of what would come of traitors.

"I know you're up for the job," Hancks offered. "That's why I'm picking you."

Quinn had no choice. Maybe this would be the adventure he was disappointed not to find when he first landed at Mackinac. Yet he would be leaving a place he had come to know where he might actually have faced his old enemies, the English, in combat.

In no time, it seemed, *Friends Good Will* was unloaded and provisioned for passage to Fort Dearborn. Quinn found himself standing uncomfortably on the pitching sloop's deck as the island fortress receded from view. He suspected he would never see this place or these people again. The sloop beat against the wind, and the choppy waters were compressed and speeded along as they funneled through the narrow straits. Suddenly the sloop emerged from the strait's confines and into Lake Michigan. Quickly, the two shorelines so clearly visible port and starboard spread out, giving the sloop welcome room to maneuver. Just as quickly, a sense of isolation and foreboding closed in.

23 July 23 1812

On Lake Michigan

Quinn wanted to shoot a Brit; he told Master Lee as they sailed toward Fort Dearborn, "Probably won't be a Limey in sight there. Wish I could've stayed and picked some off at Mackinac." He neglected to mention that he'd never killed—or even shot at—anyone.

"You've got a chip on your shoulder, lad. What did the Brits ever do to you?"

"Murder my uncle. My father's brother, my godfather. Took him out on the street and shot him like a dog. Him and thousands more murdered. Or maimed or dragged off to rot in filthy English jails. I was just nine then. Saw it for myself."

"Why'd they do such a thing?"

"Why? Good God, Master Lee, they shoot the Irish just for being Irish. My uncle Will stood up and said he had rights, but they didn't think so."

Quinn fell silent. It was just a momentary break in the arduous task of sailing a sloop through the choppy Lake Michigan waters, a chance for Lee and Quinn to sit on the forecastle and watch Lake Michigan's eastern shore slip by. The prevailing winds had piled the sand into huge dunes on the shoreline, some high enough to blot out the land behind them. As the wind pushed the sands farther inland, they buried brush and trees.

"They call them walking dunes," Lee explained, "because of how fast they move. Takes but a day or two for some of 'em to completely cover a bush, like it was never there"

Quinn liked Lee. Behind the gruff exterior was a kindly and wise man. He knew that the old sailor worried about him and about his hatred of the Brits. So Quinn decided to share with Lee as much as he wanted to know—chapter and verse, the whole sorry saga of England's exploitation of the Irish.

"My uncle Will was one of the Men of Ninety-Eight, the uprising. The English took our land, took our language, tried to take our faith. The French were supposed to support our rebellion, but weather and God knows what else worked against us. They failed to show up, and we paid for it.

"When Uncle Will was killed, my folks gave up and came to America. My father was an expert linen weaver in Dublin, but his business was failing."

Linen, Quinn explained, was an ideal product for Irish manufacture, thanks to a welcoming climate for flax. But the English favored the linen makers of Ulster in Northern Ireland who were transplanted English Protestants. English tariffs and import policies discriminated against Catholic weavers, and then cheaper cotton fabric came in from America's South.

Quinn's father, John, sold his looms, his house, and his furniture to buy passage to America for his wife, his four sons, and tiny daughter Anne.

"They had us good," Quinn said. "When my father sold everything, they had him by the balls. They got everything real cheap. Otherwise he'd just have to leave everything for the poachers."

The crossing to Baltimore was a nightmare—cramped, damp quarters; meager rations; hostile crews; virulent diseases; violence; and death. Little Anne, like a good many others, did not survive the passage.

"We had to give her up to the sea. Watching her body sink under the waves—I don't think Mother's ever been the same."

"I'm sorry, lad," Lee said quietly.

"There's more," Quinn continued. It was more than a business decision. The English stripped the Irish of virtually all rights—the right to vote, to own property and weapons, to serve in the military, to sit in Parliament, to be educated, to assemble, to exercise habeas corpus. Of course, they could reclaim some rights by renouncing their Catholic faith. Church property was confiscated or destroyed; priests went into hiding. Catholics had to tithe to the Church of Ireland, which was in fact the Church of England.

"The Irish had their own language once," Quinn said. "Gaelic. They took that away too. You talk about slavery in America. Tens of thousands of Irish Catholics were sold into slavery. This Cromwell fellow who killed the English king...he called himself the First Lord Protector of England, Scotland, and Ireland. He protected a half million Irishmen to death.

"Mark my words, Master Lee. We haven't seen the worst yet. Now the Irish are living on potatoes while everything else gets shipped out of the country. If the potato harvest fails, the Irish are doomed."

"Lad, I think you need to rest now." Lee's voice carried a note of concern. "Your color's up, and I can see why, but you've a long journey ahead. Save your strength, and husband your anger."

For a moment, the bow cutting through the water and the wind strumming on the gaff rig were the only sounds.

"My uncle, the one who was in the uprising? He got no trial. His friends found his body in a gutter. The rats had eaten his eyes and were working on his guts." Quinn shook his head. "You're right. The anger of it wears me out, it does."

Lee was studying him quietly, lighting his pipe, cupping the flame against the wind.

After a moment Quinn asked, "What do you think we'll find at Fort Dearborn?"

"Well, no Brits, I don't imagine," Lee replied with a wry grim. "You'll find plenty of savages, though, and you'd better figure that most of them side with the Brits. They communicate regularly with the Potawatomi and other tribes. It's a mystery how word can get around among them faster than I can sail the distance.

"Them Indians remember their defeat by Mad Anthony Wayne and their losses at Tippecanoe a year back. This chief, Tecumseh, is a smooth talker and has a lot of the tribes siding with him, meaning with the Brits. He tells them that the American government wants them off their lands, and there's not much they've seen to dispute that.

"The Potawatomi and them have been pushed back from the East, and now, by their reckoning, they're shoulder to shoulder, back to back, without enough land to keep them in meat and berries. Tecumseh gets promised a lot by the Brits in Canada. If he helps them drive the Americans back across the Appalachians, they'll protect the tribes and keep the Americans out for good."

"And the Indians believe them?"

"A lot of them do. You saw it up at Mackinac. But here's the thing—if Mackinac falls, assuming the worst, word will get back to the Indians and prove the Brits right. Fence sitters will jump to join Tecumseh. Detroit, Fort Wayne, Dearborn—they're all in peril. All the way down to Kentucky."

"Doesn't look good then."

"God, lad," Lee said, shifting thoughts, "it's a hundred fifty dangerous miles of wilderness between Dearborn and Wayne. Especially for a greenhorn like yourself, no offense intended. Indians, bears, what have you. Of course, them Indians at Dearborn say they're friendly, but really, you never know.

"So, here's the thing—get to know their ways. Don't show no cowardliness. They respect that. 'Specially if they think you can give as good or better than you get. Try not to insult them. Call a brave a squaw, and he'll take your heart out before you know it."

"How much farther?" Quinn asked, although he had an idea from studying the charts that Lee unfolded during the ensign's navigation lessons.

He knew they were hugging the eastern and now the southern shore, so it couldn't be long. Cutting diagonally across the lake and following the western shore would have been quicker, but Lee wanted to avoid the hostiles at Green Bay. The eastern route took longer because it required *Friends* to beat against the prevailing westerly winds at the bottom of the lake, winds that rose to batter them as they put out from a tiny trading camp at mouth of St. Joe's River. Almost directly west lay Fort Dearborn in Illinois territory.

Now more dunes came into view off the port side as they closed on the shores of the Indiana and Illinois territories. Soon, Quinn knew from the charts, the shoreline would turn north and Fort Dearborn would appear.

Suddenly Lee sprang to his feet. A half dozen war canoes were closing on the *Friends* and looked headed for the same destination—Fort Dearborn.

The sight of the Indians chilled Quinn. The canoes were no match in speed for *Friends*, but they had a better angle on Fort Dearborn, so they would arrive at virtually the same time.

Instinctively, Quinn went below to grab his musket, his pistol, and his scabbard with the officer's sword his family had given him. *Friends*, a commercial vessel, wasn't equipped with anything bigger than small firearms. And those would be deployed only if, by some horrible mistake, Lee sailed *Friends* into a spot where he had no room to maneuver.

The rest of the crew also broke out arms. Fort Dearborn, with its two blockhouses on its eastern and western walls, popped over the horizon. The canoes sliced through the water at surprising speeds. Were these Indians hostile? Or were the braves just eager for a race? As they drew closer, Quinn could see that they weren't painted for war, but he would follow Lee's advice—the first rule of the wilderness is to show no fear.

Lee sailed as close to the wind as possible, but the nearer he came to the shoreline, the more the wind shifted, forcing him to tack to port. The canoes were running so close athwart that when *Friends* tacked, the sloop cut off the canoes, spilling its crew of braves into the water.

Lee's face glowed with satisfaction as he guided *Friends* to the shore. He barely glanced at the Indians. *Lee actually enjoyed this dangerous game*, Quinn thought. Was that what it took to fight a war? A readiness to play when the stakes were so high?

23 July 1812

Fort Dearborn, Illinois Territory

"*L*ee, you're an idiot!" shouted Captain William Heald.

Lee nodded at the commander of Fort Dearborn and shrugged. "But a *live* idiot."

A cordon of soldiers had hustled Lee and Quinn off the sloop and hauled them into the fort to face Heald, by all accounts the most cautious, by-the-book, regular army officer in the Northwest.

"We're sitting on a powder keg here. Your lunacy could have started a slaughter." He turned to Quinn. "Why are you here?"

"Sir, Lieutenant Hancks sent me with his compliments. We may have lost Fort Mackinac to the British. When I left—"

"What do you mean, may have lost?"

"Sir, when I left I was sent to warn you on the eve of what we expected to be an outbreak of hostilities. An alliance of Indian and British troops were forming at Fort St. Joseph for an attack. They outnumbered us by hundreds. Hancks was certain that we had no chance."

"So you fled in the face of the enemy?"

Quinn saw his worst fear coming true and bristled. "No, sir! I was *sent* here"—Quinn's voice dripped with indignation—"to warn you. If I'd had a choice, I'd have stayed to fight the Limies—and let you *guess* what was happening up there." Quinn surprised himself at his boldness, but he wouldn't be called a coward. His thin lips twitched slightly as he considered why the world should be filled with so many fools.

"Ensign, just tell me what happened."

Quinn complied, starting at the beginning—the months of ignorance and isolation, the criminal failure of superior officers to update the outpost, the gathering of hostiles, all of it.

"I'm sure Lieutenant Hancks will find a way to send you word if events have turned out better," Quinn said. "Maybe a week or two will tell."

"A week or two." Heald sighed.

Lee broke in. "That doesn't help me much. Cap, I've got to decide what to do after I'm done here trading. Go back or hang around. Every day I'm tied up here is a day I don't make money. Going back could mean sailing into the Brits' hands. I could try to run past Mackinac and race 'em to Detroit. But what if the Brits have taken Detroit?"

"I don't know. It's your business, Lee," Heald said, turning back to Quinn. "As for you, ensign. You'll stay here. We need every man."

"Excuse me, sir, but my orders are clear. I'm to proceed immediately to Fort Wayne to warn them. If I sail back to the trading post at the St. Joe River, I might get a horse there. Otherwise I'll go on foot. Can't wait here—people could die if I do."

"People already are dying here, *ensign*. We lost almost an entire family to the savages just a few weeks ago. The Martins. They worked their crops upriver, less than two miles from here. Tomahawked in their cabin and their scalps taken. Still alive while they done it, judging from the amount of blood. Only a daughter survived.

"The local tribes, the Pottawatomie and Winnebagos, tried to tell us it was the work of some renegade scalping party down from Rock River or Green Bay. But who can you trust, eh? You saw Indians paddling past Fort Mackinac to St. Joe's? Here they're paddling right up to our gate. Every day there're more of 'em. Some's got fire in their eyes."

Lee interjected, "Figure that the Brits have stirred them up?"

"What else? Them and Tecumseh. They got the poor saps thinking that they can to take back the entire Northwest Territories."

Now he fixed Quinn with a steely look. "Ensign, as far as I'm concerned, the war's already started here. Look around you. We've never had so many Indians camped around the fort. We might as well be under siege."

Lee grunted agreement.

"They're still boiling about the whupping they took at Prophets Town down there on Tippecanoe Creek. You know about Prophets Town, ensign?"

"Well, I heard about it—"

"Hearing and knowing are two different things. If you're going to soldier in this wilderness, you *better* know about it if you're going to understand what makes these aborigines tick."

Quinn bristled at being treated like an ignorant fool but hid his displeasure.

"See, Tecumseh was going to unite all the tribes to fight the great white scourge. Said he'd drive us all back across the Appalachians. Idiotic. The tribes been killing each other off for centuries, uniting them all would have been quite a trick. Still, he was making progress."

Heald shook his head then glared at Quinn..

"Now, the last thing that we wanted was Indian nations uniting against us. So we made some concessions— promises to respect their territories and whatnot. In return, some chiefs ceded over three million acres. Didn't go over well with Tecumseh and other chiefs who weren't a party to it.

"The treaty created lots of jealousies, and Tecumseh used them to instigate raids on our settlements. Indians figured the best way to scare the settlers away was to kill every last one, women and children too.

"Fellow called William Henry Harrison was governor of the Indiana Territory. He was furious. Wanted to drive every last Indian out. Commenced the cleansing with the Indian settlement at Prophets Town. Place was named after Tecumseh's brother, kind of a crazy man named Tenskwatawa. Claimed he had magical powers. Said bullets couldn't hurt him or his braves. Turned the whole thing into a kind of religion."

Now Heald was on his feet in full voice.

"So when Harrison camps his troops a couple a miles away from Prophets Town, Tecumseh's lunatic brother surprises Harrison's boys with a nighttime raid. Lots of maiming and killing, a real frenzy till Harrison rallied his men and drove Tenskwatawa off and burned Prophets Town to the ground."

"Sounds fair to me," Lee said.

"Mind you, this was only a year ago. Some braves you see camped outside here might've been at Prophets Town. So you see, ensign, why I need every last man, especially a commissioned officer. Get on out there now, introduce yourself to the other officers, and see how you can help with drilling the men. I expect an attack at any time."

25 July 1812

Fort Dearborn

Sally Martin had found refuge and solace at John and Eleanor Kinzie's cabin after her family's slaughter. That day she had been alone in the field, checking the corn for blight when she heard those awful screams coming from her family's cabin. She could do nothing but lay quietly in stark terror among the stalks. After silence again descended on the cabin, she found her family had been massacred, her mother and two sisters raped, her father and brother brutally beaten and scalped. Suddenly her whole world was gone.

Now she went through the motions, helping Eleanor cook and clean, doing anything to fill the time. Never far from her thoughts was the fear that something waiting in the forest would burst upon her without warning. Another part of her mind was filled with anger, yet another turned to practical matters. At seventeen she was deemed quite marriageable. But a single young woman with no family could rely on the kindness of friends and neighbors for only so long.

Soon, very soon, the Kinzies and others would begin gently but firmly pressing her to choose a husband. She knew three eligible men: John Jackson was as old as her father, Paul Merryman had already worked two wives to death, and Smithfield Rogers was—may God forgive her—surely the homeliest man in the entire Northwest Territory. And, of course, the soldiers at the fort...but most of them had left wives back East, and the others...

Life on the frontier left no room or time for self-pity. So when John and Eleanor asked her to come with them to the fort to get whatever news Heald might have acquired from the new arrivals, she reluctantly agreed.

Kinzie, a trader who had settled on the north bank of the river, had established close ties to both the local tribes and the military. As early pioneers, the Kinzies enjoyed the run of the fort where they were introduced to Ensign Quinn and summoned by Heald to his office.

Sally looked frankly at Quinn's boyish face, noting his dark-blue eyes and his narrow mouth. Not bad looking, but ordinary. It was the uniform that lent him distinction—the blue coat, short in front but extending to tails in the back; the epaulette; the high collar that nearly reached his ears; and the officer's sword dangling from a decorative belt. A uniform like that, in Sally's opinion, could make *anyone* look good, but she had to concede that Quinn's bearing was impressive. And there was something interesting in his eyes—sadness but not defeat.

So she was not displeased when Eleanor Kinzie invited him, along with Heald, to dinner.

Quinn, in turn, had been charmed at once by Sally. Her face was soft and unblemished, miraculous on the frontier where many women aged beyond their years. Her strawberry curls were pulled back from her face in a fashion now passé in the East but much in vogue around Fort Dearborn. The pert nose and those green eyes—surely a cailin, surely Irish.

So absorbed was he that Heald coughed sharply then repeated, "Isn't that so, Ensign Quinn?"

"I...yes, sir..."

Heald smiled. "The situation at Mackinac...I have reported it accurately to Mr. Kinzie?

Quinn turned to Heald. "Oh. Yes. Yes, sir. At least, that is all we know at the moment."

Kinzie smiled too then took his leave and escorted the ladies out of the office. When they were gone, Heald lit his pipe.

"A very pretty girl."

Quinn blushed. "Yes, sir."

"Are you married, Quinn?"

"No, sir."

"Engaged? Do you have an understanding with a young woman back East?"

"No, sir."

"You're sure?"

"Absolutely sure, sir, but—"

"Because Sally Martin has had quite enough to deal with in her short life, and she doesn't need to be trifled with."

"Sir! I—"

"Before you get all indignant, ensign, recall what I've told you about the fate of the Martin family."

The following evening, Heald and Quinn found dinner waiting at the Kinzies' cabin. John Kinzie presided over the table with Quinn on his left and Heald on his right. Eleanor sat next to Heald and placed Sally next to Quinn. Little John Kinzie sat at the other end of the table where, presumably, he would interrupt the proceedings as little as possible. A lamb roast smothered in gravy and baked potatoes and beans fresh from the field delighted Quinn, who'd eaten his last home-cooked meal months ago in Baltimore.

At first their conversation was stilted and self-conscious, but then Eleanor asked Sally about her books. She was a prolific reader, and her parents, proud of her accomplishments, had allowed her to order books from back East. She would race to meet any sloops that might be carrying the latest batch.

Quinn was enchanted. He had not expected to find a quick mind under those red-gold curls. Her breasts rose and fell more rapidly as she spoke, and Quinn, taking in the sight in sidelong glances, was thankful that the meal was progressing slowly.

This, of course, was not Sally's first conquest. She knew he was more than a little attracted to her. Indeed, Eleanor's little smile indicated that she believed she had made a match. But Sally had questions, the same ones Heald had asked. Many a soldier had dallied with a young woman he met in the wilderness before returning home to his true love.

She did not demur when Mrs. Kinzie dispensed with a chaperone's formalities and suggested that Sally and Quinn take a walk. Quinn was uncertain whether to accept, but Heald waved him off, assuring him that he and Kinzie had old war stories to tell.

They walked in silence for several minutes. Quinn felt he should ask about her family, but he hesitated to upset her. She solved the problem for him.

"Let's stay along the river, Mr. Quinn, if you don't mind. I avoid the woods as best I can since my family was killed." She stopped walking and turned to look at him directly as if she expected a response.

Quinn was silent for a moment, looking at the ground. Then he met her gaze and said, "I think you are the bravest young woman I have ever met, Miss Martin. When I was only a boy, I lost my country and my sister, and I know that pain. I cannot imagine the depth of your loss."

In silence, their eyes met. Quinn saw tears swell in hers, and he experienced a powerful urge to draw her to him, in comfort and understanding. Quinn also saw something else in her eyes, but the young man was too inexperienced to understand what it was.

5 August 1812

Canada, Opposite Fort Detroit

Sergeant Major Judah Frake, along with the thousands of troops under the command of General William Hull, had spent months on the march. Some, like Frake, had come from Kentucky, some from Ohio, but all were fed up and tired. They craved action, and here, finally, was their chance. Hull took his troops across the Detroit River into Canada and was pleasantly surprised not to be challenged. Not a shot was fired, and in minutes the Stars and Stripes were flying over Canadian soil.

Then Hull's army stopped in its tracks.

The general ordered his troops to hunker down. Days of inaction dragged on. Puzzlement and doubt gave way to restlessness and anger. They had marched hundreds of miles to sit on a riverbank?

Their first objective, on paper anyway, was Fort Malden, which guarded the mouth of the Detroit River where it emptied into Lake Erie. Malden was undermanned, undersupplied, and insufficiently fortified, a plum waiting to be plucked. At last Frake and other senior noncoms began voicing their discontent to junior officers. Frake warned that the troops were losing their edge and their motivation.

Some were talking about going back home and to hell with their enlistment contracts. Many, like Frake, were independent-minded and skilled backwoodsmen whose frontier experience had taught them the fatal consequences of dallying and indecision.

Pressured by his staff, Hull belatedly sent out Bravo Company under the command of Major Elijah Chase to assess the situation. Not ten miles south of Hull's camp, Chase sighted a bridge across the Riviere Aux Candards guarded by Canadian militia. The militiamen saw Chase's detachment about the same time but didn't move. Frake figured they were ignorant of the danger they were in. Or just too cocky for their own good. Maybe Chase was reading Frake's mind.

"Sergeant, do you think you can pick off one of those strutting peacocks?"

"Yes, sir," Frake replied confidently.

The closest Redcoat was more than two hundreds yards away, and no one could predict what a musket ball might do as it blasted and spun out of a smooth barrel. A ball shot from a smoothbore had half the accuracy at half the distance of a tightly spinning bullet shot from the spiral grooves of a rifle barrel.

Nevertheless, bracing his flintlock against a tree, Frake instinctively reckoned the distance and the wind. He took and held a deep breath and pulled the trigger, releasing the hammer. It dropped onto the frizzen, shaving off just enough iron to create the sparks that ignited the gunpowder. Through the musket smoke, Frake saw a militiaman spin, as if hit in the shoulder, and fall from the bridge.

"Good shot, sergeant."

"Yes, sir, if I do say so," Frake said, knowing how lucky he was. "Lookit those varmints run."

"Regular British soldiers would never abandon a wounded comrade like that," Chase said. "Must be Canadian militia. Let's move out."

Chase and his men crossed the bridge in pursuit of the fleeing men but were wary of being lured into a trap. Getting and holding the land between the bridge and the fort wasn't the goal; getting in sight of Malden to gather intelligence was.

"Gawd almighty, look at this," Chase said as they neared the fort. "This place is wide open. Unless it's a clever ruse, the place is ripe for picking."

All the signs were there, Frake agreed. "No pickets stopping us from walking right up to the fort to give them a howdy-do. Not much smoke from inside the fort, unless the Brits eat their possum raw."

Now Chase called most of his men back to the bridge and told them to dig in, posted skirmishers on the perimeter to intercept any returning Canadians, and placed sharpshooters to catch the enemy in a deadly crossfire.

To his assembled staff, he said, "I don't think we need more than a single battalion to take Malden if we do it before it can be reinforced. Hull can take the rest of his troops and push on up the peninsula into the heart of Upper Canada. Men, God just handed us a gift."

"General, sir, Major Chase sends his compliments." Frake snapped to attention, but Hull didn't bother looking up from his papers as he sat at his makeshift desk in the hot and humid command tent.

"Yes, yes, what is it?"

"The major wishes to report that Bravo Company has secured the bridge over Riviere Aux Canards with no casualties, excepting for a dead Brit too stupid to take cover."

"He took the bridge?" Now Frake had Hull's full attention, as he looked up for the first time.

Frake hesitated. Hull didn't sound pleased, but surely... "Actually, general, he did more. Having secured the bridge, the major reconnoitered Fort Malden and found that she's ripe for pickin'. The place is a shambles, and here's the clincher, we practically rode up to spittin' distance, and no one came out chasing us. It's a pushover."

Hull waved away the smoke from his stogie and narrowed his eyes.

"A battalion would be more than enough to take it, sir," Frake went on. "That's what the major reckons. The only hitch is a sixteen-gunner that the Brits could move up the Detroit River to control the bridge unless, as the Major suggests, we get there first."

Hull's face reddened. Frake was only the messenger, but he caught Hull's full fury. "Sergeant major, you ride back to Major Chase and tell him he exceeded his orders and endangered his men by approaching Fort Malden. Tell him he is to personally report to me at once with an explanation for his carelessness! And, by God, if he tries any more such stunts, he'll be facing a court martial! Understood?"

"Sir?" Frake didn't think he could have had heard correctly

"And tell him he is to bring Bravo Company back with him. He is not to stay at the bridge. I will not have men under my command dangling on a thin string so far from the main force. He is to pull his troops back to Turkey River and hand over his command to Colonel Findlay."

Now Frake knew he had understood perfectly, but he was still baffled. Had Hull lost his mind?

"Sergeant Major, did you not hear me?"

Frake couldn't miss the disbelief on the faces of Hull's staff, and they couldn't miss the amazement on his.

As Frake left Hull's tent to mount up and give Chase the bad news, a junior officer and his one-man escort galloped into camp and drew up in front of the tent. The junior officer, a lieutenant, was unfamiliar but was clearly on urgent business. Before his lathered horse had fully stopped, he dismounted and turned to Hull's orderly, who was rushing forward to grab the reins. Near breathless, the young officer said, "My compliments to General Hull. Tell him that Lieutenant Porter Hancks, commander of Fort Mackinac, is reporting." He might have added, "With bad news."

13 August 1812

Fort Dearborn

Well past nightfall the friendly Pottawatomie chief Winnemeg arrived with twenty of his best warriors, after riding hard from Fort Wayne. Winnemeg barged into Heald's headquarters, interrupting a strategy meeting. The chief withdrew a sheaf of papers from a leather pouch and handed them to Heald.

"Orders from General Hull." Winnemeg's face was inexpressive, his dark eyes burning.

Heald studied the papers briefly then looked up. "The United States has declared war on Great Britain. At last we know. Hull has led a force into Canada from Detroit, but Mackinac has surrendered." Everyone knew what this meant: the surrender would mobilize thousands more Indians, and now Hull's northern flank would be exposed.

"General Hull orders us to abandon Fort Dearborn, remove all civilians, and distribute to the Indians all government stores in the stockade and those in the custody of John Kinzie. We're to go to Fort Wayne."

Heald looked around the room. Winnemeg leaned against the doorframe, his face impassive, his eyes fixed on the floor. Lieutenant Linai Helm had paled and was chewing his lower lip. The wiry Ensign Ronan—Georgie to his mates—frowned. The surgeon, Dr. Van Voorhees, looked to Quinn as if he had seen a ghost.

Quinn was worried, confused, amazed—and furious. If Mackinac was so goddamned important, if its fall so imperiled the Upper Canadian campaign and with it the entire war, why had Hull left it so isolated and so uninformed? Why hadn't he reinforced the fort? If the United States had declared war on Canada, why hadn't Mackinac been manned and supplied? Whose side was this fool Hull on?

The silence broke under a flood of questions.

"If the fall of Mackinac exposes his flank, what about his rear if we abandon Dearborn?"

"Sir, if we leave, won't even more disaffected tribes join the Brits?"

Winnemeg nodded agreement.

"Sir," Ronan said, "we're safe here. Helm and I have our wives and children with us. And what about civilians with women and children? How do we get them safely to Fort Wayne? It's a hundred and fifty miles away!"

"Ronan's right, sir. This is suicide," Quinn blurted. He wanted to ask whether every senior officer was a fool, but thought better of it. For the moment.

"Captain," Helm said, "we've got enough provisions to hold out for at least six months, enough arms for even longer. We can survive a siege. I respectfully suggest that we send a message and tell Hull we're holding the fort. Doesn't the order say that evacuation should take place *if practicable?*"

In fact, the orders did contain the standard qualification that takes a senior officer of the hook in case an order backfires, but Heald shook his head. "Gentlemen, we have our orders. And by the Almighty, I intend to follow them. In time, you'll see to the distribution of supplies to the Indians. It will be viewed as a peace offering. A treaty, if you will. We will meet with them in council and open up our storerooms in exchange for their promise of safe conduct."

Helm protested. "I mean no disrespect, but the Indians don't have to bargain for our stores. Once we leave, they can walk in and take them!"

Heald nodded. "But they don't *know* that we're leaving. In council, we say that we're making an offering of fellowship because we wish for peace. We ask what they can offer in return—perhaps safe passage *if* any or all of us decide to leave."

"And you think they'll keep their word?"

Helm's incredulous question was left hanging as Kinzie burst into the room. Winnemeg's braves had told a few settlers of the ordered evacuation, and the word had spread like a contagion. So much for keeping the order secret.

"What the hell is this I hear?" Kinzie boomed.

It was an unfortunate beginning. Heald and Kinzie may have dined together, but they had a tenuous relationship.

"I hear Hull has ordered an evacuation. By God, has he lost his mind?"

"Mr. Kinzie, this is a military installation. You may not interrupt this meeting."

"Piss on your rules. For you this is an *installation*. For me this is *home*. By what right do you order civilians around? Fella named Washington took *that* question up with some Brits, as I recall."

"I don't intend to discuss history with you, Mr. Kinzie. I have my orders. If you refuse to obey them, you'll suffer the consequences. I will not be responsible for the lives of people who remain behind. This garrison consists of only fifty-seven men under arms, entirely insufficient to hold off the hundreds, even thousands, that could come against us."

"Thousands is about right," Kinzie said. "Word's already spread about the order to evacuate. Captain, the Indians hold all the cards. Stay. You've got stores enough to last the winter. Leaving will invite a slaughter!"

Kinzie was pounding the table now, and Heald responded with equal vehemence. "I will not, gentleman. I say I will *not* face the censure of my government for brazen disregard of orders. Hull is right. If we stay here, we're doomed."

The argument was interrupted by a clatter outside. Captain William Wells and his band of braves were arriving with their usual bravado.

"What we all need now," Heald muttered.

Wells had been kidnapped as a boy, raised by a chief of the Miami tribe, and kidnapped back by his white relatives. He eventually returned to the tribe and became a chief. Both sides questioned his loyalty, having fought for and against white settlers, but he had rushed from Fort Wayne to Fort Dearborn when he heard of Hull's orders. He meant to help defend the fort in case of a siege or the garrison and civilians during the trek to Fort Wayne. Meanwhile, another debate was underway in a clearing upriver from the fort.

14 August 1812

Council Fire Outside Fort Dearborn

"We are the First Peoples, the great Algonquin family." So spoke Sunawchewome, a young Pottawatomie chief. "This is our land. Once our families populated it from the rising to the setting sun. But the white man schemed with the Iroquois to drive us off the land. Here we live on top of one another with barely enough land for each tribe to take the fish and the fowl and the game to feed ourselves. Now they push us again. We must not allow this.

"If we fail, our forests will be destroyed, our prairies ravaged," Sunawchewome continued. He was tall and thickly muscled, a man in his prime. His voice was firm. "They will build fences across it, forcing us to give up our God-given hunting grounds. If we flee, we will defile God's gift to his people. It will be divided up to be squandered and destroyed.

"We take only what we need from the land. Then in the great circle of life, we move on and return to it only when it has been replenished. These whites know none of this—of how God had planned abundance for his people. They cut down the trees to burn them! They spread the seeds of plants that God did not intend to grow here. Instead of harvesting only what they need, they send what they grow to feed distant people who return nothing to the depleted land."

He heard low grunted agreement.

"We helped the white man when he was not so numerous. We told him where to hunt, how to trap the best beaver, how to survive the winds and snows of winter. We gave him our food in his deprivation. We counseled him of the dangers—the bear and the wild cat.

"For this, how have we been rewarded? We are driven from our fathers' honored resting places. We are as the deer in the woods, fleeing before the ravenous white people or slaughtered. We are denied more than the means of our sustenance—we are denied respect for our families, our homes, our chosen way of life."

He paused, and into the quiet came the voice of Kesegowaase, his aged face illuminated by the council fire. "You well speak the truth, but eloquence will not stop the white man. We have heard the words of the great Tecumseh, and we have seen the destruction the whites have brought. Our sons and daughters murdered. Our elders dishonored. Our women raped. What can we do that Tecumseh has not advised?"

Sunawchewome turned to face the older man directly. "Tecumseh has spoken, but have we done more than listen? This time we can unite in a strong spirit and a strong body. We can ally with the British who seek our help. We can show the white chiefs that only danger and death face any who cross the mountains. We can mark as ours the plains and the prairies, the hills and the forests from the eastern mountains to the great Mississippi. They will learn to respect a people united in their fight for freedom. We cannot afford to fight among ourselves—the Iroquois, the Fox, the Miami, the Illini."

"You speak about united peoples," another chief, Chechawkose, interrupted, "but such talk is meaningless. We do not know whether other whites are on their way here even now. Will these soldiers leave their fort, or is this a trick? Will this uniting help us when the sun rises tomorrow and the white people leave? What are you suggesting?"

"Have you not heard with your own ears the weakness of the Americans?" Sunawchewome demanded. His voice was louder now, and the muscles of his thick neck tensed. "Hundreds of braves from many tribes are here now at She-gog-ong. The British hold Mackinac. We can do as we please. The fort is ours."

There were murmurs of approval, but then Chief Mawkawbe-penay, known to the white settlers as Black Partridge, rose to his feet. He commanded the respect of every chief at the fire, and he spoke with authority.

"I am puzzled, brother. Why must we *do* anything? As you say, the fort is ours. The whites are leaving in the morning. Captain Heald has promised us provisions and arms. Do you exhort us to bloodshed? There's no need. The whites are running away in fright. Let them run. Let them tell their people in the east of our determination."

"Yes, they are leaving," Sunawchewome conceded. "But they'll be back, tenfold, one-hundredfold. Letting them go shows weakness. We must show our strength instead."

Black Partridge chuckled. "How? By attacking an empty fort? The soldiers and the settlers will be gone no matter what we do. Show our strength, but how? By attacking soldiers after we have pledged them safe conduct? By attacking women and children? Do you seek a bloodbath? Are we no better than the whites, who have killed our women and children and set fire to our villages? You call this *strength*? Is this your idea of honor? Of courage? These are words spoken by of a fool. I spit on them."

Sunawchewome's eyes flared at the insult, and he got to his feet. "Enough! We do not fight women and children. We fight the soldiers. It is an honorable fight, because they are armed. No harm shall come to the women and children we put under our protection. "

"And how is this to be done? So you will ask them to please leave while we kill their men? They will not. They will fight. Your bloodlust will bring terrible retribution upon us. *Our* women and children, *our* families and villages will be sacrificed to your vain dream."

But the faces around the fire showed that Sunawchewome was gaining support.

The younger man knew it too and shot back, "So we are to wait here for them to come and drive us off our lands? Be patient and docile while they destroy us? Go like cattle to the slaughter? Do I want their blood? Yes! We will wash ourselves in their blood, and they will give up! They will see that the price they must pay for taking our homes is too high."

"Brothers." The voice of Chawcawbeme was calm, devoid of rancor. If his people had bestowed titles beyond chief and shaman, his would have been Wise Elder. He had seen much, had won and lost battles, and knew the costs of both. He was a brave warrior and a skilled strategist, but he knew when patience was needed.

"Our people are troubled, and in our sadness we see only more suffering to come. The Father seems to have assigned this fate to us. We must ask ourselves—do we want to increase that suffering tenfold by tenfold? It is within our power to do so. We can. We can bring butchery down on ourselves, and we will if we break our promise of safe conduct. And then we must tell our peoples that the greatest of our troubles were of our own making."

"You speak as a weakling speaks, old man!" shouted Sunawchewome, daring to break the ancient convention of respect for tribal elders. "The white man cares not the droppings of a field mouse about honor. He understands only savagery."

Chawcawbeme smiled. "And you imagine to speak of all our peoples united in a momentous victory against the Americans. Yet look not far from where we sit. The Miami are here to escort the white people to Fort Wayne. Do we fight them too?

"The past is gone. We cannot recover it. Look at this man who leads the Miami chief, Captain Wells. Born of a white man, raised by our people, he has fought for and against us, for and against them. Today he wears the uniform of our enemies, and the Miami, who share the blood of our fathers, follow him. His wife is the daughter of Little Turtle, and Wells is a Miami chief. *This* is our future. The lines between them and us will blur. They are many, and we will become them."

This last observation struck even Sunawchewome silent. It had the sound of a prophecy, as though the old man had somehow seen the future. When they began to speak again, Sunawchewome did not resume his rant. For more than an hour, the talk continued—sometimes heated, always intense. This decision would have long consequences—but no decision was made. Unlike the whites, who answered to a general or a governor or a president, the tribes sought consensus, and when that proved impossible, each faction went its own way.

Some tribes determined to provide the promised protection, but the belligerent vowed to march alongside the travelers as well. Five hundred braves would escort a hundred and forty-eight soldiers and civilians.

15 *August 1812*

Fort Dearborn

*Q*uinn didn't put much stock in omens, but when the fifes struck up the Dead March from *Saul*, Handel's celebrated funeral processional, he shivered. The column of soldiers and civilians leaving Fort Dearborn did look like a funeral procession. The brilliant sun in a cloudless sky did nothing to lift their spirits but appeared to hearten their Indian escorts.

Quinn and the other officers had heard that Black Partridge had personally warned Heald of the likelihood of an attack on the column of soldiers and civilians somewhere on the road to Fort Wayne.

"Those savages can hardly wait until we leave," Quinn muttered to Ronan just before their final briefing. Heald had assigned Quinn, the most junior officer, to mid-column, effectively in charge of no one. He would serve as a troubleshooter, stepping in wherever needed. Heald probably just wanted him out of his sight, and that was fine. What was expected of him in case of an attack, he did not know.

Wells and half his Miami braves were in the column's vanguard, meant to anticipate the Indians' intentions.

The rest of his braves constituted the rearguard. Behind Wells at the head of the column rode Heald with most of his regulars and twelve militia. Next came a half-dozen wagons carrying stores and any civilians too young, ill, or old to travel on foot. A dozen or so small children shared a single wagon under the watchful eye of Sally Martin. Their families marched nearby.

Altogether, the column consisted of about a hundred and ten souls. Another dozen—mostly members of Kinzie's family—would sail in Lee's *Friends Good Will*, staying close to shore. Lee had delayed his departure, considering how to sail past Mackinac to Detroit. He would deliver the Kinzies to the settlement at the St. Joseph River where the family would join the march to Fort Wayne. That Wells had smeared his face with black war paint troubled Quinn, though the others assured him that the captain had a flair for the dramatic. Heald ignored Wells's posturing but was unsettled by the change in the mood of the Indians outside the gate. They had to know that at the last moment Heald had decided to dump what arms, gunpowder, and whiskey that couldn't be taken on the journey into the fort's well and the river. He could see powder floating on the river's surface and smell whiskey, signs obvious to the Indians, confirming earlier rumors.

Precisely at 0900, the column passed through the gate and between two flanks of Indians waiting to claim the fort. When the last of the column went by, the Indians surged in, and another column of Indians moved slowly alongside the marchers. They were the escorts, among them Potawatomi, Wabash, and Winnebago.

Quinn positioned himself near Sally and the children, watching the Indians with growing trepidation. They were moving toward a high point on the beach where prairie grasses met the sand. Heald's column was positioned between the Indians and the waterline, which troubled Quinn terribly. On one side lay the lake and on the other the Indians—no hiding place, no escape route.

"William?" Sally jumped down from the wagon as the horses struggled to pull it over the soft sand. "Is this wise?"

Sally had seen too much to be placated with false assurances. She deserved an honest answer.

"I don't know." Quinn kept his voice low so the children wouldn't overhear. "We're outnumbered, encumbered with children and noncombatants. God help us."

She met his gaze and did not blink. "We'll need more than prayers, William. My pistol is loaded. I'm carrying extra rounds and powder. I've got my dagger. But I can't defend these children alone. You'd think that Heald would put more guards around them than just *you*." She blushed. "I don't mean it that way."

Quinn shrugged. "I know what you mean, and I agree. I'll do all I can."

Sally smiled and returned to the children.

Already the August sun was baking the marchers. A month of this would be unbearable, Quinn thought, and then he forgot his discomfort. The Indian escorts had disappeared behind the dunes. He could climb up to see where they'd gone, but he decided to head to the column's front to ask Heald to send outriders to survey the situation.

The captain sat on his horse, staring ahead at Wells, who was waving his hat in circles above his head, galloping back toward the column, shouting, "The Indians have us surrounded! They're getting ready to attack!"

What in the blazes is he doing? Quinn thought.

All eyes shifted to the ridge of sand dunes, but there was nothing there. Then, as if the moment had been choreographed, a column of Indians appeared on the ridge. Half-naked and painted, they were a terrifying sight.

Quinn was breathless. In minutes, Indian runners had reached the escorts, confirming the destruction of the weapons and whiskey. They were furious, and Quinn cursed the captain for that decision. But would leaving them the arms and liquor have mattered? Many of these tribesmen had traveled hundreds of miles. The local Potawatomi knew the soldiers and settlers, had even intermarried with them, but they were outnumbered and unlikely to keep the rest in check.

Wells had halted about a hundred yards ahead, forming up his own braves as if to charge.

Quinn was no military expert, but he was dismayed. Wells could fight like an Indian, but he was a commissioned captain in the regular army, and he'd adopted the white man's method of combat: form a line abreast, two or three deep, and march in the open toward the enemy. Scare him to death or overwhelm him with firepower—a strategy designed to fight an enemy like the British. Indians preferred swiftness and stealth, firing from behind rocks, trees, and dunes. Hit and hide. Hit again. Hide again then strike quickly elsewhere.

Quinn couldn't tell who fired the first shot, but barrages followed it from both sides. A couple of Wells' men fell, blood streaming from their heads and torsos. Had any Indians been hit? Now Wells led a charge up the dunes and into the middle of the Indian line. More men and horses fell.

Quinn watched, horrified, as dozens, scores, hundreds of Indians rushed, singly and in groups, toward the column. Pell-mell, they came, streaking toward the forward regulars and militia. The soldiers, caught off guard, barely had time to react. Their officers issued conflicting orders.

"Form a line and fire at will."

"Move back and circle the civilians."

They were too widely strung to form a defensive knot and pour concentrated fire on the Indians. They couldn't retreat to the fort. They were, as Quinn had feared, trapped in the open with their backs against the lake. In minutes, Wells' men hunkered down on their knees or stomachs or crouched behind their dead horses at the bottom of the dune. The Indians flanked them, raining down a deadly crossfire of bullets, spears, arrows, and tomahawks. Above them on the ridge, more Indians joined the assault.

Why had Wells charged the enemy up the middle without protecting his flanks? Quinn, for his part, knew what *he* had to do.

Some settlers and militia were pulling the wagons to the water's edge. Any man who was armed took a position in the front, facing the Indians running toward them. It was mayhem, and Quinn was an attractive target, alone in his colorful uniform as he sprinted toward the children and Sally. A musket ball whistled past his head as he rushed down the beach—his drawn sword in his right hand, a pistol in his left.

He saw a fallen soldier, flat on his stomach, pinned down by a painted Indian's knee planted squarely between his shoulder blades. The Indian clutched a clump of the soldier's hair in his left hand, his scalping knife in his right. With swift, surgical precision, the warrior sliced across the forehead, past both ears, and around the nape of the neck. In one practiced motion, he tore the man's scalp from his skull. When the soldier tried to jerk free, he spurted more blood on the warrior's knife and hands.

Quinn tried desperately to stop the butchery, but the harder he ran, the deeper he sank into the sand, as if in a nightmare. The warrior, pleased with his gory souvenir, looked up too late to see Quinn close on him with his pistol cocked. Quinn's momentum threw him against the Indian, and as they fell, the pistol discharged, spraying Indian blood and gray matter across the sand.

Quinn was stunned. He'd been boiling with rage at the bungling army officers responsible for this debacle, then horrified at the scalper's brutality, and finally amazed that he had killed another human being. Until now, he'd thought that killing a man would create feelings of either revulsion or bloodlust. Instead, he was enveloped by an eerie calmness and a surge of self-confidence.

Despite the dying soldier's frightful cries, Quinn couldn't stop. People—women, children, civilians, soldiers—were huddling together in panic. With nowhere to hide, some had formed small protective clusters, but their attackers fell upon them without mercy, leaving the dead and wounded sprawled in the sand while they moved on to the next knot of victims.

In panic, parents scrambled through the slaughter to rescue their children in the wagon, only to be struck down. At the wagon, Sally had been carrying on her own resistance. The driver had abandoned the wagon and its pair of Morgan horses and taken off for the lake. An Indian, recognizing the value of the horses, started for them, ignoring Sally and the children. Sally caught him in mid-stride with a round from her pistol, blowing him off course and sending him, already dead, tumbling at the feet of the team.

As she was disposing of the horse thief, a grinning adolescent had climbed into the back of the wagon and attacked the nearest and easiest target, a three-year-old girl. The flat side of his tomahawk collapsed her skull.

Still too far away to help, with musket balls whizzing past him like hornets from a broken hive, Quinn stumbled on an Indian standing over Dr. Van Voorhees. The doctor was on his knees, begging for his life. Still running, Quinn drew back his arm and swung his sword in a long arc, catching the Indian in the neck. In the same motion, he pulled the sword back and was gone before the dead man fell onto the startled surgeon.

On the wagon, Sally turned to the screaming children. The bloodthirsty lad was selecting his next victim, a little boy who had bravely stepped in front of the other children. Focused on the child, the Indian failed to notice Sally pulling her father's hunting knife from its sheath under her dress. He dodged her first thrust, suffering only a superficial scrape across his chest. He smirked and lunged at her. His first swing went wild but caused Sally to lose her footing and fall backward. His smirk continued as he knelt over her, giving Sally the opportunity to thrust her knife upward into his soft belly tissues. She pulled the knife out and struck again as he fell atop her. Quinn had run him through from the back with his sword.

Quinn shoved the dead man aside and pulled her up. The children had fled, some into the arms of their parents, others into the blood and confusion on the beach. Quinn and Sally jumped from the wagon into chaos. There were no battle lines. Shots rang out. Bodies fell and were hacked to pieces. Cries of agony and lost hope interrupted the war whoops. Some yards back sprawled the lifeless body of Dr. Van Voorhees, who had fallen to another attacker. George Ronan was down on one knee, thrashing wildly with his sword as Indians closed in on him. Abruptly, a spear pierced his throat.

Quinn frantically searched for an escape route. The lake?

In the surf, he saw Mrs. Helm struggling against an Indian, who appeared to be trying to drown her. Oddly, she did not look frightened. She caught Quinn's eye and nodded toward the Indian. Suddenly, Quinn recognized

Black Partridge. He wasn't trying to kill her. She was only pretending to struggle. Sally and Quinn waded into the lake.

"Mrs. Helm, we must move you to safety," they heard Black Partridge say.

15 August 1812

On Lake Michigan

"Take off that stupid coat!" Black Partridge barked at Quinn. "We will be seen."

Wrestling himself out of the drenched coat, Quinn threw the gaudy jacket into the surf.

"You must gain the sloop. My braves are claiming the boat and everyone on it as my prizes. They wait at the mouth of the river. Do not look at the beach. Keep your heads down. You are my prisoners."

Quinn obeyed uneasily, but they had no choice. The beach was certain death. Small groups of soldiers standing back to back stabbed with their bayonets at any Indian who approached, but arrows toppled them one by one. Some men sought their wives or children, but they too fell to the sand like broken toys.

A young warrior spotted the three white people struggling through the surf with Black Partridge. He did not hesitate to challenge the older man.

"Why do you have these three? We of the Algonquin tribe have traveled many miles, and we will not leave empty handed. I will take the woman, the young one."

Black Partridge struck like a wildcat, silently. The blurred shadow of the tomahawk was the last thing the Algonquin saw before it split his forehead. Other Potawatomi had observed the affront to their respected elder and ran to his aid.

Quinn's head ached with anger and guilt. He was being rescued—along with two *women*—by an Indian. Why wasn't *he* fighting and dying with his comrades on the beach? He would have turned back but for the strong arms of Black Partridge.

"Do not draw more attention," the chief hissed. "You endanger all our lives."

All our lives. Quinn turned to Sally. What he saw in her eyes frightened him—not terror, not panic, only icy anger. Given any chance, Quinn imagined that she would try to avenge not only her family, but all this day's victims. She had seen more violence in her short life than many others in a lifetime. Quinn feared what she might do in the chaos and tried to reassure her. "Let's get to the boat. Get out of here." He wanted to say that God would exact vengeance, but at the moment, he wasn't sure he believed it.

Quinn helped Sally and Margaret Helm up the rope ladder and onto the boat. More than a dozen men burst out of the oak forest and fled into the water, but their pursuers were upon them at once. A half dozen others, who had reached the lake a few steps ahead, struggled aboard just as Lee unfurled the sails.

Breathless, they reported that Heald had survived and was headed to the Potawatomi village to negotiate a surrender of the survivors. The day's only blessing was the stiff offshore wind. The sails billowed, and *Friends Good Will* surged forward. Before the Indians could launch war canoes, the sloop was hundreds of yards into Lake Michigan and pulling away.

Lee's passengers looked dazedly at one another. Some were in shock, glassy-eyed. Many were sobbing, others retching and vomiting. Some clutched the arms of people to whom they had never spoken. Most were blood splattered. What little help could be given was focused on the wounded.

As they began to speak, it became clear that perhaps half the soldiers had surrendered. The rest were killed, the lucky ones quickly. A dozen women and children had been taken captive. Maybe a third of those who had left the fort that morning would still be alive.

"Master Lee," Quinn asked, "I assume you're heading for the St. Joe's River encampment?"

"Stopping there, yes."

"You mean you're going farther?"

"As far as I can get. You think those savages were pleased to see us sail away? I give them a day or two to follow us to St. Joe. Been thinking what I should do, what with the English holding Mackinac. But them savages made the decision for me. Better to be in the hands of the Limeys."

"Detroit then?"

"I hope to run for Toledo, maybe even Buffalo—anything on Lake Erie. I'm ruined anyway. If the Brits capture me, they'll confiscate *Friends* and turn her into a warship. So will the Americans, but maybe at least they'll compensate me for her. Care to come along for the ride?"

Quinn shook his head. So far he'd been run out of Mackinac and Fort Dearborn. The humiliation was bad, but the sense of failure—even though none of it was his fault—was worse. Go with Lee and get captured by the British? Never. Too much like being back in the old country where the English could push an Irishman around. He hated being on the losing side—the side, by all that's just, that *shouldn't* be losing.

He glanced at Kinzie. The settlers weren't on the warpath against the Indians; they just wanted a better life. Whatever wrongs they had committed—selling them whiskey, tilling a few acres of their hunting grounds—could that warrant the slaughter he had just witnessed? Maybe they had a fair bone to pick with people in Washington, but not with the Kinzies. Not with the Martins. Quinn was ready for a fight.

"Thanks, Master Lee, but I've got other plans."

"Such as?"

"Doing what I was sent to do. Moving on to Fort Wayne."

"What, to warn them that war is coming? I think they already know."

"Yes, but I want to fight alongside my countrymen." He looked to the stern of the sloop, but there were no pursuers in sight.

Lee smiled. "Honorable sentiments, lad. I wouldn't try to change your mind. Might do the same if I was in your shoes. What's your plan?"

"Drop me at St. Joe's settlement. I'll make my way to Fort Wayne from there."

"On foot?"

"If I have to. Maybe I can requisition a horse or a canoe. I've been studying the maps, and St. Joe's River meanders a long way into Indiana territory. I could go a good distance by canoe and walk the rest of the way."

"What about me?"

Sally had edged closer to Lee and Quinn.

"What *about* you?" Quinn asked.

"After this"—her jaw was set—"I'll do what I can to get even."

"Just how will you do that, missy?" Lee had seen feisty frontier women who could handle a musket with the best of men and had no compunction about sending a savage off to the eternal hunting grounds.

She didn't hesitate. "I'm going back with Quinn to Fort Wayne."

"What?" Quinn couldn't believe it.

"I'm going back with you. You think you're the only one who can fight?" Her green eyes blazed.

Quinn shook his head slowly. "Can't. What do you know about the wilderness anyway?"

Quickly realizing that she knew a lot more than he did, and that she might be an asset, Quinn relented, but only grudgingly. "Okay, you can come."

"Kind of you to say, Ensign Quinn, but I don't need your permission."

"Maybe not, but I'll be moving fast. I can't get slowed down by petticoats."

"We'll see who needs to keep up with whom, sir," she retorted.

Lee laughed outright. "Gotcha there, lad."

16 August 1812

Indiana Territory

*Q*uinn chose a birchbark canoe built for two men with Sally still insisting that she could pull the weight of at least one man. At St. Joe, they left Lee who along with the Kinzies and other refugees, headed north for their uncertain fate. The dozen or so trappers and traders at the post, upon hearing of the massacre from the refugees, disappeared into the thick woods.

Quinn and Sally scrounged what they could from their leavings. Since there'd been no women there, she made do with a small pair of men's trousers and a leather shirt.

She proved an expert paddler, pound for pound more skilled than Quinn.

"Martin," he had begun to address her as he would a colleague, "take it easier. We're going to need a burst of energy if we encounter any hostiles."

"Hah!" she said. "That's just an excuse. Can't keep up, can you?"

They were paddling upstream, but there was little current here where the river meandered through flats and marshes. Mostly, they glided through woodlands that reached to the muddy riverbanks, exposed now in the August heat. Where the heat had dried up the shallow riverbed, they carried the canoe. In the wider stretches and in places where the river widened or opened into a lake, they clung close to the shore, passing unseen in the shadows. Nights were miserable. Fire would attract Indians, so they did without—even so, the mosquitoes found them.

Their shared trials were working to bring them closer together. They exchanged stories of their families, Quinn telling what prompted his family to flee to America and Sally what opportunities her family sought by settling in the marshy flats of Illinois territory.

"My father had a vision," she explained as they sat on a sunbathed, grassy flat that somehow had survived the forest's march. "His vision was of a great portage from the Great Lakes to the Mississippi River. He deeply believed that it would become a great commercial center, a gateway to the vast undeveloped regions along the Mississippi and to the West. Everything—grains and pelts—everything else would flow through there to the East.

"Farming was just a way to support us while waiting for the growth that he knew would come. He wanted to be there when it happened."

"I'm so sorry that he never would get to see his dream fulfilled."

"My father was an intelligent and educated man. He wanted the same for his children, which is why we all were taught to read and to relish the arrival of new books."

Quinn saw the tears welling up in Sally's eyes and sought to comfort her.

"Hey, Martin." But that's all he could say. That's all that he knew to say. The legendary Irish gift of blarney utterly failed him. He moved to touch her shoulder. She started to move away, but then allowed his hand to gently rest there for a moment, but only a moment. Now she was on her feet.

"We're never going go to there if we sit here jabbering."

"You're something else, you know that?" Quinn followed her to his feet.

"What do you mean?"

"Uh, I guess I don't know what I mean."

"Then you should keep your trap shut." She giggled as she turned toward the canoe.

"You're a smartass."

"And you're a puffed-up peacock. I knew if from the first time I saw you in the fancy getup. Why do they make you wear that anyway?"

The ribbing grew more good-natured as the two pressed on. Quinn had to do everything in his power to keep up his end of the sparring. Yet the memories of the violence were never far behind. More than once, Sally woke up from night terrors, screaming, with Quinn rushing to quiet her in fear of betraying their presence. Only in these times did she allow any but only the most fleeting physical contact. Still, Quinn's appreciation of her intelligence, sly humor, and physical stamina grew.

Three days in, they ran out of river. The rest of the trek would be overland. The men at St. Joe had advised him before they skedaddled that, for the last thirty miles, they would go on foot along a narrow animal path. They hiked for a day, then another, consuming hardtack and hoping at any moment to see the fort. Instead, they were seen.

A pair of eyes in a weathered face sized them up as they trudged along; then the watcher purposefully rattled a bush and just above a whisper said, "Friends."

Quinn thought he was imagining things, but Martin grabbed him from behind by the collar.

"Ssshh."

"What?"

"Hush. Listen."

"Friends," the voice was a little louder.

Quinn's hand went reflexively to his sword.

"Don't. I mean no harm."

"Then come out where we can see you."

"Here I am, your honor. Hold your water."

A ragged, dirty figure stepped into the clearing. He wore the britches of an enlisted man, but nothing else about him was military. Not his buckskin shirt, not his wild thatch of hair and beard.

Quinn blurted, "What the hell?"

"Well, I ain't Satan, but the way y'all was tramping through this forest, you mighta met 'im. Frake's the name, Sergeant Major Frake of the Kentucky volunteers," he announced, resting the butt of his musket on the ground and leaning cross-armed on the barrel. "Yours?"

"Quinn, Will, and this is Sally Martin."

"Pleased to meet you, ma'am." Frake looked at Quinn and recognized his officers' britches. "Sir? If you don't mind me asking, what are you two doing so far from the fort?"

Quinn wasn't going to admit they were lost. "I could ask you the same."

"Well, I assume you and the miss ain't just strollin'. I'd hazard y'all are lost."

"And you aren't?"

"No, sir, I'm on my way from Fort Detroit to Fort Wayne. Don't remember seeing you at Detroit, but wherever you're from, you look like ya left in a hurry."

Sally laughed bitterly. "We did. There's been a slaughter at Fort Dearborn, and we're heading to Fort Wayne too."

"A slaughter? What happened?"

Between them, Quinn and Sally told the whole horrific tale. Sometimes Will heard her voice quaver, but she soldiered on. He broke in occasionally with the military part of the story—Heald's stubborn misjudgments that caused the debacle. Then it occurred to him that he outranked Frake and should be hearing explanations from *him*.

"What's the news from Detroit?"

"Well, it ain't good. Fort Detroit surrendered, and I'm on my way to warn Fort Wayne that the fighting is heading their way—"

"Detroit surrendered? Why?"

"Couldn't say, sir. Hull just gave it up."

Quinn was incredulous. Detroit was the strongest U.S. fortification in the territories, a garrison of several hundred permanent regulars and a couple thousand militia Hull had brought in.

"Well, they ain't gonna pin no medal on that crazy, drunk old buzzard." Frake didn't seem to mind he was speaking to an officer, albeit a junior one.

"Start from the beginning. Please."

Frake explained how Hull had crossed into Canada unmolested and then settled in for weeks, racked by indecision. He described the encounter at the Riviere Aux Canards bridge, leaving out his feat of sharpshooting. Quinn listened, fascinated.

"So when that lieutenant from Mackinac, Hancks, showed up, it was like Hull went crazy."

"Hancks! At Detroit? He was my commanding officer at Mackinac! He sent me to Dearborn to warn them. Tell me what happened at Mackinac."

"Appears that Hancks had no idea that the war had started. One morning, he wakes up and the British from St. Joe's have a couple a cannon aimed down their throat. One from a hill overlooking the fort and one at the front gate.

"Not to mention a couple a hundred Indians hooting and a-hollering outside the fort. Hancks had no choice but to give it up. Not a shot fired."

"Did the townsfolk ever get inside the fort for their protection?" Quinn asked, mindful of his last day there.

"Didn't happen. Hancks said something about a crafty old trapper, named Flint, as I recall, that had talked the townsfolk out of going into the fort. Turns out the old coot had made a secret deal with the British to neutralize the townsfolk. He knew all the time that the British was coming."

"So, how'd Hanks get to Detroit?"

"The Brits paroled Hancks and the others, sent them packing for Detroit. Hanks said the British officer who accepted the surrender couldn't believe that the U.S. brass had left him hanging like that. Respected Hancks for not causing any unnecessary bloodshed.

"But the lieutenant, he found hisself in a passel of trouble with the general. Told him he was gonna court martial him, shoot him maybe."

"Sounds like Hull should be the one that's court martialed."

"That's the truth, ensign. Hull frittered away his advantage. Inside the fort he coulda withstood anything the Brits throwed at him. Instead he gave up in some kind of drunken panic. Me and some a' my Kentuckians slipped out the back as he was raising the white flag. No sitting in a British prison camp for me."

"Hancks captured for a second time in weeks! Thanks to Hull. Had Hancks been court martialed, like Hull wanted?"

"He wasn't."

"Thank God for that. Why not?"

"Never had a chance. He took a cannon ball the Brits shot into the fort. Cut him in half."

A man Quinn had grown to respect now mangled beyond imagination. Scores of innocents slaughtered or enslaved at Fort Dearborn. Quinn was so shaken that he didn't hear

Frake suggest they move along because delay could prove to be deadly.

Sally pulled on his shirt, yanking him back to reality. "Uh, yes. Uh, sergeant, please lead the way." The trio pushed ahead. Quinn, shocked into silence, followed blindly behind Sally, trying to absorb all Frake had reported. Mackinac had fallen because no one cared, Dearborn because of stupid orders from an inept officer, and Detroit because of cowardice and incompetence. Virtually the entire Northwest Territory was under British control, and the war had hardly begun.

Only Fort Wayne lay between the British and the Ohio River Valley. If the British captured the valley, they could attack the United States from the rear along its mountainous spine. And the utter brutality of it all. Quinn thought he had seen everything in Ireland, but even that hadn't prepared him for this. "Ensign, sir," Frake said suddenly, "you might want to watch where you're stepping." He pulled Quinn back just before he stumbled into a patch of poison oak. "You'd be in for a mighty rash, Mr. Quinn."

"Yes. Yes, thank you."

The crack of a musket shot interrupted his thoughts.

"I reckon it's about three hundred paces away," Frake whispered as they ducked for cover. "I reckon we're close to the fort."

19 August 1812

Fort Wayne

"Best we reconnoiter," Frake whispered. "Now drop and crawl. No more talking."

He went first, sliding his musket along close to his side. Sally followed, then Quinn, slithering through muddy low spots and around scatterings of fallen leaves, whose rustling could betray them.

After almost an hour, their muscles had tightened, their bladders filled, and their clothes caked with filth. The mosquitoes feasted.

They heard neighing ahead. Horses. No hoofbeats. They kept crawling. Presently, a small, sun-dappled clearing appeared through the trees and thickets. There, a string of Appaloosas was tethered to a rope tied between two trees. A brave sat on his haunches, his back to the horses, looking toward the sound of gunfire. Bored or resentful of his task of guarding the horses, he had relaxed his guard. Frake turned back to Quinn and Sally, raised his index finger to his lips, and motioned them to stay put. In an instant, he was on top of the brave, slitting his throat with one smooth swipe. Then he motioned the others forward.

"These will come in handy," Frake whispered, nodding at the horses. "I'm going ahead to scout the situation. Give me maybe fifteen minutes, and don't come after me if I'm late. Grab a horse and break for the fort."

He was back quicker than expected. "As I thought. They're hunkered down on the forest edge about seventy-five paces apart so's not to draw concentrated fire from the fort. Their shooting's not doing any harm. Just thwacking into the log battlements. Folks manning the walls are mostly not even firing back."

"So how do we get in?" Quinn deferred to the enlisted man's experience.

"There's about a hundred yards from the forest edge to the fort that's been cleared of trees and brush. It's an open field—a killing field. Helps repel any attackers, but it gives the Indians a clear shot at us if we try to cross it."

Frake paused courteously to give Quinn a chance to make a command decision then coughed and went on. "Sir, might I suggest something?"

Cautiously, they untied the rope to which the horses were tethered. Each selected a horse to ride on a mad dash to the fort. Riding bareback on Indian ponies would be no problem for Frake or Sally, but it would for Quinn. In Baltimore, he was familiar only with draft horses, powerful but slow animals bred to pull heavy wagonloads. Or docile creatures bred and saddled to carry folks in comfort and safety. But these ponies were bred for speed and quick turns. Only about fourteen hands high, they were muscular and intelligent, able to anticipate a rider's intention by the slightest twitch of his thigh muscle.

Quinn visibly blanched. *What the hell is there to hold onto? No saddle or saddle horn. I'll fall off the blasted thing and get trampled to death. If I don't get shot in the back first.*

Frake put a supportive hand on his shoulder. "Just grip with your thighs, not your calves. Don't look down at your horse. That's a sure way to fall off. Look at where you want to go. Believe it or not, these ponies can sense from the movement of your head where you want to go. You'll hardly have to use the reins."

Quinn swallowed and looked even more panicky, but he was listening to Frake.

"We ride as a group, leading the other horses, so your horse will know what to do." In fact, if Quinn panicked and confused his horse, there would be a disastrous pile-up.

"We'll get halfway across before the Indians know what's happening and begin firing. Crouch low and we should be all right as long as no trigger-happy moron on the fort wall shoots us."

Quinn felt his bladder loosening but caught himself in time.

"That path yonder leads to the forest edge. There was another Indian there, but I disposed of him." Frake cupped his hands and helped Quinn mount.

Frake and Sally held the lead lines of the riderless horses, mounted their own ponies, and set out slowly with Quinn between them.

He was amazed at how quietly the horses moved. They were unshod, but they were also bred for stealth. They reached the clearing, and Quinn expected to pause a moment. Instead, before he knew it, they were bursting out of the forest and thundering toward the fort.

Ahead, Sally was skillfully leading her string of ponies, but Quinn couldn't focus on her or on anything else. No matter how tightly Quinn pressed his thighs against his horse's sides, he seemed to be losing his balance. He desperately clutched the pony's mane. Halfway across the clearing, Quinn heard the first shot ring out, followed by a hail of gunfire. The last horse was hit in the haunch, breaking his rhythm. Frake felt the strain on the lead rope and let go. The wounded horse pulled up, but the others followed Frake.

As the thundering riders slowed for the gate, another horse was hit, reared, and fell behind. Soldiers on the parapets were returning the Indians' fire now—ball for ball, bullet for bullet—and then the fort's six-pounder joined in.

Quinn took in none of it. He barely realized that they had galloped through the gate. Before they recovered their breath and the gate closed behind them, a crowd gathered and questions flew.

"Who are you?"

"Where'd you come from?"

Dismounting, Quinn nearly collapsed as his right foot touched the ground. Someone grabbed his arms as he struggled to regain his balance.

"We're here…" he rasped out. "We're here…an important message. Your commanding officer? Where?"

"Ya better listen to the ensign," Frake chimed in. Here at the fort, the seasoned sergeant major let it seem that the young officer was in charge.

A corporal stepped forward. "This way, sir. And ma'am."

He led them across a small quadrangle inside the perfectly square fort with a dozen curious soldiers in their wake. Running from the ramparts were two young officers who had directed the covering gunfire. Lieutenant Philip Ostrander and Ensign Daniel Curtis caught up to the group on the porch of the commanding officer's quarters. Quinn wondered why the commanding officer was still inside.

He didn't have long to wait for the answer. Captain James Rhea was sozzled, almost too drunk to stand. The room was dark and stank of body odor, cigars, and booze.

"What?" Rhea growled.

Quinn saluted. "Sir, Ensign William Quinn, late of the garrison of Fort Mackinac and by way of Fort Dearborn, reporting. I have urgent messages."

"What the hell are you doing here?" Rhea muttered, turning to Curtis. "Who are these people?" He waved an arm at Frake and Sally. "They have no business in my quarters. Remove them."

Quinn spoke sharply. "Sir! We have business here, and we will not be removed." He had had it with idiots and morons. And now a drunk. "Together we will relate to you the fall of Fort Mackinac, Fort Dearborn, and Fort Detroit. Fort Wayne is next." Surely, *that* would get his attention.

Ostrander and Curtis exchanged looks, and Ostrander spoke up. "Please, sit. I'll send for food and water. After we're through here, I'll see that you're set up with clean clothing and places to rest. Please go on."

They did, repeating the sorry stories of ignorance, bungling, and bloody carnage. Rhea barely reacted, but the two other officers didn't miss a word.

Quinn's loathing grew. Hancks at Mackinac betrayed by superior officers. Hull and Heald. And now Rhea, too besotted to understand the consequences for Fort Wayne.

"Lieutenant Rhea, you are about to be overrun by hundreds of Indians fired up by the British and emboldened by the fall of other forts. It won't be long. They'll be coming from the west, north, and northwest. There's no time to waste."

"Ensign, I won't be lectured by an inferior officer," Rhea shot back.

Jesus, Quinn thought, *what difference does rank make now?* He resolved not to stand helpless in the face of fools. Ostrander and Curtis would have to take over.

"If there's nothing else, sir, we need food and rest."

Rhea nodded and mumbled, "Dismissed."

The other two officers followed Quinn out. "What *is* this, lieutenant?" Quinn asked as they walked toward the mess.

Ostrander described Rhea's steady physical and mental decline. He couldn't say whether the decline set off the drinking or vice versa, but gradually Rhea became commander in name only. Now that Ostrander knew of the coming attack on Fort Wayne, he told Quinn that he was glad he had sent a messenger south at the first sign of Indian hostilities. Brigadier General William Henry Harrison was encamped at the fort named for him 250 miles to the south, the only hope for reinforcements.

5 September 1812

Fort Wayne

Fort Wayne had plenty of food, water, and ammunition, though Quinn wished mightily that they had more powerful artillery pieces. He thought of the twelve-pounders at Fort Dearborn and hoped the Indians hadn't transported them here to breach the walls. Again and again, he cursed Hull. Then he cursed the fools who'd sent a letter by regular mail to inform him that the United States had declared war on Great Britain.

By now the hundreds of Indians prowling the woods outside the fort were no longer wasting ammunition with ineffective potshots. Frake said he reckoned that a strong leader had arrived and imposed discipline on the restless warriors. Wayne's perfectly square fortification offered no obvious weak point, so the enemy would likely turn to subterfuge, perhaps request a meeting to seek peace and thus get a few braves inside the walls.

Frake quickly settled in with the enlisted men and Quinn was given an officer's perquisite of a separate room.

"Miss, um, I'm sorry, I didn't catch your name," an orderly said when he was about to lead Sally off to the women's quarters.

By custom, a few soldiers were chosen by lot to bring their wives along on deployment. The army viewed these women as calming and stabilizing influences and valuable additions to the workforce. Still, their presence created tensions, disturbing both the bachelors and the husbands who'd left their wives behind.

At Wayne there were also women who'd survived massacres and the widows or orphans of soldiers killed in action. These sought shelter while awaiting transport back East. And then there were the camp followers— adventuresses, girls desperate for a place in the world and dreaming of romance or marriage.

"It's Mrs. Quinn, and I'll be staying with my husband, Ensign Quinn."

Quinn and Frake had exchanged startled glances, and Frake muttered, "Ain't you the lucky one."

"Very well, Mrs. Quinn, we'll see to it."

Quinn was stupefied and about to speak up when suddenly he realized the dilemma that Sally had created.

If Quinn denied her, her living arrangements would be the least of her troubles. She'd be mocked by the other women and eyed in a different way by the soldiers. A single woman traveling alone with two men, even in wartime, was suspect. She would be considered little better than a camp follower. If he went along with the charade and was discovered, he could end up in a stockade.

After all she'd been through, he couldn't deny her. He reached his arm around her shoulders and hugged her briefly before they were shown to a room in the officers' quarters.

When the door closed, he turned to her. "I understand why you did this, Martin. I wish you'd given me some warning, but don't worry. I'll sleep on the floor." He smiled, expecting thanks for his gentlemanly behavior.

She smiled too. "That'll be fine, William. Plus I'll be sleeping with my long knife."

In spite of himself, he laughed. "Yes, ma'am! 'Course you'd have a time explaining the bloody corpse tomorrow morning."

She laughed too, and all the tension and horror and fear they'd been holding in check erupted in gales of hysteria.

That night, though, Quinn awoke to Sally's sobs and screams. "Stop! Stop!"

Quinn rushed to her from his assigned spot on the floor.

"What is it, Sally"

"Don't you hear it? The horses. They're coming for us. I can't..."

Sally was bolt upright in the bed, her eyes betraying panic as they searched the darkened room. His hands reached for her shoulders. He gently shook her.

"Sally, you're dreaming. Sally you're safe now. I'm... we're here."

As she came out of the nightmare, her eyes focused on Quinn.

"It's the dreams. I think I dreamed about...about our cabin and...what I found there of my family. And then Dearborn...and the children...and that stupid Heald!" Now she was sobbing again, and he held her till she quieted.

And then it simply happened. She lifted her face to him, and his mouth covered hers while his hand slid to her breast. In time, his lips moved onto her hardened nipple, and she uttered a soft moan. In an instant he was upon her, and in another instant it was over. Or perhaps, more accurately, it had begun.

In public they tried to appear as just another ordinary married couple, but in private it was another world, a world both returned to eagerly whenever they could. Both understood the risks they were taking, but in this surreal world, they cared little. Neither thought of what would happen if they got out of Fort Wayne alive. Quinn did not know whether this was love, but it sometimes took his mind off his anger. And he thought it could take Sally's mind off her memories for a while. For the present, that would do.

"Do you think we're fooling anyone?" Quinn asked after another bout of energetic lovemaking, his head propped up on his hand. Even though it was midday, they had boldly retired to their quarters.

"Who cares?"

"That's why I like you; nuts to 'em."

"Just *like*?"

"Well…" The word she was looking for stuck in his throat.

"That's all right. I like you too. But someday this must end, and then what?"

"I don't know," and another word stuck in his throat. *Is she pushing this into marriage?* The thought was automatic, not to be suppressed in a culture that valued purity.

"Don't worry. Leave it to war to blind everyone to the future. Let's first make sure we get out of this alive.

She can read minds too.

She pulled him closer, and they started again.

One morning the Pottawatomie chief Winnemac rode up to the fort's wall with a half dozen warriors under a white flag, claiming to be on a mission of peace. Their terms were clear: the soldiers were to turn the camp and its provisions over to the local tribes and tell the white settlers that they must abandon their homes and leave the territory. If not... A white Indian agent captured a couple miles from the gate had been tortured for information and then scalped. The farms and settlements abandoned by those who had fled into the fort had been burned to the ground. Any settlers captured henceforth would be killed or taken into slavery.

"You can leave now. It is your only chance," Winnemac said. "I have five hundred warriors. I will hold them off while you consider my offer. But know this—every moment you delay brings the Redcoats nearer with their cannon. It will make kindling of your log walls."

The warning about the Redcoats and the possibility of capture jumped into Quinn's mind. Until now, his worry about hanging at the hands of the hated English had been pushed into the background. Now he could not escape the possibility that with the approach of British forces, it would be the first direct confrontation with his sworn, lifelong enemy.

His ruminations were ended as soon as the Indians departed and Ostrander nodded to Quinn and Curtis to follow him. He led them along parapet out of earshot of sentries. "We must take command of the fort from that drunken fool," he said.

"How?" Quinn asked.

"The captain won't be a problem. When we're attacked, he'll cower in his quarters, probably too far gone to know what's happening. If the garrison realizes we've taken over, they'll be grateful for competent leadership. Their lives depend on it. Gentlemen, are you with me?"

Curtis nodded. Quinn weighed the consequences—possible charges of mutiny or treason, and death before a firing squad. Or certain death. But he could not leave his life and Sally's in the hands of another incompetent.

"Yes, sir, captain. We'll have to count on the message getting through to Fort Harrison and pray for relief. If Fort Wayne falls, more Indians will side with the British, and the Limeys will be in control all the way to Pittsburgh and beyond. We can't let that happen."

Quinn was surprised by his own vehemence.

Now the planning began in earnest. What if the Indians attack with flaming arrows? Who will put out the fires? What if the Indians feign a full-scale attack on the west wall to cover a real attack on the east wall? Who would command which wall? Who would manage emergency maneuvers if the gate or a wall was breached? Who would direct the offensive if ever they could take one?

They then convened small groups of soldiers and civilians. Everyone—women and children included—had an assignment. Stores and munitions were checked and double-checked meticulously.

The next evening Winnemac reappeared, seeking another meeting with Rhea.

"Over my dead body," Ostrander whispered to Quinn. Then he turned to Winnemac. "Leave your weapons, chief!" he shouted from the parapet. "And instruct your warriors to withdraw. My men will search you and then admit you to the fort."

"Maybe we should tell him to crawl in on his hands and knees." Quinn smirked.

"Maybe," Ostrander replied, "but not yet. Watch."

He leaned over the parapet again. "Perhaps you have further insulting demands. Or perhaps you have thought the situation over and you wish to return to your lodges."

"Are these the words of Captain Rhea?" Winnemac shouted.

"They are the words of the United States government. Do what you must, but you may take your demand for surrender to hell."

"You will regret this!" Winnemac screamed.

"And you will regret opening hostilities against this lawful facility of the United States government."

The chief spun his horse around and galloped back to the forest.

"No need to inform the captain of these events," Ostrander said.

In any case, there wouldn't have been time. The attack came immediately, and everyone hastened to his or her post. They were vastly outnumbered, but the braves were restless and overeager, and Winnemac was too enraged to act strategically.

A volley of flaming arrows set the roof of the enlisted quarters and mess on fire, but the fire brigade responded rapidly. A bucket line was formed, mostly of able-bodied women and boys. They passed along pails from the well, dousing the flames, and Sally found herself between a camp follower and Ostrander's wife, all social barriers down.

Winnemac then tried an obvious feint at the west wall, and Quinn ordered soldiers and militia to reinforce the east wall. There was, he found, an advantage in having smaller artillery pieces that could be easily moved from one position to another.

The clearing that surrounded the fort became a virtual shooting gallery for the defenders. The warriors did not advance in tight formations but came helter-skelter, making more difficult targets. But because they did not fire volley after volley at the walls, the soldiers had time to fire, reload, and fire again and again.

Civilians not needed in the hospital or cookhouse manned the walls to reload the muskets. Attackers who scaled the earthen redoubts were unprepared for this kind of fighting. They had no ladders, and the smooth logs offered few hand- or footholds for climbing. Some used ropes to scale the walls by lassoing the sharpened ends of the vertical logs that extended above the parapets. But the slap of the ropes gave early warning to the men above who then dropped rocks or logs or poured down scalding water.

Despite their bravery, Winnemac's warriors made no progress, and he called retreat. He had lost upward of one hundred men, while Fort Wayne's casualties were minor in number and degree.

Once Rhea wandered out of his quarters to ask about the gunfire, but a civilian gently guided him back inside with assurances that everything was under control. He dozed then, and when he did send for his officers, they ignored the summons, and he soon forgot about them.

Twice over the next days, the Indians attacked, but the initial approach was always the same—rush the walls and try to scale them and overwhelm the defenders. Each attack was rebuffed, and each time their losses were greater. Winnemac would have to regroup.

At dawn on the sixth day of the siege, as the early morning mist cleared, two lookouts spotted what appeared to be a couple of cannon poking out of the forest and sighted on the fort. It was Quinn's worst fear: that the Indians would drag the Fort Dearborn artillery 180 miles and use them to punch a hole in Fort Wayne's walls. The presence of cannon might also mean that the British had arrived. Defending the fort against Winnemac was one thing, but confronting cannon, cavalry, and British troops was another.

In time, riders approached under a white flag. "Captain Rhea must come to the wall," they said.

"Let them wait," Ostrander said. "Ensign Quinn?" He passed his spyglass over. "Tell me what you think."

Quinn focused on the cannons. He shook his head. "Lieutenant, I saw the guns at Fort Dearborn. But...look at those wheels. They don't look large enough, they don't seem to be spoked, and they aren't steel-banded like they should be. If they dragged them here, they might have lost or damaged the wheels and had to improvise. But something else is wrong."

"What?"

"The muzzle. Mind, we're a long ways away, but... Maybe the muzzle's too thick or the bore's too small. I'm no expert, but those aren't like any cannon I've ever seen. And they're not glossy enough. You know how the Brits love spit and polish."

Ostrander nodded then turned and shouted down at the Indians, "Go ahead and shoot your cannon!"

"What?"

"You heard me. Shoot your cannon. Go ahead. I'll be waiting here."

Quinn heard gasps from the men around him. Had Ostrander lost his mind? But Quinn had seconded his observations. They *weren't* real cannons. They were something made to look like cannons. Hollowed-out logs, maybe? Coated with some dark resin? And now Ostrander was calling their bluff.

Winnemac responded with threats about the loss of innocent lives warnings of the power of twelve-pound cannonballs, but the war party turned back into the forest. The last word they heard from the chief was "cmokman."

Quinn grinned. "It sounds something like, 'you white man.' Anyway, it wasn't a compliment."

But Ostrander wasn't smiling. "No, I imagine not. But I'm taking a chance here with everyone's life. I'd like to see some humor in it, but I can't."

But the troops along the parapets seemed amused. Laughter broke out and catcalls followed Winnemac all the way back to the forest.

12 September 1812

Fort Wayne

*W*hen Brigadier General William Henry Harrison arrived with two thousand men a day later, he found no Indians near the fort. They had abandoned their siege, and Harrison's scouts found only traces of their villages, abandoned along with vital stocks of corn and blankets. Once assured of the fort's security, Harrison met with Ostrander and the other officers. A short interview with Rhea confirmed the reports of his drunkenness and cowardice, but Harrison declined to bring Rhea before a court martial. What would an execution accomplish? The fort had been saved by its officers, and Rhea was a wreck of a man. His resignation was demanded, rendered, and accepted, and he was summarily dismissed.

Days passed before scouts dispatched north toward Lake Erie returned with news. A large force of artillery and foot soldiers under British General Isaac Brock had moved down the Maumee River to within fifty miles of Fort Wayne then inexplicably turned back toward Detroit. What was the British general up to? Even an incompetent like Hull could have seen that Fort Wayne and the surrounding territory were sitting ducks.

Whatever the reason, Harrison was more than ready to take advantage of Brock's hesitation. He summoned Quinn, Sally, and Frake.

"I've been impressed by your actions," he began. "I'd thought to send one of my men east to describe what's happening here on the frontier, but I believe I have a better option. Washington needs to know *exactly* what we're up against. The men at the top have badly miscalculated the strength and cunning of the enemy. We've lost Dearborn, Mackinac, and Detroit. Without Ostrander and the rest of you, we'd have lost Fort Wayne as well. I want them to feel the urgency of the matter. I want to send them firsthand accounts."

At last! Quinn thought, *A general with brains.*

"That's why I'm sending you three."

Quinn was startled, Frake unimpressed, and Sally stone faced.

"Sending us where?"

"To see the president."

"President Madison?"

"He's the only one we got right now, I believe."

The three were stunned.

"Have a seat," Harrison said, pointing them to the chairs ringing his desk. "Don't want anyone fainting away here. Now I suppose you've got questions, especially *why you?* As I said, I don't think the president and his people really know what's happening out here. They need the unvarnished truth, and I can think of no one better than you three to deliver it."

Looking directly at Quinn, Harrison said, "There's no better way that you can serve our cause, ensign. Sure, I could keep you here, send you out to shoot a few Brits, as I know you are itching to do. If I led a platoon as determined as you, I'd sweep all the way to Montreal without stopping to water the horses." He smiled.

"I can't impress upon you how important your mission is. I could put all this in writing, but you will be more effective." He pointed the stem of his pipe at them. "You will go directly to the president, *not* to War Secretary Eustis. Eustis is a Republican from New England, a war supporter from the belly of the Federalist opposition. Madison hoped his appointment would bring more New Englanders to the president's side, but it hasn't. Eustis is loyal to Madison, but he's not the right man to run an army."

Harrison sipped his coffee and leaned toward them. "Now, you're going to hear things about Eustis—how he botched the job of strengthening the army, for example. We entered the war with just five thousand troops, and those are scattered all over. Congress sat on its hands, leaving the preparation to state militias. But men with muskets don't add up to a trained and disciplined army. Worse yet, some in Congress thought *they* should get the supply contracts." He shook his head.

"I don't know how long Madison will stick with Eustis. The Republicans want to put a Southerner—some War Hawk—in the job, so there's political pressure. In the meantime, Eustis won't put anyone in overall command. He's split the job between Hull and Dearborn, God knows why." The reference was to General Henry Dearborn, a veteran of the War of Independence, military commander in New England, and namesake of the fort Hull, ordered abandoned.

Harrison looked sternly at Quinn and Frake. "No overall commander means no overall strategy. Do we go first for Montreal or Ontario? Do we march through Upper Canada? Do we use New York as one prong of our pincers? Too much bickering, too much politicking, not enough communicating."

The general leaned back and shut his eyes for a moment then sat straight again and relit his pipe. "You three must inform the president about the mess they've created here. Tell them *everything*. Answer any questions honestly. I don't want you to speak my thoughts or anyone else's. The facts will speak for themselves, and you know the facts."

Frake coughed. "Um, general, I reckon you know your business, but I can't see an old backwoodsman like myself bein' much help back East. Miss Sally and Ensign Quinn are real good talkers. I don't figure I'd make such a good impression."

"Sergeant major, you're not going there to make a good impression. You're going to bear firsthand witness. Your country has already asked a great deal of you, but this mission is vital."

The general's tone left no room for further discussion.

15 September 1812
The Great Warrior Trail

*O*nce on the trail to Washington, intimacy between Quinn and Sally ended. Both had realized their dilemma when Harrison ordered them to brief the president. For Quinn that meant a visit to his family, something he'd never expected in the middle of a war. He'd thought to remain on the frontier under Harrison's command with time to work out a real marriage under less chaotic conditions—or not.

They had considered letting Quinn present Sally to his parents as his wife—a grave lie that would weigh heavily on his conscience, as did the knowledge that, according to his Catholic faith, he was living in mortal sin. For Sally, the problem was a good deal more than spiritual. If their charade were discovered, she would be branded as a loose woman.

What's more, they would be standing before the president of the United States as liars. So at last they decided to go to Harrison with a request. They approached the general with great trepidation, bringing Frake along as backup.

"Yes, what is it?" Harrison looked up from the papers spread across his desk, but the irritation in his tone softened when he saw his visitors.

"Ah, come in, come in. Sit. Sit." He motioned to the chair in front of his desk. "Coming to say good-bye?"

"Yes, sir." Quinn took a deep breath. "General, I have a personal...a very personal...request." He gulped and plunged ahead. "Could you change the orders?"

Harrison's eyebrows rose, and his jaw clenched, but before he could thunder, "No!" Quinn rushed on.

"Sir, it's not what you think. It's...Sally and I aren't married."

Harrison's face and body relaxed. He closed his eyes for a moment, opened them again, smiled, and chuckled.

"Well now. You know, I can't say I'm surprised, ensign. 'Course I never brought it up, but I did wonder. It's been a long while in the wilderness," he said softly, and Frake nodded.

Out in the territories, civil or religious authorities were not always on hand to perform marriages, so common-law marriage wasn't unusual. Nor were couples who attached themselves to each other, sometimes temporarily, in the interests of mutual support and security.

"You two looked too much in love and too happy to be married," Harrison joked. "So you don't want the orders presenting you as a married couple? I understand. For what you two have gone through, this is the least I can do. Sergeant!" Harrison called to his orderly outside the door. "We've got to rewrite some orders. Bring more paper."

And they left with orders introducing Ensign Quinn, Sergeant Major Frake, and *Miss* Sally Martin.

A fortnight had passed since Harrison had dispatched them, but Quinn and Sally were still torn over their decision. The Great War Trail that crossed the new state of Ohio and into the Appalachian foothills was a network of Great Paths made by the Potawatomi and other tribes as they conducted war and commerce. For miles after leaving Fort Wayne, the trail ran under a vaulted ceiling of trees that had not yet succumbed to the settlers' axes. It was barely wide enough for a horse and rider, so they rode single file—three escorts leading and three following Quinn, Sally, and Frake.

Nearer the settlements, the path showed signs of wheeled transport, and eventually parallel ruts marked the trail. When they came upon isolated cabins, a shouted, "Hello-o-o-o! The house!" alerted the occupants of the strangers' approach. Most settlers were glad to welcome a troop of soldiers, and the travelers were profoundly grateful for indoor shelter.

Beyond those scattered cabins lay the approach to Pittsburgh and a smattering of inns, really little more than large log cabins. Finally, at the last inn before Pittsburgh, Sally and Quinn left the others and walked to the edge of a nearby stream.

"Did we do right?" Sally asked. "Maybe we should have gone on pretending to be married."

Didn't feel much like pretending to me, Quinn thought. "Believe me, Sally, it's been on my mind just about every moment on the trail."

"And what do you think?"

Quinn paused. "I thought perhaps we might…"

"Actually get married?"

"Well, yes… If that's what you want."

"If that's what *I* want?"

Quinn cringed. "What I mean is that you've known me for such a short time and under such unimaginable circumstances. What we did was only natural."

Sally's eyes flashed. "I'm not talking about...*that*. But I suppose *you* are. *That's* what it means to men, I guess."

"No. Hell, no! Come on, Sally. What I'm trying to say is do *you* want to commit to spending a lifetime with *me*? This hasn't been exactly an ordinary courtship. What will it be like between us in normal times?" He paused then. "But, Sally, I do love you."

"Will, I don't want you to marry me out of pity or sympathy or..."

Now a new concern crept into Quinn's mind. "Maybe we should get married in Pittsburgh. Think about it. When you arrive in Washington as a single woman, what will you do?"

"What do you mean?"

"I mean, you don't know anyone there. Were you planning on coming back with me to Fort Wayne?" She looked startled but shook her head. "So then what will you do? Find work as a housemaid?"

"But I know how to read and write. I could teach."

"Yes, you can read and write, but you don't have any credentials or any experience beyond your own family. You'll have no one to—"

"I'm not a child, Will. I've made up my mind. I can't go back to the frontier—even when this awful war ends. My mother was an old woman at twenty-five. And dead in a nightmare a few years later. Women have some freedom in the West, but they pay a high price for it."

"Maybe..." She turned back to Quinn. "Will?"

"Yes?"

"How about your family?"

"You mean can you stay with them?"

"It would be better than staying with relatives I don't rightly know. I know you, and what you've told me of your family, they're good people."

"Sally, sweetheart, they'd take you in a moment, as my wife or as my friend. But I have to go back to the war."

Tears were streaming down her face now. "Oh, Will, curse this war!"

Quinn held her against him then. He stroked her hair and whispered, "Oh, Sally, without this war I'd never have met you. I can't imagine that."

19 September 1812

Pittsburgh

Stopping in Pittsburgh, Quinn found a letter waiting at the army post in his mother's familiar handwriting. She kept in touch faithfully, and Quinn thanked heaven for the Irish priest who had risked his life to teach Catholic children like his mother to read and write. That was a business asset to her husband and a blessing to her boys. He opened the letter eagerly and saw that it was dated a month earlier.

> My dear son, I have such bad news to report to you I don't know where to begin. Your father died tonight of the ghastly wounds I described to you in my last letter in July.

Quinn froze. He had received no such letter, and he felt his legs go weak beneath him. It would have been posted to Mackinac and by now destroyed or in British hands. Sally, seeing his hands tremble, stepped to his side and read along with him.

Since the night he went down to the wharf to protect the linen in the warehouse against the mob of zealots, his pain and suffering have been dreadful, and we could not grieve to see it end. Dr. Howard warned us that his wounds were fatal, but you know how determined Papa was. He hated to think of dying at the hands of an American mob when he had endured so much at the hands of the English. His spirit burned fiercely, but the fractured ribs, the mangled hands, the bruised and torn flesh overcame even his strong will. In his last hours, he let me bring Father O'Malley to give him the last rites, and he died at peace. Your brothers and I were there, and he asked us to tell you of his pride in you.

Since last I wrote, we have learned what provoked the attack on him. A crowd had gathered at the warehouse after someone spread the rumor that the linens were being traded with the British. They set upon him viciously and would not listen to his protests that he was a true Republican, a supporter of the war with his own grudges against the English.

I do not understand. Surely his brogue must have proved him Irish. But a mob is mindless, and they destroyed every bale of linen, set the warehouse afire, and left your father for dead. Thank God for the Negro wharf workers who pulled his poor, battered self from the fire.

Now I fear for your safety. My precious son, I have received no word from you, and I cannot but imagine the dangers you are facing from beasts and savages and the heartless English. Forgive me. Mothers are born to worry. Your brothers and I keep you in our prayers and trust that you hold us in yours.

Until we are reunited,
your loving mama.

Quinn was trembling. Sally looked up with tears rolling down her cheeks, and Quinn squeezed her hand.

"More death. More heartbreak. My poor mother! When will it end? Is there no peace in this world?"

Now he was seething with rage. He pulled himself from Sally's arms and went looking for someone who might have news of events in Baltimore. It was Frake who struck up a conversation with other travelers at the inn and found Oliver Wimsatt, a tinsmith from Virginia and a tireless talker.

The scholarly looking Wimsatt had sisters living in Baltimore, and when Frake told him of Quinn's loss, he was pleased to share what he could.

"You see, son," he began, seating himself beside Quinn on the long bench, "the mob started out by wrecking Hanson's office. Fellow who published the *Federalist*?" He shook his head. "Called it a newspaper! Nothin' but propaganda against the war! Anyhow, he set to stirring folks up against the war, but that got the pro-war people riled up too."

"What happened to Hanson?" Quinn asked.

"Oh, he sneaked away, but they threw all his paraphernalia out the windows, wrecked every bit of it. 'Course the Federalists set him up in business again. All those folks made money doing business with the British, so they don't want a war. They don't care if American sailors get hauled off their ships by the British. There's plenty that need jobs who'll take the place of those sailors.

"It was closing the ports, you see," Wimsatt continued. "If Jefferson and then Madison hadn't closed the ports, trade would have continued and the Federalists wouldn't have got in a dander and…well, lad, your old dad'd still be with us."

Quinn smiled sadly. "My father'd suffer any fate rather than buckle under to the English. Thank you, Mr. Wimsatt. It helps to know."

With that, the tinsmith took his leave. Quinn sat silently, and his two friends didn't interrupt his thoughts as they nursed their tankards.

His earliest memories were of his father—seated in his office at work, taking his son to walk along the River Liffey, grieving over his murdered brother, mourning his lost little girl. Death was no stranger to William Quinn, but he had not expected such stunning sorrow. As a soldier, he had sometimes envisioned his own death and imagined how it would affect his family. True, it usually fell to sons to bury their fathers, but for his father to die in a mob action that betrayed his new country's ideals was so unjust.

Sally gently covered his hand with her own. Quinn was lost in thought. They would pass within miles of Baltimore but could not stop. Their business with the president was urgent.

Suddenly, he smiled. How proud his father would have been! Imagine, an Irish immigrant in the president's house, meeting with the leader of the new nation.

"After we meet with the president, Sally, I want you to meet my mother."

21 September 1812
Washington, D.C.

*T*he travelers' first glimpse of Washington D.C. from the heights of neighboring and prosperous Georgetown revealed a national capital that left much to be desired, even for a fledgling nation. As they nudged their horses forward, they descended past brush and wetlands flora and into a motley collection of homes, boarding houses, and shops. Unlike the capital cities of Europe, Washington was ironically at once a city created by edict *and* dedicated to the revolutionary idea of self-government.

In jarring contrast to the city's primitive state, the elegant, white, marble-domed Capitol building still under construction rose on a low hill to the east. Beyond it, along the Potomac River and its eastern tributary, lay assorted military facilities, armories, and a navy yard. The streets—some rudimentary crushed limestone lanes, others no more than muddy paths—stretched in diagonals like the spokes of a wheel. A few were ridiculously wide, more suited to the traffic of Paris or London. The ambassadors assigned to represent their governments in this godforsaken swamp were accustomed to sumptuous European accommodations and found conditions here appalling.

Quinn's party arrived in September as heat and humidity settled in a damp cloud over the entire city.

"Christ, you can hardly breathe without drowning," Frake muttered.

Soon the travelers spotted their destination, a building that dominated its neighbors, but not so impressive as the Capitol. The executive mansion was more modest, a reminder that its occupant served at the people's pleasure.

They reined in their horses at the grand north entrance, looking more as though they'd come to shovel out the stables than to be received by the head of state. In the foyer a relaxed army captain sat at a small cherry writing table. Quinn presented his papers and his orders under Harrison's seal and waited for the captain to read them.

"Give me a moment, gentlemen, miss," he said and disappeared into another room. He had almost asked them to be seated, then thought better of it. The furniture was new.

Soon, First Lady Dolley Madison appeared. Her plump chin seemed to rest on a fluffy lace collar, and she beamed at them as if they were long-lost relatives. "Oh my, how exhausted you must be! Please, please let me show you where you can freshen up and revive yourselves with some food," she said.

The woman in the pale-blue gown was utterly charming, but orders were orders. "Please don't count us discourteous, Mrs. Madison, if we ask to present our information to the president first. I'm sorry—"

"Of course. The president is with Mr. Monroe, discussing affairs of state—or so they'd have me believe." She winked at Quinn. "But I'm sure that he'll want to see you at once. Please follow me."

Everything he'd heard about Mrs. Madison was true, Quinn thought as she escorted them toward the president's office. Bosomy and blue eyed with black curls and ivory skin, she had been a catch as a young widow when then-Congressman James Madison proposed to her. No match seemed more unlikely. She had set aside her reserved Quaker upbringing and become fashionable, flamboyant, and popular—a highly sought-after guest at local soirees. Madison was seventeen years older than Dolley, had never married, was often somewhat cranky, and was, in the words of his political opponents, a runt.

But Dolley was as shrewd a judge of character as she was a brilliant hostess. She saw that what Madison lacked in grace and stature he made up in intelligence and political skill. In those respects, he was a giant. And a good man. A son of Virginia, he had served in the commonwealth's assembly and in the American Continental Congress. His framing of the Virginia Constitution provided a model for the national document. He was only thirty-six at the Constitutional Convention, but his frequent and substantial contributions to the debates, his important role in the creation of the Bill of Rights, and his authorship, along with Alexander Hamilton and John Jay, of the Federalist Papers were instrumental in securing the states' approval of the new form of government. He was, indeed, the Father of the Constitution.

He and Monroe, no doubt, had a score of serious issues before them, but Dolley knocked firmly, stuck her head in, and brandished Harrison's letter.

"Mr. President, General Harrison has sent a party of messengers with eyewitness accounts of the…developments in the Northwest. I knew you would want to see them at once."

Madison rose from his desk and Monroe from his armchair to greet the visitors. They exchanged a glance at the sight of Sally, but promptly recovered themselves.

Quinn stepped forward and saluted. "Mr. President, we were dispatched here from Fort Wayne and ordered to report directly to you. Not to Mr. Eustis."

"Mmhmm." Madison nodded and turned to Monroe. "James, perhaps you would remain for the briefing. Please be seated." Resuming his own seat, he took the letter from Dolley and read for a moment then looked up at his guests. "Ensign William Quinn and Sergeant Major Judah Frake. And Miss Sally Martin. A pleasure, I'm sure."

Dolley, having sent for refreshments, took a seat next to her husband.

"Where do we start? Um, perhaps Miss Martin?"

"Yes, sir. Well, I'm not sure what the general felt I could add to this, except I do know the Northwest. My family came to the Illinois Territory when I was a baby." Sally had had time to consider how to tell her story, and she spoke calmly, even about the loss of her family and the attack on Fort Dearborn. But her jaw tightened when she spoke of Heald and Hull and Rhea. She ended with Harrison's directive, and only then did tears fill her eyes.

Dolley reached across and squeezed Sally's hand.

Madison turned then to Frake. The frontiersman drew himself up in his chair.

"Seems like you ought to know what happened at Riviere Aux Canards, Mr. President." From there the tale seemed to tell itself—the vulnerability of Fort Malden, Major Chase's initiative in holding the bridge, Hull's vituperative rejection of Chase's plan to seize the advantage and advance on the fort, the near mutiny of Hull's officers, the unwarranted retreat to Detroit, the shameful capitulation.

Quinn listened with new respect for his companion. He'd half expected to hear more of the sergeant's views on the blockheads in Washington and idiot generals. Instead, Frake spoke slowly, as though he'd been a disinterested observer of the string of catastrophes. He never exaggerated, but he never downplayed what he'd seen and heard. This was the chance of a lifetime to set things right, to bring the trials of the common soldier and the incompetence of some field commanders to the nation's highest authority.

When Frake stopped speaking, Quinn stepped in without a pause. "To begin with, sir, Lieutenant Hancks at Mackinac was never informed that we were at war."

Madison and Monroe looked stricken.

"That's why he sent me to Dearborn, to learn what was going on and to warn the others of what the British were up to. The attack took them by surprise. Hancks hadn't a prayer." Like Frake, he remained objective, but his lip curled as he reported Heald's negotiation with the Indians and later when he confirmed Frake's opinion of Rhea. "Without Ostrander and Curtis, the three of us would be dead by now."

Throughout these recitations, the president, the secretary of state, and Mrs. Madison sat mesmerized and appalled. No one interrupted with a question. Madison and Monroe had received preliminary reports of the fall of the three outposts, but no details. These accounts, from people who had been on the scene, brought the situation to life. When the questions came, they came in a torrent.

"How many dead altogether at Dearborn, do you think?"

"How many wounded or captured?"

"Where is Hancks now, do you know?"

"Have we any chance of recovering the forts?"

"Where would we begin? And how many men do we need?"

"Are *all* the Indians allying with the British by now?"

Then Dolley broke in. "Mr. Madison, husband, see, you have exhausted our visitors. You can continue this later,

I'm sure. For now, let me show them to their rooms." She turned to Quinn. "You must stay with us at least tonight."

For a moment Quinn thought of saying he must go to Baltimore, but his duty for now lay here. He bowed slightly and ushered Sally, along with Frake, out the door to follow their hostess.

21 September 1812

The White House

*D*inner at the White House was a revelation. Butlers. Fine china and real silverware. Food appearing from an unseen kitchen. Quinn and Sally were awed, and Frake was suspicious. He preferred to see his food prepared so he'd know what he was swallowing. Still, it looked and smelled tempting.

It had been easy enough to offer fresh uniforms to Quinn and Frake, but Sally had presented more of a challenge. In time, Mrs. Madison recalled that one of the housemaids was nearly Sally's height and only slightly more plump. The simple dark dress suited her well, and she was glad it wasn't more elaborate.

"Sally, what are your plans now?" Dolley Madison asked.

"I really don't know, ma'am. I have relatives in Pittsburgh, though I really don't know them or know if they'd be willing to take me in." Sally lowered her eyes as she felt tears rise.

She had come to Washington aware that her future was uncertain. If Quinn's family didn't welcome her…? Might she, in this new city, find some work to support herself— maid, cleaning lady, cook, or with luck, teacher or tutor?

"Maybe we can think of something," Dolley said.

Looking at Sally, Dolley said, "I have been searching for someone to assist me in my official duties. Planning for events. Handling correspondence. Receiving visitors." Mrs. Madison smiled. "Would you be interested in such a position?"

The question nearly left Sally sputtering. "Ma'am, I don't know how I could help you. I read and write, of course, but I know more about handling rifles than about handling fancy forks."

Dolley laughed. "Well, these days handling a rifle might be useful. No, clearly you would need to learn a great deal very quickly, but I believe you could. And this may seem trivial to you after what you have seen and done, but I cannot overstate the importance of a smoothly functioning executive mansion. I don't expect you to answer immediately. I know I have caught you off guard. Meanwhile, you are a welcome guest in our home."

Sally was stunned. To be scratching out a living with her family in the wilderness one day and seated at the president's table a few months later was hard to grasp. But to be invited to be a paid member of the household... Had the moon fallen out of the sky?

She accepted with grateful tears.

Madison turned to Quinn and Frake. "Now I have orders for you, a mission of the greatest importance. General Harrison wanted you to return immediately to Fort Wayne, but I'm superseding his authority. I need someone I can trust, someone without political axes to grind. Things are going very badly in the Northeast. My generals can't agree on a strategy for a Canadian campaign. Do they go through upper New York? Down the St. Lawrence River? Over Lake Champlain? The lake is our highway north, but it could become the British highway south, cutting off commerce and communications. With the world's most powerful navy, they can cut off our sea links too. Our coastal trade among the states was critical in the War of Independence, and we suffered badly when the British damaged our commerce at sea."

The president paused long enough to soak up a bit of gravy with a slice of bread. Dabbing his mouth with his napkin and returning it to his lap, he resumed.

"Now we can build faster pilot boats and create havoc among the British men-of-war, so I'm optimistic about our navy. Our privateers harass British shipping, and the *Constitution* acquitted herself well against the British frigate *Guerriere*. Captain Hull—uh, no relation to the general— pounded the *Guerriere* into surrender. Imagine the shock in the British Admiralty! By God, I wish I could have seen it!"

Quinn and Frake were puzzled and apprehensive.

"All this is preface for what I want you to do," he said as the stewards refilled the diners' coffee cups.

Finally! Quinn thought.

"Yes, please, cream for me," Madison said without breaking stride. "You know about General Henry Dearborn?"

Both men nodded.

"Fought at Ticonderoga, was Jefferson's secretary of war, tried to get the army organized. An uphill battle because Americans are leery of standing armies, and the Federalists dominated the officer corps. Henry replaced those he could with Republicans. I don't like a politicized military, but Federalist officers were deliberately flouting administration policies.

"Finally, Henry wanted out, so Jefferson put him in charge of the customs office in Boston. I managed to persuade him to come back as senior major general of the army. He's in Boston, building up shoreline defenses, recruiting, and whatnot.

"Please try this cake. It's marvelous," Madison said, taking the biggest piece from the proffered tray. "The problem is this—nothing's happening. Communications are a disaster. His subordinates are at loggerheads about their approaches to taking Canada. I'm no general, but I know you need mighty good reasons—*not* personal ambition and petty jealousies—to divide your forces in the face of the enemy. Dearborn needs to knock some heads together and take control."

Madison washed down a bite of cake with a gulp of coffee. Neither Quinn nor Frake could eat.

"I'm going to put all this and more into a letter that you gentlemen will place directly into Henry's hands. Know that this is my highest priority, and do whatever you must to convey my concern."

"When do we leave?" Quinn asked, resigned to his new orders.

"On the morrow, first thing," Madison said. "You'll have fresh horses and experienced guides who'll get you to Boston as fast as possible. It's been a joy to meet people who understand what we are fighting for. Be restful tonight."

With that, he rose from the table and shook hands, first with Frake then with Quinn.

"Mr. Quinn, I know that your family is in Baltimore, and Miss Martin has told Mrs. Madison of your father's cruel death. Curse the mobs! They won't be happy until they have torn this country asunder! When you stop in Baltimore on the way to Boston, convey Mrs. Madison's and my deepest sympathies to your mother. Mr. Quinn is a martyred patriot. Unfortunately, you must not stay there more than a night. Your mission is most urgent. Good night, gentlemen."

Frake, Quinn, and Sally made their way to their respective rooms, too exhausted to speak.

21 September 1812

Alexandria, Virginia

While the president was pondering the nation's future in the White House, in Alexandria just seven miles to the south, a different drama was playing out. A family of slaves, headed by Henry, was about to go on the block. The night before, while Quinn, Sally and Frake slept comfortably in the White House, Henry's mother, Emma, hanged herself. It was the only way to escape the slave auction, but the sale of Henry, his wife Flora, their fourteen-year-old son Matthew, and their daughter Mattie—only eleven—would proceed as planned as if nothing had happened. Henry's blood boiled, and his bowels twisted and groaned, but his face remained impassive. He would not shame himself or his family in front of these devils.

Henry's family was the last to be sold because all four were prime stock. He had never imagined this nightmare. His owner, Mrs. Harriett Lindsay, widow of a wealthy merchant, died of old age. She was a decent person who treated her slaves with kindness, civility, and dignity, and though far from an abolitionist, she would never have split up Henry's family. But she died childless, so the estate passed to distant relatives. Unfortunately for her slaves, these kinfolk were Deep South tobacco planters financially strapped by the British blockade and in need of capital. The slaves were simply assets, like cattle, to be converted into cash. Why had she not thought to free them?

Henry was a fine shoemaker. From just a sketch of the latest European fashion in boots or shoes, Henry could duplicate the footwear flawlessly. Thanks to Mr. Lindsay, he could also read and calculate. Many people disapproved, but Lindsay saw that this added to Henry's value, because he could requisition goods and fill orders. Henry would not have been destitute once free. He could have opened his own business, and Emma and Flora were house slaves who could have found work as seamstresses or…

They had seen this dark day coming and had attempted to prepare for it. An appeal to Mrs. Lindsay's relatives had been ignored.

"I know the Lord awaits me on the other side, and that day will be my liberty day," Emma told Henry, and the night before the auction, she twisted her clothing into a rope and hanged herself.

Flora was as devastated as Henry and briefly wished to follow her mother-in-law into the promised land. When she broke the news to Henry, he only sighed softly, relieved that his mother's suffering had ended. Perhaps now she could intercede with the Lord to help them.

The slaves were led to the well and required to strip and wash away the urine, rat dung, and other foulness they'd picked up in the filthy holding cells. New arrivals from Africa were among them, puzzled and frightened.

Handbills announcing the auction had gone out the day before throughout Alexandria, Washington, and environs proclaiming the "Sale of Negroes," along with "mules, hogs, farming and mining tools, and wagons and carts."

The city was a gateway from the Chesapeake into the slave-holding South—a center of the slave trade. Men, women, and even children passed through the slave pens and auction platforms a few blocks up Duke Street from the wharfs. Some of the young nation's most renowned proponents of the rights of man regularly dined and lodged in Alexandria, and if their consciences cringed as they passed chained slaves being herded to the auction blocks, the founding fathers didn't show it.

Now the excruciating moment had arrived. Matthew stood with the auctioneer.

"Here is a fine, young boy, fit for immediate service of the most laborious or domestic kind. Observe his muscle tone and skin condition, which speak of his prior good treatment and his submissiveness to good order. His masters kept the finest household in Alexandria, and he knows his place. Speak, boy. Show your refinement."

Matthew didn't know what to say, and the auctioneer poked him roughly with his riding crop.

"Sir?"

"Your name, boy. What is your name?"

"It is Matthew, the same as the Savior's apostle."

"Aye, mayhap you'll write a gospel, just like your namesake." The auctioneer smirked at the crowd. "Gentlemen, what am I bid for this prime field hand or refined house nigger? He has an entire productive life ahead of him, and he's not yet in his prime. Consider potential for studding. I tell you, you don't often see such valuable property. Take advantage of this rare opportunity. Fifty dollars? You, sir?"

Aggressive bidding confirmed Matthew's value before the auctioneer closed it at an eye-popping $1,235. His new master, judging by his elegant clothing, was a Deep South aristocrat. So Matthew would be taken far from Virginia. It broke Henry's heart to see the boy hold back tears, lift his chin, and be led away.

Flora begged the auctioneer not to break up her family, but he snarled, "Shut up, nigger, or you'll get the lash."

It was an empty threat. He would no more beat her than he'd whip one of the horses he was selling—a beaten animal brought a lower price. Still, she fell silent.

The auctioneer motioned Flora and Mattie to the block. Henry seethed with rage at the description of the "property."

"Come now, gentlemen, need I show you *all* the fine points of these two specimens? Not until the bidding rises. These two come from the same fine household as that nigger lad. What's your name, girl? Flora?"

He turned to the crowd with a wink. "City born and regular bred, skilled in the art of French cooking, needlework, and...other skills. Firm breasts," he said, cupping them from behind. "Gentlemen, you will find no finer piece of pussy in the Old Dominion. A few years left in her for breeding." With his crop, he lifted her shift above her stomach, exposing the dark, triangular patch below to the lecherous crowd.

"What's more, this nigress comes with a bonus. This here is Mattie, who'll ripen right soon. Hard to resist already, isn't she?" He grinned and ripped away her thin shift.

Flora moved to shield her, and Henry shuffled forward but was roughly yanked back.

The auctioneer pointed to Mattie's prepubescent nipples and her near-hairless mound. "Gentlemen, what am I bid?"

The bidding went on for what seemed a lifetime to Henry. The gavel fell at last on a winning bid of $2,100 from a planter whose lust was absurdly obvious. From the banter between the auctioneer and the bidders, Henry discerned that the lecher hailed from Virginia's Piedmont Lowlands, just west of the Blue Ridge Mountains. He would not forget. He would escape and find his family. Or die trying.

Henry, in turn, brought an impressive price because of his shoemaking skills. He went to a merchant from the nation's capital and so would be taken farther from his family, but it moved him no farther from Tangiers Island.

The British used this low-lying tract in the middle of Chesapeake Bay as a staging area for troops *and* as a refuge for escaped slaves. George Cockburn, admiral of the British fleet patrolling the Bay, had issued clearly seditious handbills promising slaves freedom if they joined the British. They could fight under the Union Jack and then find transport to Canada or the East Indies—to freedom!

Escape to the island seemed to Henry a first step to freedom. It would take careful planning and incredible luck, but it might just be possible.

29 September 1812

Baltimore and Boston

Agnes Quinn nearly swooned when she opened the door and saw her son. Oblivious at first to Frake at his side, the little woman fell into her boy's arms, sobbing softly.

"Ssshh, Mother," Quinn crooned. "Your letters caught up with me late. I know about Father, and I am so sorry I was not here to comfort you both."

She stepped back then and held him at arm's length, looking him up and down and smiling through her tears. "Willie!" she cried. "It is truly you, not an apparition. Oh, merciful God, you have returned my son to me. How can I thank you? Where have you been, William? Are you unhurt? When our letters went unanswered, we feared the worst. How did you get here? Please tell me that you are you unhurt."

Quinn wrapped his arm around her shoulder and led her and the others back into the house. "I am whole and hale, Mother, though we have had adventures, to be sure. Mackinac has fallen, but I was sent elsewhere. But first let me introduce my friend, Sergeant Major Judah Frake. To him, I owe my life. Are my brothers near at hand?"

Agnes nodded. "At the weaving mill or the warehouse. I'll send for them at once. So nice to meet you, Mr. Frake. Please, please, sir, don't stand. You look famished. And, William, invite in your other friends. Where are your manners?"

Frake spoke to their three-man escort, but the soldiers said they would find a nearby tavern and let the family gathering proceed without them.

The heartbroken woman who had met them at the door was now a bustling housewife. She sent a neighbor boy to fetch Quinn's brothers, set about making tea, then sent Frake and Quinn to wash up at the pump behind the house. They had scarcely finished when Cavan rode up, leapt from his horse, and engulfed his brother in something between a stranglehold and an embrace. Will pulled back, laughing.

"Sure, I might have known you'd barge in first," he said. "Frake, this clumsy bear is my younger brother Cavan. He's bullheaded, but he means well." Then he looked more closely at his brother's face. "Fall off your horse, did you?"

Cavan grinned sheepishly. "No. It's this new game around here. Bare-knuckle fighting, they call it. And it pays a bit."

Will frowned. "Well, if it's fighting you want, lad, the army—" But he was interrupted by the arrival of another horse and rider.

The boy who dismounted was shorter and stockier than his brothers, but he had their blue eyes and strong chins. What Aengus lacked in height, he more than made up in wit and the gift of gab.

"Welcome home, Will," he said, and to Frake, "Bless you, sir, for bringing him back to us. Lord knows he could get lost between here and the kitchen left to himself."

"Aengus! Let's have some respect for your elders!" Will grabbed the youngest Quinn and turned him to face Frake.

"Now, sergeant major, this youngster is Aengus Quinn, Mam's baby and the darling of her heart."

"And is herself killing the fatted calf this very moment?"

The voice was deeper than Will's; it belonged to Malachy Quinn, the third brother and the oldest, to arrive. He shook Frake's hand then slapped Will on the back, and Frake realized that he was an even bigger man than Cavan. The brothers Quinn would constitute a force to be reckoned with.

Once settled in the kitchen, though, Malachy became the man of the house, explaining to Will about the rebuilding of the mill and the warehouse. Agnes kept apologizing for the dinner she was serving. Having had no notice of their arrival, she had simply stretched their usual dinner. It was a traditional Irish stew—potatoes, bits of lamb and bacon, salt and pepper—with a few extra potatoes added to accommodate Will and Frake and a loaf of Irish soda bread. The Quinn boys spontaneously burst into song as the stew was placed on the table.

> Then hurrah for an Irish stew
> That will stick to your belly like glue.

"Behave yourselves!" Agnes scolded. "We've a guest in the house. Will, you say grace."

Quinn complied then looked up at Agnes and said, "Mam, you'll never know how I've longed for a taste of this."

Frake grinned, looked around the table, and asked, to the laughter of all, "What, no squirrel?"

He and Will talked as they ate—the surrender of Mackinac, the massacre at Dearborn (muting some of the horror), the surrender of Detroit, the victory and rescue at Fort Wayne, the journey to the White House, the meeting with Madison, the dinner, the guest rooms, Mrs. Madison, Secretary Monroe... Scheherazade never had an audience more enthralled.

"Oh, your father would have been so proud, so proud!" Agnes Quinn beamed. "To think that our boy was welcomed into the greatest house in the nation. It'd never happen in the old country."

At that Quinn's face darkened. "I confess, Mother, to some bitterness that our own countrymen—men of our own city!—murdered Father. The Lord and Mother Church must forgive my thoughts of revenge. Have these men been brought to justice?"

She shook her head. "I don't know, William. Father O'Malley has promised to keep me informed, but..." She shook her head then, and a cold silence settled over the room.

Frake broke it. "Seems to me, ensign, you left out something pretty important." He looked Quinn in the eye and raised his eyebrows.

Agnes raised her head, alert to the new tone. "What would that be?" Then she grinned. "Might it have to do with this Miss Martin?"

Quinn shot a glance at Frake, who must have briefed her while she was preparing dinner. Quinn blushed, feeling like a ten-year-old. "Well, ah, yes." He fumbled for words as his brothers whooped and hollered.

"Why are you hiding her?" Aengus asked, and the others chimed in.

"Is she pretty?"

"Is she Irish?"

"When will you marry?"

Agnes shushed them. "William, she sounds exceptional and gallant. When can we meet her?"

"I don't know. I have my mission now, and she has hers. We go on tomorrow to Boston with important instructions for General Dearborn."

Agnes was crestfallen, but she smiled, carefully folded her napkin, gathered herself up, and said, "You needn't explain duty to me. I have had duties aplenty in my life. You will be gravely missed, but go do your duty, and we will do ours."

It took them six days to reach Dearborn's headquarters where they had to wait for more than an hour in an ante-room. Dearborn was a crusty old coot who thought himself superior to his superiors. When Quinn and Frake were finally ushered into his presence, he left them standing while he read Madison's letter.

> General, you have received no fewer than five dispatches from Secretary of War Eustis or his subordinates telling you to engage the enemy in an assertive campaign to capture and hold critical British fortifications and cities. You have been repeatedly enjoined to acknowledge that the northeast and northwest frontiers are under your command. You have been ordered to secure necessary militia to launch an assault on Niagara, Kingston, and Montreal. You were to secure complete control of Lake Erie, denying the enemy transport of British forces and supplies. Your failure to communicate with General Hull's Upper Canadian expeditions is largely responsible for our loss of Detroit and other

important outposts. You wrote to Mr. Sec. Eustis that you did not "consider the Niagara frontier as coming within the limits of my command," despite express instructions to the contrary. Your ill-advised armistice with the enemy allowed him to position and reinforce his troops, and your inaction has jeopardized ours. The loss of the Niagara River corridor and / or Sackets Harbor would permanently cripple the war effort.

These are written orders, carried to you at my direction. You are to act now, beginning with the assault on Niagara. Ensign Quinn is fully apprised of these matters and empowered to speak for me. You are to treat Mr. Quinn and Sgt. Maj. Frake with all due respect as my personal couriers.

This extraordinary dressing down from the commander in chief, bypassing the secretary of war, and conveyed by a junior officer authorized to elaborate on it if need be was a blow. A deep embarrassment and an insult—as it might have been meant. Quinn braced himself for the general's reaction.

"You know the contents of this letter, ensign?"

"Yes, sir," Quinn replied. "President Madison ordered me to read it so that there would be no misunderstanding of its intent or content, sir."

Dearborn was fuming. He did not take kindly to a civilian such as Madison lecturing him on matters of command. Quinn heard him murmur under his breath that perhaps Madison ought to come and conduct the war himself.

But in a moment the general recovered himself. "I trust the president impressed on you that this communiqué is confidential and not to be discussed outside these walls, ensign?"

"Yes, sir. We have not discussed these matters with anyone, including our escort. We wish only to fulfill our mission. We have orders to return expeditiously to General Harrison's command. We will, with your permission, take our leave."

Quinn and Frake knew they were caught in the middle of a high-level contest of wills. Their best option was to appear as unthreatening as possible and then to disappear into the wilderness with their discomfiting information.

But they had miscalculated.

Dearborn shook his head. "You won't be returning to Harrison's command." Casually he swiveled in his chair and looked out onto the leafy Boston Common. "I've got more important work for two such...qualified emissaries. Stand down for a couple of hours while I compose a confidential message for General Van Rensselaer on the Niagara front. When you have delivered it, you'll be assigned to him. He's short of junior officers. Obviously, you've impressed the president, so I'm sure you'll have an equal impact on Van Rensselaer."

Quinn had had more than enough of the eccentricities of the high command. "Sir, I don't think I made myself clear. President Madison has endorsed Harrison's orders. With all due respect, I don't believe you are empowered to overrule him."

Dearborn smiled thinly. "Well, ensign, let me educate you. The president isn't here, and a field general has the discretion to make and alter assignments in the best interests of the campaign. It is my judgment that your services are needed at Niagara. Dismissed." And he turned back to the window.

Quinn stiffened, but Frake nudged him out of the room.

Once outside, Frake took a deep breath. "Will, this man will defy the president and send us into combat because dead men can't tell tales. You don't want to take on a man like that. Not now."

3 October 1812

Niagara

*J*unior officers, Quinn learned, had no monopoly on anger and frustration. Major General Stephen Van Rensselaer was assigned to defend the Niagara River—whose thirty-five miles bordered Canada—with one thousand ill-trained, ill-equipped, ill-housed, and ill-fed troops. For months the general had been petitioning Dearborn for more men, more ammunition and stores, more of everything he needed to make his army battle ready. .

Dearborn ignored each and every request. True, Van Rensselaer had been appointed by the New York governor as commander in chief of the state's militia with no military training or experience. The scion of a wealthy Dutch family, he was a Federalist, not pleased to be leading the state's militia into Canada. And the regular army officers and men in his command were reluctant to serve under an officer of the militia.

The letter Quinn and Frake delivered contained the final blow. Dearborn was sending Alexander Smyth to Niagara as second-in-command, empowered to operate independently of Van Rensselaer. As the general read the communiqué, Quinn saw his face grow red then nearly purple.

"Tell me, Ensign Quinn, what exactly does it mean to be second-in-command if a man needn't answer to the first-in-command?"

"I...don't know, sir. It seems odd."

"Do you think so? Well, here is something a good deal odder. I am required to take Upper Canada by winter or face great and dire consequences." He looked Quinn in the eye then. "I wonder what those consequences might be. I'm relatively certain that if we invade Canada with the men and supplies we have now, we are likely all to be dead. Will that be dire enough, do you think?"

Brigadier General Alexander Smyth was even less qualified for command than Van Rensselaer. A political hack whose main accomplishment was cribbing the French army field manual and successfully passing it off as a new U.S. Army field manual of his own creation was enough to get himself appointed by Eustis as army inspector general with the rank of brigadier. Not content to remain at a desk and do minimal damage, Smyth insisted on a field appointment.

Faced with this untenable problem created by Dearborn in the chain of command, Van Rensselaer called a council of his senior officers to plan the invasion. Quinn sat fascinated as Van Rensselaer and his staff developed a strategy: have Smyth stage a feint attack at the northern end of the Niagara River on Lake Ontario. Van Rensselaer's soldiers would cross upriver opposite Queenston on the Canadian side. Quinn left the meeting feeling hopeful—Van Rensselaer listened to his staff—but Smyth later rejected the strategy out of hand. He sent a dismissive memo in which he said he would stay camped near Buffalo to await a better plan. In effect, it was a stunning refusal to obey a superior officer's orders, a court martial-worthy offense.

Will it never end, Quinn wondered in one of his steady exchanges of letters with Sally that had begun immediately after his departure from the White House. Sally wrote excitedly about her experiences in the nation's executive mansion and capital city; how much she—an ordinary American frontier girl—was surprised and fascinated by the politics, backstabbing, and machinations that were part of the everyday routine in the District of Columbia. In his turn, Quinn unloaded his frustrations with having to deal with the bungling and hubris of senior officers that every day rolled down to crush the readiness and spirit of the lower ranks. Each complaint made Sally increasingly uneasy about his fate.

Yet their feelings for each other in the letters were strangely muted. Once on the most intimate of terms, their expressions of endearment had become less passionate. Caulk it up, perhaps, to the stresses of war and uncertainty of the future. Or their shared fear that someone might intercept the letters and expose past behavior that might have been regarded as inappropriate. However conscious they were of the subtle changes and whatever its cause, the seeds were being planted that perhaps this once-inflamed relationship might now be cooling.

11 October 1812

Washington, D. C.

As Henry's new owner, Caleb Kilfoyle, led him off, the slave was determined to find freedom. A new owner unfamiliar with Henry's habits and thinking should be easy to fool. And this war was another advantage.

Still, getting safely out of Washington, finding the British, surviving the risks of war—it would not be easy.

"Come, Henry, sit up here with me. We've got a lot to talk about," Kilfoyle said.

"Mister Kilfoyle, sir, I'm just doing fine back here."

Henry was stunned. Slaves, even free blacks, don't sit up front with the master or a white person. "Do you think it's right? Someone might see me sitting there."

"Nonsense, Henry. We're out of sight of that slave pit. You're coming with me to the nation's new capital!"

It was an interesting insight into his new master's attitudes.

Unlike many slaveholders, Kilfoyle derived no particular pleasure from owning other human beings. For him it was simply business, the advantage of cheap labor. He was a Washington merchant who saw vast commercial opportunities in the new capital. He planned to open an emporium and use Henry as the house shoemaker. "You are a very talented shoemaker," Kilfoyle went on, whipping his horses into a canter on the road along the Potomac up to Washington. Kilfoyle was a man who knew where he wanted to go and wanted to get there in a hurry.

"Yes, sir," Henry said straight away without embarrassment or embellishment. "I can make any kind of footwear you desire—high tops, high-lows, boots, fancy heels for the missus."

Kilfoyle grinned. "Well, Henry, I aim to put you up in my new store and give you an opportunity to ply your skills. You'll have a shop there among all the other craftsmen I can assemble. Silversmiths, coppersmiths, jewelers, clothiers, upholsters, you name it. We'll sell food there too. Fresh meat, fresh bread, fruit when it's in season. Lord, lord, it's a new world."

Kilfoyle stopped the team. Henry wanted to hear more; he climbed up front to hear. Once Kilfoyle got his team moving again, Henry, from the corner of his eye, assessed the man—no slave looked directly at the master.

"So, Henry, what do you think, eh?"

No white man had ever asked for Henry's opinion, but he answered firmly, "I think you're on to something, Mr. Kilfoyle."

"My God, yes I am! And you'll be a part of it." This man's exuberance, if Henry wasn't careful, could be catching. His plans didn't include lining Kilfoyle's pockets. First opportunity, he'd be gone.

He had been in Washington on errands for the Lindsays and knew that blacks, free or slave, were a common sight on the street, so he wouldn't stand out. And he had other advantages: he could read and write. Dressed for work and with the manners he'd learned from his mother and the Lindsays, he could easily pass as a free black man. No one would stop him on the street, as they would in the rural South, and demand to see his papers.

"It's a beauty, is it not, Henry?" Kilfoyle said as they drove into the city.

Henry nodded. "Yes, sir."

Kilfoyle looked at him keenly, sensing the tension. "The races might never be equal, Henry, but this is our country—yours and mine—and we can't let the English take it back. We'll all be slaves then—won't have no freedom at all."

"Yes, sir," Henry agreed, thinking, *It will take a few days to make my plans, then I'll be through with this fool.*

11 October 1812

Washington, D.C.

*S*ally was amazed at how rapidly letters to the nation's executive mansion were delivered. She had Quinn's letter in her hands in less than a fortnight. In the privacy of her room, she ripped it open and consumed the words. He had signed the letter, "Your fondest friend."

My fondest friend? William Quinn, is this all I am to you? Out of sight, out of mind? Then she took up her own pen.

Now added to her fear that Quinn would die in combat was the fear that he didn't care for her anymore. His letters to her were so full of military matters and so impersonal. She had given herself to him first in pain and loneliness but then in love. For her, attraction and friendship had deepened into something more. But for him?

So her own letter echoed his impersonal tone.

> And I was aghast to learn that slaves were building the new Capitol and to find here in this Great House slaves ministering to the president, the first lady, and their guests.
>
> Mrs. Madison keeps me fully engaged with my duties, and I regard this as a demonstration of her

growing trust in my competency. She is most discreet, of course, but she shares some of her concerns, and I absorb much from overheard conversations. Mr. Madison is frustrated and conflicted.

I am indeed "your fondest friend." You know all my foibles and dreams. I think perhaps only my sister knew me so well. My thoughts and prayers are with you. Your mother kindly invited me to visit her, and I was able to reciprocate by inviting her and your brothers here to meet the president and first lady.

They know that I write to you frequently—Aengus says he can't see why I bother—and always ask that I send their love to you.

Sally.

Now it was Quinn's turn to wonder. In his absence and in the whirl of Washington politics and social events, was she now cooling on him, a mere Irish immigrant with comparatively fewer prospects compared with the movers and shakers she now was encountering?

13 October 1812

Niagara

Quinn was monitoring intelligence reports for General Van Rensselaer, reports that indicated that the British force comprised 1,500 regular and militia troops, plus 250 Indians. The Americans numbered some 3,650 regulars and 2,650 militia. Acknowledging his own military shortcomings, the general had put someone else in command of the main invasion force. True, it was his nephew Colonel Solomon Van Rensselaer, but he was an experienced soldier who served under Mad Anthony Wayne, the Revolutionary War hero. Solomon Van Rensselaer had thirteen large boats, enough to carry a total of three hundred and forty armed men with each crossing. He had hired local boatmen to ferry them through the treacherous eddies below the great Niagara Falls. Captain John E. Wool, commanded the first boat, and Quinn commanded the second.

The attack was launched at 5:30 a.m., October 13, 1812.

The boats were spotted almost immediately. The big guns and Canadian riflemen on the bluff poured fire down with alarming accuracy, but the British and Canadian volleys were instantly returned by American artillery.

Officers stood in their boats. In the stern next to the boatman, Quinn hoped his men were too worried about their own safety to notice the moisture running from his crotch down his leg.

The oarsman immediately in front of him took a ball to his head and fell across his bench. Men were wounded or dying in the other boats too. Their cries were drowned out by the continuous roar of gunfire. One boat took a cannonball directly amidships. It was instantly gone in a geyser of bloody body parts and splinters.

Some boats were turning back. Quinn's own instincts urged him to retreat. His mind told him instead to seek shelter below the steep bluff on the Canadian side, hidden from the enemy under the rocks and overhangs. Quinn shouted, cajoled, and nearly pleaded for his men to move forward. Seconds later their boat bumped onto the rocky shore, and several others boats quickly followed. Colonel Van Rensselaer was shot multiple times as his boat neared the shore. Gravely wounded, he was transported back across the river, leaving Wool in charge.

Officers and men hugged the base of the rocky cliff until another boat made it across. Its boatman edged nearer to Wool and Quinn.

"Sir, I've got an idea!" he shouted over the roar of cannon and musket. "I'm from these parts. A little ways up the river is a small path. Fishermen get up to the heights and the village that way."

"But what if it's guarded? We could be ambushed," Wool said.

"Yes, sir, but not everyone knows about the path, and I'd bet most civilians are ducking for cover right now."

The artillery from both sides was deafening. Wool hesitated then turned to the boatman. "Lead the way. Come on, boys!" he shouted to Quinn and the men.

They followed a zigzag path, their movements hidden from British view by the steep cliffs and the scrub bushes and trees that clung to the rocky face. When they reached the top unchallenged, they found themselves at the edge of a forest, looking across a fifty-yard clearing at the backs of the British who were firing from the top of the cliff on the American boats below.

For a moment the Americans simply marveled at their good fortune. It was all the officers could do to keep their men from whooping and shooting at once. Under Wool's direction, they lined up at the edge of the woods, hidden behind trees and bushes, then counted off by threes. The first group of three was ordered to fire, then the second and then the third, creating an almost continuous volley.

It devastated the British ranks. Men fell, mortally wounded. Others were sprayed with the blood of their comrades. Deafened by their own muskets and artillery, the British at first had no idea where the shots were coming from. At last they spotted the puffs of smoke along the forest's edge and ran in panic to find cover. Some stumbled pell-mell from one tree to another, ignoring their officers' orders to form a line of combat. Others simply took off toward Queenston village below. Within seconds, the officers themselves fled. It was a complete rout. In moments, the Americans occupied the heights. Young Wool remained composed and steady and prepared for a British counterattack. He set up defensive lines and assigned positions to the men who were now trailing up the fisherman's path. Quinn watched, learned, and realized that Wool, who kept glancing back to the path and the woods, was troubled. Fewer men than he had expected appeared. At last Frake, who had crossed the river with Winfred Scott, an up-from-the-ranks lieutenant colonel, in the second wave, arrived.

"What the hell happened?" Quinn asked.

"Weasels saw the boats from the first wave returning with their wounded. Arms shot off, holes through the head. Not what they thought war was gonna be like."

Quinn sighed. "None of us did." He glanced at the bloodied British wounded being removed from the clearing and the redoubts and realized that the Americans had suffered not a single casualty in clearing the bluff.

But Frake was still fuming. "Some of them said they didn't have to cross the river into Canada because they was state militia and didn't have to fight outside New York. I thought Scott would take some of their heads off right on the spot." Frake was still trying to catch his breath from the long climb and at the same time, take in as much of the battlefield as he could.

"So then?"

"We rounded up enough to load a few boats. Sometimes at bayonet point. Told 'em they're gonna die right here right now for certain, or they can take their chances across the river. I don't know if I would have run 'em through, but I guess they thought I would. Some was purely shamed into it. But I wouldn't have been surprised if Scott hadn't shot a few of those maggots."

Altogether, something short of a thousand men had crossed the river and would have to face whatever the British might throw at them.

Something caught Frake's eye while he was ranting. "Looky down there. Ain't that General Brock?"

"Where?"

"Down the hill, toward the village."

By now, the last of the gun smoke had cleared.

"You mean that showy officer?"

Quinn focused on a man, riding straight and tall in the saddle, wearing gold epaulettes and a gold-trimmed, bright-red coat. To make sure that no one on either side could miss him, he wore a flashy scarf rumored to have been given to him by Tecumseh. Everyone on the American side knew about Brock—his courage, leadership, and intelligence. It was bad news.

Frake spat. "Makes for a better target."

He was more worried about what was behind Brock. Several companies of Redcoats and militia. That they could have reformed so quickly was testimony to the danger the Americans faced from Brock.

Brock had several companies moving straight up the hill with obvious flanking movements on each side. It was Quinn's first taste of this form of attack, and it looked suicidal. Shoulder to shoulder, with the officers and colors at the front and drums beating out the march cadence, they were an awesome sight.

Indeed, the mere sight had been known to panic an enemy into a hasty retreat. In columns and rows, the moving phalanx wheeled this way and that with extraordinary precision. When this massive serpent stopped, the first row knelt and unleashed a hail of balls and bullets that would rip through the enemy's lines. As the first row reloaded, the second fired and then the third.

Such formations were impressive and could be overwhelming, but they were less so when the enemy was dug in or behind fortifications above. The attackers were out in the open. Now the Americans had that advantage. At least in theory.

Brock had more men and several more cannon. The American situation was quickly deteriorating. Indian warriors had driven American skirmishers back to the main body and were threatening to fold back the American left flank, a classic battle tactic that opened the center to attack from the side and back. On the right, Quinn and Frake were facing a much stronger British force that threatened to turn that flank also.

On the American side, Scott was now in command. At six feet five inches tall, he looked like a leader, and he had both courage and brains. In the turmoil, he leaped onto a tree stump, fully exposing himself to the enemy, and rallied his men.

"Who dares to stand?" he challenged.

They all did, and it seemed their renewed spirit might drive the British back a second time. Quinn marveled that in such dismal situations, men—including himself—could be induced to offer up their lives. But the revival was short lived.

The next British attack was more carefully planned. Two hundred British regulars and Canadian militia with one hundred Indians crept through the woods west of the Heights until they could spring on the American left flank. Only about three hundred able-bodied men remained in the American fighting force.

Despite Scott's appeal, some ran from the sound of the braves' war whoops. The main body began to fall back. Some fled into the woods where—if they were lucky—the British found them. Those who fell into the hands of the Indians were hacked and scalped. Others scampered and slid down the escarpment, clinging to bushes and outcroppings as they descended. Some were driven off the precipices falling or leaping to their deaths on the rocks below or drowning in the river. Many gathered below the cliffs on the water's edge, waiting for rescue boats that never came.

Soldiers under the white flag of surrender were granted safe passage under the rules of war, but Indians killed two such envoys sent by Scott. The British victory might have rivaled the Fort Dearborn massacre, but Scott and a small entourage made their way to the British commander to surrender. British riders were sent to all quarters of the fight to order a halt to the slaughter and to take prisoners.

A musket ball to Quinn's arm had sent him spinning to the ground. The wound was superficial, and he tried to rise but found himself looking into the muzzle of a British gun. All the old hatreds rose in like bile in his throat. Quinn thought, *I'll die right here rather than be taken prisoner.* Quinn's worst nightmare suddenly was real. In a flash, he saw himself being led to a scaffold in London in a show hanging of what happens to traitors. No chance of a prisoner parole or exchange at the end of hostilities. He'd rather die on the field of battle, fighting to his last drop of blood against the tyrant king.

But before he could move, Frake intervened.

"Don't be a fool," he said. "It's not over. We'll fight another day."

"Yeah, Yank, listen to the wizened fart there," the Brit said through his smirk. "Nothing would please me more than putting one in your heart for General Brock, a better man than any of you swine."

Quinn gritted his teeth. Just once he'd like to give these Limeys what they deserved. Bastards, all of them, but every time they came out on top. What was the use? Anything he did now would get him killed, and Frake along with him. His determination to die a martyr's death suddenly was overcome by his will to live—and extract vengeance upon the English.

He surrendered.

"Fine then, Yank. I'd shoot you just for the fun of it, but my lieutenant would have my stripes. Get over there with the rest them."

Quinn rose and allowed the Brit to shove him toward a knot of American prisoners. There he learned that Brock had been killed by American sharpshooters. Inflamed by their hero's death and the audacity of an American attack on Canada, the British guards were in a foul mood. "No telling what they'll do," Frake whispered. "Try not to provoke them."

Quinn couldn't remember whether he had killed or wounded anyone. He remembered firing his pistol, but... he wished he could recall, because it might give him some sense of purpose. Rage sizzled in his limbs, in his gut, in his head.

As the prisoners were formed up and marched away, Quinn quickly discovered that a battlefield is a busy place after the fighting. The wounded searched for and attended to. The dead carted off. Weapons and munitions recovered. Official reports taken while memories were fresh. Winged scavengers filling the sky. Disembodied orders and moans of the wounded. The horrified cries of women and children discovering the grisly remains of their husbands and fathers. The smell of blood, innards, and death.

As the prisoners were marched past the open-air hospital, Quinn saw the wounded and near dead lying on stretchers. In the bright afternoon sunlight, surgeons were sawing legs and arms from screaming men. He spotted a pile of dismembered limbs and another of uncovered corpses under assault by swarms of green and black flies. A captured American in the marching knot of prisoners suddenly doubled over and vomited on the pants and shoes of the man in front of him. Everyone else, guards and prisoners alike, retched and gagged.

"Frake, I'm just as good as dead."

The rules for prisoners were clear. War was a gentlemanly business, a civilized matter, a profession. Accordingly, militia officers and men, deemed civilians, were promptly paroled. They could return home if they promised not to fight again, a vow most gladly given and readily invoked if ever they were called on to take up arms again.

Regular army and navy combatants were another matter. Imprisoned officers were accorded a gentleman's comforts— agreeable housing, limited freedom of movement, decent food. The enlisted, however, were imprisoned and often badly treated. Occasionally, prisoner exchanges were arranged. The return of an American general might require one hundred British privates. A British colonel could be traded for fifty privates. A sergeant major—two privates.

"Frake, I've got to get out of this. They'll hang me for being a traitor."

"How so?" As they were marched, Quinn cautiously looked around him and spoke quietly, hoping no one would notice him. "Under British law, no Brit can ever swear allegiance to another country. If you're born in Great Britain, the crown still considers you a British citizen. I was born in Ireland, don't you see?"

"They don't have to know that."

"But they will. Haven't you noticed my Irish brogue? I might as well as hang a sign around my neck, 'Come and get me.'"

"We won't let that happen."
"How are you gonna stop them?"
"Don't know, but I'm already working on it."

29 October 1812

Washington, D.C.

*S*ally learned of the Niagara rout as soon as President Madison. He and the first lady had been taking tea in the sitting room of their personal quarters, where Dolley had been going over the latest dinner invitation list with Sally. While there, War Secretary Eustis was ushered in with the latest dispatches.

In his face, Sally read disaster.

"It's the attack across the Niagara," he said.

"Yes, man, out with it." Madison nearly tossed his teacup onto the tripod table, spilling its contents on the embroidery. Sally's hands went to her mouth.

All that she heard were the words "failed...dead... prisoners...wounded...retreat."

She couldn't repress the cry that escaped her mouth and shook her body.

Dolley was instantly at her side. "Come, dear, we must let the president and secretary assess the damage. But I'm sure that your young man will be fine."

Details trickled in. The names of those killed in combat, taken prisoner, and unaccounted for, but there was no word of Quinn's fate. Sally was inconsolable.

She felt the sense of isolation she had felt at the slaughter of her family. She had known more heartache and loss than many twice her age, but now she felt like a lost child. *Who, she thought, is my family? Who can console me, understand me, and share my pain?*

True, she could rely on Mrs. Madison and on the Quinns of Baltimore. Dolley did not pity her, and that was a blessing. Instead, she grew to appreciate Sally's intelligence and spirit and to gradually give her more responsibility. The Quinns were fond of her too. If she loved Will, well then … But Sally did not feel a genuine part of either family.

Sally received permission from Mrs. Madison to dispatch a rider to inform Quinn's family of the battle's outcome and urge Mrs. Quinn to come to Washington. When she arrived, she and Sally fell into each other's arms, their tears mingling.

Sally was certain then that it was not just attraction, not just shared suffering, not just deep friendship. She really was in love with Will Quinn.

Late October 1812

On Lake Ontario

*S*ome Englishman had said, "Depend upon it, sir, when a man knows he is to be hanged in a fortnight, it concentrates his mind wonderfully."

Scott, Quinn, Frake, and eighteen other officers and noncommissioned officers, along with a few hundred enlisted men, were marched north to the Canadian village of Newark near the mouth of the Niagara River. There the officers were quartered under guard at a tavern to be transported by cartel—a ship designed for moving prisoners—to Quebec, where Quinn was about to realize his worst nightmare.

Clearly, Quinn must avoid speaking, even to his fellow prisoners who might be spies or turncoats. He trusted only Frake and Scott.

"Maybe we can get you talking like you're Kentucky fed and bred," Frake suggested, but in the meantime he stayed nearby to answer questions directed at the ensign.

The crew of the cartel wasn't much interested in this human cargo, so Quinn was eased, though silent, on the eight-hundred-mile trip over land and on water to Halifax, Nova Scotia. There the prisoners would be confined while exchanges were negotiated. And there, without a good deal of luck, Quinn would hang or be shipped to London for the deed.

On the way, the prison ship stopped at Quebec to board several British officers and a squad of marines. The luck of the Irish now deserted Quinn. The officers mustered the prisoners, including Quinn, on deck, and a British major began to question each in turn.

"Where are you from?" he asked the first, listening for any hint of a brogue or a burr or a Cockney twang.

"Boston, sir."

"How long have you served in the American army, lad?" The questions came rapidly now, meant to fluster the interrogated. "Where's your family live? Can you read? The names of your brothers and sisters? Weren't you born in Ireland?"

Unsatisfied with the man's answers, the major ordered him grabbed from the ranks and placed under guard at the ship's rail. That drew murmurs then loud objections and shouts from the other prisoners.

"Silence, you scum traitors!"

"But he's a native-born son of the Commonwealth of Massachusetts!" came a yell from the ranks. "His parents are from the old sod, but he was born here. You have no right!"

"On my mother's eyes, I'm a born American," the soldier pled, only to be dropped to the deck with a single blow to the back of his head from a rifle butt.

"Who's next?"

In short order, the major plucked twenty-three "traitors" from the ranks and lined them up at bayonet point along the ship's rail. From there they would be loaded into a whale boat, taken to the major's brig anchored nearby, and transported back to England for a trumped-up trial and the gallows. Quinn's heart sank.

"Now, this looks like a fine Irish face, if I ever saw one." The man was staring straight at Quinn and seeing his fear. "And here we have an officer traitor. Speak up, ensign. Tell me your name."

Quinn was about to open his mouth and try a Kentucky drawl, when he heard, "Silence! Ensign, do not say a word! What in the name of God is going on here?"

Scott had been below decks, afforded certain privileges as the most senior officer. Hearing the growing commotion on deck, he rushed up the ladder to investigate. Even though a prisoner of war, as a lieutenant colonel, Scott outranked the major. The major snapped to attention.

"Explain yourself, major. What are you doing with my men?"

"You, sir, are interfering with the lawful arrest of British traitors. Please step aside."

Scott was silent for a moment.

Then he pulled his face close to the major's. "You will not question my men," he said firmly. He turned to the formation and roared, "All of you, every last man jack of you will remain silent. You will not speak a word, not a syllable."

"Colonel, you are not in command. You are on a British warship. I am carrying out lawful orders to—"

"Your orders be damned." Scott pivoted back to face the major.

Quinn noted that the man was no longer enjoying himself.

"Your orders, as you call them, are *not* lawful. Sir." The last word squeezed from between Scott's lips as if it were foul juice.

"I order you again, colonel. Go below before I resort to force. Do. You. Understand?"

Scott stepped so close to the major that their noses nearly touched. His voice was low now, just above a whisper. "You dare force a showdown with a superior officer? You dare to debase the traditions of the British army and navy? There are mutual accords still in force—unless perhaps *you* have the authority to repeal them?—that prohibit the questioning of prisoners of war except to ask their name and rank. *You* are prepared to force retaliation by the United States against British prisoners of war? Well? Speak up, major, it's your turn now."

The men, still at attention, leaned forward. Whatever Scott had said, they saw the major waver.

"Colonel, I ask you with all due respect, do not interfere. It is the law that a British subject cannot expatriate himself."

Scott actually smiled. "Indeed it is, sir. And we are fighting this war over that very law. And I do not propose to concede the issue here on the deck of a prison ship." He smiled again. "Although, if you insist, choose your weapon. Pistols? Swords?"

Scott's sheer presence prevailed, but the major blustered anyway. "Very well, colonel, your men may be silent, but those I have identified as traitors are still my prisoners and…wait, where are you going?"

Scott was already striding toward the twenty-three men who'd already been shackled. "Men." Again, his voice was low. "You know I cannot unlock your shackles, but your fate has not been determined. I pledge to God himself that I will not rest until you are released unharmed into the arms of your country. I will be exchanged, rest assured, and by God I will bring your case directly to President Madison, if necessary. The British know that harming you will set off a round of retaliation that will be hard to stop."

The first year of the war ended for Quinn in humiliation and bitter defeat at the hands of the seemingly unbeatable English. He had seen battles and massacres he could never have imagined, come close to death, dined with a president and slept in the president's house, and met and loved a sweetheart. For him, the war was over—for now and maybe forever. He was a captive, and his adopted country looked to be crushed once again under the English boot.

1813

The New Year, 1813

Washington, D.C.

$\mathcal{S}$ ally was given leave by Mrs. Madison to spend Christmas in Baltimore with Agnes Quinn and her boys. They still had no word of Quinn or Frake. Were they missing? Imprisoned? Dead? Washed away by the turbulent Niagara?

With the New Year, Sally returned to her White House duties. She had come to enjoy all the comings and goings and to feel that her efforts were actually helpful to the first lady. Receiving and answering correspondence, helping prepare for elegant dinners and smaller luncheons and suppers given over to serious talk—it all took energy, a quick mind, and a certain expertise, which she'd begun to acquire under Dolley's tutelage. And it was exciting to rub shoulders with politicians, generals, and businessmen.

Some of her duties, however, were quite mundane. One blustery winter day she bundled herself up and rode in a White House carriage to Washington's newly emerging commercial district. Mrs. Madison had ordered some new dress fabric and some stylish new shoes, and Sally enjoyed these errands. The hubbub, the crowds, the activity—all delighted her.

Today she was going to the Columbian Emporium, a purveyor of fine goods and services, popularly known as Kilfoyle's. The place was irresistible. Visitors were greeted by a labyrinth of colors and a swirl of aromas. There were perfumes and leathers, knitted goods and fabrics, and chandeliers for sale, placed in such a way to highlight the merchandise. The freshly laid pine floor reverberated with the shoppers' footsteps.

Caleb Kilfoyle was an early practitioner of imaginative visual merchandising—placing manufactured goods in plain view of the shopper whose senses came alive—and purse opened—with the color and feel of the merchandise. Always colorfully dressed, the rotund little man was himself an attraction, cheerful and eager to please. He bounced about his emporium, spotting prosperous customers and steering them to his latest imports. Sally, known as the first lady's emissary, was such a customer.

"Ah, Miss Sally, how wonderful to see you," he said, delicately taking her gloved hand to his lips. "How charming that this budding flower brightens a dismal winter day."

Sally smiled and blushed. She knew Kilfoyle was a master salesman, but she was uncomfortable with such effusive attention. She swallowed a giggle.

Other shoppers turned to look.

An elegant women whispered to her companion, "Missus Madison's protégé. She's a darling, but such a tragic history! Well, apparently some savages…"

Kilfoyle paused with Sally in front of a display of dresses and fabrics. "What might I interest you in today, Miss Martin? You must tell Missus Madison that the cotton twills so popular in Paris are available now."

"Yes, Mr. Kilfoyle, I certainly will, but I'm not here today to buy anything. I'm picking up some materials and shoes that the first lady has ordered."

"Ah, yes, my dear. Follow me, please."

Henry was stitching a new sole onto a man's boot.

"Henry," Kilfoyle said, "Missus Madison's shoes, if you please."

The shoemaker leafed through a stack of orders on the counter in front of him. "Um, yes, ma'am, here they are," he said, reaching behind him to a rack of new shoes.

The first lady had selected a very fashionable pair made of white kid leather rising from the sole to the upper heel and trimmed with metallic braid.

Sally examined them in awe. "These are so beautiful! Did you make them yourself, sir?"

"My name's Henry, ma'am."

"May I ask your full name, Henry? I'd like to tell people of your wonderful handiwork."

"It's just Henry," interjected Kilfoyle. "No last name. He's a slave."

"A slave?" Sally said. Her eyes widened. How could this talented workman be owned like a horse or a dog? The slaves she had met were laborers, personal attendants, or housekeepers, but this was a craftsman, even an artist. And he could read.

Of course he was black, but she had presumed he was a free man, plying his trade at Kilfoyle's. This was a new insight into slavery. Even some abolitionists believed that Africans were a lesser breed, suited for fieldwork and perhaps housework but not for anything mentally taxing. And yet...

Henry looked down; Sally could tell that he was deeply embarrassed.

Kilfoyle regarded Henry as a valuable asset and indeed quite liked him, so he stepped in quickly. "Well, thank you, Henry. You may return to your duties. The fabric you are looking for, Miss Sally, will be just down this aisle."

Sally followed, but her mind was elsewhere as she collected the rest of Mrs. Madison's order and was escorted back to her carriage. She would ask Mrs. Madison to explain. The White House slaves were there, in part, for political reasons. And Kilfoyle kept Henry for business reasons. It was all so confusing. She hurried into the house, and then, before she could even put down her purchases, a housemaid rushed toward her.

"Oh, Miss Martin! Your young man is alive!"

3 January 1813

Quebec

*I*n Quebec, the victorious British began sorting out the prisoners taken at Queenston and Detroit. State militiamen were paroled at Detroit, Salem, and Boston. Regular army enlisted men were shipped to the brutal Melville Island prison in Halifax, some to be transported to England.

General Hull and other officers were exchanged, but the Americans had won so few battles that they were short of prisoners to barter with. Most of their prisoners were crews and passengers of British ships captured by American privateers.

Quinn and Frake were among those exchanged.

Frake was now a brevet officer, promoted to ensign by Scott for his courage under fire. So Quinn celebrated their release and Frake's promotion at the nearest alehouse after crossing into American territory. But the celebration was brief, because orders awaited the newly exchanged officers. He and Frake would finally return to Harrison's forces in the Northwest.

Quinn had mixed feelings. He was disappointed not to return to Sally and his family but relieved not to have to brief the president on what went wrong at Niagara. That job would fall to Winfield Scott, whose bravery at Niagara had already made him something of a national hero.

Indeed, everyone in Washington wanted to be seen with Scott, who would prove as adept at socializing as at leading soldiers into battle. He kept his pledge to fight for the release of the twenty-three captives, and Madison sent a message to the British government that any harm done to prisoners of war would bring severe retaliations.

Along with Quinn's orders came packets of delayed letters from Sally, all proclaiming her love. The latest:

My dearest William,

I feared that I had lost you forever. What horrors the mind can conjure up! This made me realize what you mean to me—your comforting touch, your sympathetic ear. Without you, misery would follow me for the rest of my life.

Forgive my boldness, but some matters require openness and honesty. If you are offended that I should put my sentiments on paper, then so be it. Will, I love you...

Quinn's mind was awhirl. Shouldn't *he* be writing this to *her?* Wasn't that a man's place? During his captivity, he had thought of telling her he loved her, but she was in Washington, probably meeting important men and...what if she'd rejected him?

But she risked rejection. Was she, then, braver than he? Perhaps so. He did love her. He would tell her so, and they would marry. She had given herself willingly at Fort Wayne, and now he had left her wondering whether he was abandoning her.

I must fix this, he thought, *and I must not die, for her sake.*

22 January 1813

Michigan Territory

Quinn and Frake caught up with Harrison's army at Upper Sandusky, Ohio, a tiny village occupied mostly by runaway slaves. Harrison wasn't settling in for the winter but planning to retake Detroit and invade Upper Canada.

Frake was delighted to find two thousand fellow Kentuckians with Harrison, though most were untrained volunteers. He knew some—Deskin, McCommas, Hatfield, Dinges, Toney, Locke, and others of the Anglo- and Scot-Irish stock who had followed the trail of Daniel Boone and made Kentucky the first western state. All told, an astonishing two-thirds of the able-bodied men came from around Frankfort, the young state's capital, and others from much smaller towns, had trudged hundreds of miles north to fight—toting rifles, tomahawks, knives, cartridge boxes, bayonets, canteens, knapsacks, and blankets.

Their eagerness to fight sprang largely from what they and their elders had seen of the British during the War of Independence, but also from their belief in a manifest destiny—America dominating the continent and the hemisphere. They were more than ready to march on Detroit.

As an added bonus, from their stock of arms, Frake was able to exchange his smoothbore musket for a rifle. The spiral-grooved barrel made for a much more accurate weapon, and a sharpshooter like Frake an even more dangerous soldier.

Harrison split his army in two, half led by himself and the rest by Brigadier General James Winchester of Tennessee. Winchester marched his forces north to the Maumee Rapids and encamped there on January 10. On the twelfth, Quinn and Frake joined them. Four days later, messengers came from Frenchtown, a settlement straddling the Raisin River where it entered Lake Erie.

They reported that a group of British and Indians—smaller than Winchester's force—had occupied the village, taking whatever they pleased. The French settlers there, angry and spoiling for revenge, wanted American help. Driving out the despoilers, the messenger promised, would be easy pickings. Winchester couldn't resist.

Attacking Frenchtown at Raisin River went against Harrison's orders. It would distract from the coordinated attack on Detroit and Fort Malden. It would take Winchester's men deep into enemy territory. At a council of officers that night, Winchester's decision met with strenuous protests, but within hours the general dispatched seven hundred men to cross snow-covered terrain and frozen Maumee Bay to attack Frenchtown.

A quarter of a mile from Frenchtown, the detachment formed up to fight, but no British or Indians appeared. They remained inside the town so the Americans would have to root them out, man by man. Deadly, dangerous work. At three o'clock, the Americans began the grueling house-to-house and hand-to-hand combat. By sunset the enemy had been driven two miles into the woods, but it was morning before Winchester, back at his camp, learned of the outcome. The celebration would be brief.

Eager to share in the victory, he departed that morning for Frenchtown with some two hundred men, surely enough to repel any British counterattack. But British regulars and a contingent of four tribes headed by Wyandot chief Roundhead—in all, about five hundred men—were crossing the frozen Detroit River to surprise Winchester.

At Frenchtown, Winchester scattered his troops haphazardly in homes and barns throughout the village, though his officers argued that it weakened them in the event of a counterattack.

"Nonsense," Winchester huffed. "They won't be back for days, if ever. Ten dollars says they are hunkering down for the winter in Malden."

Quinn was wondering if he was bold enough to protest this foolishness, but higher-ranking officers beat him to the punch.

"Have you intelligence on that point, sir?"

"Have you sent spies?"

The officers knew that the west coast of Lake Erie was buzzing with reports that the British would return to Frenchtown, but Winchester silenced them.

"*I* am an honored veteran of the War of Independence and an experienced officer. I *won't* explain myself."

With that, he installed himself in the comfortable farmhouse of one Francis Navarre, a full mile from his troops—and mysteriously took all the spare gunpowder with him, leaving his men with only ten cartridges apiece.

Quinn and Frake were outraged. They scrounged any ammunition they could find and bivouacked with some Kentucky riflemen on the outskirts of the town. Before long, more Kentuckians joined them. Out in the open, shivering in the cold, they kept watch in four-hour shifts, sleeping whenever they could. They set no campfires that might alert the enemy. They gritted their teeth and waited.

Meanwhile, Colonel Henry Procter's one thousand British regulars, Canadian militia, artillery, Indians, and even sailors from the sloops frozen into the ice of the Detroit River arrived at Frenchtown about two hours before sunrise. Approaching cautiously, they saw smoke from chimneys but no activity.

Quickly and quietly, Procter formed his troops into two main attack groups, with their left and right flanks covered by Wyandot allies. The rhythm of the Americans' reveille drum was followed almost instantly by shots from sentries who had spotted the advance.

The Americans leapt to action, and the British cannons responded with a seemingly endless barrage. Quinn and Frake were on the American left flank, not in the direct line of attack. They waited.

At the farmhouse, the sound of gun and cannon fire finally penetrated Winchester's sleep. Throwing coats on over their nightshirts, he and his staff galloped toward the conflict, but battle lines were shifting so rapidly he didn't know where to set up his command post. Settling on a small rise that afforded a view of the battle, he sent messengers to order his besieged infantry to retreat across the frozen river and there make a stand.

The officers and men, however, weren't waiting for orders. They fled helter-skelter as Winchester watched helplessly. Each time the Americans tried to stop and form up, Indians on horseback outflanked them. Small, defensive circles were quickly overwhelmed. Scores fell dead or wounded; scores more were captured. Some were scalped where they fell. At last, Winchester and his staff were surrounded by Canadian militia and Indians.

"Well, look at what we have here." A young lieutenant chuckled. "Yankee brass. Give up now or you're dead men."

The general was the first to throw down his sword and sidearm, and the rest quickly followed.

"Under the laws of combat, you guarantee our safety," Winchester said shakily. He was mesmerized by the Indians, who were talking excitedly among themselves and glancing at the captives as if coveting the scalps of the most senior officers.

"Well, Yankee, we'll see. Pretty hard to keep these savages in line." The lieutenant signaled the Indians to tie the captives' hands. "We'll take a little walk. Tecumseh will be glad to see you."

Tecumseh? Here? Winchester was clearly terrified, his staff variously fearful, determined, resigned, or rueful. No one looked hopeful.

Quinn, Frake and his men, still on the left flank, hadn't surrendered.

Not if I have any say! Quinn thought furiously.

The enemy moved into range of the Kentucky sharpshooters, and the rifles that the British had dubbed the widow makers.

Quinn believed they could hold their positions indefinitely with enough ammunition, but they were undersupplied. Should they stay and fight with bayonets?

The minimally trained militiamen would likely be slaughtered. Then should he call retreat? Could the sharpshooters keep the enemy pinned while the others fell back? There were no easy answers.

"Get down!"

Quinn's warning came too late: the musket ball caught the private in the face, exiting the back of his head in a gush of brains and blood. Quinn had been lying flat behind a snowbank when the out-of-breath private dropped on one knee beside him. The boy had come with a message, but Quinn wasn't pleased to have his position given away. After a moment, the private slumped slowly onto his side across Quinn's legs. There was no time to be horrified.

"What was he going to tell me? Who sent him? Blast it all"

Now enemy rounds whistled overhead. Even lying flat in the wet snow and spread as far apart as possible, they were vulnerable. And now they were running out of ammunition.

"Thank you, Winchester, you blockhead, for putting us in this fix," Quinn muttered, gripping his saber in anticipation of hand-to-hand combat.

The ball entered Frake's left shoulder, ripping the protective tendons and ligaments away from the ball-and-socket joint before slamming into the bony mass. Heavy bleeding began immediately. "Damn fool," he said to himself. "I shudda known better than to stick my head up for a better look. Someone, for sure, got a better look at me first."

"Probably a lucky shot," a nearby corporal said. "Gotta stuff that wound with something. Here." He dug in his knapsack for spare socks. "Hope you don't mind a little rotten-foot stink."

Both knew what a wound could mean: amputation, infection, and a painful death or life as a cripple.

"Idiot." It was Quinn.

"Idiot, yourself. You coulda had your manhood shot off comin' over here. Getting yourself killed wudda pissed me off good."

"I know. Look, we've got to get everyone outta here. Think you can walk?"

"Well, I ain't about to stand up and try it."

"Okay, okay. But we gotta retreat. They've come at us three times, but if they try again, we'll get overrun."

"Don't worry. I've got enough blood left. Where we heading?"

"There's a mill not far up the road. I figure Harrison eventually will send some pickets here or come himself. He could be on the move now, so if we can hold out in the mill for a while, we've got a chance."

"Look! Look! A white flag!" The shout came from down the line, where the British main assault had been focused.

Sure enough, someone was carrying a flag of surrender from the British lines.

"What, *they're* giving up?" Quinn was incredulous. The American center and right was in a shambles. "What are they up to now?"

The puzzlement didn't last long. As the rider and a small escort approached, he saw that it was an American officer,

Winchester's aide Major James Overton, carrying the flag. British officers, including a colonel, accompanied him.

"Ensign Quinn, sir," Quinn said, standing to meet the party.

"Quinn, may I present Colonel Procter of the British Army. We have come to give you a written order of surrender from General Winchester. All men are to immediately lay down their arms." He handed the paper to Quinn.

Cries of protest arose from the Kentuckians.

"Never!"

"Tell Winchester to suck my cock."

"After he kisses mine!"

The cries spread up and down the line as Quinn read the order. *More eyewash*, he thought as he crumbled the paper.

"Son." It was Overton. "Take this...well, call it *advice*. You're about the only ones left. You've put on a good fight. No one questions your dedication or bravery. We admire your purposefulness. But the colonel is becoming increasingly irritated with your resistance. This engagement is a lost cause. Believe me."

Quinn turned to Frake. "What do you think?"

"I think it's all a crock."

"Colonel Procter, will you ensure the safety of my men if they surrender?"

Procter raised himself high in his saddle, looked down at Quinn, and hissed, "Boy, do you mean to dictate to me?"

"No insult intended, sir."

"I might have the lot of you hanged for obstreperousness, ensign. I will not mince words with you. I will tell you quite honestly, sir, that you are in no position to negotiate. If you do not surrender, you will be killed. If wounded, you will *wish* you had been killed, because you will be dealt with by Chief Roundhead's savages, and the town will be burned."

The Kentuckians shouted back.

"Then let it be so!"

"Up yours, Limey."

"Ensign Quinn," said one Kentuckian, "we choose an honorable death in combat rather than the disgrace of surrender only to be massacred anyway. Sir, don't do it."

"Colonel." Quinn turned back to Procter. "You see for yourself the mood of my men. If I hear a promise of safe conduct, I may be able to persuade them to surrender. Otherwise more of your own men will die at their hands. Your men's lives are in your hands just as surely as ours are. The choice is yours."

Procter shook his head. "So this is what comes of the republican revolution. The great experiment in self-government leads to insubordination and the lack of good order. Very well, ensign, you've got my word. All prisoners, including the wounded and their property will be protected if you surrender. You've got half an hour. Send word with your major here when you decide." With that, he turned his horse and rode away.

Now, for the first time, Quinn felt the burden of command. On his own, he would fight rather than submit again to capture, though he thought of Sally and knew he didn't want to die. But his decision would affect these other men, so he laid out the same choices: die now or live to fight again. Martyrdom didn't really achieve anything.

Overton spoke quietly. "Look, I shouldn't have to tell you what you're facing here. These people are bloodthirsty. They quite enjoy inflicting pain. They told us they were taking us to Tecumseh, to scare us. It turned out to be Chief Roundhead, their little joke, but Roundhead was no bargain either. Made us remove our uniforms and parade around in our undergarments. Even Winchester. Luckily, one of Procter's staff officers stepped in. If Procter unleashes his savages on you…" He trailed off.

"Men." Quinn had made his decision. "I can order you to surrender, and if you are of a mind, you can ignore my order. But you'd be throwing away your lives for no good reason."

The men began to murmur.

"Shut up!" It was Frake. "He ain't no Kentuckian, but he sure is as good as what comes in second."

The murmurs stopped.

"Look," Quinn continued, "you've come here because you felt it was your duty to protect your families, to keep the British from coming through the Cumberland Gap and sitting their asses right on down in Boonesbourgh with George the Turd telling you what to do again."

"Turd. You got that right!" someone shouted.

Laughter broke the ice.

"No one wants to beat the British more than me. But if we're going to beat them, we have to be smarter than them. We can't let them back us into a corner or egg us into doing something stupid. To die here as heroes isn't smart. If we die now, who will take our places? Your sons will. And their sons."

Quinn heard murmurs of agreement, but he still had doubts. Was it foolish to surrender? Should he change his mind? And again, he was thinking that his capture could end in his execution.

Frake decided it. "I'm throwing in with Ensign Quinn. We were captured not three months ago, and here we are fighting again. Besides, they've got Winchester, and when he sees me, when he sees you, captured, I want him to know it's all thanks to him."

Quinn looked to his right and to his left, up and down the line, and he saw heads nodding in agreement. But he wasn't relieved; he was even more deeply troubled by his decision.

And here Quinn was, arguing for surrender, once his greatest fear and a certain death warrant. He thought of any captured Kentuckians who might share his "traitor's" punishment. He thought of Sally, his mother and his family. But he also had thought of blood in the snow and men dying because of his own fears. Maybe he had done the right thing. Maybe not.

Late Winter 1813
Raisin River, Michigan Territory

Quinn looked ruefully at his fellow American prisoners sitting and shivering under guard in the snow. The longer he waited for word to come down from the British to start marching north toward Canada, the more anxious he became. At last, the British sent a junior officer, Captain William Elliot, to relay the surprising orders to the prisoners.

"You're leaving the wounded behind in the *care* of the Indians?" Quinn shouted at the captain. "You can't be serious!"

"I am, ensign," Elliot said, his breath turning to vapor as soon as it hit the cold air. "All able-bodied prisoners are marching to Fort Malden for transport to Halifax. The wounded can't march, so they'll stay here until we can have some sleds sent from Malden to carry the wounded. The sleds should be here in a day or two."

"This is not what we understood would happen," Quinn said, his voice rising. "You know very well that leaving anyone here, especially in the so-called care of Indians, means death. I protest strongly!"

"Protest all you want, ensign, but that's how it is."

Quinn's mind boiled with questions. Did Winchester agree to this? Why weren't he and his senior officers protesting? Why couldn't the British wait a day or two until the sleds for the wounded arrived?

"At least leave your physicians behind," Quinn pleaded after a moment's pause. "We've got two of them, but they can't care for more than one hundred wounded men by themselves. Some of them certainly will die without proper care."

"We can't spare any doctors. But the Indians are excellent doctors." Elliot smirked.

"Well, they're certainly well practiced in the surgical arts. How many scalps do you think they'll take?"

"Me and my men will be staying here to protect you."

That didn't calm Quinn. He suddenly announced, "I'll be staying here with the wounded too."

"What's one less crazy American ensign?" Elliot muttered.

While the wounded prisoners were moved out of the weather and into the town's homes, the uninjured American captives were herded into whatever tents were left after the battle. Frake was ensconced with two other wounded Kentuckians in the house of John Anderson, a fur trader who had volunteered for the militia after the surrender of Detroit.

The two American doctors, John Todd and Gustave Bower, along with Quinn, had been doing the best they could, going from house to house in the cold night to attend to the wounded. A few had died in the night, others were in great pain, but little could be done for them. Some, like Frake, had been weakened by their wounds, but they would make it. The three did the best they could to keep everyone's spirits as high as possible. Medical supplies were limited; food was more available, but the three couldn't handle all the preparation and distribution required. It was a medical and logistical nightmare.

At sunrise the next morning, Quinn was startled to find Elliot and his men gone. Quinn was appalled and frightened by this stunning betrayal. He realized that he didn't have much time before the Indians got it into their minds that more than one hundred scalps were waiting their knives. *Think, think!* he told himself.

Quinn was torn by indecision. Don't tell the wounded of Elliot's abandonment to avoid adding to their anguish? Or tell them so they could try their best to hide or scrounge whatever weapons they could find in the homes. He decided to tell them; after all, he planned to tell Frake, and what knowledge he deserved to have, Quinn figured the others did too.

Some were alarmed, others terrified. Each prepared to meet his fate in his own way. Some cried, and others became resolute. Some looked for hiding places; others started to weigh their chances in the wilderness. Others couldn't move or be moved; still others were too damaged to understand what was happening. Quinn could do nothing to organize any resistance, and the full weight of his decision to surrender and to encourage the others to do likewise now came crashing down on him.

His hope that Harrison would send a relief column faded. Harrison was too far away and the weather too bad. By ten a.m., a couple hundred Indians started to move into Frenchtown. When Quinn came out to confront them, their leader rode forward and dismounted.

"Where is Captain Elliot?" the Indian asked. Obviously, the Indian didn't know that Elliot hadn't stayed.

"Not here," Quinn replied, wondering if there was a way to bluff him.

"Where?"

"Somewhere else."

"Elliot said he would be here," the Indian said.

"He's not."

"Why not?" the Indian asked.

"Don't know. Ask him."

"When did he leave?"

"Can't say. Sometime between sundown and sunup."

The Indian thought for a moment then asked, "The wounded are still here then?"

"Some."

"Why didn't they take the wounded with them to Malden."

"They said they didn't have enough sleds," Quinn replied. "Besides, General Harrison is on his way here, so they hightailed it out of here. Cowards."

"What?"

"Did you think that General Harrison would abandon us here? You and your braves might want to skedaddle too," Quinn said, hoping the Indian would buy the bluff.

"Damn English. Why did they tell us to come back here?"

"You'll have to ask the English."

Again, the Indian paused for a moment, as if deep in thought. Then: "We will have to kill the wounded."

"What? The hell you say!"

"Many braves were killed by your Kentucky long rifles. To keep our honor, we must avenge those who were killed."

"Honor requires no such thing. Squaws kill the wounded, men who cannot defend themselves. Are you squaws?"

Quinn's interlocutor looked down to his belt to reach for his tomahawk; Quinn used the unguarded moment to knee him in the crotch with such force that the unsuspecting Indian was nearly lifted off his feet. As he crumbled to the ground, Quinn beat him to the tomahawk and grabbed his musket for good measure.

Quinn could have finished him off, but taking the time would have sacrificed the advantage of surprise. By the time the other Indians figured out what was happening and raised their muskets, Quinn was around the corner of a building, heading for the house on the other side of the village where Frake was holed up.

The carnage began.

The Indians began ransacking the houses, taking whatever they could find of worth and stripping the wounded of personal belongings. The most grievously wounded they stabbed, tomahawked, shot, or scalped. The less seriously wounded were taken prisoner for ransoming or as slaves.

Quinn had outrun his pursuers, who had been diverted by the easier pickings. Only the Indian who had been disarmed by Quinn continued the chase. As Quinn wound his way between houses, sheds, outhouses, and barns, the pleas and screams of the butchered caught up to him. Those who tried to run were quickly overtaken and hacked to death. Those who thought they'd found safe hiding places inside the houses were burned out as the Indians began torching every structure in the village. Those who couldn't climb out of their beds burned to death; others were tomahawked as they crawled from the infernos. A few who sought refuge in the homes of Frenchtown families who had stayed were turned away for fear of retaliation. Limping from house to house, they soon were overtaken by the rampaging Indians and murdered.

Quinn had rounded a corner of one shed, waiting for his pursuer. The Indian had gotten careless in his haste, and as he rounded the shed's corner at full speed, his own tomahawk split open his face.

Quinn, wasting no time, headed for the Anderson trading post on the edge of town, where Frake and two other Kentuckians had spent the night. As he barged through the front door, he saw that Frake had already begun mustering whatever defense he could.

"We're getting out of here," Quinn gasped between breaths.

"Easy, Willie. McCook here has a ball in his leg. Clark's eyes are bandaged. How far are we gonna get? You planning on outrunning those savages with a gimp and blind man tagging along?"

"Wait."

It was Elizabeth Knaggs Anderson—Lizzy to those who frequented the post. She was alone with her baby, Frances, because her husband, John, had hightailed it earlier when the Indians had threatened to cut out his tongue and lop off his hands.

"It's taking a big chance, but I've got an idea. I don't know what else we can do."

She led the four to the trading post's back room, where she pointed to a trap door. It opened into the cellar where her husband hid the whiskey he traded for pelts. Quinn helped the three wounded men down the ladder then followed and situated himself last among the kegs, casks, and bottles.

When the trap door slammed shut behind him, they were immersed in pitch darkness. He could hear a scraping sound above and figured that Lizzy was pulling a stout chest over the trap door. In that chest were the family's valuables, including keepsakes from the old country, and she was using it to protect these men.

"Shush, shush," Lizzy murmured to baby Frances, wrapping her tightly in one of the cozy blankets the local Indian women traded for needles, pins, and other manufactured necessities. Then she planted herself and Frances firmly on the chest, waiting.

Only seconds had passed before Indians, besotted with victory, broke into the house. Whooping and hollering, they emptied their pouches of the bloody scalps they had collected, spattering fresh blood all over the merchandise. They were counting out their spoils when one looked up and saw Lizzy staring at them from the other room.

They were accustomed to seeing white women scream and flee before them, but this one just sat calmly on a wooden chest, soothing her baby. They glanced at one another and silently decided they could not let this challenge pass. With raised knives and tomahawks, they moved menacingly toward her, expecting her to run in terror at any second. Still, she didn't move; their approach only intensified her steely gaze. It stopped them cold.

"Get up, leave!" one shouted.

"Go, squaw, away from this place."

Again, she would not budge, and now she raised her finger, extended her arm toward them, and spoke solemnly in their own language. "Shame. So many Indians fight one squaw. And her infant. Shame!"

She was hoping that they feared the pointed finger, as if it were about to hex them.

Instead, they looked at each other, shrugged, and ignoring the crazy woman, began the business of ransacking the post. Arms loaded, they left the place in shambles. Lizzy knew that the others would soon come to scrounge what was left, so she stayed put. When the other looters arrived, they went about their business, not even bothering to look at her. The first invaders must have warned the others about the crazy white woman who might steal their spirits.

"They're gone," she whispered at last, lifting the trapdoor slightly. "But don't come out yet. Wait until dark. You can make your escape then."

"Don't that beat all," Frake leaned over and whispered to Quinn. "That woman's got balls."

When the shadows lengthened, turning the still air frigid and dry, Quinn and Frake slunk away, taking the few surviving prisoners fit enough to walk. If there were others still in hiding, they were left to the mercies of the townspeople when they returned from hiding in the woods.

As the four set out to find Harrison's camp, they stumbled through deep snow and scalped bodies; sometimes they seemed to be wading in blood. Footprints of the pursuers converged on the scene of each slaughter, leaving the dead

Kentuckians in craters of snow. Some footprints led to the edge of the village where a few despairing soldiers had sought cover in the forest or marsh. But those trails were also followed by multiple footprints and also ended in bloody depressions in the snow. No one, it seemed, had escaped.

But Quinn, Frake and the two other lucky Kentucky survivors did manage to escape—into the woods and along the road toward Harrison's encampment. As they struggled through the snow, they were discovered by pickets that Harrison had sent out to ascertain what in the blazes Winchester was up to in Frenchtown. Upon hearing of the massacre, Harrison decided to spend the rest of the winter in a defensive position by building a fort along the Maumee River Rapids, several miles upstream from Frenchtown. Days after Quinn, Frake, and the other two Kentuckians were rescued as they struggled through the snow—fleeing Frenchtown—a letter arrived from Sally. She reported that after the disastrous defeat on the Niagara River, General Van Rensselaer had recognized his own failures, resigned, and turned over command on the Niagara to the disloyal General Smyth. Smyth, true to form, had accepted the position with such pomposity that he quickly became an object of ridicule on both sides of the river. His men loathed him.

But Smyth, to no one's surprise, so botched his own invasion that he was booted out of the army. Not accepting his fate, he appealed to Congress to restore his command so he could "die for his country." One congressman replied, "May it be ordered that the prayer of the petitioner be made so."

Then Sally, not knowing of the Frenchtown massacre and Quinn's and Frake's lucky escape from death, got down to more serious business:

My love, I miss you so and pray for your safety every day. I anxiously await every day for a new letter from you, but often in vain. I understand, as you must know, the travails of life on the frontier, especially in time of war. I only look for your reassurance that our love is mutual. I know that my sojourn at the executive mansion must end some day, as must this war. My dreams are of that happy time when we can be reunited and our lives once again entwine.

Quinn's second captivity, his brush with death, and Sally's avowal of love had put him in an unsettled state of mind. Her proclamation of love clearly was an entreaty for him to respond in kind—with as much ardor and passion that had gripped her.

Since his escape from Frenchtown, his letters to her concentrated on the drudgery of soldierly routine. Despite the Irish gift of blarney, many Irishmen were like Quinn and kept their emotions to themselves. None of his brothers, as far as he knew, had even contemplated matrimony. In the old country, poverty had discouraged many marriages, and now life was so terribly uncertain. Marrying, having a family…it seemed risky.

My Dearest Sally,

I offer no excuses, only apologies for my failure to respond properly to your heartfelt sentiments. Perhaps it is in my Irish nature to move slowly in matters of emotion. In any case, I earnestly seek to improve in that regard. Some say the Irish shy away from attachments because they have an ingrained fear of loss.

I can imagine no greater pain than the loss of your affection. Your love is more than I ever dared to hope for. Therefore, I pledge you now my everlasting love. I would be honored if you would marry me. I promise to protect you to my last breath from all hazards, real or imagined.

This falls short of what convention and my own heart demand, so I promise to ask you in the proper way when this war is over and we are reunited. If your answer then is no, I will be sad beyond words. But I will understand.

Quinn could barely breathe in the weeks it took to receive Sally's response. Frake went from teasing him about being off his feed to looking genuinely worried. At last her letter arrived.

My dearest, loving William,

Yes, of course I will marry you, though my joy is tempered by the wait. If I could have my way, I would travel to you and marry you on the spot and be at your side through all your travails and share all dangers with you.

Will this war ever end?

Before he could answer her, almost before he had stopped grinning, another letter arrived.

I could not wait for your response. I have such good and important news.

Perhaps this melancholy business of war, as Mrs. Madison calls it, will soon end. We have received word from John Quincy Adams, our esteemed envoy to Russia, that Czar Alexander has offered a mediation to end the hostilities. The president is encouraged but cautious. The czar hopes to end our war because he and other European powers have formed a grand alliance against Napoleon. The less attention Great Britain focuses on the Americans, the more it can help defeat Napoleon.

Mr. Madison thinks Napoleon will lose. He has exhausted his armies, and Mr. Madison says the czar was a crafty fox, drawing Napoleon's armies deeper and deeper into Russia.

The removal of the twenty-three prisoners from the prison ship at Ontario for trial in England has caused an uproar. The president has warned the British government that any harm done to those men will seriously jeopardize the health and welfare of all British prisoners of war in our custody.

Dearest Sally,

Such joyous and wonderful news—that you accept my expressions of love—has buoyed me beyond imagination. And the hope for peace is a boon to my spirits in these long and tedious winter days. Harrison, I am happy to say, is a professional soldier through and through. Having decided that the Maumee River Rapids is the best place to build a fort, he has plunged into the project with a passion. He calls it Fort Meigs after the Ohio governor, and he sees it as a base from which to launch his assault on Upper Canada.

The work of building the structure is heavy and wearying, and the entire garrison is on a strict regime of physical and military training: daily exercise, full manual of arms, and maneuvers outside the fort's walls. Young boys imagine military service as one heroic adventure after another, but most of it is sheer drudgery. The training is exhausting, but the men are becoming more professional by the day.

I pray daily that this war will soon end and we will be united.

The war would not and they would not.

17 February 1813

Washington, D.C.

For a while the work was plentiful and Kilfoyle a benevolent master, and Henry nurtured the hope that he might be able to *buy* his freedom. Now that hope was gone. Some enlightened slaveholders did allow craftsmen like Henry to keep some portion of the money their work brought in and use it for their own purposes. Sometimes that meant saving it up until they could purchase release. For Henry that would have been an immense amount, considering what Kilfoyle had paid for him. But Henry had the patience, the willingness, and the ability to manage it. He still had no idea where the rest of his family had been taken, but he was determined to save enough to buy their freedom too.

He had already raised the question with Kilfoyle three times. The first time Kilfoyle was too busy to consider it.

"Come back, Henry, when I have time, and we can talk about it." The second time, the merchant dismissed it as nonsense. The third time he said a firm no. Now the refusal was more threatening. Behind Kilfoyle's agreeable façade lay greed so intense that it would astound all those who thought they knew him.

So there was no option but escape.

Late Winter, 1813

The Northwest Territories and Washington D.C.

Madison, with the advice of Monroe and other trusted cabinet members, finally decided to replace Secretary of War Eustice. The appointment was puzzling, and especially with information Sally provided to Quinn and supplemented by the grapevine.

"General John Armstrong? What was Madison thinking?" Quinn asked as he got to the relevant part of Sally's latest letter.

Frake looked from his soup thickened with meal, flour and whatever meat and vegetables could be acquired. "I'm sure the president wants to know what we think. What difference does it make?"

"No, wait. You should hear what Sally says. She says that Armstrong is cantankerous and thickheaded. At least that's what she hears."

"Just like most of the rest of 'em running things, eh?"

"Madison supposedly wanted him because he's a Revolutionary War veteran and has been around a long time. Served as minister to France, until he pissed off Napoleon and had to resign."

"All of which makes him highly qualified," Frake scoffed.

"Well, Madison thinks that he's some kind of administrative genius and will be able to organize the army's campaigns better, Sally says. Oh, and wait, maybe this is the real reason: Armstrong is a northern Federalist. Guess Madison thinks he'll help with the anti-war Federalists."

"Doubt it."

"This is even better. Listen to this: Armstrong threatened once to march on Washington in some kind of uprising because he thought that Congress had reneged on its promise of lifetime pensions for Revolutionary War veterans. Took George Washington himself to diffuse the whole thing."

"Just another muggins. Nothing to do with us."

But at officers' call next morning, they discovered otherwise. One of Armstrong's first acts was to order Harrison to drop any plans to retake Detroit. He was instructed to "take a defensive position." In other words, to sit out the war.

"Got to be professional jealousy," Frake whispered to Quinn. "Makes no sense otherwise."

"And there's more," said Harrison, who was obviously restraining his frustration while further explaining the orders. "Secretary Armstrong says that the focus of the land campaign will be the taking of Montreal. It will be a two-pronged assault from the south from upper New York by way of Lake Champlain and from the west down the St. Lawrence from Sackets Harbor on Lake Ontario. Armstrong has assigned General Dearborn the overall command of the Montreal operation."

"No mention of how we can help in that invasion?" a voice from the back of the room asked.

"The idea, I gather, is that by taking Montreal, we can choke off the British and Canadian forces on the lakes, I mean Ontario and Erie. That will deprive them of supplies and reinforcements; they'd have to surrender."

"So we're supposed to just sit here?"

"Maybe, maybe not," Harrison said enigmatically.

"But Armstrong does have a role for some of us, at least. I'm to send one thousand of our best fighters to assist at Sackets Harbor." When he said it, he was looking directly at Quinn and Frake.

27 April 1813

York, Ontario, Canada

"He's trying to get us killed," Frake, who was now fully recovered from his Frenchtown wounds, fumed.

At first Quinn agreed, but then it seemed to him impossible that a man as powerful as Henry Dearborn was out to get the two of them. When he raised the question, Frake snorted and shook his head at such naiveté.

"I don't say he'd shoot us in the head while we're sleeping." Frake grumbled. "But he asked for us *by name.* How many times does a senior major general do that?"

"Well, we are pretty damn good."

"It's no joke, Willie. He wants us in combat under his command. He's still smarting because we delivered Madison's scolding to him. He probably thinks we've spread that story all through the ranks. Why else are we ordered to lead the charge? Why are we in the first coupl'a boats?"

Frake had a point. It was April, and the ice was gone from the lakes and rivers of the Midwest. The war would be heating up again, and the two men had been dispatched with one thousand Kentucky riflemen to Dearborn's command at Sackets Harbor, thirty miles south of Kingston in Canada. The general had initially planned to make Sackets Harbor his base for the assault on Kingston, and then down the St. Lawrence to Montreal—until he learned that the British were preparing to preempt the attack. Instead, he stayed away until the ice broke up and the British attack failed to materialize.

Meanwhile, he reconsidered his plan. He wrote to Armstrong that Kingston was too heavily defended so he would turn his attention first to York, on the northern shore of Lake Erie, and then to Fort George, the British garrison guarding the mouth of the Niagara River on Lake Ontario. At York, a regional capital, he argued, the British were building a thirty-gun frigate, the *HMS Sir Isaac Brock*. Also, two smaller warships had wintered there. Strategically, York supplied Detroit, Mackinac, the Niagara peninsula, and other forward positions, so its warehouses of arms, ammunition, and stores would be a prize.

Despite its importance, York's garrison was relatively small—several hundred regulars augmented by Canadian militia and Indian allies. Its capture by a superior force would be comparatively easy and would restore some of the army's luster.

Both sides keenly appreciated the importance of the inland waterways and so had entered into a fierce shipbuilding competition. This raid was to be America's first joint army-navy operation of the war. Dearborn was in overall command and would actually be present at the battle, riding the *Madison,* a twenty-four-gun corvette. Commodore Isaac Chauncey, the naval commander, would direct the transit and the amphibious landing.

Dearborn designated Brigadier General Zebulon Montgomery Pike to lead the assault ashore. Pike had made a name for himself out West after the Louisiana Purchase and had boldly attached his name to a mountain peak, but his courage was as formidable as his ego, and his troops were proud to be led by him. Quinn and Frake were assigned to the first wave of longboats, the vanguard of some 1,700 men, more than enough to overcome the small garrison.

Unfavorable winds and choppy waters complicated the assault and gave York's garrison ample warning. The selected landing site was an old French fort three miles west of York where the land had been cleared of the dense forest that could give cover to British riflemen. But winds blew the boats a half mile farther west onto a narrower and more dangerous beach where the trees grew closer to the shore.

As soon as the first longboats came into range, the air whistled with rounds from Indian sharpshooters hiding in the thick woods. A volley from the six-pounders aboard the *Madison* silenced the rifles briefly, long enough for the first longboat to crunch onto the beach and offload its men. Quinn and Frake led the way into the dense brush and began to lay down covering fire for the arriving boats. Pike was aboard one of them.

Commanding the enemy forces was Sir Roger Hale Sheaffe, the British general who had directed the successful defense of Queenston after Brock's death. Sheaffe had ordered Grenadier reinforcements to back up the Indians and repulse the landing. But the Grenadiers arrived late, allowing Pike to land his men with only a few casualties and no deaths.

Such good fortune was brief. As Pike formed his troops to march to York, the Grenadiers arrived. Twenty Americans fell at the first salvo. Two hundred and fifty British soldiers rushed from the woods, bayonets fixed, and descended on the embankment. Too surprised to return fire, the Americans quickly shifted to bayonet combat at close quarters. Gradually they gave ground, some retreating as far as the boats, but Pike turned to his bugler and ordered not retreat but charge. That bugle call convinced the confused soldiers that other units up and down the line must be winning. It turned the tide.

"C'mon, boys, we've got them on the run!" Quinn shouted over his shoulder as he led his squad back up the embankment.

The bugle call startled the enemy as well, and the British and their allies fled back into the woods with the Americans in hot pursuit. It was all Quinn and Frake could do to keep their men from charging ahead and losing contact with the rest of the Americans. In moments, they passed the old French fort. Pike made sure that the main body, traveling up the road to York, was protected by skirmishers in the woods, but they encountered no one. Sheaffe appeared to have ordered a retreat.

Quinn and Frake's squads were in the lead, accompanying the colors. Sheaffe ordered his fifes and drums to play the mocking strains of *Yankee Doodle*, and a pair of old British eighteen-pounders opened up on Quinn and his men. Chauncey's schooners, meanwhile, had reversed their course back to York and countered the British guns. There wasn't much to bomb: one blockhouse and a wooden palisade surrounded by a dry moat. Quinn, from his forward position, calculated that maybe a half dozen guns, six-pounders and twelve-pounders, were attempting to engage Americans on land and in the schooners. Now the schooners were pouring on an impressive display of broadsides.

It had been two hours since the amphibious landing, and Quinn could see the enemy weakening. *My God!* he thought. *This might be his first taste of an American victory.*

When American forces arrived on the outskirts of the town, the Union Jack still flew at the fort and the governor's mansion, so Pike proceeded cautiously, sending Quinn and his men to scout ahead. The general expected an attack and was anxious to interrogate a captured British sergeant who had been brought to him.

"Sergeant, I will assure your proper treatment and, in turn, I request certain information. I do not expect you to betray your forces, but you can help us reduce the coming casualties."

"Sir," the sergeant replied, "you know that I can only give you my name and the name of my unit."

Pike took a seat on a tree stump and was about to reply when the earth shook with a horrific explosion. He looked toward the sound, and a flash like a sun exploding blinded him. At the same instant, an immense black cloud rose above what had been the magazine and rolled toward Pike and his prisoner. Some men instinctively ran; others fell or were blown flat on the ground by the concussion and the scorching heat.

A deadly shower of debris rained down on them—rocks, bricks, and logs from the destroyed magazine; parts of weapons and munitions; dirt from the massive hole the blast created under the magazine; and then body parts. Pike was struck on his head and back by what appeared to be a remnant of the magazine door and its hardware. For impossibly long seconds, the debris continued to fall.

When at last the deadly hail abated, the wounded—those that still had their wits—cautiously surveyed the scene.

Frake's squad, which had been covering the flank away from the river, quickly arrived. Some men, devastated by what they saw, fell to retching violently. Others began tending to the bodies that were whole, stanching their wounds before blood loss proved fatal. Far too many were beyond help. A rifleman's eye had been obliterated by a shard of rock that still protruded from the socket. Blood and tissue oozed so profusely from Pike's wounds that he seemed lost until they gently rolled him on his side and detected a slight pulse and light breathing.

Men ran back and forth, some out of control, screaming and sobbing. Others sat dazed, cradling an arm or leg or shoving clothing into a gushing abdominal wound. A few were frantically searching for missing limbs. Most expired quickly. Frake did what he could to restore order and assign the able-bodied to identify the dead and wounded so that when the surgeons arrived they could begin their gruesome work at once.

Stretchers, a part of every assault force, began arriving from the rear, but there weren't enough. Some of the wounded were simply picked up and carried to the shore. Chauncey, seeing the explosion, had immediately maneuvered his ships into position and launched whaleboats to pick up the wounded. Even the battle-hardened had never seen such carnage.

In the confusion, U.S. Colonel Cromwell Pearce began shouting orders. Pearce had been standing only fifteen yards from Pike and was briefly stunned by a blow from the sky. Coming to his senses, he saw that the panicked Americans would be easy pickings for a smaller force sweeping down from the town. He assumed that the Americans had fallen for one of the oldest military tricks. Convinced they had the enemy on the run, they had been suckered into a trap. Unaware of the explosion at the garrison, he believed they had been drawn into a huge landmine's killing zone and would soon face a counterattack.

In minutes Pearce had restored some order, creating a makeshift front of two ranks with a single rank on both flanks. They waited, the first rank kneeling and the second standing behind.

Frake was there, assuring his men. "Those cowardly squirrels soon'll come out of hiding, and y'all can get your revenge." But where was Quinn?

26 May 1813

Fort Niagara

Quinn felt as if he were flying. As long as he could keep swimming, doing a breaststroke, he could stay in the air. He was at once terrified and exhilarated. Below him, the battle raged; puffs of smoke marked each side's front lines. To his right were Chauncey's warships, heaving cannonballs into York's fortifications. As he swooped lower, he saw Dearborn on the *Madison's* quarterdeck, peering through his glass at the battle.

The general turned his glass on Quinn, and he felt himself losing altitude. He swam harder, but now his arms were heavy. They felt tied to his sides. Now he couldn't see; he was in a darkened tunnel with only Dearborn visible, Dearborn laughing.

Quinn woke. Or he thought he did. The tunnel disappeared, but nothing looked familiar. He heard a high-pitched ringing, loud and piercing. He tried lifting his hands to his ears to block the sound, but they were immobile. Then darkness returned, and a windmill was turning in the distance while women jigged to a familiar Irish tune.

Then the floor below them was gone, and below it was a cellar, dusty with age.

There was his father, urging, "Son, we've got to do this," and Quinn was ashamed that he couldn't. He didn't even know what *this* was.

He turned and found himself between rows of buildings that bent down to enfold him. Then an awful smell. He wanted to retch but resisted because he was at a table with Sally and the Madisons.

"Willie, it's me." Quinn heard the voice but thought it was part of the dream. "Willie, I know you're in there. It's Malachy."

What the hell? Where was he? Malachy? He struggled to open his eyes.

"He's awake."

"Thank God."

There was the voice again. "Hey, brother. Open your eyes. Wake up."

Wake up? How could he? He couldn't fly. Maybe he never had left home. Never visited the White House. Dreamt the whole thing: Mackinac, Queenston, blood in the snow at River Raisin, York, and Dearborn's threatening eyes.

First came light, then images, then a face—Malachy's.

"Thought we had lost you for a while there, brother. Thought you were a goner."

Now he was fully awake, but he couldn't think. "I can't remember," he said, touching his head where the pain was. Bandages? Pain like he had never felt before. Then more pain in his arm now. His left arm? No, his hand. And the ringing in his ears…no, in his head…nearly drowning out what Malachy was saying.

"At York you were injured, wounded."

"How? What?"

"First, just be easy. Get your strength back. Eat something."

Something was wrong. He didn't like what was happening.

"Tell me," he demanded, his voice stronger. He raised his eyes and saw other figures.

"Thought you was gonna get outta the rest of the war, did ya?" It was Frake's voice like a splash of cold water, bringing Quinn to his senses.

"Surely this must be a nightmare. No one can be that ugly."

That brought laughter from everyone, breaking the tension.

"Glad you haven't lost your edge, cap, but Dearborn wants to know when the hell you're gonna get out of that rack."

"What happened?"

"Got your bell rung but good. The sawbones can explain it all better, but you walked into the biggest 'splosion I've ever seen. You're lucky to be here."

"If you felt like me, you might not think so. Jesus, Mary, and Joseph, my head hurts. What hit me?"

"Somethin' the size of a house. Them Brits set off their arsenal just as you and your squad was getting there. You walked right into it. You don't remember?"

"Nothing." He frowned. "The last thing I can remember was Pike sending us to reconnoiter." Quinn shifted, trying to find a comfortable spot in his rumbled bedclothes.

"Well, that arsenal was buried between you and the fort. If you'd got there ten seconds later, you wouldn't have left so much as a grease spot. Some of your men got flung through the air like ducks on the wing. Some others was smashed into pulp. All told, a couple a hundred killed or wounded."

"Who made it out?"

Frake rattled off the names. Some lost limbs in the blast; others lost them later under the surgeon's saw. Some were blinded or deafened.

"You were on the ground, shaking like a wounded varmint. The docs called them spasms or somethin'."

"You had a concussion." The military doctor pushed past Frake.

Malachy was silent on the bed's other side.

"When you take a blow to the head, it creates a swelling between the brain and the skull," the physician said. "That causes the pressure and the pain that you're feeling, son."

"Will it go away?" Quinn asked.

"Eventually, if you stay quiet and rest. If the swelling gets too great—and it still can—you could die. The pressure squeezes your brain so hard it stops working."

"Well, doc, you're sure doing a fine job of setting his mind at ease," Malachy interjected.

"The ensign deserves to know how serious this is and how important that he follow my orders," the doctor responded testily. "Luckily, whatever hit you wasn't big enough or going fast enough to penetrate your skull. You're a fortunate man."

"My hand hurts like hell."

"We've given you laudanum for the pain but not too much, because you could become addicted." The doctor eyed Quinn steadily. "I'm afraid you've lost two fingers of your left hand."

"You won't be picking your nose and shooting your gun at the same time no more," Frake said.

Malachy smiled. The physician didn't, and neither did Quinn.

"Which fingers?"

"Your ring finger and middle finger. You've still got your little finger and—this is the good news—your thumb and index finger. That means you've still got good use of the hand."

"Lucky me. What else?"

"That's about it. As I said, you're a fortunate man."

"How long have I been here?"

"Going on four weeks."

"Four weeks! How can that be?"

"Can't explain it, son, but it happens. You were in what's called a coma, and there's no way of telling when or if you were going to come out of it. It's still a mystery why some people wake up and others don't. You just happened to do it while we were standing here. Maybe you sensed the presence of your friends."

"I was laying here all that time with you all not knowing if I was going to die? God, I'm sorry." For the first time, Quinn felt tears welling up.

"Nothing to be sorry about, lad," the doctor said. "You've got good friends by your side. Your brother here came all the way from Baltimore. Been here more than a week now. You're lucky you've got people who care about you. I've seen too many men suffer and die in here alone."

"He's even luckier than you know, doctor," Malachy said with a wink. "I've got letters here for you direct from Miss Sally."

30 May 1813

Fort Niagara

Quinn hurt something beyond awful. Malachy, who had come fearing that he'd be bringing his brother's body home, had left with the good news. The letters from Sally, full of love and sympathy, had lifted his spirits but saddened him too for the worry he must have caused her. He had been awake a week and was still trying to learn the details.

Frake filled him in. His Majesty's regulars had hightailed it back up the peninsula, leaving the locals and the Canadian militia behind to surrender. On their way out, the British had ordered the shipyard burned and with it the half-finished *Sir Isaac Brock* in order to deny the Americans another warship and the stores housed there.

By most accounts, the British commanding general had deliberately destroyed the arsenal, but the Canadians denied it and claimed that one of the Americans had set it off accidentally. Not likely, since none of them knew the arsenal's location.

Pike had died while being rowed back to the *Madison*.

Frake picked up the story:

"Dearborn had briefly come ashore, not to take personal command of the troops, but simply to survey *his* victory. He'd quickly looked around then scooted back to the *Madison*. Didn't issue a single order about what to do with the prisoners or the town. Didn't stay to negotiate a ceasefire or surrender with the Canadians. Everything turned into chaos. Our guys were red with rage over the arsenal explosion. They set to plundering the village; Dearborn failed to put up enough men to guard the town. The next day, we and them Canadians jawboned for six hours about the terms of surrender. You'd a thought that they'd won the battle. When they got about to agree to something, Dearborn shows up and starts insulting 'em."

"Jesus."

"I don't know," Frake continued, "maybe it helped, because things started to happen a little later. The British wounded and captives held at the garrison finally got tended to. And we started loading everything we could find onto the ships: ammunition, provisions, every government document lying around the governor's mansion and the government buildings. Thousands of pounds of sterling trucked out of the provincial treasury. Didn't miss a thing of value until the ships were so loaded you woulda thought they'd sink." Frake took a swig out of a jug of Kentucky hooch that he had mysteriously obtained and snuck into the hospital. "Getting parched doing all this talking. Sorry, I forgot my manners. Want some? It's the genuine cure." He held it out, but Quinn waved it away.

"Our sailors managed to refloat a dismantled schooner, the duke of something-or-other, but I hear we missed another prize, the *Prince Regent*. It sailed off just a couple a days before we got there."

"But why didn't Dearborn step in to stop the looting?" Quinn still couldn't believe that the senior officer present allowed the pillage to continue.

"Dearborn wasn't much worried about what was on the Canadians' minds—stopping the looting and violence. He went on back to the *Madison*, and it all started again. Someone even robbed a church. All the government buildings were torched. Dearborn could see the flames against the night sky but didn't do nothin'. Places burned to the ground. *Then* Dearborn shows up saying as how he's appalled—by his own troops, mind you—and pretty near admits he has no control. Tells the civilians it's their job to protect their own property."

"Unbelievable."

"Yeah. Once there wasn't much left to loot or torch, it all finally simmered down. I pushed for court martialing the looters, but Dearborn didn't want to sully *his* victory with anything messy. Folks back home are just hungry for any kind of win, 'specially on Canadian soil, and Dearborn figured they wouldn't tolerate any punishment."

Quinn wondered what he would have done if he hadn't been knocked cold and had witnessed the attacks on civilian life and property. He still liked to think that he was fighting on the good side and that the Limeys and anyone who stood with them were the bad guys. His earlier doubts about war were reinforced, and he contemplated what his own role should be...as if he had a choice. An officer simply didn't walk away from his sworn duty. That would make him a deserter, no better than a savage whose word you could never trust. Of course, Quinn's own government had broken its share of promises to the Indians.

Temporarily diverted by those thoughts, Quinn returned his attention to Frake's story.

"Fact is," Frake continued, "I don't know why we bothered with York. We didn't stay to occupy it. We lost ten times as many men as the Brits. I guess they thought we just went up there to disrupt their shipbuilding, not to claim it as American territory, because the whole invasion force went right on back to Fort Niagara, which is how you got here."

"So we're right back where we started from," Quinn said.

"Pretty much. But some things went right. A lot's been happening whilst you been taking your ease, my friend. We finally took Fort George across the river. You shoulda seen it. The guns here and Chauncey's cannon pounded the fort to smithereens. Then our old friend Winfield Scott—he's now a full-bird colonel—landed and captured the Union Jack at the fort. We drove the Brits outta Queenston up river.

"I'm glad to say that we control the entire frontier along the Niagara, from Lake Ontario to Lake Erie, meaning we pretty much control both lakes and access to the whole Northwest. If we wanted, we could march all the way back along Lake Erie to Detroit and retake what that fool Hull gave away. We could have all of Upper Canada. Problem is, it doesn't look like we want to. Fact is, Dearborn didn't bother pursuing the British regulars when he had them on the run at York. Didn't at George neither.

"Just a second, I need another swig," Frake said, lifting the jug to his lips.

"The Brits we chased out of George now are holed up somewhere inland, at a place called Burlington Heights, and all we've done is settle down around Fort George. But the Brits don't lay 'round. They've been sending in skirmishers for hit-and-run raids on our outposts, sometimes with nasty results. Seems like there's ambushes every night, especially on the supply and reinforcement lines. The outposts are at least a mile away, and there's no way to protect those routes.

My riflemen are manning most of the outposts, and you can hear 'em grumbling about having to sit there waiting for the Limeys to attack. Just like Dearborn likes it, if ya ask me."

Sounds like Dearborn is actually trying to lose the war, Quinn thought.

"Listen, that's not all," Frake continued. "While we're fiddling around the Niagara, the British have their sights set on Sackets Harbor where most of our shipbuilding is going on.

"The Brits come at it with somethin' like a thousand troops, outnumbering the garrison there. They had an eye to take all the stores and burn the big, new thirty-gunner, the *General Pike*, we're building there. All the stores Dearborn liberated from York were at Sackets Harbor—lots of canvas for sails, hardware for ships. The place was a treasure trove."

"What happened?"

"A bloody fight, from what I heard. Captured the town, burned the stores, and torched the *Pike* and an old schooner that Chauncey had taken at York. They withdrew, and when Chauncy got there, he figured the *Pike* construction would only be set back three weeks, maybe a month. But word is everyone's worried that the attack tipped the balance toward the Brits in who gets to control Lake Ontario. Last anyone heard was the British fleet was standing off Burlington Heights hereabouts. Even with Chauncey's fleet challenging them, it'll be a lot harder to dig them out of Burlington."

"So now what?"

"I think they're going back to the idea of attacking Montreal and cutting off Upper Canada's supply routes. We take ahold of Upper Canada and make it a part of the United States or trade it for something big. Assuming the war ever ends."

Yet, for all the blood and dying, what had been accomplished? Despair, in addition to pain, now overtook Quinn. He became aware that Frake was searching his face.

"What?" Quinn asked.

"Was looking like you were slipping back into your coma there for a minute."

Quinn tried to grin and keep Frake talking. "So how do you *know* the strategy has shifted back to Montreal?"

"Doesn't take a genius to figure it out, Willie. We're going east. Most everyone here is being redeployed to Sackets Harbor or beyond."

"And leave the Niagara open? Give it all back up? Mother of God."

"You're coming along as soon as you're well, and if you're not missing a leg or an arm, they consider you well."

"No surprise, I guess," Quinn said, suddenly conscious of the throbbing where his fingers should have been. "Where are we heading?"

"My riflemen and me are going a good deal east into Major General Wade Hampton's command. We'll be attacking Canada from the south and east through upper New York."

"And me?"

"You, I saw your orders. Quinn, you've been assigned—because of your, ahem, condition—to staff work. As soon as you can travel, which I reckon will be in a month or so, you'll work for Major General James Wilkinson."

"Wilkinson? Wilkinson!"

"You know of him, Will?"

"Every regular army officer does. He may be the most treacherous and traitorous man ever to don a United States Army officer's uniform. His reputation is that he never won a battle but never lost a court martial.

"In the Revolutionary War, he somehow got himself made a brigadier general at twenty. That ought to tell you something. In thanks, he joined the Conway Cabal— some senior officers tried to dump George Washington as commander of the Continental Army."

"Think I'll need 'nother poke of this," Frake said, hefting the jug again.

"Obviously, the conspiracy failed, but Wilkinson went on to better things. Like the Burr conspiracy to create a new nation out of western territories. When that looked like it would fail, Wilkinson turned on Aaron Burr, denouncing him to President Jefferson. Actually fabricated some evidence against Burr. Wilkinson's fake evidence was discovered; he even faced a court martial for it but was acquitted."

Quinn paused for effect, signaling that the worst was yet to come.

"Incredibly, he was handed command of New Orleans and our Gulf of Mexico shores. Camped his couple of thousand troops in a swamp, of all places. Men died not just from swamp fever, also from the rotten food, sold to the army by a supplier that gave Wilkinson kickbacks. Word reached Eustice, and he ordered the men to a healthier site. But Wilkinson jammed them on boats described as 'hell ships.' Many as one thousand supposedly died, but no one could really tell because of Wilkinson's sloppy records."

21 June 1813
Washington, D.C.

"He's Armstrong's friend."

It didn't take long for Sally to dig out the answer from the Washington gossip mills. The capital city, she discovered, was buzzing with incredulity and disgust about Wilkinson's appointment. The people of New Orleans, however, heartily approved and were glad to see him go. Sally wrote:

> Armstrong and Wilkinson served together at the Battle of Saratoga. Even Mrs. Madison is appalled by his appointment, but the president felt he had no option. The pick of quality senior officers is slim indeed. Most are War of Independence has-beens. Mr. Madison says he prays for the quick seasoning of young officers, and for that reason he is much distressed by the death of General Pike.

Sally was getting accustomed to the dark intrigues of Washington and had grown more accepting of the idea of something untoward happening behind the scenes. She was able now to concede that bad judgment—if not something darker—could be at work even in the White House.

> Wilkinson was ordered to proceed from the South to Sackets Harbor with all deliberate haste, but he seems determined instead to celebrate his appointment. In Washington, where he never should have stopped because it is out of his way, he has been attending an endless round of congratulatory soirees. The man is a disgrace.

With her loss of naiveté came a growing interest in and understanding of public affairs. She was in the House gallery when Madison spoke to a special session of Congress and hinted—astonishingly—at a possible end of the war. She described the renewed peace effort with the appointment of a three-man commission—Gallatin; John Quincy Adams; and James Bayard, an anti-war Federalist—to attend talks in Europe sponsored by the Russian Emperor Alexander I. To Sally, the speech sounded overly optimistic.

> My love, we know how those who have actually witnessed battles at York and elsewhere know that optimistic descriptions of those events are twaddle. The overlong guerrilla war conducted by our enemies against Frake and the other brave souls at Fort George gives rise to the most grievous fears. But Mr. Madison had to say such optimistic things, because the most immediate problem is the lack of money to press the fight to its successful conclusion. That accounts for why he is proposing a new tax, a direct tax.
>
> The debate that resounded through the halls of the Capitol was so vexed that I feared the very walls would tumble from the reverberations of angry voices.

Nobody is for a tax unless it is on someone else, and this direct tax is upon just about everyone. It would tax land, imported salt, stills, retailers, auction, sugar, carriages, and banks notes. It is supposed to raise $5.5 million, about three times what Mr. Madison said was in the nation's treasury.

The president clearly tires easier and has begun to suffer intestinal distresses. Mrs. Madison frets daily about his state of health and asks us to join in prayer for him. The raids on the Chesapeake Bay towns by an admiral named Cockburn have added to his worries. The British blockade of our ports hobbled trade and made merchants restless—as your own family well knows. Now shortages of all kinds are driving prices up. Worse yet, the attacks around Chesapeake Bay make us all fear for Baltimore.

At times, I confess that I despair that this war will ever end. My fear for you is so great that I wonder if we ever will live together as man and wife. I am true only to you, and I remain your constant and everlasting love.

22 June 1813

Chesapeake Bay

Rear Admiral Sir George Cockburn, 10th Baronet and commander of a fleet of British vessels sent to harass American towns and interfere with commerce along Chesapeake Bay, placed his pocket watch on the table in front of him.

"You have ten minutes to get whatever valuables you want out of the house before it goes up in flames," he told the three women who had been sitting quietly at tea when he burst through the door.

He had plopped himself uninvited at the table. Behind him stood Royal Navy Captain Sir Peter Parker, 2nd Baronet and cousin to poet Lord Byron. Outside waited two companies of Cockburn's marauding marines armed with muskets, pikes, cutlasses, and fireballs. Their intent was clear.

Like other unfortunate women and children in the villages along the bay, Agnes Heathman, with her daughter Pauline and her sister Grace, had stayed behind when others fled. Under the rules of civilized engagement, civilians and private property would not be assaulted, but Cockburn was not a man for niceties. His orders from the British

Admiralty were to hunt down and destroy American ships, arms, stores and instruments of war, but also to burn and pillage the bay communities, encourage slave revolts, and demoralize Americans. Cockburn, in a series of hit-and-run raids on anything in sight of the shoreline, carried out those orders with considerable exuberance. His obvious enjoyment of this assignment troubled many of his officers.

Tonight was another such exercise. The warm fire in the cabin that chased off the evening chill was a beacon for Cockburn. That single light in the gathering dark lured him to muster the marines, launch the longboats, and go ashore himself.

"But why?" Agnes asked, genuinely confused.

Cockburn silenced her with a raised hand. "Because you have dared to challenge the British Empire!" he shouted. "Because your own soldiers have inflicted unspeakable depravities upon His Majesty's capital of Upper Canada at York. Because"—he took a breath and then lowered his voice to a mocking whisper—"I *like* to see houses burn, if it please your ladyship.

"Besides," he went on, now in a conversational tone, "I have it on good authority that your husband is a colonel in the local militia, and for that treasonous conduct he will return to find his home in ruins. Our directives are to burn every abode, every warehouse. Why should your house—a shelter for the king's enemies—be spared?" He glanced from face to face, hoping to find sheer terror in the women's eyes.

"There's no use denying what you say, sir, even though it is not true," Agnes replied. "But surely even in warfare certain civilities remain. Cannot a gentleman, a civilized person such as yourself, see the distress that you bring to us? Everything we have is here."

"I can only promise you will be spared bodily harm if you do as you are told. You have less than eight minutes left." As much as Cockburn enjoyed sitting in the warm cabin, he did not care to debate his victims. This bothersome woman should accept her fate, obey him, and leave. Dealing with beggars was tedious.

At that, Pauline—Cockburn judged her to be about sixteen and a girl of uncommon beauty—fell to her knees before him and wept.

"Please, sir," was all she could say.

Cockburn's expression reflected both boredom and irritation. As an English noble, he felt it appropriate that she should kneel to him, but... He stared impassively at his watch.

"Seven minutes." He sighed.

Now Agnes and Grace approached Parker, whose handsome face revealed a certain amount of sympathy and decency. Parker seemed about to speak till Cockburn shot him a fearsome look.

"Time's up," Cockburn said briskly, though more than four minutes actually remained. He had enough, and now he was appalled to see tears in Parker's eyes. He rose and stepped to the door.

"Lieutenant!" he shouted. "Torch this place."

He'd had quite enough nonsense, but suddenly the young girl wrapped her arms around his knees, nearly tripping him.

"Curse you, peasant," he said, pulling away and striding haughtily out of the cabin.

"Please, sir, please, rescind your order," Agnes called as they followed him out. "It's not too late."

The marine with the torch paused almost imperceptibly, as if Cockburn might indeed change his mind.

"Insolence will get you a court martial and a noose," Cockburn told him, waving the marine and two other torchbearers into the house.

Almost instantly, the house was ablaze, the fire lighting their way back to the beach and their longboats. As Cockburn climbed in, he could see the three women silhouetted against the flames of their home. Minutes later from the rail of Cockburn's flagship, *HMS Fantome*, dying flickers of flame and glowing embers still marked the place. If the women still were there, they could not be seen, not that Cockburn was looking for them. *Ah, time for a brandy to chase the night air,* Cockburn thought as he headed below to his quarters.

17 July 1813

Sackets Harbor, New York

*A*s Quinn regained his strength in Sackets Harbor, his spirits declined in equal measure. He wrote to Sally.

It is impossible, my dearest, for me to fathom that we sit here idle on the northern frontier while the British are causing such devastation on the Chesapeake. I hear from my family that Baltimore feels itself under siege, and the linen business is near a standstill because of the British blockade. So far business within our country keeps my family from poverty, but Baltimore depends on trade. Sentiment there would be entirely for ending the war but for the Cockburn's devastation of the bay communities. He already has made several feints toward Baltimore, which is now preparing for an invasion. I hope that they are blessed with better commanders than I.

Speaking of which, Dearborn has been removed from command. It was for failure to follow up on his victories at York and Fort George and because of ill health (whose causation is to be found more in a bottle than in contagion).

Sadly, though, the command of the campaign against Montreal has been divided between two generals who despise each other. Wilkinson you know of, and General Wade Hampton, who has a fine reputation and who detests Wilkinson. This is hazardous, because close cooperation will be required. The pincher movements of the two commands must be highly coordinated. For the moment Wilkinson is not even here. You probably have a better idea of his whereabouts than his staff does! Delays already have prevented us from undertaking the campaign before the onset of winter. Mark my words. We will be spending our winter encampment not in Montreal, but somewhere in New York State.

Meanwhile, we are still attempting to keep the troops fit and prepared, but it is difficult to keep morale high. Gnats, mosquitoes, flies, spiders, June bugs, lice, beetles, and glutinous insects of all types— flying, crawling, biting, and digging—assault us on every front. It is worse at night when the light of a candle to write home—or simply to check for wee beasties in our bedding—attracts varmints from nearby marshes and forests. Frogs and other creatures inhabit our tents, which often have to be moved, because they become mired in the mud from the supposedly unseasonable rains. Without Wilkinson to fight for our share of logistical support, provisions are not what they should be. Flour and other provisions that escape the ever-present rats are infested with weevils.

Many of the troops are little more than recruits. Few have seen battle. I have acquired a reputation as the most battle-scared veteran in the entire brigade. This appellation I could well do without. My thoughts at such times naturally turn to the eternal. Being a Catholic in a largely Protestant country is not without difficulties. I am often referred to in disparaging tones as Romish or papist. I know these notions are not representative of all Protestants—certainly not of my own beloved—I pray that when this war is over we will overcome the old enmities that poisoned our ancestors.

5 October 1813

Moravian Town,
Near Ontario in Upper Canada

ortunately, the war wasn't entirely in the hands of the army. U.S. Commodore Oliver Hazard Perry had strengthened the Lake Erie fleet with an ambitious shipbuilding effort and forced the British ships to seek safe harbor near Amherstburg. When the British tried to make a run for it, Perry's squadron engaged them in an hours-long running gun battle. After his victory, Perry messaged D.C.: "We have met the enemy and they are ours."

The stunning defeat allowed General Harrison, now released from Dearborn's stand-in-place order, to hotly pursue the British and his Indian allies along the north shore of Lake Erie, following the route that the disgraced General Hull was to have taken. British promises to Native Americans led by the great chief Tecumseh to create an independent buffer state for them in Northwest Territories were collapsing.

Pessimism reigned as British Major General Henry Proctor tried to inform Tecumseh and his chiefs that they were now on their own. Tecumseh sat expressionless as he heard Proctor say, "You are freed of your obligations to us.

You may return to your villages and families. I have given the men of the Canadian militia the liberty to return home and to save themselves."

With all the dignity that he could muster, Tecumseh rose and addressed the general:

"Father, listen to your children. When war was declared, our father in London stood up and gave us the tomahawk and told us that he was then ready to strike the Americans—that he wanted our assistance and that he would return the lands the Americans had taken from us.

"Father, your ships have departed, and now we are much astonished to see you tying up everything and preparing to run away without letting his red children know what his intentions are. You always told us to remain here and take care of our lands. You always told us you would never draw your foot off British ground. But now we see that you are drawing back, and we are sorry to see you doing so without meeting the enemy. We compare such conduct to a fat dog that carries his tail on its back, but when affrighted, drops it between its legs and runs off.

"Father, listen. The Americans have not yet defeated us by land. Neither are we sure that they have done so by water. We therefore wish to remain here and fight our enemy, should they make their appearance. If they defeat us, we will then retreat with our father.

"Father, you have the arms and ammunition that our great father sent for his red children. If you have an idea of going away, give them to us. Our lives are in the hands of the Great Spirit. We are determined to defend our lands, and if it be his will, we wish to leave our bones upon them."

Tecumseh's words were prophetic, for soon, Harrison would catch up to Proctor's troops and Tecumseh and his braves at a settlement called Moravian Town. Harrison decimated the British with a daring cavalry charge, leaving

Tecumseh and his warriors standing their ground in a nearby forest.

Tecumseh had taken cover behind a stand of oak trees and was drawing a bead on a squad of advancing Americans. As he aimed, he heard an American voice from a slightly different direction yell out a warning: "Look out, an Indian is aiming at you!"

They were the last words that Tecumseh heard, as an American bullet from another direction caught him in exposed chest and found his heart beneath. The chief fell dead and with him, the dream of an American federation.

17 October 1813

Sackets Harbor

With the British defeat at Moravian Town the Americans retook control of the Northwest Territories and the western end of Upper Canada. It was a stunning turn around in a war that had gone so badly for the Americans. Harrison could march unimpeded throughout the Upper Canadian peninsula, his lines of supply and communication assured by Perry's newly won control of Lake Erie. With America in virtual control of Upper Canada, perhaps the British could be expelled from Lower Canada and the North American continent entirely. The smell of victory at last was in the air.

But not if Wilkinson could help it. Quinn was flabbergasted by the towering incompetence and ego of the man Armstrong had put in charge of the western assault on Montreal.

Wilkinson's army vastly outnumbered the British regulars and Canadian militia forces at Kingston, so Armstrong believed Wilkinson could easily overwhelm Kingston and capture a mammoth fleet of three hundred flat-bottom boats for the two-hundred-mile trip down the St. Lawrence to Montreal. Meanwhile, from the East, Hampton would transport his four-thousand-man American force to the upper reaches of Lake Champlain, drive his way some fifty miles into Canada to the St. Lawrence River, and prepare to strike Montreal. It was an intricate plan requiring precise timing between two large forces hundreds of miles apart.

Sadly, Wilkinson and Hampton seemed to regard each other as the enemy, instead of the British. Quinn had written Sally as autumn started to turn the air chilly.

> Wilkinson arrived here much too late. Then, instead of concentrating on preparing his troops here for the Montreal campaign, he took a grand tour of Fort Niagara, where Winfield Scott was in command. Scott is widely praised for his exploits at Queenston and elsewhere, so that windbag Wilkinson had to bring him down a peg. They say he ordered Scott to stay at Fort Niagara so he wouldn't share in any of the glory Wilkinson expects to reap at Montreal. And to make matters worse, Wilkinson has snatched the bulk of Scott's troops.
>
> It seems that Scott served as a junior officer under Wilkinson in Louisiana. When he saw what the general did there, he called him a traitor, a liar, and a scoundrel. Not the thing to do in the army, so a court martial—reluctantly—convicted Scott of unofficer-like conduct and suspended him from the service for a year. It was a mild punishment, because the court didn't want to sanction Wilkinson's behavior. Anyway, there's bad blood between them.
>
> Sanitation isn't good here. Hundreds have come down with some sort of malady. It appears that the mess cooks made bread dough with water taken from too close to the latrines. Without a real command presence, every senior officer wants to be

in charge, but no one wants to take responsibility. How important is leadership! Thousands of men must march hundreds of miles and must be properly provisioned and trained! How will they follow into battle a man whose reputation is as sullied as Wilkinson's?

He seems to suppose that all the cannon, ammunition, arms, and provisions have appeared here by magic. Lumber, of which there is an abundance in this region, is the only thing that didn't have to be carted over hundreds of miles of barely passable roads or floated or manhandled around rocky portages. His lack of appreciation grates on the men.

I had hoped Armstrong would send us Harrison, but it appears he again will be held in check in the Northwest, although there's no immediate threat there. Again, there seem to be personal differences. My God!

Wilkinson is not going to try to take Kingston, which is the lynchpin for the entire campaign. He intends instead to make a feint at Kingston but bypass it and proceed directly to Montreal. This will pose a serious threat to our rear and could trap us between forces from Kingston and Montreal. How this campaign can ever be successful, I don't know.

24 October 1813

Washington, D.C.

*H*enry had planned carefully. He had accumulated a few pennies skimmed from Kilfoyle's shoe business, as well as some surreptitious tips from satisfied customers like that nice Miss Sally from the White House. He had studied a map he found in Kilfoyle's stock room. His feigned obedience had established him as a trustworthy nigger, never troublesome. No one would be suspicious if he was seen leaving the store. Now he only needed Kilfoyle to leave town on business.

Henry, like every other slave, knew that liberty's path led north to free states and on to Canada. Yet the path was incredibly difficult to navigate, and for southern blacks, the road necessarily led through Virginia and Maryland, home to nearly half of America's 1.1 million slaves. Against the odds, a network of sympathetic abolitionists had created way stations and safe harbors along the way.

Now the war was providing new opportunities. The forests along the Chesapeake Bay's western shore became crowded with men, women, and children waiting for the chance arrival of a British raiding party and a ride out to the fleet and freedom. Indeed, so many were fleeing that plantation owners petitioned the Virginia commonwealth for reimbursement for such losses. Rumors of massive slave uprisings and the slaughter of masters, though unfounded, were widespread. *Interested citizens* formed slave patrols—often little more than rogue posses—to hunt down runaways. They were inclined to shoot fleeing slaves on the spot, but that would deprive them a juicy finder's fee, delivered by the owners. A runaway might have an ear sliced from his or her head. Repeat runaways lost both ears or a tongue or a penis. Never an arm or a leg—amputees were not so useful.

So the night Henry slipped away, his goal was Point Lookout, an arduous seventy-mile hike southeast from Washington to the bottom tip of the Maryland peninsula that juts into Chesapeake Bay. British raiding parties had made it a frequent stop, according to the rumors Henry had picked up, so the woods were full of escapees waiting for their chance.

Unfortunately, the rumors had also reached the ears of the slave patrols, which made a practice of scouring Point Lookout's environs more frequently than the British checked in. Henry took a calculated risk that, traveling light and by himself, he could evade the patrols. But because of the uncertainty of when or where the British might come ashore, a man might wander the forests and marshes for months before he encountered a landing.

He moved at night on back roads and across fields, sometimes encountering a bog, forcing him to backtrack a mile or two. He traveled light, because a black man carrying provisions and changes of clothing surely would be marked as a runaway. He had planned for it, taking just enough clothing to wash out before sunrise in a marsh or stream, letting it dry during the day while he slept. For food, he pilfered fruit and vegetables when he could. He never went hungry…but neither did the mosquitoes.

On the third night, exhausted and discouraged, he encountered a family of runaways—the mister, missus, and four children, looking to be from about six to sixteen. To his further amazement, he learned from them that he wasn't where he thought he was—on the way to Point Lookout. Instead of traveling southeast from Washington, he had been walking east by northeast and was now a few miles from the Chesapeake, north of Annapolis.

"Lord, you sure confused," said the woman, Tilly. "Don't you know that moss grow on the north side of trees?"

Henry shook his head.

"I can tell by the way you dressed that you ain't no plantation slave like us. Else you wouldn't be wandering lost about the countryside, like you some city slave waiting to be plunked or plugged by the night riders."

Her man, Ampy—they had jumped the broom together—explained, "You been misled by the heaven signs. If you ain't familiar with the nighttime sky, like us who knowed the nighttime sky because we sleep under it for a breath of cool air in the hot summer, you end up not knowing north from south. See up there, that's what we call the North Star, and there's the Big Dipper."

Henry took it in but didn't think he'd need it, an attitude that Ampy could read.

"Well, this here is your lucky day I'd say, Lord Henry."

Henry didn't particularly care for the appellation. Ampy was joking, but Henry felt ridiculed. "Lucky? How is that?" Henry asked.

"Go just a few miles south of here, and you would have found yourself in the middle of Annapolis, where they don't cotton much to runaway slaves. If they don't hang you right there, you'd find yourself packed and shipped back to whatever city you come from. Washington or Baltimore, I reckon, because I don't think you could make it this far from anywhere else. 'Course, I can't rightly criticize you for not knowing about these parts, because you ain't from here…and where did you say you're from?"

"Alexandria, I mean Washington," Henry corrected himself

"That ain't here nor there." Ampy took off again.

The man does have a working mouth on him, Henry thought.

"What's important is where you is now. See here, just beyond that pinewood is this little town called Pasadena. Beyond that the marshlands start. Ain't as bad as it sounds— plenty of paths take us out to the bay shore near Gibson Island, kind of at the mouth of the Magothy River."

Don't need a geography lesson, Henry thought. "So, what?"

Ampy cocked his head like he had just encountered the year's biggest fool. "It's where the English boats is coming. Once a week. Tonight could be the next."

"How do you know all this?"

"Because it keeps happening, and we kept hearing about it."

"How do you hear?"

Now Henry was starting to get on Ampy's nerves. He sighed: "Word gets back to us. The folks who leave the master don't come back to him."

"How do you know they met up with the British and not with some night riders?"

"They'd be back then. The riders get a handsome reward."

Henry was getting flustered. Was this man so naïve that he didn't consider the possibility that the runaways had run into foul play?

"Listen," Henry said. "What if the British don't come? I mean, how long have you been waiting here? How long can you wait? What happens if you have to leave? Where can you go?"

Ampy was about to tell Henry that he was on his own if he continued so high and mighty, but then took into account Henry's naivete: "We've figured it out. We go north, meet up with some folk who will get us through Baltimore. And then more north into the free land."

"Do you know these people, the ones you're supposed to meet?"

"I know of them. I know where to meet them. Near a place called Glen Burnie. A farm just this side of it."

"But who are these people? White folk?" Henry asked, immediately even more suspicious of the information that he was receiving.

Ampy looked away, then, patiently stroking the stubble on his chin, turned back to Henry, "No, black. Free people. Their former owner done freed them."

"They got a name?"

"Name's Cavanaugh."

"Can you trust them?"

"Have to."

"And what if you can't?"

"Got no other choice. But that's why we're waiting here for the English. Not so many things to go wrong this way."

Henry had to give him that. Obviously, Ampy thought it through, evaluated the risks, and came up with a plan. That he could have gotten this far and remained safely in the woods for a week with his family told Henry something about Ampy's abilities.

"All right, let's go," Henry said, as if he had a choice.

Not even a thank ye, Ampy thought.

25 October 1813

Gibson Island, Maryland

"What'd I tell you? Them are sails are out there." Ampy was pointing to a small frigate, illuminated by the moonlight, standing off the shore a good ways out.

The British warship already had launched two boats that were being rowed toward an unoccupied spit of land called Gibson Island.

"You was right. I'll give you that," Henry said. His heart had leapt at the sight, and his mind could hardly comprehend that freedom was near at hand, heading his way.

"Those are the glory boats. Those be the liberty boats, coming over River Jordan to take us to the Promised Land on the other side, yes, sir!" Ampy wasn't at all hesitant. He turned to run back for his family.

"I'll wait here," Henry said to Ampy's retreating back.

He had tucked his family safely away in a grove of pines rising from the marsh. As Henry turned back to watch the boats slide through the water, something caught his eye at the intended landing spot on the island. It was a lit torch.

Then came another. Whoever was waving them was marking the spot where the boats should land.

We're not alone, Henry thought. A sliver of anxiety poked into his elation at the thought of approaching freedom. Would there be room in the boats for everyone? If not, would the British risk making two trips?

Worse, Henry feared that the boats would pick up whoever was waiting, leaving him and the Ampy family behind, unaware that they too wanted to be picked up. How long would they wait for Ampy to round up his family? Should he expose himself now?

It was as if Henry's legs made the decision for him. He popped out of his hiding place and started rushing down the beach. From another direction, he heard yelling. "Wait! Wait! We're coming too!" Ampy had spotted them too and was running toward the torches with the same thought of being left behind.

As the two boats crunched onto the sand still some distance away, Henry heard a pop, then others in rapid succession. Someone on the beach, he could tell by the flashes, was shooting. At him? He slowed then froze.

He was only a couple of hundred feet away now. He heard no bullets whizzing past him, nor could he see sand being kicked up around him. Flashes now were coming from the boat. Whoever was on the beach and the British marines in the boat were shooting at each other, Henry quickly realized. He was dumbfounded. Why would escaping slaves be firing at the marines?

His puzzlement lasted only a few seconds. It was a trap. Those weren't runaways on the beach; they were Maryland militia or maybe a citizens' posse shooting at the British. Whoever they were, they were no friends of runaway slaves. Word of an escape route to the British ships, widely circulated among slaves, couldn't have been kept secret forever. The posse had lured the British close to shore with the torches. Now the outnumbered marines, caught in the open in their boats, were getting the worst of it.

As Henry stood frozen, he watched marines crumble or fall into the water. Then the firing stopped, replaced by the moans of dying men. Now from the British ship came the thunder of its nine-pounders firing back, followed by the whoosh of balls in the air and the thumps of them landing harmlessly on the sandy beach. The Americans melted untouched back into the darkened marsh. They had melted in the direction of Ampy and his family.

It seemed to Henry that suddenly he was alone in the world, exposed and vulnerable. His instinct, ridiculous and fleeting, was to swim out to the frigate. His elation at the approach of freedom now was replaced by fear, the kind of fear that reaches down into the belly and then explodes back up and out. His mouth filled and quickly emptied of vomit. He feared that had he revealed himself just moments earlier, he might have made the biggest mistake of his life. Henry didn't even remember starting to run; he found himself in full flight, sprinting back toward the grove where the family was. Or had been. Surely, they'd heard all the shooting and commotion. He had to find them, warn them. Where would they go? Dread rose again from his belly as he ran. Now his lungs were burning in protest, but he couldn't stop.

If the shooters had seen him, they would be close behind. Maybe he shouldn't look for the family. He'd just be leading the pursuers to them. Shit. Shit! What should he do?

The sound of screams and then more gunfire halted him. Somewhere off to his left. Right where Ampy would have taken his family on the most direct route to the landing point. They had rushed directly into the slave hunters who had been retreating from the ship's guns. Perhaps Ampy's family had stopped at the sound of gunfire and couldn't see what was happening on the beach. Even if they had fled at the first crack of a rifle shot, the slave hunters still would be on them. Henry could only imagine their terror. They must be captured or dead.

Going to their rescue would be folly, but Henry struggled with his conscience anyway. Should he try to help them? Surely he'd be shot down or captured too. What was the use? What did he owe these people he'd just met? Maybe he owed them a lot. He'd been lost, on the way to being hanged in Annapolis, according to Ampy. And they'd given him an alternate plan in case the British landing failed. That might be the most valuable gift of his life. So would he use it now?

28 October 1813

Near Chesapeake Bay

The dogs made up Henry's mind. He could hear them chasing around in circles now, but soon enough they'd pick up his scent. They must be well trained, because there was no sound out of them during the shooting or during the capture of Ampy and Tilly and their children. Guilt was choking Henry, but he ran from the dogs. He'd never plowed a field or done heavy work, never pushed himself this far physically. With each step, a stabbing pain pierced his lungs, and his leaden legs ached. But now he was sure the dogs had his scent.

What had Ampy said about the North Star and the Big Dipper? He could see them when he emerged from a stand of trees and stumbled through a tobacco field. He ran for the star, but so did the dogs. He knew his best chance of losing them was to erase his trail by wading or swimming across water.

At the end of the tobacco field, woods loomed dark and mysterious, and he plunged into them, tripping over dead tree limbs and other detritus. Suddenly, he was skidding down a muddy embankment and falling on all fours into a shallow stream. He began running, still trying to follow his

Savior's star in the northern sky. Sometimes the water was only ankle deep, and other times up to his waist. The going was difficult, and he could still hear the dogs barking.

Were they were closer or farther away now? If they followed the river south from where he'd fallen in, he would be a lucky man. But if they came north, as they probably would, they would pick up his scent where he climbed out of the river, and they'd be on his trail again.

How to confuse the dogs? He climbed out of the water, still wondering. By instinct, he ran into the underbrush then circled around and stepped back into the water about one hundred feet from where he left. Another hundred feet, he climbed the bank on the left side and repeated the circle another hundred feet up the stream. Maybe the dogs would get confused. Maybe not.

Fear of vicious dogs and more vicious slave hunters renewed his energy. He could hear men's voices cursing, hear them crashing through the brush. Now Henry held onto a tree trunk, catching his breath. He listened. Silence.

Had his pursuers stopped to listen too? He held his breath. Only the sounds of crickets and the occasional owl's hoot. He waited, still as a statue. Five minutes turned into ten. If they were playing a waiting game, hoping for Henry to betray his position, he decided he'd outwait them forever if necessary.

Had he slept? What of dawn? How would he find his way when the North Star disappeared? Think. He remembered Ampy had told him to follow the rivers and the fence lines. Never travel during the day (he'd known that already). He forced himself to stand and began stumbling north.

Soon he came to a cornfield, the ears just about ripe for a late harvest. Eagerly he shucked one and gobbled it raw. Then another. The corn stalks blotted out the horizon, and he knew he mustn't get lost in the field. He could still see the North Star, and he followed it till he stepped into a clearing near a road. In the distance, he could make out the silhouettes of houses, barns, and outbuildings. It would be sunrise soon. He needed refuge.

Ampy had told him to look for certain signs. He looked more and saw a candle burning in a second-story window of the farmhouse. That was the sign of a safe house, according to Ampy. Or someone was just up early. Maybe slave hunters were using the sign as a decoy.

He would have to risk it, trust that the Lord was guiding his steps. Fearfully, he moved quietly toward the house. Please, God.

Cautiously he stepped onto the porch. His tap on the door was tentative and faint, maybe too quiet to be heard. His mind swirled.

A man cautiously opened the door. Stinking, disheveled, and trembling, Henry crouched, prepared to run. In a flash, a strong arm reached for Henry's sleeve and yanked him inside.

"Relax, son, you're in safe hands now," the man said.

Only then did Henry realize he was trembling. Gently, the man led Henry to the fireplace where a pan of water, a towel, and a dry set of clothing waited. In the firelight, Henry was astonished to see the man was black.

Now Henry was sobbing. "Thank you, thank you," Henry said in a voice that mixed exhaustion, fear, and relief.

"We have food and water. Coffee if you prefer."

Henry stammered. "Are you Mr. Cavanaugh?" He remembered the name even though the conversation with Ampy seemed to have occurred months ago.

Now Cavanaugh was suspicious. It was not unheard of for slave hunters to pay black men to pose as runaways. "Who told you my name?"

Henry told him about Ampy and Tilly and his own narrow escape. "They know of you through the network. If they got away, they might still turn up here," he said.

Cavanaugh looked Henry directly in the eyes. Apparently satisfied, Cavanaugh then nodded and led him to the kitchen. "We'll get some food in you. Then you must rest. We'll wait a day or so to see if Ampy's family turns up, and then we'll send you off. Congratulations, Henry, you're on freedom's road."

Cleaned up and fed, Henry was led to a hidden room in the cellar.

"We have to keep you hidden. You never know who'll turn up."

Inside the room were two pallets, but they were clean. Henry thought how crowded it would be if Ampy and his family appeared and was as quickly ashamed at the thought.

When he awoke, he was refreshed but anxious. Alone in the darkness, he had no idea of the time, but he dared not leave the room. Presently Cavanaugh appeared with a candle.

"You've been asleep all day and almost through the night," he said, sitting down on the other pallet.

He was prepared for the usual flurry of questions and patiently explained how he and his family came to be emancipated and what it was like to live a free man. He and his family had been given their freedom and this piece of land by their owner, Richard Cavanaugh. It was beyond Henry's comprehension that this man would risk his own hard-earned freedom by helping runaways. He couldn't imagine putting Flora and the children in such danger.

"There's been no sign of Ampy and his family, I'm sorry to say. You should not stay any longer, so we must prepare you for the next leg of your journey."

He led Henry to the kitchen where a hot and satisfying meal was waiting. Other than the two, the house seemed empty of the family that Henry had assumed lived there. Better not to involve the children, he figured.

When the sun came up, a wagon was waiting, its horses already hitched. Henry lay down in the wagon bed, as instructed, and was quickly covered with an old sheet and then with layers of hay. There was just enough room at the edge of the pile for him to breathe. Without delay, the wagon rolled out of the farmyard. Henry was hot, itchy, and uncomfortable but eager to be moved on.

He couldn't see, but he could hear and feel, and presently he knew that they had traveled from a rutted lane to a gravel road and from the quiet countryside into a bustling city. Stop and start. Stop and start. His stomach rumbled ominously, but at last the wagon stopped and stayed. Hands reached in to haul away the hay—friendly hands that then pulled off the sheet and helped him down from the wagon. He was in an enclosed area behind a house, somewhere in a city. Cavanaugh led him gently to the door and knocked.

A woman opened to them, and Cavanaugh said, "Good day, I've got another traveler for you, Mrs. Quinn."

8 November 1813

On the St. Lawrence River

*I*n the army's view, the battered Quinn was fully recovered, so he was assigned to lead a rifle company at Sacket's Harbor. He had quickly adapted to the loss of his two fingers, but the headaches and maddening ringing in his ears persisted. Moreover, the monotony of the endless drilling, as well as the heat and bugs and dampness in the bog where they were camped, and now Wilkinson's noxious presence, were taking a toll.

Quinn thought he had taken a shortcut to hell. Wilkinson's incompetence was on display the moment he arrived. His ego, his disdain for logistics, his inability to see beyond his own narrow interests, his constant delaying of the Montreal invasion—it was all Quinn could do to keep his men disciplined and ready for battle. Without thoughts of Sally and her affectionate letters, he couldn't have gone on.

The only other bright note was the assignment of Colonel Scott by Armstrong to Wilkinson's command. Wilkinson was not pleased, but Quinn believed that Wilkinson, bullheaded and irrational, could not ignore Scott's intelligence and experience, nor withstand his forceful personality.

In any case, they were finally on the move and, despite worsening late-fall weather, the men were grateful to leave the miserable camp. Quinn and his squad of riflemen were sent to guard the rear of Wilkinson's five-mile-long flotilla of flat-bottom boats floating down the St. Lawrence River. Even traveling on foot, the rear guard easily kept pace with the flotilla, slowed by the river's rapids. This slowness, though, made them vulnerable to constant British and Canadian fire. Quinn felt in perpetual retreat, always liable to get pinned down and lose contact with the main body.

"Ensign, sir, I'm sorry. I'm sorry. I tried to recover Dunston's body, but the Limeys tried to ventilate me. They was lurking about, just waiting for someone to fetch him."

Kentucky volunteer Private Jack Duncan dutifully informed Quinn of Private Coby Dunston's bloody demise, but the report was more than a duty. He was seeking forgiveness.

"I had to leave him where he died," Duncan continued sorrowfully. "Sir, he was my closest friend! Our families been friends in Boonesboro ever since we came over the mountains. We were supposed to keep watch over each other. How can I tell them I didn't? How can I face them?"

Quinn had spotted the pair's affinity. Good company commanders noticed friendships—or enmities—among the men. For Kentucky frontiersmen like Frake and Duncan, kinship, friendship, duty, and patriotism were more than words. They laid down their lives simply because it was their duty.

"Listen," Quinn said, turning to the boy. "First of all, it's *my* duty to write his kin with the bad news. I aim to do it soon as we catch up with the rest. I'll tell them of your loyal friendship. You have no cause for regret. Look at me. Private, you hear me? You. Had. No. Choice. You were duty-bound to save yourself."

"That sounds like crap," Duncan said as the two pushed through the undergrowth, trying once again to catch up with the rest of the riflemen after the latest skirmish.

Their conversation was on the run and continued only as they stopped and gasped for breath or to try to figure out the best way to go.

"Does it?" Quinn panted. "You promised to take care of each other? Well, *could* you have saved him? No. And would he want you killed dragging his dead body back? You are completely blameless, Duncan."

"I should have been watching closer."

"Oh? How many shots do you have in your musket?" They took off again, running, ducking under fallen tree limbs and skirting bramble bushes.

Now they came to a rocky crag and paused to see if they'd been followed.

"Even if you'd seen the danger you two walked into, you *might* have killed one of them. But there were half a dozen? Were you going to take the rest out single-handedly with your bayonet? If there's a fault, it's mine for sending you two out alone."

They were moving quickly again, their hushed conversation interrupted by their labored breathing.

"Sir, I know what you're trying to do. But I ain't blaming you."

"Then why are you blaming yourself?"

"'Cause my friend is dead."

"Look, Duncan, when the war is over, you can go take the blame for anything you like. Watch that branch." Quinn stopped and turned to the young man.

"Right now, I don't need you moping around. I need every man's talents—and you have many—to keep us alive. Unless you keep all your wits about you, more people are gonna die. And self-pity won't bring Coby back."

Quinn heard a twig snap and paused to listen. It might be the footfall of the enemy or just an animal prowling for food. After a moment, he went on.

"But there's plenty you can do to get the rest of us, including me, out of this war alive. For that, I'll be beholden to you."

Every junior officer eventually found himself having to balance sympathy with straight talk. Keeping that equilibrium in front of the troops took daily effort; how well an ensign or lieutenant managed it could mean the difference between life and death. And most of them were plagued with their *own* doubts. Having the most combat experience among the junior officers, Quinn was looked to as an example, and he knew it. He'd seen too many officers seek solace in the bottle. Others froze in indecision. He'd seen the disasters that it could cause.

He lived with his subordinates, heard their complaints and questions, and knew his answers could destroy or build morale and discipline. His greatest dilemma was how to ignore the obvious incompetence of superior officers while maintaining discipline. If he tried to justify neglect and foolishness to his men, he would destroy his own credibility. If he promised better times and better decisions that never came, how could he be trusted?

Wilkinson blamed others for any setbacks. But now, moving on Montreal, his incompetence was on display. Moreover, as the march toward Montreal progressed, he appeared increasingly afflicted with an illness the physicians could neither diagnose nor cure (though he found whiskey medicinal). At last he declared himself incapacitated and withdrew each night to the comfort of his tent.

The current of the St. Lawrence was so rapid that a log set adrift would cover the one hundred and eighty miles from Kingston to Montreal in two days. Thanks to Wilkinson's many and manifest failures, the column had covered eighty miles in eight days, ample time for a modest British force to overtake them. By the time Wilkinson's army reached the difficult Long Sault Rapids—still one hundred and twenty miles from Montreal—two British gunboats and five hundred well-trained regulars and militia under the command of Colonel Joseph Morrison had caught up with the American rear. Morrison now posed a real threat to the mission.

Wilkinson didn't want his boats to come under fire while shooting the rapids, so once camped on the American side, he ordered Brigadier General John Boyd to clear the river's north shore where Morrison's men could be seen gathering. That wet and cold November morning, Boyd and some twenty-five hundred men crossed in boats to the north bank to confront the enemy. It should have been a cakewalk.

11 November 1813

Crysler's Farm, Ontario, Canada

Shit, I knew it! Quinn thought as he struggled through the underbrush with Duncan close on his heels. *We've lost contact with the main body.*

Duncan was badly shaken by his friend's death, but Quinn regretted letting himself be diverted. They had missed the river transport back to the main force. They might have been given up for dead or captured. Whatever the case, the rest of the rear guard had headed downstream without them.

Here on the river's north side they were likely to run into British and Canadian troops. Sure enough, after about an hour, he heard commotion ahead—voices, horses, and wagons moving. Quinn and Duncan crept forward and peered through the trees at hundreds of British regulars and Canadian militia setting up for battle. Colonel Morrison had established his headquarters in the Crysler family's homestead, and his men were digging in, a defensive tactic.

Quinn and Duncan's arrival behind the Canadian formation was a stroke of luck. They could assess the size, position, and armaments of the enemy forces and inform the American command across the river or the troops across the clearing. *If* they could get to them.

The two turned back and headed to the river, ready to signal the Americans to send a boat for them, but the opposite bank was too far away for them to signal without giving away their position. If he and Duncan ran along the riverbank, British regulars and their gunboats would spot them. Instead, they faded back into the trees, searching for a route that would skirt the British to the north and bring them to the Americans on the east side of the field.

The terrain was difficult. The British left flank was protected by a thick, black oak swamp but was otherwise unguarded. The enemy's force consisted of seven to eight hundred men, Canadian Fencibles and Voltigeurs, Provincial Light Dragoons, the regulars of the British 49th, and scores of Indian braves. It was a far smaller force than Wilkinson had sent to confront them, but most of the Americans were green and untested. The Canadians had a few field pieces and several cannon mounted on a small flotilla of gunboats anchored in the river on their right flank. They spread themselves in a line two deep across the seven hundred yards between the river and the swamp. In front of them were two ravines, which the Americans would have to cross to reach the British position.

Boyd, Quinn knew, would recognize the enemy's advantage. He scanned the ranks for Wilkinson in vain— probably back in his tent with his whiskey and laudanum.

Quinn and Duncan slogged through the swamp. The Americans needed to know that the entire enemy force was deployed on the field. No British reserves lurked in the woods, and that flank seemed wonderfully vulnerable. Also, the British regulars were wearing their grey winter coats and might be mistaken for inexperienced Canadian militia.

Boyd sent a brigade into the swamp to attack the British left flank from the north while the main body of his troops began a full frontal assault. Quinn, still splashing through the marsh, glimpsed the American battle line and winced. There was so discipline, no focus. Some whooped and cheered. Some knelt and fired before the enemy was in rifle range. Others advanced in ragged lines or rushed forward before the order to charge.

Meanwhile, the disciplined British and Canadians stood shoulder to shoulder, perfectly still. The Americans reached the ravines, and still the disciplined enemy held fire until, as the Americans advanced up the incline, British officers shouted in perfect unison, "Ready. Present. Fire."

Those were the last words dozens of the Americans ever heard. Some fell dead or wounded. The rest hesitated or bolted as a second volley hit them. More fell, and those who didn't, panicked, running until they were well out of range. Boyd did his best to regroup.

By this time, the American brigade aimed at the British left flank was in position. Formed up in the swamp where Quinn and Duncan were heading, they fired a series of volleys that ripped into the British lines. Unfazed, the men of the British 49th reformed again, shoulder to shoulder, and on command executed a perfect backward wheel with a precision more characteristic of a parade ground than of a battlefield. Suddenly, the Americans were looking down the barrels of four ranks of British regulars. The first rank fired and reloaded while the second rank fired. An instant later, a volley exploded from the third rank—and then the fourth, and then again from the first.

Just then, Quinn and Duncan arrived in the chaos. The two most senior officers had been killed immediately, leaving Quinn the most senior officer present. Staring up at the British muskets, he knew it was hopeless. If they were to be of any use in the attack on Montreal, they needed to get out now—and quickly. He ordered retreat.

The British officers, seeing the threat to their left dissipate, promptly returned their full attention to the front. American reinforcements had arrived and were regrouping for another attack. Wilkinson, who had been observing the disaster from afar, had committed more than a third of his eight-thousand-man force to a useless battle for ground he had no intention of holding.

The fighting went on for hours until darkness, cold, rain, and sleet convinced both sides that they had had enough. The Americans went back to their boats, and the British and Canadians remained in the field, exactly where both sides had begun the day. Quinn and his bedraggled men plodded through thigh-high muck to rejoin the main force and continue down the river to Montreal.

It was a pointless battle. Wilkinson had not put a stop to the harassment; the pesky gnats were still nipping at his behind. He had wasted men, ammunition, and arms. He had lost the confidence of the men. And he had jeopardized the timing of the joint attack on Montreal.

It was a disaster, and every man under his command knew it. Of course, the general blamed everyone but himself. Rumor had it that he might call off the attack on Montreal, but that would be both a logistical nightmare and another disgrace for him. He had no choice but to push on.

Eventually, the army reached Cornwall on the Canadian side, about ninety miles upstream from Montreal. Quinn was surprised to find Frake waiting there with the even more surprising news that General Hampton had deferred the assault on Montreal and settled into winter quarters in New York to plan a new attack for spring.

12 November 1813

Cornwall, Ontario

*W*ilkinson called a council of war to decide whether to proceed or to abandon the Montreal campaign. Actually, he had already decided.

"Gentlemen, you know that the cowardly and disloyal Hampton has sabotaged this campaign," he began. "I should arrest him and proceed to Montreal without him!"

He stared into each face to see if anyone dared contradict him.

"Sir, I don't think you can have him arrested." It was Winfield Scott, in an attempt at tact.

"Yes, I can. I'm his superior officer!" Wilkinson hissed, but Scott knew better.

He had been a party to the discussion between Armstrong and the two contending generals when the secretary of war had agreed that Hampton would report directly to him.

"Yes, sir," Scott conceded, "but perhaps we should simply ignore General Hampton. As you say, we've got sufficient force to move on Montreal ourselves—eight thousand men, six hundred bateaux, sufficient provisions and ammunition. We've traveled so far that it's only a short way now to Montreal. And we believe it's lightly defended."

General Boyd spoke up. "Perhaps we outnumber them, but we could be caught between the troops that outfought us at Crysler's Farm and those that sent Hampton retreating. We could be surrounded."

Now Quinn unexpectedly stepped forward from the cluster of junior officers. "Sir, I have it on good authority that the force Hampton fled from was small, only about one thousand men."

"Your name, ensign?" Wilkinson asked coldly.

"William Quinn, sir."

"And who is your good authority? That messenger fellow, Ensign Jake?"

"Frake, sir. Yes."

"Why the hell isn't Rake here?" he demanded. "I summoned all officers. Bring him here."

"Not possible, sir," Quinn said.

Wilkinson whirled on him. "Why the hell not?" he bellowed.

"Because he has already left."

"Without my permission? Captain," he shouted to his aide, "send men after that deserter!"

"Sir, he's militia, and his enlistment has expired, so he's a civilian and out of your reach. I expect he's halfway back to Kentucky by now."

"*I'll* decide who's answerable to me! Captain, get started. Chase him all the way to New Orleans if you have to, but get him back here. *Now.*"

"Sir, if I may. I've known Frake for more than a year. We fought together at Fort Wayne, Queenston, Frenchtown, and York. If he says there were only a thousand enemy there, then that's a fact."

Scott stood silently by, watching Wilkinson waver. Scott suspected, with good reason, that Wilkinson didn't want to attack Montreal by himself, but if only one thousand men stood in the way, he had no choice. He must go to Montreal or face humiliation and ridicule. If Frake hadn't shown up... if Quinn had kept his mouth shut... But every officer in the room now knew what had to be done: push on to Montreal.

"General, if I ma—" Quinn ventured, but Scott cut him off before he could get himself court martialed.

"No, Mr. Quinn, you may *not*," Scott barked, then turned to Wilkinson. "Sir, we are unprepared to winter in this region. By spring—"

But Wilkinson's gaze clung to Quinn, and his voice dropped to a sinister whisper. "Tell me, ensign, how you know so much about warfare." He smirked and glanced around at the other officers. No one met his eye.

"Ensign Quinn, be silent!" Scott ordered, but it was too late.

"With respect, sir," Quinn said, his voice rising. "I've seen enough mismanagement to choke a horse. I'm sick of self-important, ignorant, petty, jealous—"

The stunned silence was broken by Wilkinson. "I'll have you court martialed, you insolent *boy*."

Quinn could tolerate no more. He exploded, all caution now forgotten. "Perhaps, but a court marital would be no greater disgrace than serving under your command, *sir*. You turned near-certain victory into disaster. If anyone should be court martialed, you should for all the wasted blood on your hands."

Scott had never heard a superior officer so brutally dressed down so directly by a subordinate. Everyone shifted uncomfortably and stared at the floor. The disagreement over the Montreal attack had been respectful till now. Some, like Scott and Quinn, favored attacking at once. Others wanted to defer the battle till spring. But this was a different matter entirely.

Wilkinson ordered Quinn arrested and secured in one of the outbuildings.

As soon as the door slammed behind the ensign and his guards, the general snarled. "I will convene a court martial, and all of you will, by God, testify to what has occurred here tonight."

Scott shook his head. The three court martial officers could not be drawn from the same pool as the witnesses, so protocol would require that three independent officers be summoned from Hampton's command. But Wilkinson would never allow any of Hampton's officers to sit in judgment in his command, especially when Wilkinson's own actions would come under scrutiny.

This, Scott thought, *is all too familiar.* As a lawyer's apprentice in 1806, he had attended Aaron Burr's trial for treason. Wilkinson had been the government's star witness, and Scott had never wavered in his belief that Burr was guilty—and that Wilkinson was in on the plot.

He turned to the general. "Sir, may I have a word? In private, if you please."

"See me in my quarters later," Wilkinson said. Rising unsteadily on his feet, he addressed the other officers. "I have decided...I have decided that we will proceed to winter quarters. No more discussion. You are dismissed."

Back at his rooms, Wilkinson greeted Scott coldly. "I'm not going to change my mind."

"About what, general?"

Wilkinson was caught off guard. Had Scott come to urge an attack on Montreal or to plead Quinn's case?

"State your business, colonel, or get the hell out."

How do I mollify this fool? Scott wondered as Wilkinson called for his orderly.

Ignoring Scott until the orderly entered, the general muttered, "Private, get me my, um, medications."

"Yes, sir. Should I summon the surgeon?"

"Curse your eyes, private. Do what you're told."

"Yes, sir." The private saluted and departed.

Now the silence intimidated Wilkinson.

"Spit it out, Colonel Scott. What the hell is on your mind?"

Scott drew himself up. "Give me a brigade, and I'll take Montreal. You get the credit, and Hampton gets shamed."

Wilkinson stared. He wanted time to think, but Scott wouldn't allow it.

"And while you're thinking about that, general, let me suggest that you go easy on Ensign Quinn. We can't lose our heads over this matter."

"*Which* matter?" Wilkinson asked. "Montreal or Quinn?"

Scott nodded thoughtfully. "A half dozen years ago, you court martialed another junior officer for conduct unbecoming."

Wilkinson's head was aching. He was ill. He knew he was ill, and the surgeon was an idiot. He glared at Scott. "What about it?"

"He called you a scoundrel," Scott said. "He threatened to bomb you."

"I don't remember."

"Sure you do. It was I."

If Wilkinson *did* remember, his pride made him deny it. "I don't recall. But what of it?"

He had played right into Scott's hand.

"Well, sir, how important was it if you don't even remember? Why concern yourself with Quinn's insolence?"

"Are you asking me to ignore—"

"I'm asking you to send him with me to Montreal. That will shape him up."

"No one's going to Montreal, Colonel. Not you *or* that insolent ensign. I plan to have him shot."

"I don't think so," Scott said. "You'll have a hard time convicting an officer with his record. Quinn has been on the front lines, been shot at, been taken prisoner, lost some fingers, and was nearly killed at York. And need I remind you that those officers sitting in judgment of Quinn—and you—have to be from someone else's command. Like Hampton's?"

But Wilkinson's jaw remained stubbornly set.

Scott sighed then spoke quietly. "Here's what you are going to do. You will release Quinn from custody and drop any thought of a court martial. You've botched this campaign, and going after Quinn will be the final straw. If you proceed against him, you will answer directly to President Madison, and your friend Armstrong won't be able to save you."

"Madison? What the hell are you talking about?"

"If you knew the men whose lives are in your hands, you would know that Ensign Quinn has a special relationship with the White House. He corresponds with a young lady who works for Dolley Madison and lives at the executive mansion. Quinn and Ensign Frake have dined with the president and were his overnight guests. Mr. Quinn is not a man who would use his relationship with the Madisons to save himself. But I would. You will drop this matter, or I will take Quinn's case directly to them."

By now Wilkinson's face was deep crimson, but Scott went on. "I'm in an accommodating mood. Obviously, Quinn cannot remain under your command. I will take him with me to Montreal."

Wilkinson sat down heavily.

"If I cannot take him with me, give him the same deal that I got from my court martial," Scott said, "suspension from the military for a year and forfeiture of emoluments."

That would be a bitter pill for Quinn, but his outburst directed at Wilkinson couldn't be tolerated without diminishing respect for every senior officer. But after suspension from the army for a year, the ensign could return to military service, and Scott was confident that Quinn would do very well.

Wilkinson was cornered and angry, but even he could recognize a face-saving out. The court martial board would approve Scott's recommendation, but the general would not allow him to march on Montreal. Wilkinson and Hampton were dug in for the winter.

As 1813 ended, the war dragged on. And Quinn returned to Baltimore, in disgrace.

2 January 1814
The White House, Washington, D.C.

Quinn's presence at the White House was announced as Sally and Dolley were checking the list of ambassadors invited to the next White House reception.

The first lady rose at once and said to Sally, "Go. Freshen up; take your time. Then meet us in the side sitting room. I'll keep Mr. Quinn occupied. It never hurts to let a young man wait a bit. And don't fret. You look absolutely stunning."

Sally smiled gratefully and hurried to her bedchamber. She supposed he had stopped to see his family. When he'd written to them about his court martial, his mother had been devastated and his brothers furious. They'd assured him there was always room in the linen business, but Sally knew he was uncertain about what to do next.

When Sally entered the sitting room, Dolley turned to her.

"Mr. Quinn was telling me so many interesting things about our war on the northern frontier," she said, but Sally's eyes were locked on Will as if they were alone in the room.

War, she knew, changes people, and she saw alterations in Quinn. His fair Irish face had coarsened. The long months in rough weather, the scars of combat, and the stresses of prison had turned it leathery and creased. His hair had thinned, his body grown more sinewy. Unconsciously, it seemed, he kept his left hand with its two missing fingers in his pocket. And she recognized something troubling in his eyes—a distance, as if he focused on a place apart. That unseen place would have to be approached cautiously and with permission.

He stood, and then she was in his arms, weeping.

Dolley left them together and shut the door behind her.

Quinn held her tightly, renewing her confidence that he was still the man she loved.

"We should sit," he whispered.

They sat on the nearest divan, turned to face each other, and kissed deeply. During all those months, lonely though rarely alone, she had wondered, *Would he still care?* All the tears she had suppressed flowed now, and Quinn, staid Irishman that he was, didn't know what to do about all this weeping.

"Just hold me," she whispered and then laughed softly. She turned her face to him, and he brushed away her tears. "Please tell me you are all right, you are whole, you are the same person," she said, touching his wrist.

"Yes, lass, I am who I was. My God, you are wonderful to see. You are so…beautiful."

"You too." Now her tears gave way to laughter. "You must tell me everything."

"In due course." His voice was husky. "But for now there are things I want to forget." He sighed. "I'm angry. I can't help it. So many dead. Men left without legs and arms. Some with their eyes blown out. They'll never see again. This infernal ringing in my ears—but at least I can still hear. Some are totally deaf. What will their lives be like?"

She had no answer, and he went on.

"The worst of the wounded were carried to the surgeon's tent. Some even managed to walk there, God knows how. The doctors were overwhelmed. They had to treat the ones with the best chance to survive. The others waited outside on stretchers or on the ground, dying like dogs next to the piles of arms and legs the doctors had sawed off."

He saw her horror. "But, Sally, they *had* to do it. They couldn't risk gangrene. Some screamed they'd rather be dead. Those piles of arms and legs…the ones who just died waiting…" His voice trailed off.

Sally felt him pull slightly away from her. It was selfish, she knew, to want him as he used to be. They had shared their nightmares back in the Northwest, but now…

"Sally, I'm sorry," Quinn began, and she caught her breath, afraid he might be saying good-bye. "I'm truly sorry that I told you all that. I shouldn't burden you."

She was so relieved she nearly laughed again. "Oh, I don't want you to carry your burdens alone. You mustn't." After a moment she asked, "Do you want to tell me about, um…?" She didn't know exactly how to refer to his court martial.

He nodded, knowing what she meant. "I won't say I didn't deserve to be disciplined. The army can't allow insubordination. I wouldn't tolerate it from a man under me." He looked down at his hands. "I don't know what comes over me. I hear my words as if they're coming from someone else, someone so angry it scares me."

"You had a right to be mad."

"But not like that. It started out…I was just trying to urge Wilkinson to act. But the military is full of people like him who won't abide any disagreement."

"He should have listened."

"But he didn't, and I should have known I couldn't reason with him. As if shouting at him would do any good! He was too besotted with whiskey and self-importance. I should have left it to Scott."

She said nothing for a moment then tentatively said, "So now when you feel like blowing up at someone, you'll remember Wilkinson. By the way, he's been removed from command and will face a court of inquiry. The president's orders."

Quinn grinned and looked for a moment like his old self. "Good." He looked up at the lacquered crown molding as if he had just noticed where he was.

Sally couldn't hold back the question at the forefront of her mind. "What are your plans?"

Quinn paused. "I don't really know. The army's out for now. Maybe the family business? I never wanted that, but my notions of settling out West are gone after what I've seen of the frontier."

"I'm not much for returning there either," Sally said. "But you know that."

"Sometimes I feel as if it doesn't matter what I do. Plans always get overturned, so why even make any? I made a lot of plans and some rotten choices. Fighting in a war run by idiots. Getting myself run out of the army. What's the use?"

Sally looked away. "What would Frake say to that?" she asked.

"Well, I said it to him too, and…well, I can't really tell you what he told me."

"Oh, I can imagine." She giggled and eased the tension. "How is he?"

"He's okay. Staying with my family in Baltimore."

"What's he doing there?" She was surprised, presuming that he would return to Kentucky.

"His enlistment was up. He's trying to decide what to do too. He doesn't have much family left in Kentucky. You know Frake. He's most at home when he's on the move. He figures a good war won't come along that often, and he can go back to hunting possum anytime."

Sally smiled again.

"Actually, a lot of Kentucky riflemen *have* gone home. They didn't join up to hang around some camp while generals bumble around. Before long, the twelve thousand we started with will be down to less than half that many."

"I thought you and Frake were separated when he got assigned to Hampton."

"We were. But Hampton sent Frake to tell Wilkinson he was deferring the attack. Wilkinson blamed Frake for the bad news and dispatched a squad to bring him back. But he was still secretly in camp. They probably got all the way to Kentucky before they gave up." Quinn chuckled, relaxed a little, and went on to tell Sally about his court martial.

Suddenly he stopped talking. "I'm sorry. Here I've been talking about myself all this time. What about you? How have you fared here?"

"From frontier family to the White House in less than a year. It is astonishing," Sally said, straightening in her seat. "I certainly wasn't prepared for it. But Mrs. Madison is wonderful. She includes me in just about everything. I keep her schedule. She has *no* free time. I don't understand where she gets her energy. I help her with her correspondence, and there is a mountain of it. You know she writes regularly to Abigail Adams? She's friends with the wives of most of the important men, so she knows things that are very helpful to the president."

"Yeah, I bet," Quinn said, wondering what she might know about Armstrong.

"You know," Sally continued, "because Jefferson was a widower while he was president, and Madison was his secretary of state, Dolley was already acting as the nation's hostess. Everyone knows about her balls and receptions. Ladies imitate the way she dresses."

"Really?" Quinn tried unsuccessfully to look interested.

"Oh, you," she said, playfully poking him. "But listen. She's got great political instincts, and Mr. Madison values her advice. Some people in Washington would be truly upset to know how much he listens to *a woman*. Perish the thought! Of course, he doesn't *always* take her advice, but he always respects her opinions. She just has a natural ability to charm people, to calm them. Whenever there is friction at one of her soirees, she can always settle things down."

"*Soiree?*"

"Well, Willie, there's more to life than shooting squirrels." She giggled.

"Yeah, shooting Brits."

"What I'm saying is that what she does so well publicly, she also does privately."

"So what is she advising the president about the war?

"I don't exactly know, but I've overheard dining room banter and such, and she agrees with Monroe that Armstrong should go."

"Any chance?"

"I don't know. But they're all worried about Washington. Armstrong thinks the British aren't interested in the place."

"For God's sake, can't the president of the United States, the commander in chief just tell Armstrong what to do? Or do it himself?"

"It's not that simple," Sally said. "It's about politics. If he removes Armstrong, he upsets the Federalists, and their support is already shaky. They talk about seceding from the Union and ending the war on their own terms. That could mean a civil war."

He nodded. "I know it's complicated, but we've got thousands of men under arms, thousands dead or wounded, and we don't have the guts to finish what we started. Maybe the Northeast *wants* the Brits stopping their shipping and grabbing their sailors and hijacking their ships."

She sighed. "It's a mess. But the president and Mr. Monroe may just go around Armstrong. They want to establish a separate military district in and around Washington and appoint someone who'd report directly to the president. That makes the defense of Washington purely an internal matter. It's roundabout, but William, you have no idea how close we are to having the country come apart at the seams. Southern planters don't think they have anything in common with Northern farmers and merchants, and the other way around."

"Speaking of southern planters." Quinn lowered his voice. "There's a runaway slave hiding at my family's house."

"What?"

"Truly. Imagine my surprise when I got home." He shrugged. "But that's my mother. I take it that she never told you either."

"No, and I'm surprised. I thought they considered me a member of the family. I can't imagine where they got that idea," she said, looking slyly at Quinn.

He cleared his throat, quickly returning to the subject of Henry. "He's working in the business, mastering the loom. Used to be a great shoemaker and makes some money on the side fixing boots and shoes for folks."

"Wait, wait," she said, holding up her hand. Something in her mind clicked. "Where did he come from?"

"Washington, I think."

Sally's expression went from puzzled to amazed. "I think I know him!"

"The slave? How could you?"

"What's his name? It has to be Henry."

Now it was Quinn's turn to be surprised. "How did you know? I mean, it was, but he's changed it. How do you know him?"

"If he's a shoemaker, he escaped from Caleb Kilfoyle, the merchant. He's free! Thank God!"

She now was bouncing in her chair as they shared descriptions—old enough to have a young family, handsome, well spoken, able to read and calculate. Definitely the same man.

"But...how in the world did he end up with your family? Isn't it dangerous? Won't they find him? What will happen if they do?"

"One thing at a time! When he saw what his prospects were in Baltimore, he decided to stay on for a time. My mother and brothers recognized him right off as a hard worker. It's risky, but it's just as risky traveling north with a war going on."

"But what if he gets recognized? Won't Kilfoyle try to find him?"

"Maybe. But the slave hunters by now might figure he died in some swamp where they lost him. Besides, there's a lot easier game out there with so many runaways trying to sign on with the Brits. We've fixed him up with proper papers that say he's a freeborn black whose mama was freed by a kind mistress. Baltimore is full of free black folks, not like the Deep South."

"What would happen to your mother and brothers, though, if he were found?"

"Up to now, they've just given them a place to rest and sent them along to the next safe house. Never kept anyone on before. In Maryland, the penalty is usually just a fine, 'cause the main idea is to return the property to the rightful owner. Anyway, after the war, he can get to Canada or England. Funny thing, a black man can be free in England, but an Irishman can't be free in Ireland."

Sally wanted details now. How did Henry get away? Quinn had heard the story directly from Henry, and he answered all her questions. When he came to the sale of Henry's family in Alexandria—his mother's suicide, his wife and daughter sold to the lecher, his son to God-knew-what—Ampy's family, the slave hunters, the dogs and his narrow escape, Sally sat strangely mesmerized as if by some grisly accident. She couldn't have dreamed such a nightmare.

"Sally, I've upset you again. I'm sorry," he said.

She did not see the hand he extended to her. How was it possible that people could do this? How take away a man's wife, his children? It was savage! It was... She thought of her own family and wondered whether their slaughter had not in the end been more merciful than the fate of Henry's wife and children. She thought of Henry earning money for Kilfoyle.

"This, this cannot be!" she said, hoping that Quinn would take it all back, as if it were a bad joke, a tale to frighten children.

Quinn was flummoxed. He ought not to have told her all this. He had come to talk with her about their marriage, but a passionate discussion of slavery was a poor preamble to a romantic proposal.

"Sally, please." He began the speech he had memorized for the occasion, but he simply blurted out, "I came here to ask for your hand in marriage. I wrote you that I would do it proper."

She was still absorbing Henry's tragedy, but now her mouth fell open. "Wha...? You said...I'm sorry, what?" She sank back onto the divan.

"I planned this. I kind of memorized a speech. I didn't mean to spring it on you, but then you asked about Henry and..."

Sally's mind was swirling with outrage about Henry, with surprise about the Quinns, with the sight of Will. And it was that that overcame the rest—the sight of Will. She fell into his arms, sobbing, her whole body shaking with powerful emotions.

"Yes, yes, of course I will."

"I'm...I'm sorry. I had planned to get down on one knee. I had this poem with me..."

"You silly! If you had read me a poem, I would have thought that it was someone else proposing. And I would have said no."

"Please don't say no now."

She kissed him deeply then pulled back to look at his face. In it she saw caution, uncertainty, a qualification. "What is it, William?"

Quinn was again groping for words, wondering why he'd not been blessed with the gift of blarney like his brothers.

"I want to marry you, but...not right now."

3-8 January 1814
Washington, D.C./Baltimore

Quinn had left and Sally was dabbing her reddened eyes with a handkerchief when Mrs. Madison encountered Sally in the hall, rushing back to her room.

"He didn't ask you to marry him?" Mrs. Madison demanded. A look of disbelief, sympathy and—was it anger?—crossed her face. "I just assumed he'd arrived to sweep you off your feet with his surprise. How romantic that would have been!" She could have bitten her tongue before the words were out. "I'm so sorry, my dear." Dolley enfolded Sally in her ample bosom.

Sally pulled back from the embrace, sniffled, and said, "He did propose...in a way. He just doesn't think it's the right time...the war...the court martial. He says life is too uncertain."

"Life is always uncertain, child. For all of us." Dolley sighed. "We have to take our happiness where and when we can. I hope Mr. Quinn learns that very soon."

"He thought," Sally said, gasping for air, "that maybe I wouldn't love him after the war was over. That maybe he'd be horribly disfigured. Or maybe that he'd die." The word intensified her crying. "He said he couldn't leave me a widow, that it wouldn't be right."

"I thought his fighting days were over after the court marital. Why would he even think about returning to fight?"

"He and Frake want to join Commodore Barney's bargemen fighting the British on the Chesapeake."

"What? Why?"

"Something about unfinished business. Mrs. Madison, he has changed. I expected that, but I didn't know he would become so vengeful. He is so bitter. It's as if he doesn't know himself anymore. Do *I* really know him?"

"War changes men, my dear. Something inside gets altered in a way that we who don't fight can't quite understand. Just give him time." She didn't quite believe her own assurances, but she had been a widow herself. "Look at me, my dear. If my first husband had lived, my life would have been much different—better? worse?—but we must live the life we have."

At the linen mill, Quinn's thoughts could be drowned out by the clanking and growling of the Spinning Jennies, Spinning Mules, and other newfangled machines spawned by what people were calling an industrial revolution. A steam engine could power textile works even in regions lacking the rapid rivers and waterfalls of the Northeast.

The Quinn brothers had stepped into their father's shoes, saving and working other jobs to buy the latest machinery. Quinn headed to the back office, watching out of the corner of his eye the women observing him—the other brother, the soldier. A shadow fell across his path, and Malachy grabbed him by the arm, hustling him into the office.

"What sort of fool are you?" Malachy asked.

"Not you too! Mother just finished giving me the same dressing down. Mother of God, when will everyone stop trying to live my life?"

"Maybe when you start living it yourself. We all have lives, brother, but we wouldn't be doing you a favor by keeping our mouths shut. I've heard this load of guff about the war and how you can't commit because of the uncertainty. I know better. What's really going on, huh?"

Quinn wasn't taken aback. He paused, cast his eyes down on the pine planking, and shuffled his feet. Turning, he looked out the door at the women and the machinery then turned back to Malachy.

"I want to fight."

"What?"

"As simple as that, I want to fight."

"Because they're Limeys?"

"Sure. Partly. But I don't think that's the main reason."

"What the hell you talking about?"

"I don't know. It's just something that I feel, real deep."

"You mean you want to go out and kill men?"

"It's not the killing itself. No, I get no pleasure from that."

"Then what is it? You're not talking sense."

Quinn plopped himself in one of the office's rickety wooden chairs. "I can't explain it. But ever since I've gone into battle, I've had this feeling. I can't describe it."

"You've got demons, brother. You ought to go see Father O'Malley."

"Demons. Maybe you're right. I don't know. It makes as much sense as anything else. All I know is that this war, this bloodletting, has done something to me. It's like I have to do it. Like I have to work it out. Almost like I don't care anymore if I get killed. I mean, look at me—missing two fingers, got my head battered and nearly died. Constant damnable ringing in my head. Yet I need to go back. It's like there's nothing else I want to do."

"Well, fortunately, the army won't have you just now. So you can put those thoughts aside."

"Actually, there is something me and Frake have been discussing."

"Frake." Malachy let out a sigh. "How long does he plan to hang around here anyway? Business is good enough that we could put him to work in the mill." He shrugged. "So what are you two talking about?"

"You know about the British raids on the Chesapeake, out on the bay?"

"Gonna paddle out in your canoe and take on the whole British fleet, is that it?"

"Maybe you're closer than you think. We've heard about gunboats that slip out there and harass the Brits. Might not do all that much damage, but at least we can get some licks in."

"So this is all about getting even with the Brits for everything they've put us through?"

"I don't know. But Frake and I are going to scout it out anyway."

"Willie, you're not the man I knew when you left Baltimore a couple of years ago. You're hesitant, confused. I think you're going off half-assed, but I don't know what to tell you."

"Then don't tell me anything."

16 August 1814

St. Michaels, Maryland

$\mathcal{S}$t. Michaels was small but important. From its boatyards came the vessels that privateers sailed to harass the British on the bay and to run their blockades. A dozen miles directly southeast of Annapolis across the Chesapeake, the town nestled unobtrusively among the marshes and lowlands where the Miles River emptied into the bay. And there Joshua Barney built his fleet of gunboats.

Barney was an old salt who had gone to sea before the War of Independence. As a teenage apprentice, he found himself in command of a merchantman when its captain unexpectedly died. During the war, he captained a privateer and later served in both the Continental and the French navies. That service with France made him ineligible for an American naval command.

So when the War of 1812 began, he returned to privateering with spectacular success: eighteen enemy ships sunk or captured. Those taken, along with their cargoes, were valued at an impressive 1.4 million dollars, and he accomplished all this in a mere four months with his thirteen-gun schooner *Rosie* and a crew of one hundred

and twenty men. When he returned and saw Chesapeake
Bay at the mercy of British marauders, he fired off an
indignant letter and a plan of defense to Secretary of the
Navy William Jones.

There were eight thousand British seamen off Chesapeake
Bay on eleven ships of the line, thirty-three frigates, and
thirty-eight sloops. That kind of force was meant to do more
than merely frighten a few villages, Barney knew. Its larger
purpose was to attack Baltimore, Norfolk, Alexandria,
and Washington itself. In his memorandum to Jones,
he suggested creating a squadron of gunboats to harass
the British.

> A kind of barge or row-galley, so constructed as to
> draw a small draft of water, to carry oars, light sails,
> and one heavy long gun… Let as many such barges be
> built and manned, form them into a flying squadron.
> Have them continually watching and annoying
> the enemy in Chesapeake Bay, where we have the
> advantage of shoals and flats. We could harass them
> day and night, keeping up a constant barrage, and
> induce them to finally quit our waters.

The craft would be under sail but manned by fifty
oarsmen who could maneuver the boat through shallow
waters. Barney knew those waters intimately. The British
did not. It was perfect for hit-and-run warfare. Blessedly,
an entire squadron could be built for the cost of a single
man of war and in far shorter time, with fewer men and less
material. As expected, deep-water admirals opposed the
venture, determined to devote every penny to constructing,
provisioning, and manning traditional warships to fight on
the high seas.

But Jones bought it. He endowed Barney with a sloop flagship, fourteen gunboats, six hundred men, and a title—commodore.

Barney needed experienced men, and Quinn's court martial mattered not at all to a man who had a history and a temper of his own. Plus Quinn had learned a little about sailing from Master Lee on *Friends Good Will*. Barney planned for each boat to carry fifty sailors and a squadron of twenty-five soldiers or marines. He was looking for men of mettle with proven ability to take chances and to fight, so Quinn and Frake fit the bill.

"Lads, good of you to come," Barney greeted them in his makeshift office in the St. Michaels shipyard where the two had been waiting. "I hope I haven't kept you too long— got to keep a close watch on the progress of my boats, you know. Can't have you running off. I need some hearty boys to give what-for to the Brits."

"We're your men," Frake offered, and when Barney raised a quizzical eyebrow, he added, "Our feet just started heading this way. Just seemed natural."

"Natural?"

"Yeah," Frake said. "With Limeys shooting up the countryside, sittin' 'round ain't gentlemanly."

"Fighting comes natural to you, does it?" Barney asked coolly.

"Yep," Frake said, but Quinn hesitated.

"I don't know," Quinn said. "Is it built into us, or do we learn it?"

"I don't know either, son," Barney said. "Don't matter, seeing as you got the itch to fight, and I hear you're good at it. That Wilkinson set-to don't bother me none. I figure to put each of you in charge of a gunboat."

"Well, commodore, you know we're not real sailors."

"Oh, you'll have good sailors with you. Your job's to direct the fighting. Firing the cannon. Shooting." Barney went on to explain his strategy. "The idea is to keep 'em too busy to launch an amphibious attack. Frankly, we're the only ones standing between the Brits and Washington. General Smith and the Maryland militia have things pretty well covered up in Baltimore, God willing, but Washington's a sitting duck."

"How can that be?" Quinn had been asking the question since his arrival home.

"Because they're idiots!" Barney thundered, bringing his fist down on the table so hard that even Frake jumped. "Dolts! It's like the Greeks leaving Athens or Sparta undefended. The Caesars, Rome. Napoleon, Paris. Nincompoops! "

30 March 1814

Baltimore

From his post at the spinning jenny, Henry could look out the second-floor window at Baltimore's inner harbor and the roads leading down to it. What he saw on this bright, spring day sent a shiver down his back—three men armed with muskets and billy clubs approaching the linen mill.

When the men drew closer to the door directly below him, they disappeared from Henry's view. He and the Quinns had rehearsed for this, so he rose and quietly walked to the back of the building. Just beyond the looms and dying vats, he stepped through a narrow door that led to a cubbyhole behind the stairway. Feet first, he climbed into a hiding place so compact that he had to crouch uncomfortably. Cracks in the wallboards allowed slivers of light, and if Henry pressed his eye close enough, he could just see the stairs below.

Henry had never hidden like this for real. Now terror varnished his body in a thin coat of sweat. If they found him…

Praying that Henry had hidden himself, Malachy stepped out the door and stood on the wooden stoop. The visitors would have to look up at him from the dusty street, and given his size, they'd think twice about trying to shove past him into the building.

The men paused and greeted Malachy curtly. "Morning."

There was no response. The big man just stood there, arms crossed, sturdy as an oak and just as silent.

Finally, one of the men cleared his throat. "We are here on business. Is this your establishment?"

"Maybe. Who's asking?"

The man pulled a sheet of paper from his pocket. "The law."

"What law's that?"

"We are in pursuit of stolen property."

"All the property here belongs to me and me brothers," Malachy growled, and as if on cue, Cavan and Aengus appeared to flank him.

"This'd be nigger property we're hunting. Runaway slaves." The speaker removed his battered hat and smiled, revealing yellowed teeth.

One of his companions stood close behind, a huge man with rolls of fat from chin to shoulder and a tiny head, a preposterous figure but still formidable. The third remained steps behind them, a weaselly little fellow with a badly pockmarked face who had certainly not been brought along for muscle and might. Maybe he was the brains of the group.

"Not here you're not," Malachy said.

"I guess I just got to ask you straight out. You hiding any nigger slaves?"

"They your slaves?"

"Don't matter. We got the right to hunt 'em down under the law of the Commonwealth of Virginia."

"This is Maryland."

"We can hunt anywheres in the whole country. Otherwise, them niggers would get clear away."

Malachy shook his head. "This is our property and our business, and you need to leave. Now!" He turned away.

"We knowed you got one in there, name of Henry!" the man shouted. "Calls hisself Bartholomew Alexander."

Malachy turned back. "Is that so? You got proof another man's slave is working for us?"

"I ain't in a mood for explaining, but if it'll cool you down, we heard you got a nigger who's a bang-up shoemaker. Fancy stuff for the ladies and gents. Well, see, this Henry we're lookin' for did just that in Washington afore running off. We're being paid by the rightful owner. That'd be a Mr. Kilfoyle."

"That's not here nor there. This is a linen mill, not a cobbler shop, and if you try to come in, you'll regret it."

More men had gathered behind Malachy, ready to stand up for the Quinns. The confrontation also drew the attention of passersby, creating the beginnings of a small crowd. Maryland was a slave state, but abolition sentiment ran strong in Baltimore.

"That's no bluff," Malachy added.

"The law's on our side, and that ain't no bluff either," the spokesman said.

"We'll go back and git the law," the weasel whined.

Malachy smiled. "Well, while your back gittin' the law,' you better find a judge to sign a search warrant. That piece of paper you got from your boss means nothing here. The Constitution says you got no right to look inside without a proper warrant. And I'm not sure I'll let you in *with* one."

He was playing for time. The law didn't favor fugitive slaves. Self-appointed posses went about capturing runaways and reaping handsome rewards. The law ignored their abuses. Slave hunting attracted bullies, sloths, and a few sociopaths who joined in the chase more for sport than for reward.

The slave hunters turned to go, and Malachy prepared for the next step.

Up in his hideout, unable to see or hear any developments, Henry grew increasingly fearful. Bile rose in his throat, and he realized that he was covered with sweat.

After what seemed like a lifetime, he heard, "Henry, it's us. We're coming up."

Peering through the crack, he saw Malachy climbing the stairs—not, he hoped, at gunpoint. With a sigh he heaved himself out of the cubbyhole.

"Henry, we've got a problem." Malachy described the confrontation in front of the mill.

"So," Henry asked, "it's time for me to go?"

"Afraid so. And right away. Aengus is bringing the dray out back, and Cavan has your new fake documents and your manumission papers. You're Thomas Jessup now. Our friend at the capital has certified the papers."

"You sure this is best?"

"I believe it is, Henry—I mean *Thomas*. Getting to Canada is even harder now. Both sides are wary of anyone trying to cross the border. You need to follow our plan. It's all worked out."

Finally get a taste of what it's like to be free, and already I've got to run and hide again, Henry thought. But he nodded and took the papers from Malachy.

The eldest Quinn shook his hand and said, "Cavan will drive the dray. You're not traveling alone. If anyone asks, you're going to do your patriotic duty and fight the British who came ashore and killed your family and burned your house. They done a lot of that."

Henry smiled wryly and thought, *The folks I should be fighting are the Americans.* They *took my family, not the British.*

"Are you ready to go?"

The best he could squeeze through a throat constricted by fear and anger was a whispered, "I'm ready."

As he turned and began heading downstairs, Malachy whispered, "Give our best to Willie and Frake."

1 June 1814

On Chesapeake Bay

"*S*ails and oars," proclaimed the signal flag that Barney raised on his flagship *Spider*.

The flag meant that flotilla would go into battle at maximum speed, this time in a daring daylight raid far more dangerous and more complicated than their nighttime ventures in harassment. Those had met with some success, but now Barney and his men craved something bigger, more rewarding.

They had received intelligence that the British were staging their forces on Tangier Island in the bay's southern sector. The magnitude of the preparations suggested that the British were planning something more than coastal raids. Indeed, Barney expected a full-on attack on one or more major cities, and he was determined to frustrate that effort.

Standing on the stern of his boat, Quinn felt its sleek hull respond to the deployment of the fifty oars. Fifty men pulling twenty-foot-long, thirty-eight-pound oars in unison required constant practice. One rower out of sync could be catastrophic in combat, causing a cascade of colliding oars that disabled the boat and hobbled the rest of the fleet.

Quinn felt the spray on his face. To left and right, the other boats shot forward in harmony with his until the sails no longer caught the wind and were hauled down. Excitement surged up his spine and into his chest as it did when, on land, the rhythm of the drum and fife sent the troops into battle. He had been right. This was where he belonged.

Ahead, two specks appeared on the water and then grew to become two rapidly closing British sloops. Barney's advance scout boat had spotted them, and the commodore had fixed them as his target. The sloops, however, were unwilling to engage the American gunboats and began a broad 180-degree turn. To conserve the crew's energy for the actual confrontation, Barney signaled a return to sails. The sleek boats in the flotilla kept pace with the British warships heading back to Tangier Island. Then the enemy's guns issued two blasts, though they were hundreds of yards out of range.

The shots were meant as signals. From behind Point Lookout to the south sailed the seventy-four-gun ship of the line *Dragon*. The sloops were bait to lure the flotilla under the guns of one of Britain's mightiest warships and its entourage of gunboats and barges. They were more than a match for the firepower of Barney's boats, and at once the *Spider* ran up signal flags ordering a retreat. Barney would not let his grand plan be wiped out in a single battle.

Barney's goal was to make it back to the Patuxent River from where he had been operating. The Patuxent was the longest of three rivers whose course ran entirely through the state of Maryland. That and its many tributaries and estuaries made it perfect for concealing his mini fleet.

The race was on. Heading south, Barney's group had set their sails at broad reach to take advantage of the wind. Now northbound into the wind, the sails were close hauled. Back at the oars, the men hove to with energy heightened by fear of capture or death. Balls from the *Dragon*'s long guns splashed around them, some close enough to douse the men in spray.

Now Quinn fully appreciated Barney's foresight in building his boats with eight extra inches of freeboard to prevent them from being swamped. The flotilla headed northwest into the Patuxent, running for St. Leonard's Creek.

The creek was near enough to the Patuxent's mouth to provide refuge, but its mouth was unfortunately deep enough to accommodate the *Dragon*. A better haven lay farther up the river where the big ship couldn't follow. There the flotilla could slip into any of the scores of shallow-water creeks and estuaries, but it also could be bottled up.

Barney's flotilla made it to the St. Leonard's creek with the British still in pursuit. Once there, the *Dragon* dropped anchor at the mouth of the creek, while its vanguard of gunboats pursed Barney into the stream. Barney quickly formed his gunboats into a line across the creek, positioned to concentrate their fire on a narrow throat the British boats would have to navigate. The narrows also limited the number of cannons the British could bring to bear. Meanwhile, Quinn, Frake, and others led squads of riflemen—including the hastily trained Henry—into the covering foliage along the riverbanks and poured fire into the British boats.

Twice the British charged up the river and twice were repulsed, but the siege continued. Extra warships flying the Union Jack came in to stand guard, effectively trapping Barney's fleet while the British awaited four thousand reinforcements from Bermuda.

19 July 1814

Washington, D.C.

"Sally, we must make preparations ourselves."

Dolley Madison had watched, with growing frustration and alarm, her husband's apparent inability or unwillingness to protect Washington from attack.

"What does Mr. Madison say?"

"Well, Secretary Armstrong still resists any suggestion that Washington lies open to British attack, and the president still fears that cashiering Armstrong will destroy support in New York and the northeast. He cannot risk that."

"Even General Scott is having trouble," Sally observed. "And now with Napoleon defeated, more British soldiers are headed our way. Do you think that General Winder can protect us?"

William Winder, a Baltimore native, had recently successfully negotiated with the British in Canada an agreement facilitating a prisoner exchange. When Madison created a Tenth Military District responsible for the defense of Washington, he chose Winder as commander. The general was popular in Maryland—the nephew of its governor, Levin Winder—so Madison hoped that this appointment would secure thirteen thousand Maryland militia to protect the capital. Unfortunately, that militia had not been activated, and Maryland, like every other state, was reluctant to assign its soldiers outside the state. The governor's first concern was Baltimore.

Dolley shook her head sadly. "So far his performance has been less than encouraging. He rushes around hither and thither organizing but doesn't get anything done! I think he's a better clerk than a general. And now Armstrong is so upset by Winder's appointment that he's refused to help at all. It's an *impossible* situation!"

"But can't Mr. Madison *demand* that Armstrong help? He is the president, after all."

"He wishes it were that simple. Sometimes, Sally, it seems that not offending some politician is more important than winning the war. The Tories see this whole mess as confirmation that you can't run a war *or* a country with a democracy. And sometimes I wonder myself."

They returned to sorting the first lady's correspondence, but then Sally asked, "What did you mean, Mrs. Madison, about making our own preparations?"

"I mean we have to think about what to do if the British capture Washington."

"But that's unthinkable!"

Dolley frowned. "Now you're thinking like men. They don't want something to happen, so they don't think it will. But what do we do if the British march up to our front door? Open it and ask them in, 'Gentlemen, we've been expecting you. Please make yourselves at home while we select a nice claret to go with your roast'? Flee and leave everything in British hands?"

She laughed, but her tone was very sober as she said, "Truly, we have to think this through."

"This place is important," Sally reflected. "It's the people's house, like you always say, and it makes me sick to think of some fat British general plunking his fat arse down on that sofa. Excuse my language, ma'am."

Now Dolley laughed heartily. "So we're agreed. We'll go through these quarters and select what must be spirited away. We'll need to arrange for transport and choose a hiding place for our treasures."

"Yes!" Sally was tired of inaction and worry. Will wanted to be part of the struggle. Well, so did she. "Can we start now?"

"Yes, but you needn't mention anything to Mr. Madison. For the moment."

15 *August 1814*

Pig Point, Maryland

*Q*uinn had been writing to Sally from Barney's bottled-up boats on the Patuxent. He wanted to mend fences, but his letters still revealed deep-seated indecision about his future. He was focused, it seemed, exclusively on *his* war with the British. With less frequency, she wrote back about developments in Washington, avoiding anything personal. Quinn was sure that if he proposed again, she would refuse him.

Amid her reports of White House comings and goings, she casually mentioned that Winfield Scott had asked permission to call on her. Now a brigadier general, he had returned to Washington to recover from injuries received at Lundys Lane. His reputation had reached heroic proportions, and he would be a matchless catch for any young lady.

Whether Sally's allusion was calculated or wholly innocent, it wounded Quinn. He believed he had lost her to a man he unreservedly admired.

19 August 1814, 9:27 a.m.
Benedict, Maryland

As a musket ball whistled past Quinn's ear, he instinctively dived into the mud.

It was the first sign that Barney's suspicions had been accurate: the British were landing at Benedict for an overland assault on Washington. Holed up at Pig Point for more than a month, Barney had grown restless, impatient. That the British hadn't attempted to root him out had deepened his conviction that the schooners anchored at the mouth of the creek were a deception.

Waiting for an axe to fall didn't suit him, so he sent Quinn and Frake to reconnoiter Benedict and the surrounding countryside. Henry was assigned to go with them to guard the horses at the rendezvous. If either spotted anything, Quinn would rush to Washington with the news and Frake would return at once to Barney.

Quinn and Frake slipped into separate sectors of the deep Maryland forest, and now Quinn realized he had run right into British skirmishers from a larger force. Lying in the muddy depression on the forest floor with a mouthful of dirt, he was hidden from the enemy under ferns and black huckleberry, but he was unprotected from blind shots.

The shot had been fired from the thicket to the right. There was no second shot. Was this only one man? Even in experienced hands, the British Brown Bess musket could take as long as thirty seconds to reload. Fifteen if the shooter was superb.

He held his breath. There had to be more than one. Skirmishers don't go out alone. Possibly two, more likely three. So two could be primed and loaded.

If he ran, he'd get back-shot. If he stayed, he was easy pickings. They'd know he had one shot ready to fire, two if he had a pistol. They wouldn't approach him.

He tried to think. *If the one who fired is reloading and the other two are flanking me, they'll count on me trying to run. They'll never figure I'd turn the tables and charge them. I'll go for the one who's still reloading. Maybe they'll pause just for a second for fear of shooting one of their own. It might work.*

Grabbing his musket, Quinn leapt blindly toward what he hoped was the middle Brit. As he sprang from the foliage, he saw the Redcoat already ramming a ball down the barrel. Quinn moved at full speed. The Brit looked up dumbfounded—he had been the hunter, not the hunted. With no time to pull the ramrod from the barrel, he swung around and braced himself, his musket already swinging up, his arm rising with it and leaving his side open to Quinn's bayonet.

Quinn felt ribs give way as the steel penetrated the man's heart and lungs. The deadly blow pushed the Brit backward as his finger tightened on the trigger. The rod and the ball ripped harmlessly through the leaves of the forest canopy, but Quinn never heard the discharge. He was withdrawing his bayonet and swinging his musket around to face whatever was coming his way. He could only hope that the other two were equally surprised. And luck was with him.

He leveled his musket—waist high, no time to aim—at the spot where the right-flanking Brit should be. When he saw a red blur, he fired. The wound wasn't fatal, but it put the bleeding Brit out of action. Lucky.

Quinn didn't have the luxury of watching him fall. As he reached for his pistol, he felt a searing pain along his left arm. The third Brit, firing, had gambled and lost. Now he'd have to reload, flee, or charge while Quinn had time to aim his pistol carefully. And to see the man realize his mistake. Quinn had seen the look before in this damnable war. It haunted his nights. A ball to the heart ended it.

He quickly turned back to the wounded man. "I'd just as soon kill you," he said, "but I'll give you a chance to save your miserable life." Quinn took out his knife. "How many and where? Quick."

"Stick around. You'll soon see how many and where, Yank," the Brit spat.

Quinn put the knife against the man's throat, drawing a thin string of blood. "Limey scum. Last chance." In seconds the sound of the shots would bring other British skirmishers running. He pressed a little harder with the knife, and the Recoat yielded.

"Wait! Four thousand men. Cockburn's taking them to Washington."

No time to slit his throat. Quinn was on his feet, running in a crouch, his musket low and parallel to the ground. His body surged with fear and anger. Anger at incompetence! Anger at failures of intelligence! Anger at the whole bunch of idiots!

Washington was unprepared and could be ablaze in a day. And…his heart stopped. And Sally was there. In a building the Brits would burn!

He scrambled to the rendezvous where his horse and, God willing, Henry and Frake, were waiting. Once or twice he paused to listen for pursuers, but he kept moving as fast as he could manage. And from a hiding place in some bushes, a pair of British eyes watched him approach.

19 August 1814, 10:19 a.m.
Washington, D.C.

*N*ews of the British landing at Benedict spun Washington into a panic. That no one yet knew if Washington, Annapolis, or Baltimore was the target didn't matter.

Dolley Madison watched wagons and horses fill Pennsylvania Avenue all the way back to Capitol Hill. Most were headed west to Georgetown and points beyond, but others were scurrying from pillar to post, disrupting the exodus. Sally had seen panic at Fort Dearborn, and she recognized it in the faces of the jostling masses.

"Word sure spread fast," she said, letting the lace curtain she had pulled back to get a better look fall. She turned to the first lady. "What should we do?" But there was no *we*. The decision was the president's and the first lady's. "I'm sorry, that was presumptuous."

Dolley, distracted, waved away the apology. "Perfectly understandable, Sally. I don't know what the president will decide. Armstrong *still* insists the British aren't interested in Washington, so Mr. Madison is riding out to see for himself."

"My goodness. Are you worried for him, ma'am?"

Dolley sighed. "A little. Winder is still pleading with the Virginia and Maryland militias for troops." She gestured vaguely in the direction of the crowds fleeing the city. "I'm afraid some of the able-bodied men we need are at this very moment turning tail from the fight instead of rallying to it."

Sally nodded, thinking of Quinn, who always seemed to run *into* the battle.

"Secretary Jones has ordered Commodore Barney to destroy his own boats rather than let them fall into enemy hands. A bitter pill after all his effort."

"Speaking of Mr. Jones, a note has come from his wife. Shall I read it?"

"Please."

"Yes, it's about tonight's dinner. It appears she won't be able to attend. 'In the present state of alarm, I imagine that it is mutually convenient to dispense with the enjoyment of your hospitality today and therefore pray you admit this as an excuse for Mr. Jones, Lucy, and myself.'"

"How very thoughtful," Dolley said soberly.

Something in the first lady's voice made Sally, for the first time since coming to Washington, afraid. She had lost her family and seen the horrors at Fort Dearborn. What would the British do if they did take the city? She had heard reports of Cockburn's atrocities.

But Dolley's tone turned reassuringly firm. "I will not be seen fleeing in front of an army that may not come. I will not abandon my husband and this seat of government. How can we expect sacrifice from others if we ourselves falter? I will not join that mob." She turned on her heel and announced, "I am going to the roof. We must be watchful now."

Sally took pride in her own competence, knowing she could fight along with the best of them. "It's not fair," she said as they climbed the stairs.

"Fair? War is not fair."

"No, I mean that the rabble is fleeing, but we must sit here and wait for the enemy to come to us. Blast it all! I can use a rifle with the best of them."

"And use course language too, I see," Dolley chided.

Sally blushed. "I'm sorry, ma'am, but it isn't right. Women are out there right now ready to defend their homes and families, but we have to sit here like sheep waiting for the slaughter."

"Don't deprecate our role, my dear. We provide succor and encouragement when our own hearts are breaking. We demonstrate courage in our own way. We treat the wounded. We care for those left behind—the widows and the orphans."

They had reached the top of the stairs, and Dolley paused for a moment to remove a spyglass from a utility cabinet. She wanted to keep watch for her husband, because she was agitated in his absence. As they stepped out onto the roof, Dolley turned back to Sally.

"I will confide in you, Sally, that I have often felt the same. We have our role as women to bear and nurture children and to create families. I have never been ashamed of that role nor thought it inferior to what men do. But as I watch events in this capital city, I feel a certain—well, not jealousy—a certain aspect of mind that I can't quite put into words. A woman's legal rights are only marginally greater than a slave's. Our right to own property is limited. We cannot vote."

"Will it ever change?" Sally asked.

"Someday. The world changes, my dear. Slowly, but it does." She smiled. "I daresay if we were running the war, we'd have to try very hard to make a bigger dog's dinner of it." She raised the spyglass to her eye.

Sally laughed.

"I shock you, my dear?"

"Not really. But tell me—will slaves someday have their freedom?"

"Such provocative questions, Sally, and God bless you for the distraction they afford. I think I see military riders approaching...Sally! I think it's your young man!"

She turned the spyglass over to Sally. "Yes, it's Will! I see him there, riding up with a Negro. Could that be Henry? They look dreadful."

19 August 1814, 12:12 p.m.

Washington, D.C.

O nce again, Quinn arrived at the White House hot, sticky, and muddied, but this time there was no army lieutenant to ask his purpose or announce his presence. The mansion's major domo French John Sioussat answered the door and bowed him in.

Quinn looked around. "Where is the guard?" he asked.

"Sir," Sioussat replied coolly, "I believe he has departed."

"Departed? *Deserted*, you mean?"

"Quite possibly."

Quinn shot another glance around the vestibule. "Where is the rest of the command? There were at least a hundred men under Colonel Carberry."

"Gone, sir."

"Did the president dismiss them?"

"Not to my knowledge, sir. Perhaps they have gone to confront the British."

"Perhaps," Quinn said wryly. "But who guards the first lady?"

He knew enough of British atrocities—everyone did— yet here were Mrs. Madison and Sally unprotected! Was there no end to cowardice and incompetence in this war?

And then suddenly Sally was in his arms. She clung to him, amazed and relieved that he was alive and seemed uninjured. All her determination to greet him with cool reserve at their next meeting dissolved. She drew back enough to see the blood on his sleeve and felt tears spill down her cheeks.

"You're hurt, Will!"

"Not much. Look at me, Sally. I'm fine."

Behind him, she saw Henry waiting outside the open door. "Henry, thank God. You too are safe. Come on, come in."

Henry hesitated. He smiled then and stepped in but froze in his tracks when Mrs. Madison appeared.

"Dear lord, look at you," she said to Quinn. "Must you always show up on our doorstep in such disarray?" She drew Will farther into the entry hall. "Please, come in and give us news."

When Henry remained in place, she paused for a long moment then said, "You are wearing the uniform of the United States, and you are welcome here. Pay no mind to the dust. I fear it will soon be the least of our worries."

In the small drawing room, she motioned them all to be seated and sent the butler, John Freeman, for iced lemonade and tea.

Dolley was eager for information. "Now," she demanded, "where are the British?"

"I figure about four thousand came ashore at Benedict and marched north, but we didn't know where they were headed. For a while they looked like they were going northwest to Alexandria, but that was a feint. We met them near Upper Marlboro. Barney sent me, Frake, and Henry to scout and find out if they were on the way to Pig Point to wipe out his flotilla. I ran into some forward skirmishers and found out they were marching to Washington."

"Oh, dear, then it's true," Dolley said.

Quinn nodded. "I believed them, and then I got lucky—ran smack into a British deserter hiding in the bushes. Appears he slipped away from his unit during the night but underestimated how slow a man travels in this heat. He was famished and exhausted, but he confirmed it. Said a separate force was heading to Pig Point to capture Barney's fleet. Don't know if that was true. But Barney had orders to destroy the boats if the British showed up. Anyway, Frake took off to warn Barney, and Henry and I came here with the deserter."

"Have you reported to Jones?" Dolley asked.

"Yes, ma'am. He's in conference with the president, Armstrong, and Winder at the navy yard, still arguing over where the British are going to hit. I figured our intelligence would settle it."

"Well, of course!" Dolley said.

Quinn shook his head. "Afraid not. The deserter swore his information was the God's truth, and it'd do him no good to lie. But Armstrong yells, 'How do we know you're not here to bear false witness?'" Will imitated Armstrong's bluster so vividly that Mrs. Madison laughed. "'You want to make us believe Washington will be invaded while your army descends on Baltimore or Annapolis?'"

Dolley frowned. "But the others believed him?"

"Yes, and they have a plan. The east branch of the Potomac flows between here and the British. Only a few places to ford, and the British won't know them, so that leaves three bridges—Anacostia and Bloddert's bridges on the east and Bladensburg bridge about five miles upriver, northeast of here. Winder will blow up Bloddert's bridge and guard Anacostia, so they'll have to cross at Bladensburg where the route to the bridge is narrow. They'd have to squeeze through. With artillery and supporting troops, we have a good chance of holding them off."

"What supporting troops?" Dolley asked.

"Now that there's an immediate threat to the capital, Winder thinks Virginia and Maryland will help. Barney has five hundred men, and maybe we can round up five hundred more, but most of them will be untrained farmers and tradesmen—against the cream of the king's regulars, the men who defeated Napoleon."

"Wonderful," Sally muttered. Watching Quinn outline the situation, she found herself admiring his calm intelligence.

"On the other hand, those men are battle weary and not very happy, after years of Continental war, to be sent over to deal with us. They had a long ocean crossing and now this infernal heat and humidity. No telling what shape they're in or how many will desert."

Finally, Dolley asked, "What will Mr. Madison do now?"

"Ma'am, he asked me to convey his apologies. He is going to the front to personally assess the situation. He'll be with Mr. Monroe, and I'm sure they'll be protected. He says that he trusts in your understanding of the circumstances that require his absence from you."

"Nicely put, Mr. Quinn," Dolley said, forcing a smile. "So what happens now?"

"I'm not experienced enough to say, ma'am, but I suggest that you ladies evacuate."

"What did my husband say?"

"He also encourages you to leave. In fact, he—"

Dolley's eyes were narrowing dangerously.

"Well, ma'am, he *insists* that you leave this house and go to the pre-arranged gathering spot outside the city."

"He *insists*? Surely, Mr. Quinn, my husband did not *order* me out of this house?" Her tone was ominous.

"Oh...well...no, ma'am, but he's most concerned about you and your household. And I have to agree with him."

"And what will *you* do?" It was Sally.

"I'll go back to fight with Barney."

"I wish I could fight alongside you," Sally said. "You know I can do it."

Quinn rolled his eyes. "Oh, woman! Even if it were permitted, I would not put you in such danger. Besides, you're needed here. Is she not, Mrs. Madison?"

"Since we have been left virtually alone, and since we will be *staying here* at our post, as it were, she is indeed needed. A fighter will come in handy."

"Henry will stay with you," Quinn said.

Henry was silent.

"Henry is able bodied and can fight," Quinn went on. "He can also help you move to safer quarters."

Henry rose and bowed. "I'd be glad to give any help I can, ma'am."

And with that, Quinn was gone.

19 August 1814, Noon
Bladensburg, Maryland

$\mathcal{B}$ ladensburg, with its 1,200 inhabitants, was the last daily stagecoach stop from Baltimore before arriving in the District of Columbia. Roads converged on the town from all directions and merged into a single lane on a narrow bridge crossing the Anacostia River, a Potomac River tributary. High ground west of the bridge is where the Americans chose to confront the British, who were approaching from the other side. It was a well-chosen position, forcing the British to funnel over the bridge in the open, exposed to a hail of bullets and cannon balls. If the British could sustain the heavy casualties during the bridge crossing, then they still would have to fight, nearly fully exposed, and up the hill to break through the dug-in Americans. It would be both the first and last chance for the Americans to stop the British. Failing that, the British would have an open road into Washington, only five miles away.

By now the British intent was indisputable. With a platoon of dragoons, Monroe had clattered across the bridge, through the town, and down to the road that forked southwest Benedict to scout the British. It was a bad decision. After just two miles, his party approached a glen darkened by overhanging maples. In the dimness they could just see foot soldiers approaching on the run. Only when they recognized the British uniforms did the Americans rein in their horses and wheel about. In the confusion the horses collided with one another as the British soldiers knelt and fired. Bullets raked through the maple leaves as Monroe's men whipped their mounts back toward Bladensburg. By sheer luck, no one was hit and no member of the president's inner circle taken prisoner.

As Monroe's party thundered back, they passed lines of their own skirmishers who had taken up positions on Lowndes Hill on the east side of the bridge in the village. In the distance drums beat the measured cadence of British troops on the march, stirring up heavy dust clouds. Suddenly, from over a rise in the road, the first column appeared to the defending Americans, moving as steadily as if passing in review on an English parade ground. The imposing sight had its intended effect. Neophyte American soldiers watched in awe until, abruptly, the British halted, took aim, and opened fire. A few Americans returned fire without effect before rushing back across the bridge to safety. Now the full force of the British emerged from the shade of the woods into brutal sunlight. Their woolen uniforms and heavy backpacks had already taken a toll, but they marched on relentlessly.

When General Ross arrived in the village, he commandeered a two-story house. A second-floor window gave him an unobstructed view of the American positions across the river. The bridge, he ascertained, was about a hundred and twenty feet long and a dozen feet wide, allowing only one column at a time to advance. Well-positioned guns on the opposite side of the river could sweep the bridge with canisters of grape shot. Indeed, about a hundred and fifty yards beyond the bridge, the Americans had thrown up earthworks to shelter a half dozen six-pounders, a first line of defense. Guarding their right were about a hundred and fifty riflemen, a like number on the left, and some three hundred yards farther left a squadron of cavalry.

He could make out a second line of guns and riflemen behind the first. Clearly a backup, but too far in the rear to be useful.

"Fools," he muttered, beginning to accept Cockburn's view of the enemy.

Much farther behind, a third defensive line was forming. A last-resort backup in case the first two lines collapsed? How to approach the enemy? A head-on assault across the bridge would be costly—possibly suicidal—but not unthinkable.

Chewing up countless men in a frontal assault was standard practice, but to clear out the first nest of guns and rifles meant flanking their positions on the right, left, or both. Could they find a place up or downstream to ford the river? He was deep in enemy territory and didn't know the lay of the land. He estimated the size of the American force at eight or nine thousand men, compared with his four thousand—though his were experienced warriors.

In reality, the Americans had six thousand men, many of them untested. Most carried smoothbore muskets instead of the more accurate rifles that Armstrong had refused to supply. (They were "needed for the fight on the northern frontier," though in fact they were stocked in nearby armories.) In addition, few of the weapons were equipped with bayonets, leaving the Americans nearly unarmed in hand-to-hand fighting.

The placement of the American troops was changing by the minute, depending upon who supposed himself in command. Even as the troops were arriving, disputes among senior officers broke out over who outranked whom. Winder was ultimately in charge, but command had initially fallen to Tobias Stansbury, whose two-thousand-unit militia was formed to defend Baltimore.

He was dispatched to defend Washington, but once there, received conflicting orders: "Hurry to Washington at once! As quickly as possible. No, stop halfway there! No, set up a defensive line a mile outside the city. No, go back to defend Bladensburg bridge!"

He had established the defensive lines that Ross observed, but then Monroe—without informing Stansbury—moved the first back-up line too far to the rear, giving rise to Ross's puzzlement. The second line had been well placed in an orchard, but after Monroe's realignment, its guns could not effectively cover the first line.

Winder, arriving about the same time as Ross, concluded that it was too late to relocate the backup line. Armstrong himself had arrived at Winder's pleading but seemed to prefer sneering from the sidelines. Even Madison and his entourage had journeyed from Washington to watch the battle from the heights, as if on a Sunday picnic. Initially, the president's party had miscalculated and nearly crossed the bridge into British hands before a frantic militiaman risked his own life by jumping from cover and waving his arms to divert them.

Now, with Madison, his advisors, and his friends as audience, the battle began.

19 August 1814, 1:35 p.m.

Bladensburg, Maryland,
on the American Side

Frake's frustration had been rising while Barney's men were holed up at Pig's Point. Blowing up the flotilla to keep it out of British hands demolished all their work, training, and plans to stymie the enemy. The Kentuckian was only slightly mollified when they took the boat's long guns—twelve- and eighteen-pounders—with them, though it was rough work dragging, pushing, and manhandling them over difficult terrain.

Lacking horses, mules, or caissons, the men did all the hauling—some strapping on harnesses, others straining at ropes, all of them sweating as they plodded through the heat to the District's borders. Eventually, after hours of confusion about where they should be, Barney's men, including Quinn, Frake, and Henry, as well as their guns, were positioned on top of the rise where the third American line was forming.

What unfolded there astonished even the battle hardened. When the fighting started, the bridge quickly became covered with Redcoat bodies, dead and wounded. Those who survived the bridge were mowed down on the open ground in front of the forward gun emplacements. At first glance, the U.S. soldiers had put up a stout defense, sweeping the attackers off their feet in grisly numbers.

But the slaughter didn't stop professional British foot soldiers. On the next try, walking or climbing over the bodies of their dead and wounded comrades on the bridge, hundreds soon pushed their way through the withering fire. Soon they were swarming over the earthen redoubt that protected the forward American guns. In panic, the first line of American militiamen took refuge in a nearby orchard. To the left of the first-line gun placement, the American flank collapsed, sending hundreds of militia rushing pell-mell back to Georgetown along a separate road.

Part of the American panic was caused by the British Congreve rockets. As a weapon, these were dismally inaccurate, tending to fall far off target. But they created a hideous, terrifying screech, like nothing the green troops had experienced, and now the second line was giving way. A mounted General Winder had rushed up from his command post to rally the troops, but most just fled for their lives.

Commodore Barney set his naval guns along the right side of the third line. Every available man, including Quinn and Frake, lent a shoulder to position them for best effect. They were aimed directly at another, much smaller bridge crossing Turncliff Creek. The sluggish stream ran through a draw that separated the second and third lines. While the shallow gulley wouldn't present a major obstacle, it would slow the British down and make them easier targets. As each gun was placed, Barney sighted it on the spot where the enemy would appear.

Gunner mates tended to the guns, while Quinn, Frake, the marines, and any remaining militia settled in with their rifles or muskets to the left of the guns with a clear view of the approaches. Farther left, one of the generals had wisely located hundreds of soldiers, ranging them along a rise all the way to the bluff a few hundred yards away. In front of them, a dozen larger army guns, along with Barney's guns, would catch the attackers in a crossfire. To the right, on another rise, were several hundred more soldiers, some of them army regulars. In front of the Turncliff Creek Bridge, several ranks of militia stood to meet a frontal attack.

These placements would allow retreating soldiers to regroup and turn back on the enemy. The art of warfare depended as much on orderly retreats as on aggressive offensives. This last line of defense, however, was effective only if the fleeing soldiers know that it existed.

"Nobody told us."

The retreating soldier had thrown away his musket and was lugging a wounded comrade on his back. The two emerged from the brush at the bottom of the draw and were struggling up the rise when Barney's riflemen spotted them. Rushing forward, stretcher-bearers and riflemen all gave a hand.

"My name's Private George Stewart, and this here's my friend, Private Howie Cramer. If you can help him, I'd be grateful. We was on the line at the bridge, and those Brits kept coming and coming. God, it was a nightmare! We kept shooting, and they fell where they stood, but there was always more kept coming and coming like demons from hell. Howie here got hit bad, shoulder, I don't know. Kept bleeding. Nothing we could do but run. Only Howie couldn't run. Couldn't leave him there to be gut bayoneted. While I was carrying him, he got hit in the leg. Put on a tourniquet, blood coming out of his shoulder, his leg..."

"We've got you, son. Don't have to talk no more." Frake offered his canteen to Stewart. "Take a swallow, private. Not too big. We'll get you back home. Don't you worry."

"We didn't know you was back here. Honest to God, we didn't know. That there general kept telling us we had to hold the line no matter what, but people was getting killed all around. He shoulda said y'all was here and we could regroup. Folks wouldn't have run off to Georgetown if they knew. God help us."

"Lad, God help us all, but don't you worry now. You've done right. You kept your friend here alive. You're a hero, son."

Stewart shook his head. "I ain't none of that."

Rapid gunfire interrupted them. The British were concentrating on the delaying force in front of Turncliff Bridge. The American left had broken down, and British foot soldiers, having chased out or captured the last remnants, turned toward the American center. Now the delaying force retreated to the American side of Turncliff Creek.

"Private, the boys here will get you on your way back. There's other business here right now."

The first British platoon was crossing Turncliff Bridge when Barney ordered the first cannon to fire. The single ball nearly swept the bridge clean of men, leaving only the dead and some body parts behind. Behind them, the British riflemen took cover behind shrubs or trees.

Seconds, then minutes passed, while Barney held his fire. It was a standoff, and for the defending Americans that was success, however temporary. A few impatient marines in Quinn's platoon let go with isolated shots.

"Sergeant!" Quinn shouted. "Stop those men now! Anyone who fires before the order, anyone who wastes ammunition, will have me to deal with." *His* men were itchy too, ready for battle.

"Come and get it, you jake-offs," one shouted.

As if on cue, the British renewed the advance but were swept from the bridge. Those who waded the stream were picked off by a hail of balls and bullets. The rout was so thorough that several American squads broke from cover to chase the remainder off the bridge. Quinn, Frake, and the other officers screamed at their own men to stay put for the next attack.

The battle had gone on for two hours, and surely the British generals were reassessing their plan. Why would they sacrifice the finest soldiers in the empire, if not the world, to take a midget bridge in this godforsaken colony? Lose well-trained, experienced men in a vainglorious attack on a capital that they didn't plan to hold?

More time passed while British troops under a white flag scoured the bridge, creek, and draw to remove the dead and the survivors

Their gruesome task completed, they regrouped behind an imposing figure on a prancing stallion. This was no mere brigadier, but a major general well respected by his men. Ross himself.

The American cheers died, and Quinn shouted, "Don't fire until you have a shot. If you miss at this range, they'll think the man can't be touched. Wait." But he raised his own weapon, muttering, "Wait, wait. Curse your Limey hide."

Now the British soldiers, with a couple of six-pounders, had formed line after line in shoulder arms across the battlefield. The drums began the cadence, signaling the ranks to step off. They moved forward, shoulder to shoulder, step by step. No one could watch them without feeling both admiration and fear. Yes, they were easy targets, and the Americans opened fire. Volleys of ball and shot flew, opening holes in the approaching lines, but those holes were instantly filled by men who stepped up from behind or by the simple closing of ranks.

Quinn remembered Stewart's words: "They just kept coming."

Now the British front rank knelt, aimed, and fired—a thunderous sound almost as frightening as the shrieks of the Congreve rockets. The Americans returned fire from behind hastily constructed barriers. Again, holes appeared in the British ranks and were plugged with replacements. Near the Turncliff Bridge, several platoons broke and ran in single file to minimize their exposure to the crossfire. By the dozens, the British fell while acrid smoke, the screams of the wounded, and the cacophony of drums, rifles, and cannons made the place a vision of hell.

The British were concentrating their fire on Barney's guns, hoping for a knockout punch that would open the bridge. When the cannoneers fell, Barney's riflemen replaced them. The commodore's horse had twice been shot out from under him, and now he stood behind the guns, shouting orders and encouragement. To right and left, he could see the British assaulting the flanks. But the American lines held.

Then horsemen galloped through the American lines in the distance, shouting, "Retreat! Retreat! We will regroup later. Retreat! Retreat!"

Barney's men, out of earshot, could make no sense of the scene, but at last they made out the figure of Winder. As he moved along, the American guns fell silent, as if his presence was the dark shadow of surrender. The men were puzzled. They didn't appear to be overrun by the British, but officers were quickly picking up the general's orders and calling for retreat. Squad by squad, platoon by platoon, company by company, the men ceased firing and scrambled from their positions. Some stepped into the line of fire and were cut down, turning uncertainty into dread, and dread into hysteria. Others simply threw down their guns and ran with no idea where to regroup.

Barney shouted at Winder, but his curse was carried off by the sounds of battle.

Quinn saw the commodore running toward him and picking up a rifle dropped by a wounded soldier. He raised it, threw it down, and seized another that was primed and ready to fire.

"Christ, Barney's going to shoot Winder," Quinn realized and leapt forward to wrestle the gun away from him.

Barney was screaming, "Let me kill him! You traitor!"

Once disarmed, though, he calmed himself, refusing to let his command disintegrate in a fit of passion. He turned to his men. "Don't anyone move. You're under *my* command, not that, that…fool's. We're staying, and we're going to show those redcoats who they're dealing with. Can I count on you boys?"

It didn't hurt that Barney was exposed to enemy fire as he spoke. Indeed, that stoked the men's determination to stand with him. A loud cheer arose. By now, the battle was in its third hour, and for an hour more Barney's men held their line and fought. But they couldn't hold out with their left flank exposed and the British scrambling into what had been American positions. The troops on their right were out of ammunition and facing hand-to-hand combat when they finally relinquished their position. They sent a messenger to tell Barney that they had no choice. They urged him to retreat as well.

But Barney wouldn't. His men wouldn't. On they fought, as the British vise closed around them.

Then Barney took a shot to his hip. Bleeding and in pain, he fell to the ground and accepted the inevitable. "It's time, gentlemen," he said firmly. "You must return to Washington to fight again."

"Never!"

He was weakening, but his voice was firm. "That's an *order.* Spike the guns before they can be turned on us and leave without me."

"Not on my life," said one.

"Again, that is an *order.* Now get, all of you."

The force of his personality and the strength of his leadership prevailed. They dressed his wound and staunched the bleeding as best they could. Then most reluctantly retreated. Redcoats surrounded the handful that flatly refused to leave him.

"Commodore Barney, I presume?"

It was Ross, dusty but unwounded. He had ordered his men not to harm the American captives and extended his hand to Barney. When the commodore attempted to rise, Ross stayed him with a gesture.

"Sir, I have come here for a single purpose," he said. "To salute you. Rarely have I witnessed such valor. Your men have earned our everlasting respect, and, mind you, we have fought the very best. I will personally see that you and your men receive the best medical attention, and we will work quickly to arrange your exchange."

"Thank you, general," Barney replied. "Is it possible that you can spare our capital city?"

"Unfortunately, sir, I cannot, though I would gladly do so. That decision rests in more powerful hands than mine. For whatever relief it may give you, commodore, know that you are in no way responsible for what will follow."

19 August 1814, 4:15 p.m.
Washington, D.C.

*E*xcept for an occasional sniper, no one challenged the British on their march down the Washington turnpike from Bladensburg. They'd sent skirmishers and pickets on the lookout for Americans regrouping, but they found none. Four miles…three miles…two miles…and then officers spotted an edifice that must house the American parliament. They halted on a plain between that building and the Congressional cemetery and viewed the United States seat of government.

It was hardly what British soldiers expected. Except for the Capitol building and a large house in the distance, the town was disappointing—no bustling port, no imposing citadel, no clusters of incipient manufacturing. Not even dust stirred up by horses and wagons on the move. Not a person. Not an animal. The city might have been a deserted stage set. The exhausted soldiers began to poke one another and laugh till chortles grew into guffaws.

"Fine thing," one said. "Marching all this way, and no one to say hallo."

"Run off holding their skirts," said another.

"This pig sty of a place ain't worth the sweat it took to get here. Let's burn it and be done."

"Might I congratulate you, general, on your glorious victory," Cockburn said to Ross as they rode into the American capital at the head of the exhausted British column. "The capital of this sovereign nation lies at your feet. Don't let their cowardice and ineptitude diminish your achievement. You deserve full accolades."

Ross did not miss the not-very-subtle suggestion that his victory had been easily achieved, but he let it pass. A victory is a victory. The men killed or maimed at Bladensburg Bridge had not found the enemy so easy to vanquish, had not found the battle such a walkover. Ross's concern for all his men was genuine, and they in turn respected and even revered him.

Now, seeing the deserted American capital, he couldn't help but wonder what the conflict was all about. He'd been here only a few months, and he had despised the raids along Chesapeake Bay as beneath the dignity of a professional soldier, but he kept his thoughts private.

"To matters at hand, if you don't mind, admiral."

"Ah, Robert, you must learn to enjoy victory," Cockburn pronounced airily.

"I've given the order to assemble a surrender delegation of two hundred officers and men—army, navy, and marines—and to be ready to enter Washington before sunset to present our terms to the Americans."

"And those terms, general?"

"Unconditional surrender."

"And evacuation of this shantytown prior to our burning it to the ground."

"Admiral, I have no intention of ignoring my orders or the precepts of civilized war. I'm sure the admiralty would agree." Ross hoped to remind Cockburn that he was not in command here.

"We will, of course, not tolerate disruptions by civilians or rogue military units. We will fire only government buildings or structures employed to oppose us. Private property will be respected absolutely," Ross said.

Cockburn had other ideas. "Unlike the American vandals at York."

"Yes. Should we lower ourselves to their standards?"

"In retaliation, yes. An eye for an eye."

"They will suffer enough. We do not destroy the homes of women and children and turn them out into the streets. The king's purposes are well enough served by the humiliation that the Americans will suffer."

"As you say," Cockburn muttered grudgingly.

Tradition dictated that the British delegation be met by an equivalent group of Americans, both proceeding under white flags to ensure the orderly transfer of control. That the British delegation carried the makings of torches would clearly declare their intentions to the vanquished Americans—if any Americans had been present.

The British delegation had almost reached the steps of the Capitol, and still no one had appeared to meet them. Ross and Cockburn were too stunned to know what to do next. They knew how to rally men, lay out battle plans, fight, retreat, and regroup. But they had no idea how to receive the surrender of an absent enemy.

"I say, what the hell do we do now?"

Just as Cockburn shifted in his saddle to face Ross, a bullet thwacked into the head of the general's horse. The horse collapsed, first onto his front legs and then onto his side, and Ross barely avoided having his legs crushed under the beast. All turned toward the source of the shot—a two-story frame house near the Capitol.

"Burn it!" Cockburn shouted.

19 *August 1814*, *4:15 p.m.*
Washington, D.C.

"*O*h, Christ."

Quinn and Frake, crouched behind a window in a nearby house, saw the horse fall and the British platoon gallop toward the sniper's house next door.

"They'll be high-tailing it here in a second," Frake whispered.

They could see an American rifleman rush out of the sniper's house back door and take cover behind a row of sheds in a neighboring yard.

"He's heading *our* way. That idiot's going to get give us away."

Hardly a moment after Frake spoke, the sniper banged through the house's back door and bolted into the very room the two had hid in.

It was Henry.

"You trying to get us all killed?" Quinn bore down on him.

Henry hadn't expected to encounter anyone. The bayonet was fixed on his musket, and he instinctively raised it before he recognized them.

"Now, you trying to git yourself killed too," Frake said, pushing aside the bayonet. His own gun was cocked, and only his extraordinary reactions had kept him from firing. "Better hope to God you didn't draw them here, or we're all cooked."

"Shut up," Quinn suggested.

He had crawled back to the window, checking on the progress of the British searchers. They were charging into the house that had served as Henry's sniper's nest. In time, splitting doors, breaking dishware, and the various sounds of searching and plundering were heard. If they came up empty handed, they'd soon move onto to where he and Frake and Henry were holed up. Now the orange glow of flames flickered in the windows of the first house and licked up its outer walls. The place was consumed in minutes.

Quinn and Frake could hope that the British would be distracted and not notice them sneaking into the protection of the growing darkness. Or that British officers had bigger fish to fry and would turn their attention to public buildings. Suddenly, a bright flash followed instantly by an earth-shaking explosion drew everyone's attention away from the blazing house. Another flash and explosion followed, then two or three more. South, southeast. Maybe two miles away.

"The navy yard," Quinn whispered. "I thought they'd set it afire if the British got this far. A shame, place was loaded with guns, powder, supplies, ships abuilding. What a loss."

Quinn, Frake, and Henry took advantage of the commotion to slip into the darkness of the nearly deserted District. When they felt safely out of reach, they entered another abandoned house, found food and drink, and sat down to review their situation.

"Henry," Quinn asked in the darkness, "what the hell were you doing? What made you think you could take on the British army?"

"I could ask you the same thing," Henry answered.

"We was reconnoitering," Frake told him. "Everyone was in such a rush to get the hell out of town, no one was thinking about what comes next. So we was skulkin' around to see what we could see. But we didn't have no intention of shooting at a general. Why'd you do it?"

"Fed up of running."

"From the British?"

"From everything. Soon enough a man's got to stand his ground."

Quinn nodded. "That's so, but you gotta pick your fights."

"Well, then let's see. British get me, I go to prison. Americans get me, I'm a slave again." He shrugged. "Just had to take it out on someone. Shooting at Brits might get me a medal. Or better yet, my walking papers."

"We got rid of our uniforms back in that house and found some men's clothes. Makes it easier to move around."

"And get shot as spies."

"Got no intention of getting caught," Frake said. "At least not till you shot that horse out from under the general."

"If I'd got that general instead of his horse, you think that might have helped?"

"Don't know," Quinn said. "Maybe just make them madder."

"So what? They gonna burn Washington twice?"

"Anyway." Frake sighed. "Three of us is better than two. Let's find out what the Brits plan to do next. Stay here and hold the capital? Take Alexandria? Work their way up the Potomac? Skedaddle back to their ships? Attack Baltimore?"

"Winder's troops could go shore up Alexandria or Baltimore, and maybe—"

"Hate to pop your bubble," Frake growled, "but Winder couldn't put together a squad, let alone an army. Shit!" He spotted the British entering the Capitol, armed with torches. "We should get moving."

"Henry," Quinn said, "head up the road to the White House. See what you can pick up along the way. Anything— gossip, British troops talking, rumors, anything. They'll figure you for a runaway slave."

"Won't take no acting," Henry muttered.

"Frake, time for you to go huntin'. Just don't shoot no one...yet."

"And you, ensign?"

"There's a doctor's sign posted outside a house near here. I'm guessing he's tending to the wounded from Bladensburg. Once the Brits find him, they'll bring him their wounded. I'm going there and hope the Brits take me for a civilian volunteer.

"Meeting up place is the alley behind the French ambassador's house. You all know where that is? They'll be a curfew, so be careful. If you can't make it there tonight, take what you've learned and head north. Last I heard, what's left of Barney's men are heading up to Baltimore."

"Good luck."

19-20 August 1814

Washington, D.C.

*T*he flames from the burning city painted the skies above Maryland and Virginia in the red glow of defeat. Men, women, and children gathered in silence on the hills surrounding the District to watch the fires appear first from the Capitol then the government buildings and finally the White House. Low, angry clouds blanketed the early evening sky, their undersides reflecting the sinister glow.

British troops marched down Pennsylvania Avenue, fanning out with their torches and setting building after building alight. The remaining civilians heard the laughter and shouting of the victors as they turned official Washington to ashes.

Was this more than the death of a city? Was it the funeral pyre of a nation? Of democracy itself? Some turned away in fury at the president and the Congress, the men who begot this war. And at the generals who had lost it—at the British for destroying the city and the dream. Others froze in horror, unable even to imagine what might follow.

At last, though, they began to move, to seek shelter from the angry winds that suddenly whipped across the city and from the storm that followed. Flashes of lighting danced through the sky. Slashing rain followed but could not douse the fires. The flames consumed the superb woodwork, the exquisite furnishings, the invaluable documents in the public buildings.

When the flames in the Capitol finally died down, only a shell remained of the House of Representatives. The Senate fared better, its carved marble and limestone still standing but thoroughly blackened. The White House roof collapsed with a cracking and then a rumble that was heard above the roar of the storm, crushing everything that hadn't been consumed in the flames.

In the morning, though, Ross and Cockburn found their task incomplete. Soaked by the rain, some public buildings proved difficult to reignite, but the British were determined arsonists, and eventually fresh flames rose above Washington. That afternoon a storm more brutal than the first swept through the city, dousing the embers.

When the self-appointed spies rendezvoused that evening, they assessed the damage.

"Looks like all the private houses were spared," Quinn noted.

"Yeah, the only exception was the one that Henry here got burned," Frake said. "After I saw they weren't burning civilian houses, I hid in one, and they passed right under the front window. I was close enough to put one right between their eyes. So I leaned out and begged, 'Spare us, oh, spare us.'"

Quinn chuckled, imagining the grizzled Kentuckian pleading with the Brits.

"Yeah, so they call back, 'Not to fear, sir, we are not barbarians like your Jamey Madison. Your life and possessions are safe, but stay inside lest you be shot as a spy.' Had to laugh at that one. What'd you learn?" He directed the question to Quinn.

"Not all that much," Quinn said. "Most of the British camped out east of the Capitol. Three, four thousand of them. Got the worst of it in the storm. Tired and dispirited, but not as much as us."

"At least they're still an army. No telling where our side hightailed off to. Probably isn't an organized platoon left outside of Barney's men."

"I went to that doctor's house, and the British brought him their own wounded, the ones too hurt to treat in a bivouac. Some of them are messed up pretty good. Quite a sight to see the Brits getting doctored right next to the Americans. I just kind of blended in, kept busy with dressings and stuff. Kept my ears open. Some scuttlebutt about them heading back to their ships in the morning. It'd make sense—why stay here? I thought I might find out a lot more when—you're not going to believe this—Ross himself showed up."

"No."

"Yes. There I was standing right next to him, close enough to slit his throat. His men, as miserable as they were, sure perked up when they saw him. He's purely worshiped. Walked around, talked to everyone. I think they'd march through hell for him."

"So, didya find out anything?"

"Not from Ross. The men don't much care if they go to Baltimore or somewhere else, just want to go home."

"So," Frake concluded, "when they go back to their ships, we still don't know what's next? Alexandria? Baltimore? Philadelphia? Maybe New York, Boston?"

"Baltimore." Henry spoke with certainty.

"How do you know?" Frake was skeptical.

"Heard it from Ross and Cockburn."

"You just walked up and asked 'em real polite?"

"No, sir. I kept my distance and followed them to a boarding house, where they set up their headquarters. After that they headed over to the White House, banged their way in, and sat down at a table. Laughed about how the lady of the house must be expecting them. I just passed myself off as the house nigger, too stupid to run."

Quinn and Frake looked at each other, first with surprise and then admiration.

"You mean you were right there in the *same room*?"

"Us colored folk is nigh invisible. They hardly knew I was there. I just ladled out the soup and passed out the vittles, said yas sah, no sah, your grace, and all that, while they joked and talked about what they was planning."

"Right in front of you."

"Like I said, we's invisible. Ross didn't seem real convinced, but it sounded like Baltimore is next. Take it and hold it, cut off trade, strangle the country. Maybe make a separate peace with the North. Thought the rest of the fleet would make it up the Potomac to take Alexandria 'bout the same time as they to got to Washington, but no. Maybe the river slowed them up with all those shallows. Anyhow, they still count on them to take Alexandria, but Baltimore's their main target. Maybe turn back to a colony."

"Good God, they might as well written you a letter and drawn you a map."

Henry nodded sadly. "But what they did to that grand house! Plundering whatever they could find. Took the cushion Mrs. Madison used to sit on. Lord! Made a crude remark no gentleman would repeat. Even Cockburn took stuff to brag on later. Then they piled the furniture and papers, curtains and whatnot, in the middle of a room and set it a fire. Stood around outside, smirking and joking, watching it burn."

"Hear anything about Commodore Barney?"

"Took him prisoner and treated him like a hero. Admired his courage. Said they'd parole him once they get the job done. After Baltimore, I guess."

"We've got to find someone to tell all this to. Christ, no one knows where Madison is. Winder? Armstrong? God help us. We're going to have to head off in different directions and hope we run into someone who knows what the hell to do. Frake, you go south. Warn Alexandria what to expect—if it's not too late. Henry, you and I'll go north to Baltimore, Fort McHenry, and all."

5 September 1814

Baltimore

The British miscalculated. If the British thought that burning Washington would so dishearten Americans that they would plead for peace, it didn't. Word of the calamity spread in the newspapers from Richmond and Baltimore to Charleston and Philadelphia and beyond, as fast as riders could carry them. In New York, Boston, and other Federalist bastions, the effect was stunning. The war's opponents demanded retribution. The country came together in its outrage—yes, at the mishandling of Washington's defense, but more at the British. Nothing since the Declaration of Independence had so unified the nation. It was a high water mark for a country divided geographically, ethnically, and economically.

Baltimore was prepared. Maryland—unlike Washington—was a state with its own militia and with many men available for the city's defense. No need for Maryland Governor Levin Winder to plead with other states for men and arms, though several readily offered them. When the musters were called, more than ten thousand men responded, far outnumbering the four thousand British soldiers and marines available for a land assault.

The British route to Baltimore would be on both land and water. Over water, the British would assault the city on the Patapsco River. Because the river is shallow, narrow, and loaded with shoals, the British approach would be time consuming, even dangerous. The British had not sounded the river and so risked running aground while trying to maneuver under the American guns placed at Fort McHenry and elsewhere.

Over land, the British could attack from southeast or southwest, but either option required a debarkation point to put ashore foot soldiers and artillery somewhere along the Patapsco. Again, unfamiliarity with the terrain weighed against the British. Three weeks after Washington burned, the betting was heavy, not on whether the British would attack, but on when the assault would come and from which direction.

Every able-bodied man in Maryland was automatically a member of the militia. Each received an order to report with arms—ten rounds of ball cartridges, knapsack, and canteen—at regimental headquarters when the alarm was issued. Maryland's militia commander, Major General Samuel Smith, set about reinforcing the regular army units at Fort McHenry at the mouth of Baltimore Harbor. Fort Armistead on the western approach to town was strengthened. To the east, on a ridge running across Hampstead Hill, he sent troops to building breastworks and redoubts. They clogged the entrance to Baltimore Harbor with sunken and derelict ships. Citizens were required to assist in constructing earthworks, bringing any available shovels, pickaxes, and wheelbarrows. Artillery was positioned to shell enemy ships and to protect American troops on land. Smith trained and retrained his men to anticipate every conceivable British strategy. Here, he vowed, there would be no rout, no troops retreating in humiliating defeat.

Indeed, in Washington it took days to regroup and for Winder to establish a semblance of military presence. Many of the men who fled the District had gone home to Baltimore, and now they pledged things would be different.

Quinn, Frake, and Henry had reported their discoveries to the authorities. In fact, Frake had traveled south from Washington and actually encountered the president's party and was able to inform Madison himself. In Baltimore, Quinn and Henry were directed to Smith's headquarters, where they told him what they knew. Barney's troops were mustering, so the fighting was not yet over for the trio.

While waiting for the alarm of the approaching British, Quinn took the opportunity to return to his family's Baltimore home, where he was astonished to learn that his three brothers had been at Bladensburg and had come through unscathed, though understandably shaken by their first taste of combat. They knew of the bravery of Barney's forces and had worried about Will, especially after the Maryland militia abandoned the battlefield, leaving Barney's men to their fate. Now they were determined to redeem their honor and send the Limeys scurrying back to England in disgrace.

Quinn was quick to reassure them. "The fault lies with the commanders and the government," he told them.

His pent-up frustrations, fueled by the Washington debacle, were at a full boil now. So why was he still in the fight? Loyalty? Duty? Nothing really explained it. Some mechanism, he concluded, keeps men in battle till the war's end releases them.

"I hear that General Smith wants to see you," Cavan said to Willie later, after Frake joined them. "I bet he's got some special plans for you."

"That's what I'm afraid of."

"Couldn't be worse than you've already seen," Aengus said.

"It can always get worse. Just ask Frake."

Frake nodded. "Henry here knows how things keep getting worse. You planning to stay with us or make a run for freedom?"

Henry remembered running through the streams and hiding in cornfields, beset by the choking fear of getting caught.

"It's a hard choice," he replied, reminding his hosts of the stark realities he faced.

Stay and fight and get killed or maimed. Run and be discovered as a fugitive slave. Stay and fight and...come out a hero? Win his freedom? Find his family?

"Guess I'll hear what Smith has to say."

The general did indeed have a special mission in mind. "I've assigned the remnants of Barney's flotilla to breastworks on the city's east side," he explained when they reported to him the next morning. "But your talents can be put to better use elsewhere."

"Here it comes," Frake whispered from the side of his mouth.

"We've got a battalion of riflemen, Aisquith's Sharpshooters—stout men."

The three looked at each other in surprise.

"My God, general, my three brothers are in that outfit," Quinn said.

"A happy coincidence."

"Not if we all get wiped out at once," Quinn retorted.

"Well, then," Smith replied firmly, "you'll all have to keep an eye on each other. The sharpshooters have been training for this moment since the British sailed into Chesapeake Bay two years ago. They can pluck the eye out of a squirrel at one hundred paces, but they've had little or no combat experience—that's why they panicked and fled the field of battle.

"So I'd like you boys to go with them. Help Aisquith keep them under control. Show by example."

"We ain't no nursemaids," Frake grumbled.

Smith grinned. "Frake's got a point. This won't be a nursemaid job, believe me. And from everything I hear, Mr. Frake, you can teach these men a thing or two about sharpshooting. Take out a squirrel's eye at *two hundred* paces, I bet."

The compliment softened Frake's disposition from pugnacious to merely gruff. "Might could, sir."

"Look, I calculate the British will come up the peninsula from North Point," Smith said, referring to a finger of land running out from the east side of Baltimore and then south along the east side of the Patapsco River. "We *must* stop them there before they reach the redoubts and earthworks at the city. Folks see those ranks of Redcoats heading their way…could start a panic. I'm confident that the east wall will hold, but we've got to use every tactical advantage we have. And North Point gives us that."

"More than a delaying tactic, then, sir?" Quinn said.

"Yes. I'm sending General Stricker's forces to scout, delay, and—I hope—defeat whatever the Brits send marching our way. They can't take Baltimore without a land attack. Their big warships can get only so far up the river. Then they depend on the sloops, barges, and shallower draft vessels to pound their way in. We'll have them in a crossfire."

Now Smith looked from one to the other, each in the eyes. "I don't have to tell you how vital this is. We've lost Washington and Alexandria. The northern frontier was a disaster. If we lose Baltimore, we risk losing all. Any more losses up here, and the Brits will be knocking on the door at New Orleans. Without a victory here and now… But you don't need me to tell you.

"A lot has been asked of you already, I know. But every failure you've survived, every blockhead who didn't cost you your lives, has given you valuable experience. Maybe this will be the time we do it right. With God's help."

12 September 1814

North Point, Maryland

Stricker's First Brigade of Maryland militia was marching smartly toward North Point, a fact that Quinn observed.

"They seem well trained. Maybe this is a good sign."

"I have to agree," the crusty veteran said. Although he allowed, "Perhaps not as crisply as Kentucky militiamen."

"Who does?" Quinn cracked. "But you've got to admit, whatever they lack in marching ability, they make up in enthusiasm."

"Enthusiasm don't win wars. Courage does. We have yet to see."

Vivid recollections of militia collapsing under fire troubled Quinn, as did having his brothers under his direction. He felt responsible both for their safety and for the mission's success, and he feared a conflict between those duties. He had considered asking Aisquith to transfer his brothers to a different unit, but these men had trained together, and it was probably best for them to remain a unit. Besides, he didn't think his brothers would stand for it.

The brigade had marched for a day, encountering no opposition, no hint of a British landing. When they bivouacked, they were grateful for the chance to rest but fearful of what lay ahead. When? And how? And where? Was the enemy just over the hill? Waiting in ambush in the next grove?

Having settled in camp for the night, some were morosely silent, others talkative. As his brothers introduced Quinn, Frake, and Henry to the men, Quinn felt the weight of their lives in his hands. He wanted them to be nameless—and their wives and children and the towns they came from and the work they did in peacetime. Knowing them would make it harder to see their brains blown out or to leave them behind with the rest of the wounded if he had to move forward. Stop in place, and you become an easy target. He had seen too many lost that way. Nevertheless, he talked to them. Idle conversation eased their fears a little, he knew.

Private Henry G. McComas was an apprentice at the Felix Jenkins leather works, learning to make saddles, harnesses, and trunks. He liked to use his middle initial, thought it sounded more prestigious.

Daniel Wells' grandfather and namesake had fought in the War of Independence, and the boy was apprenticed to another Jenkins, Edward, also a saddler. Both shops were near the Quinns's linen business fronting Baltimore Harbor.

Private Peter Little apprenticed at the neighborhood print shop, and Corporal Casparus McGinnis was a blacksmith. Quinn matched other faces with names: William McGee, Francis Mitchell, and George Pewder. Those names and faces wandered through his dreams, and at dawn an orderly poked his head into the tent to say that General Stricker was calling his officers together in the Methodist meeting house.

The squat, whitewashed building sat alone in a harvested wheat field, not a hundred paces away. Stricker had already been debriefed by a cavalry scout who arrived at full gallop from Baltimore, followed moments later by another from the south.

"Gentlemen," he told the assembled group, "the invasion of Baltimore is underway."

The room erupted in questions, but he raised a hand for silence.

"Please, your attention, for I have much to impart. The British have landed at North Point. We expected as much, but Smith will have to contend with more than fifty warships that are now maneuvering into position. Those ships will unleash a heavy barrage of cannon and rockets.

"It's what we hoped they'd do. The British have divided their sea and land forces, generally not a wise thing to do. We know from our spies that the vanguard of the troops that landed at North Point is a light brigade. They're made up of companies from several regiments of foot. They're backed up by six field pieces, two howitzers, and several more foot regiments and marines. They appear to be traveling light and expecting a quick victory. We estimate their force at some four thousand men against our three thousand, but we know the land better, and their supply lines are stretched. General Ross is in command, and I dare say Cockburn is with him. You need not discourage your men from exacting retribution for his iniquitous behavior."

Murmurs of agreement rippled through the room.

"We expected them to move quickly to engage us, but they haven't. Ross and Cockburn are enjoying a leisurely break at the farm of one Robert Gorsuch, as if their only pending business was a Sunday promenade. Gentlemen, we will not endure this insult."

Again, there were murmurs of assent, but Stricker went on. "They are so certain of victory, so smug, as if saying, 'You Yankees, pick the spot. Wherever, the victory will be His Majesty's.' But here"—he jammed his finger onto a large map pinned to the bare wall—"*this* is where we choose to meet them."

The site was about halfway down the fourteen-mile neck of North Point where the British would have to approach over open fields. The rest of the land was marshy and flat, except for some wooded groves and a zigzag fence that could provide cover for the Americans. Flanking their position were two streams—Bear Creek on the right, and to the left Bread and Cheese Creek. The British would have to fight through the strip of the land between them, and the main American force would be waiting.

"We'll post riflemen where they'll have to ford the two streams and have ourselves a turkey shoot. To the rear of the main line, we'll place our thirty-ninth and fifty-first regiments. The sixth will be farther back"—he pointed again—"at Cook's Tavern. Our artillery will straddle the main road, Long Log Lane.

"Lieutenant Colonel Biays, you will move your cavalry—about a hundred and forty horsemen? Good— three miles up toward the Gorsuch farm. Captain Aisquith, your sharpshooters will form their skirmish lines here." He indicated a tree line about a mile ahead.

"From all indications, Ross has brought little if any cavalry with him, so he cannot send out mounted scouts. This is our chance to redeem our country, to make amends for Bladensburg, and to mete out justice for the wanton destruction of the capital. Good hunting, gentlemen." He pulled a cigar from an inside pocket of his military blouse and put a match to it.

Returning to his platoon, Quinn outlined the battle plans. Many officers kept the broader plan a secret for fear that captured soldiers could be cajoled or tortured into revealing critical intelligence. But Quinn had seen too many soldiers stumbling around in confusion thanks to their ignorance of the overall strategy.

"Keeping the boys in the dark serves no purpose but to feed panic under fire," he told Frake.

So while other junior officers conducted an inspection of uniforms—which soon would be filthy with mud and blood—Quinn gathered his around him.

"Don't bunch up. You *feel* safer in a group, but you're not. You're just a better target. You're safer on your own. Remember that when you shoot, you give away your position, so think about where you are. Is there a tree or rock to duck behind? The return fire will come before you know it. When you reload, don't expose yourself by standing up or by turning your back on the enemy.

"The truth, men, is that we're the trip wire. The sound of our first engagement with the enemy tells the main body where the Brits are. We're not here to take on the whole British army, so be ready at my signal to fall back and regroup. This is dangerous work, and my job is to bring you all back safely. Be careful out there. Now, form up."

The four platoons of Aisquith's sharpshooters were first to move out of camp. Quinn divided his platoon into two squads; he took one and Frake took the other. He put his brother Malachy in Frake's squad and Cavan and Aengus into his.

The company was already on the move as the morning sun burned through the fog and dew from the forests, bogs, and fields. Already the men were sweating.

When the sun reached its zenith, the platoon was in position on the right flank of the skirmishers, along the tree line fronting a quarter-mile clearing. The clearing ended at a rise where a road emerged from a grove of trees. No sooner had Quinn settled in than the sound of gunfire erupted from beyond the clearing, sporadic and moving.

The forward cavalry spotters had been seen and were on the run. Quinn watched horsemen in full gallop thunder along the road toward the American line then disappear into the woods.

Any minute now, Quinn thought.

A final check of the men and then he and all his men dropped into a prone firing position—Aengus ten yards to his right, and Cavan ten to his left. Beyond him Quinn could see McComas, Wells, and Casparus, along with other men, now visibly fidgeting.

They waited.

Stricker had said the British lacked cavalry, so he wasn't surprised when no dragoons pursued the American riders. But five minutes grew into ten and then fifteen. It was agonizing.

Quinn crept to his right and spoke softly to those who seemed ready to shoot. "Hold, hold. You'll know the Red Coats when you see them. Pick out a single target. Good shooting."

As he slithered back to his original position, something on the rise about five hundred yards distant caught his eye. Movement. Then the Red Coats—maybe two dozen—spreading out along the road as it descended into the clearing. This was an advance reconnaissance party, probably several hundred yards ahead of the light brigade. His scrotum tightened.

Then he caught his breath in amazement. A man on horseback rode forward, his uniform impressive even at this distance.

"Jesus," Quinn muttered, "he's ahead of everyone. Even in front of the vanguard."

Senior officers often gained their men's respect by leading them into battle, and Ross was certainly a leader. But generals did not ride with or ahead of a reconnaissance party.

He must be insane, Quinn thought. *Does he really expect to march unmolested into Baltimore?*

Whispers among the men told him they too recognized Ross.

Someone far to Quinn's left fired a single shot. Ross didn't even flinch. He was too far away to be hit, and the shooter was too far away for the British skirmishers to return effective fire.

"Wait! Wait! Pass it down," Quinn whispered to his brothers.

Don't scare him off, he thought, but no one else had fired. Ross might think some lone American was trying to take on the entire British infantry. Maybe he would come closer.

He did. By now the light brigade had reached the crest of the rise and started down, stepping along in five perfect columns. That impressive picture was intended to frighten the enemy into rash actions or retreat, and it often did. But no one moved, and soon the British would be in range. Quinn found himself hoping Frake would get off the first shot.

As Ross rode closer, Quinn heard, "I see a mark."

"So do I," another voice answered.

He turned and was alarmed to see Wells and McComas standing together under a tree. Cavan had joined them, and they were drawing a bead on Ross. Hadn't he warned them not to bunch up like that?

"No!" he called out. "No! Not together. Take cover first. Take cover,!"

Simultaneous musket and rifle reports echoed up and down the American line. Instinctively, Quinn turned in time to see Ross fall. The ball or bullet had struck his right arm, ripping the reins out of his hands, and had then apparently entered his chest, judging by the blood dyeing his uniform. The impact spun him sideways in his saddle and knocked him to the ground. Was he dead?

Even before Ross fell, British skirmishers fired at the telltale wisps of smoke that showed Wells's and McCormack's location.

"Take cover! Take cover!" Quinn shouted as the two began to reload.

Now Cavan was taking aim, as all three missed or ignored his warning. A heavy volley from the British marksmen ripped through the leaves, thumped into branches, and thudded into the soft flesh of the men.

The back of Wells's head exploded in a spray of blood, hair, and brains. McComas took one in the back. Cavan, the most exposed, was struck repeatedly as he braced his gun to fire.

Forgetting his own advice, Quinn sprang to his brothers' side. Gunfire, British and American, erupted all around him. Cavan had landed on his back, and one side of him—his face, neck, and shoulder—had been turned into pulp. Quinn vomited.

"No, don't. Get back!" he shouted as Aengus ran to them.

He rose as he shouted, and a round sliced across the side of his head. He felt himself spinning to the ground and crashing facedown onto the forest floor. The warm liquid running down his left temple and into his eye was, he knew, his blood. Then came pain, dizziness, loud ringing, and finally darkness.

12 September 1814

North Point

Quinn was moving. No...*being* moved. Someone held him under his shoulders, and someone else had his feet. He couldn't really see, but there was light and shadow as he was jostled along. Whoever it was put him down on something hard. A rock? He couldn't move...couldn't see. He could hear noises...familiar sounds. *Thump. Thwack. Crack.* Battle. Someone was fighting and screaming. Who? Where was he? Men were running, stumbling, cursing. Were they leaving him? He couldn't speak. Pain was in the whole right side of his head.

Yes. He'd been shot. Was he dying? Maybe not, but... Cavan! Cavan was dead and then—

Now he was lifted again. Had he slept? Passed out?

"We got to stop the bleeding! Put him down!"

A familiar voice—a brother. Maybe Cavan was alive, and *he* was dead. Darkness again.

Quinn opened his eyes, and his vision was blurry, but he could see. The room was familiar. He was flat on his back, and his head throbbed. Pain like at York. Darkness.

"I know this man." The voice was distant but hostile. "I saw him in Washington. He was with the wounded at the medical station. I thought he was a civilian orderly. He wasn't in uniform then."

"You sure?"

"Yes, I'm sure. He was spying, sure as hell! Shoot him."

"Now? Shoot a wounded man before we even know what he's done?"

"Yes, because he was a spy. It'll be a lesson to others."

"What others? These half-dead men? Waste of a bullet. He's going to die anyway."

Quinn heard a gun cock then a new voice. "What the hell you doing?"

"Shooting a spy."

"Not while I'm in charge here."

"Sergeant, get these men out. Any more insubordination and *you'll* face a court martial and a firing squad."

"Says who?"

"Captain James Waterford of His Majesty's surgical corps. Don't tempt me to arrest you, you insolent pug."

More darkness. When Quinn opened his eyes again, he'd no idea how much time had passed. Minutes? Days? When he closed his eyes, he saw Cavan lying in a pool of blood. He moaned and forced his eyes open again.

He was back in the Methodist meeting house, Stricker's headquarters before the battle. The map displaying the American positions was gone from the wall. The room was crowded with men moaning, asking for water, or calling for their mothers. He was lying on a pallet under a blanket stiff with dried blood and filth. He tried to get up, but strong hands pressed down on his shoulders.

"Lie still," a deep voice said. It was firm but reassuring.

The man stepped around to Quinn's side. He was enormous, and in the gown of a British medical officer, he looked like the enemy.

"You've had your head creased with a bullet. Took a slice out of your skull, almost down to your brain. Fractured your skull there, I'm afraid. Apparently, it didn't cause any subdural bleeding or you'd be dead by now."

Subdural bleeding? He remembered York. He didn't die then. Would he now?

"You're a surgeon?"

"Yes. Now you *must not* move. I've stopped the external bleeding and sewn you up, but I don't know what's going on inside that hard skull. Move around too much, and you might shake something loose. You're a lucky man, you know. Here, let me look at your bandages."

"I'm lying here. I could die, and that's *lucky*?"

"That's right, son. Not many soldiers with head wounds survive. Most of them here have a leg or an arm amputated. But you...I don't know. Surgeons made great headway in the Napoleonic Wars. They treated head wounds, tied off blood vessels with ligatures, excavated skulls to relieve pressure... Unfortunately, *I* never did any of that. I'm your regular sawbones."

"Anyone else here by the name of Quinn? Malachy or Aengus?"

"Can't say. Some of your men?"

"My brothers. I started out with three, but one was killed."

"I'm sorry, son." Waterford looked around at the wounded on their cots or on blankets spread on the floor. "There's some we don't know their names. I'll check." He waved over an orderly. "See if anyone here answers to the name Quinn. Brothers of this man here."

As the orderly moved away, Quinn asked, "What now?"

"I'll keep you here as long as possible."

"Meaning?"

"I don't know." The surgeon reached down to adjust the blanket that had bunched up under Quinn's back.

"Thank you. I reckon the Americans have retreated?"

"Yes. Last I knew, we'd fought to the outskirts of Baltimore."

"How long ago was that?"

"A day ago, I guess. Now drink this water. You must not become dehydrated."

"So Ross is about to take Baltimore?"

"Not Ross, no."

An image of Ross hit by gunfire flashed across Quinn's mind. "He got hit," he said softly.

"Yes."

"Hurt bad?"

"Dead."

"I'm sorry," Quinn said and did not add that he wished it had been Cockburn.

"Some men carried him back to us. We hadn't set up a field hospital yet, but we did the best we could. Chest wound. Couldn't stop the internal bleeding. Said something about his wife before he died. He knew it was coming— death, I mean."

"How many times was he hit?" Quinn asked, remembering the simultaneous shots, but he regretted the question when he saw the surgeon's face. "Sorry."

"Really, I couldn't tell," the surgeon answered. "Maybe more than once, maybe not. Thinking of giving out some medals?"

"No, but someone in my platoon—" Quinn thought better of saying it, but the surgeon finished the sentence.

"Shot him?"

Quinn went silent.

"I should tell you," the surgeon said. "General Ross was a soldier's soldier. The men all respected him. Maybe I shouldn't tell you this, but it can't hurt now. The fight pretty much went out of the men when he died. I don't know how they advanced as far as they did."

"They're professionals," Quinn said.

"Indeed. But we're all beginning to wonder what the hell we're doing here. It's not like your Mr. Madison is Napoleon, threatening to sail up the Thames and put the king in stocks."

"I'm wondering too," Quinn said.

The surgeon chuckled. "I don't know about your president and Congress, but I imagine the war office and the admiralty back in London are wondering the same. Not to mention the king, the prime minister and parliament. If it was up to me, we'd be long gone."

Quinn smiled then, and before Waterford could turn away, asked, "How did I get here?"

"Don't know. You were here when we arrived. Someone brought you here and left."

"Are other Americans here?"

The surgeon nodded. "About half the men here, as best I can tell."

"I remember hearing shooting and men screaming. It was—"

"Yes, it was. Well, it looks good under those bandages," the doctor remarked as he stretched the gauze back in place. "We've got to be careful of infection. Wounds get septic all the time. We'll change those bandages regularly. We can't cauterize wounds on a head."

"I've survived worse. I was at York."

Now the doctor's voice was chilly. "Were you present at that outrage?"

"You could say so, but it wasn't our fault."

"How so?"

Quinn explained that the retreating British had set off the armory, and the explosion had put him into a coma. The surgeon looked startled. "This is your *second* head injury?"

Quinn nodded.

"This isn't good. As I said, we don't know what's going on inside your head, but with a second wound, your chances of dire consequences greatly increase—going back into a coma. Losing brain function, memory, cognition. Sorry to be so blunt, but you took me by surprise. You could lose your sight, maybe your hearing. Your reason. But one thing is sure—your fighting days are over."

Quinn took a moment to consider. He was finally finished with this war. Or maybe not. Maybe he could still fight. Sally would be happy if he couldn't. If she still cared. But didn't his country need him? And how would he make a living? The linen factory? Would they need him now with Cavan gone?

Waterford smiled thinly. "Nothing's sure, son, in the art of medicine, but further injury to your head would lead to permanent impairment. You shouldn't fight again."

Maybe that was just as well. Nearly killed twice, taken prisoner... He must be the luckiest soldier in this confounded war, but now what would he do with his life?

"Will there be a prisoner exchange?" he asked.

"Too soon to say."

"If not, what happens to me, to us?"

"That depends..."

"On what? If you lose, will you leave us here?"

"We're not likely to lose. But if we withdraw, I don't think we'd take you along. Most of you are too badly wounded. Anyhow, you seem to be a survivor, and if we leave, I'm sure your countrymen will find you."

"If they get here before some of us die."

"When we leave, I'll raise a white flag over this place. That should bring them."

"Can I get a message...to my family?"

"Not now."

So the idea of capture and execution for being a traitor re-entered Quinn's mind in full force. Indeed, he already was, for the third time, in British hands. His only hope was an American victory, and that seemed utterly unlikely now. His luck at last had run out.

14 September 1814

North Point

Quinn's brain seemed to be pushing against his skull as if it would burst through the bone. He dozed, but the pain was so fierce it woke him. Hoping that movement might help, he struggled out of his cot and steadied himself against the wall, but the pain persisted. Slowly he put one foot in front of the other and tried to pace. That made the pain even more piercing, so he lay down again, resting his head on the wadded blanket that served as his pillow.

He whimpered. *God, oh God, it's worse.*

If a loaded gun had been near him, he would have blown his offending brain out. Anything for relief.

"An infection," he mumbled. "Am I going to die? If I don't get help, I *will*. Someone help me." Then louder, "Somebody help me, please."

The room was spinning, but he could make out men lying on cots and blankets, all motionless and silent. Why wouldn't anyone help? No doctor, no orderlies. The British must have gone and left them. His head hurt so much that he knew the sound of gunfire would drive him out of his mind. He sat up again, carefully, and squeezed his eyes shut.

Think, he told himself. Could he go for help? A table across the room… It looked familiar. Yes! That was where Dr. Waterford had dispensed medications. Maybe there was something…

He forced himself upright, braced himself on the backs of chairs, and staggered the impossible distance to the table. He drew a deep breath then began scrutinizing the bottles and vials, knocking some over in the process. At last he found one marked laudanum.

Uncorking the painkiller, he brought the bottle to his lips and took a sip, then two, then three. He longed to drain it completely but made himself stop, give the drug time to work. He tucked the bottle under his arm and searched the table for anything else useful, but he was too addled to think straight. He stumbled back to his cot, lay down, and felt the first soothing effects of the opium-based palliative. His head might not explode after all, he thought. Then darkness again.

Later—an hour? A day?— he awoke and noticed a spot on the ceiling. A water spot? Had it rained? The headache returned, and he passed out again. His dreams, fueled by the laudanum, were bizarre. Multicolored balls of light raced back and forth, trailing wakes of sparks. He was in a strange city street that was somehow familiar. Odd, nauseating smells assaulted him, and weird, disturbing sounds.

Awake again. Now covered in sweat, urine soaking the crotch of his pants and marinating his clothing and cot below his buttocks. The smell was sharp, like a physical presence in his nose. Then other smells—excrement, soiled clothing, pus-soaked bandages. The pain had eased a bit, but still he reached for the laudanum. Where was it? His hands patted frantically at his putrid clothing and blanket.

"Looking for this?"

The hoarse voice was surprisingly close.

"What?"

"This," the voice said, coming closer.

"I can't see!"

"That's 'cause it's night. A lamp would attract attention. No telling what's out there."

As Quinn's eyes grew accustomed to the darkness, he saw the man hovering over his cot. "Laudanum," the voice said. "Thought you was going to swig every last drop before I could get some. Had to save some for the rest of us. We're not in such good shape."

"That's the truth of it," came another voice out of the blackness.

"Who are you?" Quinn asked.

"Private Caleb Barnes, at your service. Reckon you've been unconscious on and off for the better part of the day and two nights. Thought we were going to lose you."

"What day is it?"

"Thursday, maybe. We ain't seen hide nor hair of anyone since the Brits took their leave."

"Where did they go?" Quinn rose up on his elbow and reached with his other hand for the laudanum. Barnes squatted next to the cot.

"Back where they come from. Be careful now, ensign. You gulp down too much of that stuff, and you'll be going out of your mind with craving for the rest of your life."

Quinn took a single sip and passed the bottle back. "I don't understand. The British surgeon said they were knocking on Baltimore's door."

"They was, but things musta not worked out for 'em, because the next day they went trotting down North Point to their ships. I'm hoping they sailed back to England where they belong."

"Them lobsterbacks musta gotten beat up pretty bad," a disembodied voice said.

"Well, the sky over yonder trees," Barnes said, pointing toward Baltimore, "was pretty well lit up. Rockets and cannon fire. Went on all night. Stench of gunpowder floating this way made me sick. Must have been some fight. Sun up and the guns went silent. A few hours later, the first Redcoats came marching past and kept right on going."

"I don't understand. We were losing. They had scores of gunships and gunboats. They could have pounded Baltimore from land *and* sea." His head still throbbed, but this news was penetrating the pain.

"Don't know. Heard some grumbling when the Redcoats passed by. Some were right glad to get out of here, but some were grousing that they didn't get to fight."

"Something turned them around. No time now to dwell on it. Got to get moving."

"Moving? Where?"

"I mean I have to get up. Get out of these filthy clothes. Change my dressings. Clean up."

"One thing to be grateful for—the Brits left us food and medicine. They just took off with their sick and wounded on litters. The doctor, he apologized that he couldn't do any more for us."

Quinn swung his feet onto the floor, sat upright on the cot, stood up, and passed out again.

15 September 1814

North Point

Quinn felt cool water on his face and woke.

"Christ, Willie, you look like death."

"Malachy?"

"Jesus, Mary, and Joseph, Willie, you had us worried! But here you are, taking your ease among the Methodists."

"You look horrible," Aengus chimed in.

"You're both here?" Quinn felt the pain returning and tried to sit up. "Where's the laudanum?"

"Whoa! Lie back, brother," Malachy said. "Quit jumping around like a fresh-born foal. Aengus, find Willie's medicine. Now then." He peered more closely at Will. "You're not doing so well, from the looks of you. But better than we expected. We thought we might find you dead," he said, turning away.

Bracing himself, Malachy turned back to remove the foul dressing around Quinn's head and gagged at the smell and the sight. "First order of business is to get you cleaned up. What did the Brit doctor say about your wounds?"

Quinn repeated most of what the surgeon had told him—his prognosis and the dangers of infection. He left out the doctor's admonition about returning to the fight.

Then he demanded and got a report of the battle of North Point—how the Americans retreated; how Stricker's left had panicked and fled; how that left Frake, Henry, and the Quinns exposed on the right; how Stricker was forced to retreat to the fortifications on Hampstead Hill east of the city.

"Are Frake and Henry here?" Quinn asked, looking around the crowded room at the other wounded and the men tending to them.

"Be here soon. Frake's platoon wasn't far behind us. They're fine and anxious to see you."

"How'd you know where I was?"

"We brought you. Carried you at a dead run. Bullets whistling all over the place. God Almighty, thought we'd never make it."

"And Cavan?"

Malachy averted his eyes. "We had to leave him. Couldn't carry you both."

Quinn closed his eyes and thought of crows, coyotes, and other scavengers picking at his brother's flesh, his eyes…

"We'll try to get his remains back," Aengus said quietly. "But *you're* not going anywhere except home to recuperate. Mother has been waiting, expecting to hear the worst. And Sally too."

"Are they well?"

"They'll be better when they see you. Mother's already lost a son and a husband to this war."

The impact fell heavily on Quinn, who fell into silence.

For hours the Americans tended their wounded—bathing them, changing their dressings, feeding them, collecting personal information, arranging to send them home. The dead were removed as quickly as possible to a wagon and covered with a tarp. Heavy rains from the night before made the going slippery, causing litter bearers to skid and drop their morbid burdens into the mud.

When Henry and Frake joined the Quinns, their exuberance at finding Will alive drowned out the moans from other wounded men for a time, but then Henry looked around and took in the scene around him.

"God Almighty, this is a scene right out of hell," he said.

Quinn winced a little as Malachy replaced his bandages, but he was desperate to know more. "Tell me the details. I want to know everything. Did we win?"

"Victory is ours, lad. We drove them away," Malachy replied proudly.

"How? The last I heard from the British doctor the Limeys were at the gates of Baltimore."

"And so they were. Coming by land *and* by sea—but they couldn't land their ships. You shoulda seen it. They were pouring it on. Six-pounders, twelve-pounders, twenty-four-pounders, much bigger ones, and those screeching rockets. Fort McHenry took the brunt of it."

"Don't know how anyone survived," Aengus cut in. "It went on for hours and hours. Thought it would never stop. But when it finally did, the fort was still there and the colors still flying." His blue eyes gleamed with tears at the memory.

Malachy took up the tale. "The sight of it, grown men weeping and cheering. You could hear crowds all over the city. They must have been dug in good at the fort."

Frake chimed in. "No matter where the Brits tried to land, guns were waiting. Civilians came from all over the city to man the barricades, reload, haul ammunition and supplies, and bring food and water. Never saw a sight like it, probably never will again."

"Even Mother," Aengus said and then laughed as Quinn rolled his eyes.

Agnes Quinn was not one to sit home and knit in a crisis.

"Don't know anyone—man or woman—who can reload a musket as quick as her."

"The British couldn't bring their biggest guns in closer because of the shoals," Malachy explained. "And without the cover of those guns, the British barges would be blasted out of the water."

"But Ross, I mean Cockburn, was winning. *He* could have breached the fortifications, couldn't he?"

"Might be he coulda," Frake picked up the story. "He only had five miles to go before he'd meet up with General Smith's defenses, including us. But he waited."

"Waited?"

"Yeah, the British kept trying to land barges full of Redcoats west of the fort. Wanted to draw some of Smith's troops away, but a bunch of ships had been sunk in their way, and they couldn't get around them. Got confused. Fort's guns chewed 'em up and spit 'em out. Smith didn't have to move a single soldier to defend the west side."

"Then what?"

"Well, we gotten detailed to entrenchments along Hampstead Hill where we could see them Limeys about a mile out. Getting ready to attack, it looked like, maybe waiting for the sun to set. But come nightfall, it was raining and as black as coal. If they *had* come, we couldn't a seen 'em until they was sticking us with their bayonets." He shrugged. "They never came. Not that night nor next morning nor next day. Them ships kept blasting away at Fort McHenry, so we knew they weren't making any headway. Word spread down the line."

"So when *did* they finally attack?"

"Well, see, here's the confounding thing. The sun came up the next morning, and they was gone."

"Gone?"

"Disappeared like morning mist. Musta snuck off in the middle of the night with their tails between their legs."

"Good God Almighty. Didn't even fire a shot?"

"Not a one."

"Why?"

"Can't say for sure certain, but it seems like they planned a combined sea and land assault. When the sea one didn't work, the land troops got scared off."

"Scared off? They kicked the blazes out of Napoleon, and now they just walked away from *this*?"

"Think about it, Willie. If it was me and the sea part of my invasion didn't work, I'd think twice about charging up Hampstead Hill not knowing what was waiting up there."

"Didn't they scout it out?"

"Hell, they didn't have no horses except the one Ross got shot off of."

"Ross died."

"Did he now, and how you know that?"

"The British surgeon told me. He treated Ross but couldn't save him."

Malachy looked thoughtful. "Quite the jabberer, that surgeon. Giving out critical information to the enemy."

"Figured it couldn't hurt 'cause we were beaten. Or maybe 'cause he thought I wouldn't make it."

"Fooled them, didn't ya?" Frake said, drawing soft laughs from the brothers.

"Thank God," said Malachy.

"And the surgeon. Probably saved my life. Didn't expect that from a Brit, I'll tell you, especially since he had to know I'm Irish."

"His mistake, our fortune," Frake said. "But some of us think Stickler and us wore them and Ross out here. They drove us back, but they had to trek another five hot and sticky miles to Hampstead and on. They knew they'd have to take us on again, a lot of us fresh and rested. Or at least fresher and more rested than them. And knowing Ross was dead would take some of the fight out of them. Whoever took command maybe calculated it wasn't worth risking losing more men."

"God, Frake, this was a lot different than Bladensburg and Washington, wasn't it?"

"Got that right. Something sparked in the people of Baltimore. Fear or anger. Vengeance, maybe. If them Limeys thought burning Washington was gonna frighten us off, they sure got that wrong."

"Shows what people can do when they set their minds to it," Aengus said.

23 September 1814
Washington, D.C.

The first family had moved into the Octagon House, designed a decade and a half earlier by William Thornton, the architect of the U.S. Capitol. Because Colonel John Tayloe, its current owner, had offered it as an embassy to the French ambassador, it was saved from the British torch and now served as temporary home to the Madisons and their entourage.

Dolley and Sally chose the first-floor parlor as their workspace and set about restoring a semblance of normalcy to the household. Their hearts were lightened by the victories at Plattsburg in upper New York and Baltimore and by the departure of much of the British fleet from the Chesapeake. But when they heard the president's heavy footfalls barreling down the stairs from his study, they paused and looked up from their work to see him burst through the door. He was waving a letter that could not be good news.

"Look what they want now!" he shouted, flipping the letter into Dolley's lap.

She saw immediately that it was from John Quincy Adams, her husband's ambassador to Russia. He led a peace delegation that included the war hawk Senator Henry Clay, the Federalist Senator James Bayard, and Treasury Secretary Albert Gallatin. They had traveled to Ghent in the Low Countries months before to discuss terms of peace with the British, though secret negotiations to end the fighting had been going on virtually since the war began.

The message Dolley was studying while the president paced had been written only a few days after the burning of Washington, before Baltimore and Plattsburg, where the Americans had won another stunning victory. None of that news could have reached the peace delegation by the time Adams wrote.

She began to read aloud.

Mr. President,

I regret to bring to you news of British intransigence. Our British opposites are imperious and above themselves, though of second-tier rank. The king's top diplomats are at the Congress of Vienna, trying to heal Europe after Napoleon's ravages. Still, the delegation dallied about after arriving here and then did not present themselves but sent intermediaries to inform us that they saw no urgency in "this matter"!

Initially, they proposed that we come to their quarters, but we refused this incivility out of hand. The loquacious Mr. Clay, for one, was beside himself. Then when at last both delegations agreed on a neutral site for our meeting, we were taken aback by the intemperance of their demands. One might assume from their insolence that they had personally sashayed into Washington and raised the Union Jack above the Capitol.

Dolley glanced up at her husband, then continued.

> We conveyed our terms, primarily the end of
> impressments of our sailors and an end to the Orders
> in Council. Since the latter were revoked prior to
> the commencement of hostilities, we believed that,
> apart from our retention of territories acquired in the
> conflict and pending other matters, such as agreement
> on our Newfoundland fishing rights, our differences
> would soon be settled.
>
> Not so. At our first meeting, the British demanded
> surrender of territories in the Maine district of
> Massachusetts and the territory of Minnesota,
> removal of all naval vessels and garrisons from
> the Great Lakes, creation of an Indian buffer state
> encompassing most of the Northwest Territories,
> and the British right to unimpeded navigation and
> shipping along the entire Mississippi River.

Madison leaned over Dolley's shoulder and pointed. "There, that paragraph! That one! That would require the removal of a hundred thousand American citizens from the Northwest Territories and from the state of Ohio! Are we to declare Ohio no longer a state? Give up one-third of our sovereign domain to twenty thousand Indians? And free use of the Mississippi? We'd be giving Britain control of the whole of the Louisiana lands west of the river. And they want Maine too? Are they insane?"

Dolley placed a soothing hand on his arm, stopping him from slicing the humid air. He collapsed into an empty chair next to her and closed his eyes for a moment.

"By the Christ Lord himself, do not these English know any bounds—of decency, of civility? Curse their empire and the high-and-mighty attitude that goes with it."

"Dearest James, they did not yet know that their cause had been crippled. Surely, that news will diminish their arrogance," Dolley said. "Baltimore, Plattsburg. Their plans are in ruins. Their ships have departed the Chesapeake."

"Speaking of that." Madison sighed. "It seems that wasn't a retreat. Later in this letter, Adams apprises me of reliable intelligence that has come to him in Ghent. The British fleet is headed for New Orleans, as we feared. Shall we *never* be rid of these marauders?"

"No doubt General Jackson will turn them back at New Orleans," Dolley said crisply. "I am told it is a place of swamps and difficult terrain. Its defenders have a significant advantage."

"Jackson has handled himself well," the president agreed, calmer now. "So far, at least. He has an irritating independence of mind, but it's hard to argue with his results. He's more interested in driving the Spanish out of the Floridas, and at the moment I believe he's near Pensacola. Spain isn't what it used to be, but it's still strong enough to be troublesome. Pray God Spain doesn't ally with Britain against us."

Sally had heard enough discussions—or parts of them—to know there was no qualified replacement for Jackson, certainly not one who would be readily accepted by the troops. They called him Old Hickory for his ever-present cane but also for his toughness.

"I've sent for Monroe," Madison said, "and I think you're right, my dear. Perhaps the British will be more amenable when they hear of their defeats at Baltimore and Plattsburg. My God, think of it. We beat back an armada of more than fifty warships of the world's greatest naval power. We stopped an advance of seventeen thousand British soldiers."

He paused thoughtfully. "They could be stalling for time to attack New Orleans and gain control of the Mississippi. Maybe they'll try to attain their goals simply by strangling our westward expansion." He shook his head sadly.

23 October 1814

Baltimore

*B*ack home in Baltimore, Quinn began slowly and painfully to recover. Bouts of fever had drained his energy, and enforced idleness and recurring pain sapped his spirits. He thought often of the naïveté with which he had joined the army, the suffering he had witnessed, the evils that led men to war, and death, too much death. The more he reflected, the more amazed he became at his own survival, just as the odds had been stacked against his country. Two serious head wounds, two missing fingers. He was lucky to be alive, but was there a reason for his survival? Or was it self-indulgent and egotistic to presume that he had a higher purpose? But if he didn't—why had the Almighty preserved him?

What was done was done. He must look to the future, a realistic future. One more head injury could finish him or worse, leave him a burden on his family. . Sometimes the pain was unbearable, as was the continuous, remorseless ringing in his ears. He prayed for comfort and silence.

Days and then weeks passed. His health and perspective improved. His thoughts were less jumbled, and his mind less scattered and kaleidoscopic. He was still angry with the fools he had encountered and the vanity and stupidity that had led to so many disasters. Reasonable men could have prevented this war. Failing that, it could have been won but for so many bloated egos and such incompetence. Nevertheless, democracy presented an opportunity to set matters right. People could remove fools and knaves from power. They weren't stuck with whatever king heredity bestowed on them. Somehow all those incompetents, like Hull, could be replaced by men of talent and energy.

The war had taught him a great many lessons—how to set a course, how to act within his own limited sphere, how to accept what he couldn't control and make the best of it, how to take responsibility for the soldiers in his company when some fool general put them at unnecessary risk. He had participated in historic events. It was likely someone under his command had fired the round that killed Ross and possibly reversed the direction of the war.

He sat up in bed, winced at the pain, but did not lie down again. It was not his nature to entertain grandiose thoughts. He would speak of them to no one, not even to Sally, but he saw now that both he and the nation had grown with the war and come to a better understanding of the dangers they faced, now and in the future. The war had almost split the country apart, and there were still forces that could divide it once and for all. But there were others forces that could bring it together again. These had to be reconciled; otherwise, America could disintegrate into partisan, economic, social, and geographic fragments.

And what if it did? Would the states be better off in groups with common concerns and cultures? Clearly, Kentuckians like Frake were cut from different cloth than the New Yorkers who refused to cross the Niagara into Canada. Could a common government urge these men to grow more alike, or could it benefit from their differences? Or both?

He was sure of only one thing: his own family had left a country wracked by the greed, prejudice, and malevolence of outsiders. Now they lived in a free nation, and he felt duty-bound to preserve it.

Gradually, under the loving ministrations of his mother and with regular visits from Sally, Quinn's health was improving. He said nothing of his growing desire to return to his country's service in some manner. Already, he had put aside thoughts of the linen business. It was in capable hands and would prosper as long as freedom, stability, and peace could be sustained. He wanted to be a part of that effort, but he could no longer fight. What *could* he do?

Plattsburg and Baltimore had brought the nation together emotionally as it hadn't been since the revolution. Quinn read in the Baltimore newspapers of the passion ignited throughout the land by the burning of Washington and the heroic resistance at Fort McHenry and North Point. He had read Francis Key's poem "The Star Spangled Banner" and had heard it sung by Aengus to—ironically—the melody of an *English* drinking song. Indeed, it was published and sold all over the country as sheet music. He was especially fond of its fourth and final stanza:

> O! thus be it ever, when free men shall stand
> Between their loved home and the war's desolation!
> Blest with victory and peace, may the
> heav'n rescued land

Praise the Power that hath made and
preserved us a nation.
Then conquer we must, when our cause it is just,
And this be our motto: "In God is our trust."
And the star-spangled banner in triumph shall wave
O'er the land of the free and the home of the brave!

The seed was planted. He would go into politics.

30 October 1814

Baltimore

"You're a fool!"

"You don't approve?" Quinn raised his eyebrows but expected that response. Frake had as much use for politics and politicians as he did for a constipated bear on the prowl.

"Willie, they'll eat you alive. The voters might like your war record, but the politicians will run upside your backside and downside your front side. And you won't even know they've even been there until you notice their tracks."

"Maybe that's why I need to run. Someone from the outside needs to step up and tell them when they're wrong."

"Selfless sentiments." Frake scoffed. "But why you, friend? You came into this war—I remember way back at Fort Wayne—not knowing squat, and look where it's got you. I almost had to bury you twice. Know how tough it is to be your friend, junior?"

"Can't be as tough as being your friend, Judah."

Frake was silent for several moments. "Okay," he said at last, "I'll humor you. How do you plan to get yourself elected?"

"I'll run from Baltimore. My family is known here. I'm known here. In fact, most folks think the shot that killed Ross came from our platoon." He smiled at Frake as he said it, but the Kentuckian's gaze never flickered.

Quinn had always believed that Frake's rifle fired the shot that felled the general. Both the other men who fired were dead, so Frake could easily take credit. But instead he let the families, friends, and towns of the dead men have the acclaim, for whatever comfort it might bring them.

"I know it was you, Judah."

Frake shrugged. "What's a monument good for, anyway? You can't burn them in the fireplace when the winter gets cold and long." And he meant it. The man truly didn't care about much more than the here and now and what varmint he could scope in his rifle sights.

"Anyway, some think I'm a hero for that alone, so they'd vote for me," Quinn said frankly. "And why shouldn't they?"

"You a Republican? Or a Federalist?"

"Maybe neither. Both sides have some good ideas— maybe take from both. That'd be the sensible thing to do."

"Politics don't got much sense to it."

"Listen, there's a job to do. Think how Congress stiffed Barney's men, and us too."

They hadn't been paid for months, and although the men were recognized everywhere for their heroism, Congress kept finding reasons why they shouldn't or couldn't be paid.

"Someone has to stick up for the veterans, especially Barney's, who didn't have to risk their lives."

Now Frake was nodding energetically. "Then you got to do it," he said.

"And right now, even with the British on our doorstep, Madison is still having trouble convincing Congress to fund the fight. The debt is getting out of control, and the banks are getting tough about giving the government any more credit."

"It's all politics, ain't it?"

"I guess, but it goes with democracy. Instead of a king sitting up there and handing down all the decisions, everyone's got his oar in."

"Well, you go to it then, but much as I've enjoyed pulling your chestnuts out of the fire, I don't want no part of this."

"So what *will* you do? You know you've got a job with my family. Or we could find you something else in Baltimore."

"No, thank you. I'm not much for city living. Not enough things to shoot at, least not legally. Besides, where would I hide my whiskey still so's no one would be poaching on it?"

The two men chuckled.

"What, then?"

"Reckon I don't know yet. I might just head for New Orleans. I hear that they're putting together a Kentucky rifle brigade."

"Haven't you had enough fighting?"

Frake nodded. "Never thought the day would come, but I'm beginning to think I have. Besides..." He trailed off.

"What?"

"Your woman, Miss Martin, was petitioning on my behalf, although I ain't asked her to. Sally convinced Mrs. Madison, who convinced Mr. Madison, that I'd be good to be Mr. Monroe's aide, now that he's secretary of war."

"And what would Your Highness do for Mr. Monroe?"

"Tell him how to fight the war, I reckon."

"The hell, you say."

"I'm thinking about it."

"Not a bad idea to have someone who knows what the hell he's talking about at the war department."

Frake cleared his throat. "So...what do you plan to do about Miss Sally?"

"Do?"

"She's been hovering around all this while. Coming up from the District every chance she gets. Think she's doing that because she likes the smell of a sickroom? Are you going to make her your wife or just go on like she's your handmaiden?"

"I don't know."

"This is wearin' on my nerves, boy. You've looked death in the eye, yet you can't make up your mind about the best thing in your life."

"Combat and marriage are different things, Frake."

"You're a fool."

30 October 1814

Washington, D.C

"What about your young man?" Dolley asked.
"What about him?"

"Well, you two seem so suited for each other, and you seem to be so close. It would be a shame if—"

"If we didn't get married? First, he hasn't asked me. Second, I don't know if I would accept him."

"I'm sorry to pry," the first lady said. "Please understand that I have only the best intentions. You know how people are. If a woman waits too long, she becomes a, well, spinster. Such an awful word."

"I've had a lot of time to think about this," Sally said. "I've been exposed, thanks to you and the president, to the best education anyone—even a man—could wish for. I've been on hand for some of the most important decisions ever made for this country. I see what goes into it, how the president has to play off the different interests. The traders and the planters. The Republicans and the Federalists. It would be a shame to waste that."

"It would, my dear. But how would you put it to use?"

"Well, if I could, I'd run for office."

Dolley chuckled. "Maybe someday, but right now you can't even vote."

"Where in the Constitution does it say a woman can't run?" Sally mused, her face more serious now.

"Nowhere, as far as I know. But you must take into account the realities."

"Always it's the 'realities.' The 'realities' argue against anyone fighting for the abolition of slavery."

Sally sighed. "It's not realistic to try to abolish slavery. But it wasn't realistic for thirteen little colonies to demand their independence from Great Britain. What's realistic isn't always what's right."

"I don't mean to patronize you, my dear, but you are very young. I sometimes wish that we adults could be more idealistic."

"But you *are* idealistic, ma'am," Sally said earnestly. "It wasn't realistic of Mr. Madison to take on Great Britain again, with so many other problems already before him. I think he believes in the country so much that...I confess that at times I thought the country was done for."

"Between us, Sally, so did I." Dolley sighed as she picked up the correspondence Sally had sorted.

A knock on the door preceded the entrance of a White House butler. His expression was a mix of embarrassment and amazement.

"Excuse me, madam, but there is a, uh, gentleman at the front door—a black man." His voice reflected disapproval. "He, ah, insists that he has an appointment with you, and he won't wait in the cook house."

"What's his name?"

"He says it's Henry."

"Please show him in at once."

The servant raised his eyebrows but bowed and withdrew.

"Right on time," Sally said. "You can always rely on Henry."

Dolley had invited Henry to the White House. She knew from all accounts that Henry was good and loyal and a diligent worker. He could have slipped away in the confusion, but he didn't. Her curiosity about his motives was one reason for the invitation. The other was to reward him appropriately.

She rose and extended her hand to him as he entered, and Sally followed suit.

"So good of you to come, Mr., um."

"It always been just Henry, ma'am."

"We'll have to take care of that. Please take a seat."

Henry looked from Dolley to Sally then perched tentatively on the edge of a gilded chair.

"Before we get down to business, Henry, I have to know, and pardon my directness," Dolley said, dispensing with the customary small talk. "You have had multiple opportunities to flee, to join the British, or to escape into Canada. You chose, instead, to remain and be of service. Sally has told me of your bravery with Commodore Barney's fleet. At Bladensburg you stayed to fight instead of running away as so many free men did. You acquitted yourself well at North Point. You risked your life to assist William Quinn when he was almost mortally wounded. Please tell me what inspired your courageous actions."

Henry had not raised his eyes to meet hers during her inquiry, but he did now as he spoke from his heart. "I stayed through no sense of obligation, Mrs. Madison," he said. "Fact is, I plotted to join the British in exchange for my freedom. If that effort hadn't failed, I might be right now on a British warship heading for New Orleans. I might have fought on the other side at North Point. I might even have fired the shot that brought down Mr. Quinn."

"I quite understand, Henry. I cannot place myself in your shoes, but I do understand."

"But even if I'd got the opportunity to join the British, I might not have taken it. My dearest wish is to find my beloved family. If you see loyalty to America in my actions, I will not contest that. But truth be told, it is loyalty to my family that keeps me here, the hope of finding them and finding freedom for all of us."

"You are free, Henry."

"Beg your pardon, ma'am?"

"It has been arranged. You can burn all those fake identity papers and stop hiding at the Quinns'. You are a free man, in all regards legally entitled to search for your family in these United States."

"How can that be?" Henry was stunned.

"My dear Henry, you don't think that the president and his lady would harbor a fugitive slave here in the executive mansion? Dear me, no. So we have purchased your freedom."

Dolley explained how Caleb Kilfoyle had been persuaded to sell Henry's freedom. He never knew who the buyer was, but the price was generous—his original investment plus interest plus the recovery of costs incurred by the loss of the slave plus a munificent profit for his troubles.

"Your manumission papers have been prepared and signed by the president himself. We feel confident that his signature attesting to your liberty will be sufficient anywhere. For your service in the war, the president has found the money—the ungrateful Congress has not been consulted—to recompense you. This will allow you, I think, to set up your own shoemaking business, if you wish to do so. That, in turn, should enable you to accumulate enough money to purchase your family's freedom. I should say, also, that your friends wish to invest in that endeavor to assure your success."

Henry could not speak. All his energy was directed into suppressing an unseemly emotional breakdown. It failed, and he broke into sobs.

Mrs. Madison turned to Sally with a smile. "And so, my dear, you see the realities that people of good will and high purpose can achieve."

Christmas Eve 1814

Baltimore

*D*ays dragged into weeks and months, but the news from Ghent remained depressing. The British held to their outrageous demands. The Americans chafed at the idea of yielding anything that would restrict the country's expansion. When the war started, the population stood at some seven million, and now it was eight. The country would not accept limits on its growth set down by Europeans who still regarded the Americas as theirs. Monroe especially was adamant that Europe must keep its hands off anything in the Western Hemisphere.

British attitudes remained patronizing. They tried to pry the American delegation apart by playing regional interests off against each other. New England Federalists were interested in securing Atlantic fishing rights, and the Southern states were focused on the Mississippi River.

At home these differences were feeding the nascent secessionist movement in the New England. Several governors, legislators, peace party activists, and radicals who had never been enthralled with American independence in the first place organized a convention to take place in December in Hartford, Connecticut.

They intended to draft a separate New England constitution to protect shipping and fishing interests. Some delegates were hotheads who predicted defeat at New Orleans and the subsequent unraveling of the Union. Others were equally determined to preserve the Union. Whatever its outcome, the convening of such a meeting did not bode well for Washington and added to Madison's pressing problems.

The central government was nearly broke, and war funding was uncertain. Monroe could fill only half the army slots authorized by Congress, because enlistments were drying up. He proposed—and then abandoned in the ensuing heat—conscription. With enlistments running at only ten thousand a year, the army was far short of the hundred thousand that Monroe believed necessary to win the war.

News of the American victories belatedly reached both delegations at Ghent but did not soften the demands of the British overlords. An exasperated John Quincy Adams was ready to end the talks and let the Americans take their chances at New Orleans.

It looked bad.

"I just had to come to tell you myself!" Sally shouted days later, bursting into the Quinn household late one afternoon, disheveled from her dash in the one-horse, two-wheeled open buggy. "The war is over!"

"Thanks be to God!" Agnes cried, and sent Aengus to the mill to fetch Malachy while Will called everyone into the parlor.

Sally was dancing with excitement, but she waited for the brothers. Once everyone was settled, she stood and... realized that she might have been a little hasty.

The Quinns exchanged glances as she cleared her throat. "It *looks like* the war is over," she said. "They could be signing a peace treaty in Ghent any day now, but some details have to be worked out. Mr. Madison has received a most optimistic communiqué from John Quincy Adams. The British have dropped their impossible demands and agreed to what's called restoration of status quo ante bellum, conditions as they were before the war."

The room was flummoxed. Good news indeed, but the futility of the entire war descended on everyone with immediate and full force. A father and a son dead—another son fighting for a return to good health and respect. Sally read it all in an instant and didn't quite know what to say.

"So, nothing's changed?" asked Malachy, disbelief catching his question in his throat. "Maybe you should, I mean, can you explain a little more?"

Sally didn't quite know where to begin and now wished that she could remember Adams's letter more exactly. "I'll try," she said, clearly intimidated by the disappointed faces. "It's not as bad as it sounds. It means that we don't have to create a buffer state in the Northwest, give up fishing rights, or let the English use our Mississippi as if it were the Thames. All prisoners exchanged, of course. We retain what we lost in Maine and in the Great Lakes. We can regarrison Mackinac and the other forts. The British will stop stirring up the Indians. No more impressment of our sailors. Renewal of full commercial relations. Let's see, what else?"

"In other words, a tie. A draw. No gains, no losses." It was Will, who was already recalling bloodied and maimed bodies at Fort Dearborn and elsewhere. "A waste, a damnable waste," he said quietly.

No one in the room disagreed.

Sally was crestfallen. "But, but, the killing is over! That by itself is cause for rejoicing. Is it not?"

"Certainly, my dear," said Agnes. "It is in the nature of women to rejoice at the end of bloodshed, but men"— she waved at her sons—"are different. Always some score to settle. Now, dear Sally, I am curious about how all this occurred."

"I'll try to remember," Sally said hesitantly. "Lord Casterleigh was the chief British negotiator in talks about dividing up Europe after Napoleon. He stopped at Ghent on his way from London to Vienna. He was appalled—I think that was the word Adams used—at the hard line the British delegation had taken with us, the Americans. Apparently, public opinion in England was shifting against the war. Even the British high councils were not anxious to spend more millions. Everyone was just tired of it all."

"Truth be told." Malachy sighed.

"Even Wellington. He was offered command of the British campaign in America, the government hoping he could repeat his victory over Napoleon. But Adams heard that Wellington turned it down. It wasn't worth it, he said. He meant the war wasn't worth it. He even said that the British might not win. All this folderol about victory at New Orleans and sailing up the Mississippi to split the United States in two—he didn't think much of it, and because he's a hero, his word was taken quite seriously."

"So there'll be no battle at New Orleans?"

"Well, that's the problem," Sally continued. "It took weeks for word of the proposed agreement to get here. Mr. Madison and Mr. Monroe don't think they can get word to General Jackson in time. I suppose the British might get the word quicker and stop the bloodshed. But what is Jackson supposed to do if the British still attack? Tell them the war's over, let's not fight? As if the British would believe it!"

"Christ."

"More people dying, and for what? Nothing."

Voices now filled the room with anger and frustration. Sally waited for the hubbub to die down.

"Mr. Monroe dispatched his most reliable messenger— Frake," she said to Will. "You know he'll do his best to get there on time."

"And if he doesn't?" Will said.

"Frake says then he'll just join the fight and pick off a few of them Limeys for old time's sake."

At that, the room broke out in laughter, and the celebrating began in earnest. Malachy went out to spread the word to the neighbors, and soon jubilant families were pouring into the street. Agnes, Aengus, and Malachy joined them, leaving Quinn and Sally alone in the parlor.

Quinn's excuse for bachelorhood had suddenly disappeared. Both knew it and knew the other knew it.

"William Quinn, I am not one to force you into something. You know me better than that. Anyway, I know that you love me and that I love you. Nothing else matters."

The Irish gift of gab still eluded Quinn. "I do love you," was about all he could squeeze out as he took her hands in his.

"Well, then?"

"So much is still uncertain, but I know you approve of my trying to go into politics. You can be my own Dolley Madison"—he ducked as she aimed a playful punch at his jaw—"or you can go to school if you want to. Or teach. Or—"

"I want to be your wife and your helpmate, Will, but you know I have my own mind, especially about doing something to end slavery. But for now, for right here...I love you with all my heart."

"Then, uh, maybe we should visit Father O'Malley," he said, and then she was in his arms.

Epilogue

rake didn't arrive in time to stop the Battle of New Orleans, but fighting there alongside a Kentucky brigade, he did help rout the British. On Christmas Eve, as Sally and the Quinns gathered in the Baltimore parlor, the two sides formally signed the Treaty of Ghent with the very terms Adams had communicated to Madison. Word of the signing, however, did not reach troops in the field until after Andrew Jackson secured a convincing victory over the British. Even if the treaty had not been signed, the British had been beaten in the North, the Chesapeake, and the South.

Still, the Americans had not won the war in the classic sense. They had been turned back from Canada, dashing forever their hopes of northward expansion. Yet the Americans achieved many of their goals. They took on the most powerful nation in the world and fought it to a standstill, winning worldwide respect. No longer an amalgam of colonies that had fortuitously won independence, America had emerged from its adolescence as a nation of political, commercial, and military consequence.

In the south, Jackson's move into western Florida cleared the way for the future state's acquisition. America's dominion over the western lands nearly to the Pacific Ocean would never be contested. Expansionism was strengthened, setting the stage for the Mexican-American War, the ensuing creation of an ocean-to-ocean nation, and the Spanish-American War. Interrupted only by a bloody Civil War, America's march toward global power began in the War of 1812.

In many ways, America emerged from that war more unified than ever. New England views of state's rights were altered by a nation more firmly defined as federalist. The idea of a citizen militia survived the war badly tattered, and support for a standing army began to grow.

The fundamental economic, social, political, and philosophical differences that threatened to splinter the country remained as an undercurrent, an inevitable outgrowth of such unique diversity. Politics continued to be influenced by geography, commercial and agrarian interests remained in conflict, and ideals of equality and self-government played out in the contentious abolition and suffrage movements. Indeed, though the conflicts that led to the Civil War were fought out, they were by no means entirely resolved. Slavery, after its abolition, emerged under the guise of Jim Crow and fractured the nation for decades to come. The suffrage movement gave women the vote but not full equality. Voting blocs still form along regional, economic, demographic, ethnic, and social lines.

The War of 1812 was a watershed event for the adolescent country. Just as youth shapes a person's life, the War of 1812 formed this country and revealed the strains that would tear at it for two centuries to come. If the War of 1812 taught us anything, it was that while enemies lurk outside our doors, internal disunity and self-interest are greater threats.

Author's Note

This is a work of fiction based on actual events. All the battles and disputations described here really happened—from the surrender at Fort Mackinac to the victory at Baltimore. I have concocted the characters of Quinn, his family, Sally, Frake, Henry, and a few others, but just about everyone else mentioned in this book actually lived the war. Historians (and I don't pretend to be one) may justifiably disagree with my interpretations of events and their consequences. It was not my intention to write a narrative history of the war. There are a number of excellent ones. My intent was to show how I imagined regular people would live the war and how it would change them. If anything does not ring true here, it is a fault of my imagination.

In my research, I tried to scrupulously follow events as described in a number of sources. Among my benefactors were such readable narrative histories as *The War of 1812: A Forgotten Conflict* by Donald R. Hickey and *The Incredible War of 1812: A Military History* by J. Mackay Hitsman. An invaluable resource was *Lossing's Pictorial History of the War of 1812* by Benson J. Lossing. Written in 1868, it provides detailed narratives as recounted by living participants, survivors, and direct observers of the war.

I also tried to mine original sources, an effort that afforded me the pleasure of working in the magnificent Library of Congress—whose roots, incidentally, are in the books that Thomas Jefferson donated to the library after the British burned the Capitol in the War of 1812. While there, I discovered that the electronic age has changed, if not facilitated, historical research. Many documents that would have been available in the flesh only to certified researchers are now available electronically. While waiting for documents to be delivered in the Great Reading Room, I found that I could access on my laptop loads of library documents from my desk under the library's grand rotunda. To my joy, I discovered that these same electronic documents were available offsite, so that the need for an onsite visit was, for my purposes, greatly reduced.

I also discovered a mother lode of documents on the Internet from a multitude of sources. They include old books and publications now in the public realm and available as PDF documents, such as Lossing's book. Even more fascinating is the trove of narratives and documents placed online by families, localities, and organizations involved in or with an interest in the war. They provide a plethora of views and facts not necessarily included in historical narratives.

For me, the research and writing was a most satisfying exercise and an exploration into an often-ignored phase of our history. I hope the reader enjoys the results of my efforts as I have enjoyed producing this book.